THE THUNDER KEEPER

"Coel has obvious respect for the land and people who populate it . . . She creates dense and compelling characters in complex stories to entertain her loyal fans."
— *The Denver Post*

THE SPIRIT WOMAN

Winner of the Colorado Book Award for Mystery

"Intriguing Arapaho and Shoshone history, and realistic treatment of contemporary Native American issues . . . [A] winner."
— *Library Journal*

THE LOST BIRD

"Engrossing . . . Enjoyable characters and a super mystery."
— *The Literary Times*

THE STORY TELLER

"One of the best of the year."
— *Booklist* (starred review)

THE DREAM STALKER

"Seamless storytelling by someone who's obviously been there."
— J. A. Jance

THE GHOST WALKER

"Coel is a vivid voice for the West."
— *The Dallas Morning News*

THE EAGLE CATCHER

"She's a master."
— Tony Hillerman

WATCHING EAGLES SOAR

MARGARET COEL

BERKLEY PRIME CRIME, NEW YORK

THE BERKLEY PUBLISHING GROUP
Published by the Penguin Group
Penguin Group (USA) Inc.
375 Hudson Street, New York, New York 10014, USA

USA I Canada I UK I Ireland I Australia I New Zealand I India I South Africa I China

Penguin Books Ltd., Registered Offices: 80 Strand, London WC2R 0RL, England
For more information about the Penguin Group, visit penguin.com.

WATCHING EAGLES SOAR

Berkley Prime Crime Books are published by The Berkley Publishing Group.
BERKLEY® PRIME CRIME and the PRIME CRIME logo are a registered trademark
of Penguin Group (USA) Inc.

Berkley Prime Crime trade paperback ISBN: 978-0-425-26554-3

An application to register this book for cataloging has been submitted to the Library of Congress.

PUBLISHING HISTORY
Berkley Prime Crime trade paperback edition / July 2013

PRINTED IN THE UNITED STATES OF AMERICA

10 9 8 7 6 5 4 3 2 1

Cover design by Lesley Worrell.
Interior design by Laura K. Corless.

To Mary Fedel,

my dear cousin and lifelong friend,

who left us too soon.

ACKNOWLEDGMENTS

A collection of short stories, like a child, requires a village to nurture it. I am in the debt of many people who championed these stories and brought them into print, including the editors who selected my stories for various anthologies. But I am especially grateful to Jim and Mary Seels of ASAP Publishing, who suggested the series of Arapaho Ten Commandments stories, and, over eleven years, published each story in a beautiful, limited hardback edition, then collected the stories in another limited hardback. My hat is off to Mary Seels, the technical wizard behind all of those hardback books. Another tip of my hat to my editor, Tom Colgan, and Berkley Prime Crime for believing in these stories enough to publish them in this trade paperback edition, thus bringing them to a wider audience. And a tip of my cowgirl hat to Craig Johnson, who took time from a busy schedule to write an enormously generous introduction.

To all of you, thank you for allowing me into your publications and into your lives. Thank you for having me.

CONTENTS

MORE FROM BEYOND

ESSAYS

Introduction

by Craig Johnson

Where do you start when writing about a precious gem like Margaret Coel?

Do you start with the renaissance author who whips out novels, nonfiction books, magazine articles, and short stories with incomparable ease? How about a historian whose attention to detail is nothing short of awe-inspiring? Do you talk about a woman whose place in the literary and mystery fields is unassailable?

Or do you just talk about one of the finest people you know?

A fourth-generation Coloradan with more than sixteen prize-winning novels—it's hard to not mention Margaret in conjunction with one of her mentors, Tony Hillerman, who referred to her as a master in the field. You can read some of the resonances of the old master in Margaret's work, but you can also see where she advanced from there, cutting a new path for herself and her writing.

A fellow I once worked with said there is no such thing as tough; there is just prepared. I think that's one of the ways I view Margaret's work—prepared. She doesn't do anything by the seat of her skirt; like a true student of the craft, she prepares in a way that makes other authors blush. Each work is an opportunity for study, and one she takes very seriously. I remember having dinner with her as she was doing the research for one of her more recent novels, *The Silent Spirit*. She was like a kid in a candy store—the research she was doing on the Arapaho and Shoshone involvement with Hollywood in the twenties was a chocolate truffle. I listened to her as she breathlessly relayed the information she'd uncovered about the tribe's relationships with actor/cowboy Tim McCoy in my state of Wyoming. It was hard to concentrate on the words for the amount of excitement in her voice and the intellectual enthusiasm that threatened to take her away from the dinner table that night and back to her writing desk.

Margaret is like her writing: she tends to sweep you away.

I heard about "Saint" Margaret before meeting her, and by all reports, I figured she couldn't be real. I'd been invited to the Hillerman Conference in Albuquerque, and it was one of the first literary events that I'd attended. You learn a lot about other writers in those circumstances, and the one I was most impressed with was Margaret. She was warm, friendly, magnanimous, and charming—enough so that we've remained close friends over the years.

Dark and statuesque, Margaret has fielded the inevitable question of, "Are you Arapaho?" with grace and candor. Generally they take another look at her and insist, "Well, maybe you are and you just don't know it—maybe you should have your DNA done." Margaret usually informs them that she really doesn't need to do that since the only people who've never mistaken her for Arapaho are the Arapahos. It isn't as if they wouldn't want her; in that, I suspect they love her as much as she loves them.

For Margaret Coel, love begins with interest, and the depths of her interest in the Wind River Reservation and its people have yet to be plumbed. Margaret is a writer; she's been a writer her entire life, and writers ask questions, looking for answers. Early in her life, the tales she heard were the stories of the individuals who had been there before her ancestors—the plains tribes of the Arapaho and Cheyenne.

I'll let you in on a little secret: I know why she chose the Arapaho as her main point of interest. They were the traders of the high plains, the barterers of both goods and words. Is it any wonder that the wordsmith Margaret Coel would be drawn to the storytellers?

Her first work, a magazine article on Chief Left Hand, blossomed to more than three hundred pages after five meticulous years of research—Margaret had accidentally written a book. A book, I might add, that hasn't been out of print since its publication in 1981. I'm sure Margaret considers that work to be her introduction to the Arapaho culture and its people. It was only in a chance event where she heard the aforementioned Tony Hillerman speak of his love for the Navajo and how they had enriched his life that that first spark of the novelist was seen. There in that massive ballroom, surrounded by others, she heard that small voice that speaks to would-be authors saying, "I can do that."

She'd spent time with the Arapaho, knew the elders, and, most important, had heard the stories. A student of history and an avid mystery fan, Margaret made the wise decision to write what she read.

In structuring her novels, she knew that one of her protagonists would be an outsider like her, someone who could view the Arapaho and provide the reader with an entrée into their world. She settled on a novel approach with Father John—a man who would be intimately involved with the spiritual, social, and cultural tapestry of the Arapaho tribe. Father John Aloysius O'Malley, certainly the most Irish moniker ever introduced in modern literature, would be an outsider not only to the tribe but to the entire West. Knowing full well that we like people for their virtues, but that we love them for their faults, Margaret made the Jesuit priest a recovering alcoholic, banished, certainly in the minds of his Boston upbringing, to the wilds of the Wind River Reservation.

The counterbalance to Father John is the other creation of Margaret's fertile imagination—Vicky Holden, a traditional, young Arapaho woman and a shaman of the first right in modern culture—a lawyer. A woman who escaped an abusive marriage and returned to the reservation not only for her own good, but for the good she could do her people.

In her first novel, *The Eagle Catcher*, these two elements of fire and water begin a relationship that has carried through Margaret's novels with the personal and dramatic conflict that's the stuff good writing is all about.

I don't know whether Margaret knew she'd still be dealing with this unlikely relationship after sixteen installments, or how it would ever reconcile. We did a conversation together, and I had to admit that the chronological differences in the glancing relationship between my sheriff and his chief deputy paled in comparison with the obstacles she had to contend with—the weight and breadth of the Catholic Church.

In my mind the two characters are representative of church and state, an uneasy alliance where the stakes couldn't be any higher. The more specific Margaret becomes with her characters, the more she approaches the universality of the human condition—another hallmark of great writing.

You hold in your hands now, gentle reader, Berkley Prime Crime's Short Story Collection by Margaret Coel; handle it carefully because the stories are precious stones. Some are departures, like the curious case of "The Man Who Thought He Was a Deer," or the unflinching historical "Murder on the Denver Express," containing no less than the unsinkable Molly Brown, while some contain the characters from Margaret's award-winning series, such as "The Man in Her Dreams," where we experience the character's hands-on spiritualism, and the mathematical/mystery precision of "A Well-Respected Man." In fact, this collection starts with her tour de force and my personal favorite, "The Arapaho Ten Commandments," which as a work stands alone. All of the stories are finely crafted, precious gems—just like the crowning jewel herself, Margaret Coel.

Craig Johnson
Ucross, Wyoming
2011

The Arapaho
Ten Commandments Stories

Stolen Smoke

The First Commandment:
I am the Lord Thy God;
Thou shalt have none other gods but me.

The front door on the Arapaho museum stood open. Father John O'Malley saw the massive door moving slightly in the wind as he crossed the grounds of St. Francis Mission on the Wind River Reservation. Strange, he thought. It was early, not much past seven a.m., too early for Lindy Meadows, the museum curator, to be in. He hadn't noticed the opened door an hour ago on his way to the church for Mass, but it had been dark then. Now the sun glowed orange-red in the eastern sky and cast the mission buildings in sharp relief. A gust slammed the door against an inside wall, sending a loud thwack into the morning silence.

Father John hurried up the steps and across the porch that stretched along the gray-stone facade. As he walked through the entry into the main gallery, his breath stopped in his throat. The glass doors on the exhibit cases hung open. The Arapaho artifacts were gone: feathered belts and wands, painted parfleches, tanned and beaded deerskin dresses and warrior's shirts, an ancient bow and arrow, a council pipe made of black-and-white stone. More than a hundred and fifty years ago, the Arapaho headmen had smoked the pipe in treaty councils with the government to signify truthfulness and good heart.

Still in the case where the pipe had been on display was an old photo of three Arapaho chiefs and several government agents seated in front of a tipi. One of the chiefs held a long pipe with a black stem and white bowl, a mute reminder of the pipe that was now missing.

Whoever had taken the artifacts had picked the locks on the exhibit cases. There were no shards of broken glass, no sharp edges that might have damaged the delicate skins and feathers, and for that fact Father John felt almost grateful. This was a clever thief who knew the value of what he had stolen.

Father John forced himself past the empty cases to the side door that opened onto a smaller gallery, a tight knot of dread in his stomach. The early morning sun broke through the windows and cast a pinkish glow over the diorama of a camp scene from the Old Time: the white tipi standing in the center of the wood floor; the tripod holding a black kettle over a simulated fire; the wax figure of a warrior squatting in front of a frame that held a buffalo skin. On the walls were framed photographs of Arapaho warriors, somber in feathered headdresses, and women and children sheltering in the shade of tipis that rose out of the gray, desolate plains. Nothing had been disturbed, but Father John had the strange feeling that the ancestors had looked on helplessly while the thief had looted the artifacts in the adjoining room.

He tried without success to shake the feeling as he made his way to the library across the hall. Everything looked the same: metal shelves filled with orderly rows of books and brown cartons that held old letters and manuscripts. Obviously the thief wanted only the artifacts. There was an insatiable market for Indian artifacts, Father John knew. Unscrupulous dealers who never asked questions and an army of wealthy collectors who would pay hundreds for a warrior's bow and arrow, thousands for a finely beaded deerskin dress. Once sold, the artifacts would be impossible to trace. He felt a sickening sense of loss as he picked up the phone on the library desk, dialed 911, and reported a burglary at St. Francis Mission.

"Looks like Junior Tallman's work, all right." Art Banner, Wind River police chief, was leaning over and peering at the lock on an exhibit case. "Yep. Junior can pick a flea out of a nest of rattlers."

Junior Tallman. Father John let the name roll around in his mind. Familiar, but he couldn't put a face with it. "Who is this guy?" he asked.

The chief straightened up. He was about to say something when Ted Gianelli, the local FBI agent, snapped shut the notebook he'd been writing in and started down the line of exhibit cases toward them. The chief drew in his lower lip and kept an expectant eye on the agent. Father John understood. This was a major crime, which put it in the FBI's jurisdiction, a fact that rankled the police chief. More than once, Banner had complained that the fed, who didn't know diddly-squat about dealing with Indians, got to investigate the really interesting cases while he and his officers were stuck with the grunt work. Two of the chief's "boys," as he called his officers, had already dusted the gallery for prints.

Gianelli said, "Convicted felon, did time in Leavenworth for breaking into the Ethete Museum and stealing a couple hundred thousand dollars' worth of artifacts. A neat, careful job. If it hadn't been for an informant in Denver, Junior might've gotten away with it. But we traced a couple of stolen artifacts back to Ethete and nailed him. Even Vicky couldn't get him off."

Father John stuffed his hands into the pockets of his plaid jacket. He remembered now. Vicky Holden, the Arapaho lawyer he often worked with on different cases—divorces, adoptions, getting some teenager into drug rehab—had mentioned Junior Tallman not long ago. Too clever for his own good, she'd said. He'd taken such meticulous care of a fringed shirt and feathered cape—making certain nothing was altered—that the curator at the Ethete Museum had no trouble proving they belonged to the museum. Father John felt a chill pass over him unrelated to the cold breeze coming through the opened front door. The Ethete Museum never recovered the rest of the stolen artifacts.

The police chief cleared his throat. "Count yourself lucky you never met Junior, John. Man's got the conscience of a rattler. If you'd happened by while he was at work here, he would've killed you."

"You've got to pick him up before he sells the artifacts," Father John said to the agent.

"Soon's we confirm the prints, we'll arrest him."

"Prints!" Father John moved in closer, his eyes locked on Gianelli's round, fleshy face. "That'll take time. Junior could be selling the artifacts right now."

"Let me handle this." A blue vein had started pulsing in the middle of the agent's forehead. "We can't make an arrest stick without evidence. And I have no intention of tipping Junior off that we're on to him. He'd just disappear on the rez, and we'd be months trying to find him. By then your artifacts would be long gone."

There was a tap-tap sound of footsteps in the entry, followed by a loud gasp. Lindy Meadows stood in the doorway, one hand gripping the jamb, eyes darting about the empty exhibit cases. "Where are the sacred things?" Her voice came like the wail of a siren. Then she burst into tears. Father John walked over, handed her his handkerchief, and placed an arm around her shoulders. He could sense the trembling beneath the heavy brown coat as the woman dabbed at her eyes.

"What will I tell the old people when they come to visit the ancestors' belongings?" the curator managed. "What can I say to Clint Old Bear? He comes every Friday to visit the council pipe. How will I explain that it's gone?"

Father John didn't know what to say. He'd seen Clint Old Bear in the museum just last week, standing reverently in front of the council pipe, lost in his own thoughts. Clint was a *ne:thne:teyo'u'u:wu't*, a traditional, who lived in a tipi out in the foothills and wanted nothing to do with the modern way—"the white road," he called it. What would he make of the fact a burglar had broken into the museum and stolen sacred artifacts that the Arapahos had trusted the museum to protect?

Gianelli walked over. "What I need from you, Lindy," he said, using a firm, businesslike tone, "is an inventory of everything that's missing."

The curator threw her head back and drew in a couple of ragged breaths. "Yes, of course," she said. She stepped past him and headed toward the door on the right that led into the museum office.

Father John turned in the opposite direction. In the library, he dialed Vicky's one-woman law office in Lander and waited while her secretary put him through. What seemed like five minutes passed before the familiar voice came on the line: "John? What's up?"

He told her about the missing artifacts and the clever way the thief had gone about his job.

The line went quiet. For a moment, he thought they had been disconnected. Then Vicky said, "Sounds like Junior Tallman's back in business."

"Where can I find him?"

"Wait a minute." There was the noise of paper rustling. "Junior came to see me after he got out of prison. Gave me a big story about how he was going to change his life and follow the good red road. He said he'd started studying the Arapaho Way with one of the traditionals. Clint Old Bear, I think it was. Junior was so convincing, I believed him. Here it is." Another rustling noise came over the line. "He's staying at the old cabin out on Trout Circle Road, about a mile past Driscoll Lane."

"Thanks," Father John said.

"You're going out there, aren't you?"

He didn't reply.

"Let the fed handle this, John. If Junior Tallman has plans to turn the artifacts into a lot of cash, he could be very dangerous."

"Gianelli's waiting on fingerprints. By the time he arrests Junior, the artifacts will be gone. Maybe I can reason with the man and talk him out of selling his own heritage."

"You don't know Junior, John." Vicky paused a moment. Then she said, "I'll meet you out there."

* * *

Vicky saw the black sedan rise out of the dust cloud and speed toward her down the center of Trout Circle Road. She swung the Bronco to the right, as close to the borrow ditch as she dared, and gripped the steering wheel to keep from slipping off the road. The sedan shot past. A man as small as a child was clutching the steering wheel, head thrust forward, dark cap pulled low over his forehead. The license plates were white and green. Colorado.

Vicky felt her muscles tense. What if John O'Malley was right and Junior Tallman had already sold the artifacts? She may have just passed the dealer who bought them! She considered turning around and following the sedan, but it had already disappeared from the rearview mirror. It had probably turned onto Highway 287 and could be heading north. Or south. How would she know which direction it had taken?

She pressed down on the accelerator and watched the dirt road unfurl ahead, trying to think rationally. What dealer would make the long drive from Colorado before he knew for certain that Junior had the artifacts? More than likely Junior was in the cabin now, calling contacts, making final arrangements. *I've got some good stuff.* She could almost hear the man's voice, unctuous and arrogant at the same time.

Set back about fifty feet from the road ahead was a cabin that resembled dozens of old cabins scattered across the reservation, constructed of peeling gray logs with a plank roof that ran to one side and a tilted wood stoop at the front door. Despite the brown pickup with a camper in the bed parked under a lone cottonwood tree a few feet away, the cabin had a used-up, deserted look. No sign of Father John's red Toyota pickup, but St. Francis Mission was a good forty-minute drive. It was only thirty minutes from Lander.

For a moment, Vicky thought about pulling over and waiting for the red pickup. *Junior could be dangerous,* she'd warned Father John. But she was Junior's lawyer; she'd defended the man.

She turned right into the dirt yard, parked a few feet from the stoop, and knocked on the front door. "Junior," she called. "It's Vicky Holden. I have to talk to you."

Silence. She knocked again and waited. The wind whistled through the cottonwood branches and cut little ripples over the dirt yard. She tried the doorknob. It turned in her hand, and she stepped inside. A thick smell, like that of wet leather, engulfed her. Sprawled on his back on the plank floor was Junior Tallman, half of his face gone, blood pooling around his shoulders and soaking into his denim shirt, and bloody, gray clumps of brain and scalp and hair spattered across a broken-down sofa and the shiny legs of a yellow Formica-topped table.

Vicky backed through the door and ran into the yard, doubled over, retching, grateful she'd been too rushed this morning for breakfast. She could picture what had taken place. The childlike man in the black sedan had quarreled with Junior over the price. Junior got angry, probably started shouting and making threats. The dealer panicked, pulled a gun, and fired.

Vicky made herself breathe deeply—one, two, three breaths—until the nausea dissipated. She pulled herself upright just as the red pickup turned into the yard and stopped. John O'Malley swung his long, jeans-clad legs out from behind the steering wheel. "Junior's dead." Vicky heard the sound of her own voice, hollow and shaky in the wind, as she explained—she was babbling, she knew—that the killer had passed her on the road. The look in the priest's eyes reflected her own horror. He started for the cabin. A minute passed, then another. She knew he would pray over the body, ask the Creator to accept Junior Tallman and forgive whatever sins he may have had on his conscience. There were many, she thought. She dug into her black purse for her cell phone, tapped in 911, and told the dispatch officer what she'd found.

As she clicked off, she realized John O'Malley had come back outside and was examining the camper in the pickup. He opened the rear door, and she walked over. An Indian blanket covered the floor. Arranged neatly on top were parfleches, belts and head roaches, an eagle whistle, a bow and arrow. Deerskin dresses and shirts were carefully folded in tissue paper. She recognized her own astonishment in the way Father John gripped the edge of the door and stared wordlessly at the beautiful things. The dealer had shot Junior, then left the artifacts behind.

At the FBI office in Lander, the artifacts covered two conference tables. Father John reached out and touched the shaft of the arrow. "Everything seems to be in good condition," he said in a tone edged with relief.

"Junior was clever." Vicky moved slowly down the other side of the table, then stopped, her attention diverted for a moment to the eagle bone whistle tied with feathers that fanned over the polished wood tabletop like air. "Damaged artifacts don't bring as high a price."

"Then why didn't the dealer take them?" Father John said. It was the question he'd been asking himself since he'd opened the camper door and seen the familiar items. Even Gianelli had seemed surprised to find them, after he and Banner and a phalanx of police officers had pulled into the dirt yard. Father John had watched the officers load the artifacts into boxes; then he'd followed the fed to Lander to make a formal identification and take care of the paperwork. He was glad Vicky had come along. Maybe she'd come up with some answers.

The door across the room swung open, and Gianelli walked in, waving a flimsy white sheet of paper in front of him. "Lindy Meadows just faxed over the inventory," he said. "Twenty-seven items. I suspect that's what we've got."

"I only get twenty-six," Vicky said.

Something was missing. Father John let his gaze roam over the artifacts, mentally placing each one in its display case. And then he saw it. "The council pipe's not here," he said.

"Maybe the pipe's worth so much money, the dealer decided not to bother with the rest." Something in Gianelli's tone said he didn't buy it.

"It's very old," Father John said, groping for some explanation. He felt as if he were stumbling across the open plains with no landmarks to point the way. "The pipe could have been smoked in the early treaty councils, which gives it historic value. But some of the other things are probably worth a lot more." He nodded toward the beaded deerskin dress still folded in tissue paper. "Lindy's told me more than once that a deerskin dress could bring enough money to support St. Francis Mission most of a year. Why would the killer leave something that valuable?"

The agent shrugged. "We've got an all-points out on the black sedan. The guy won't get far. You'll have the pipe back in no time."

"I hope so," Father John said.

Vicky seemed as preoccupied as he was, Father John thought. They walked in silence to the parking lot. He opened the Bronco door and waited for her to slip inside, still not saying anything, not wanting to lose the flicker of an idea that had started darting at the edge of his mind.

Vicky threw out a hand to stop him from closing the door.

"Somebody else could have taken the pipe," she said.

Father John realized she was grappling with the same idea that he'd been trying to bring into focus. He walked around and got in beside her. "What makes you think so?"

Vicky started the engine, eyes straight ahead on the redbrick wall of the FBI building. She left the transmission in park, and the hum of the idling motor floated into the quiet between them. "All the artifacts are sacred," she said finally. "They belonged to the ancestors, and they retain part of their lives, their spirits. But if the pipe wasn't a council pipe . . ." She hesitated, then plunged on. "If it was a *prayer* pipe . . ."

"It would be the most sacred artifact of all," Father John said, finishing the thought. It was his own, part of the new idea working its way into his mind. He had believed the pipe was the council pipe in the photo, but he'd been wrong. All Arapaho pipes were made of black-and-white stone.

"Junior was studying the Arapaho Way with Clint Old Bear," he went on. It was making sense now. Clint Old Bear had visited the pipe every Friday. "He must have told Junior it was a prayer pipe, so Junior decided to liberate it from the museum."

"But if all he wanted was the pipe, why steal the other artifacts?" Vicky said, skepticism in her tone.

Father John sighed. "Temptation is strong. Junior knew he could pick the locks on the exhibit cases in minutes, and he had the connections on the Indian market to sell the artifacts. Maybe he figured he'd save the pipe and make himself a lot of money at the same time."

Vicky had started drumming her fingers on the rim of the steering wheel. "It still doesn't explain why the dealer left the artifacts, unless . . ." She stopped drumming and turned sideways, allowing her eyes to bore into his. "Unless Junior was already dead when the dealer showed up. He must have found the body and beat it out of there without even looking for the artifacts. He was doing at least eighty when he passed me." She drew in a long breath and exhaled slowly. "You know what this means, don't you? Whoever killed Junior took the sacred pipe."

"Let's go have a talk with Clint Old Bear," Father John said.

Vicky shifted the Bronco into reverse, backed a few feet, then shifted again and carved a wide circle through the parking lot, gravel pinging the undercarriage, tires squealing. Father John caught a glimpse of Gianelli at the window just before they roared onto the road.

Twenty minutes later they drove down a narrow dirt path in the foothills and parked at the edge of a grove of cottonwoods. Nestled in the trees was a large, white canvas tipi. In front of the opened flap, a tripod held a heavy-looking black kettle over a smoldering fire. Smoke trailed around the kettle and drifted up into the branches. A few feet away, a man wrapped in a black and red Indian blanket sat on his haunches, facing a large wood frame that stood upright on the ground. The scene resembled the diorama in the museum, except that the frame held a pipe about two feet long with a black stem and white bowl.

Father John followed Vicky through the trees to the campsite. The only sound was that of dried leaves crunching underfoot. The man didn't move. His arms were crossed in front, hands lost somewhere in the folds of the blanket. A thick, gray braid ran down the hump of his back.

"Clint," Father John said when they were only a couple feet away.

The man twisted slightly and glanced up, past the blanket bunched at his neck. Wrinkles cut deep furrows into his dark forehead. The black eyes narrowed in sadness. "I been waitin' for you. You bring the police?"

"No." Father John dropped down on one knee beside the old man. "What happened?" he said.

"I couldn't let Junior sell the prayer pipe." Clint turned back toward the frame. "I figured Junior was up to something when he didn't come around the last couple weeks. So this morning I went out to his place. He was fixin' to load something out of that camper of his, so I went over to give him a hand, you know. Then I seen what was on that old blanket. All the stuff that was in the museum, and the sacred pipe, too, just layin' there, like it was nothing. Oh, I knew what was goin' on. Junior was gonna sell the ancestors' things. He didn't deny it. 'What the hell,' he says. 'Who cares about this old stuff anyway?' And I thought all the time he was comin' out here to learn the Arapaho Way 'cause he wanted to be a new man. All he wanted was to find out about the stuff in the museum so he'd know how much money he could get for it."

The old man tilted his head back and fixed his gaze on the pipe. "Truth was, Junior loved money more than anything, even more than the sacred pipe that sent smoke up to heaven and joined the people to the Creator Himself. Even more than that."

"So you shot him," Vicky said. Her voice was quiet behind them.

The old man had started shaking. He drew in his shoulders and dropped his head. "I didn't mean to shoot him. I said, 'Junior, we gotta talk this over.' He said he didn't have no time. I said, 'It's not the Arapaho Way, sellin' the ancestors' things.' He just looked at me and said, 'They're goin', old man.' I said, 'Not the sacred pipe, Junior. It's gotta go back to the museum so the people can come and visit it.' 'Get outta my way, old man,' he says, and starts pushing me back, pushing me hard. So I grabbed a skillet on the table and hit him on the side of the head. He went down on both knees and pulls out a gun. I hit him again, and the gun went flying across the floor. I was going after it when Junior knocks me down and starts pounding on my head 'til everything starts goin' black, but I got my hand on the gun and then I hear a noise like thunder and I seen Junior laying real still next to me."

Clint stopped talking. The cottonwoods swayed in the wind; the air filled with the smell of smoke. "It was terrible," he said.

"You didn't mean to kill him." Father John reached out and patted the old man's shoulder.

Slowly Clint began unfolding the blanket. He withdrew a small, black revolver and turned it over in his hand, examining it, as if it were some alien object he couldn't understand. Then he handed it to Father John.

"I heard everything." Gianelli's voice came from the far side of the tipi. There was the slow, rhythmic crackling of leaves under his boots.

Father John got to his feet and gave the revolver to the agent. "What brought you here?"

"The way you and Vicky tore out of the parking lot." He shot a glance at Vicky. "I figured you two were on to something, so I decided I'd better follow and see what it was." The agent stepped around the frame and leaned over the old man. "You know I have to arrest you, Clint." In a voice not much above a whisper, he began ticking off the old man's rights—the right to remain silent, the right to have an attorney present.

Clint started to his feet, struggling upright, reeling sideways. Father John gripped the old man's arm to steady him, and Gianelli took hold of his other arm. Finally the man was on his feet, still swaying, boots set a couple of feet apart. Moisture trickled down his cheeks, and he dipped his head first one way and then the other, brushing against the edge of the blanket. Throwing his shoulders back, he turned to Vicky and nodded.

"I'll be representing Clint Old Bear," she told the agent.

My Last Good-Bye

The Second Commandment:
Thou shalt not make to thyself any graven images.

WIND RIVER GAZETTE

MAN'S DEATH DUE TO NATURAL CAUSES
by Sam Harrison

Jan. 16, 1972. Lander, Wy. An autopsy on the body of a forty-year-old man found on the Wind River Reservation indicates that he died of natural causes, according to Fremont County Coroner James Goodly. Cause of death was asphyxia.

Leon Whiteman was found last Monday in the bedroom of his home on Givens Road. A police spokesman said that Albertine Whiteman discovered her husband's body at two o'clock in the afternoon. The woman told police that Whiteman had been in good health, but had complained of shortness of breath earlier in the day.

*   *   *

The one-story pile of red bricks floated out of the ice fog that had pressed down over the streets of Lander all morning. It was now almost two in the afternoon, and snow was falling through the grayness. Mounds of snow lay over the ground and weighed down the evergreen branches. Father John O'Malley left the Toyota pickup in the circular driveway that curved along the front of the hospital. He patted at his jacket for the silver compact of sacred oils in his shirt pocket, then plunged into the fog and snow, across the ice-paved sidewalk and into the lobby.

Waving to the receptionist at the desk, he started down the corridor—right, left—to the intensive care unit. He knew the way. He even knew the faint, antiseptic odors and the muffled clank of trolleys behind closed doors. How many times had he visited the hospital in the eight years he'd been at St. Francis Mission on the Wind River Reservation? Two, three hundred? He'd lost count.

He found Rosemary Morningside in the waiting area next to the oversized steel door beneath the black-lettered sign that said ICU. The old woman sat huddled inside a bulky, tan jacket, weaving her fingers through the fringe of the red scarf that hung around her neck and puddled in her lap. She glanced up, a startled look in her face.

"Oh, Father," Rosemary said, sinking back into the chair. "I thought you was the doctor bringing more bad news."

Father John set a hand on her shoulder for a moment, then perched on the chair next to her.

"How's Darryl?" he said.

It was as if a flood had started. The old woman dropped her face into her hands and began sobbing. Her shoulders shook inside the jacket. Moisture pooled around her fingers.

"My grandson's gonna die, Father." Her voice was thick with tears. "He's got the throat sickness."

"Throat sickness?"

"It's like his throat's closing up on him. Like he's being strangled." She balled her hands and began jabbing at the moisture on her cheeks.

A moment passed before she said, "Cindy's with him now. Don't matter that Darryl and her was gettin' a divorce. She come to say her good-bye."

"Divorce? I'm sorry to hear that," Father John said. The couple had been married only a couple of months. He could picture Darryl Morningside: twenty-five years old, tall and rangy, plunging forward always, never stopping to look back or question himself. Kept a job long enough to get money for a good binge. He'd visited Darryl in the Fremont County jail about six months ago after the man had been arrested on a drunk and disorderly charge. It was the last time Father John had seen him.

"Darryl said it was best." Rosemary was hurrying on, both hands lost again in the red fringe. "Said he didn't know why he'd gone and gotten himself married. Didn't hardly know Cindy, 'cause she just moved up to the rez from Denver a few months ago. He didn't mean her no harm." She was smiling through the tears now—an old woman dismissing the tantrum of a much-loved child. "Darryl just ain't ready to get himself settled down yet," she said.

The steel door moved inward. A smallish woman who might still be in her teens, with frizzed black hair, stood in the opening. She had on a baggy jacket and blue jeans that hugged her thin legs. A lattice of shadow and light fell across her face, which was hard-set like a plaster mask. She let the door swing shut behind her before she stepped into the waiting area.

"This here's Father John." Rosemary glanced between him and the young woman. "He's come to anoint my grandson."

"Well, he's all yours." The young woman—a girl, he thought—tossed her head back toward the door. "I'm outta here."

Rosemary scooted forward and lifted an anxious face to the girl. "What're you talking about, Cindy?"

"Darryl said we gotta move on, and I'm moving on. Got me a bus ticket back home to Denver today."

"Today! What if Darryl wakes up and calls for you?"

"You think he's gonna wake up, Grandmother?" The girl's laughter was quick and brief—an expulsion of breath. "Well, if he wakes up, you tell him I said my last good-bye."

She whirled about and started down the corridor, almost skipping, Father John thought, hooking her fingers into the back pockets of her jeans as she went. Her boots made a schussing noise, like a wet mop slapping the hard floor.

"What she says is right, Father." Rosemary turned to him. The anguish in her face was so palpable, he reached out and took her hand. "Darryl ain't gonna wake up."

After a moment, Father John stood up and let himself through the steel door. A series of rooms fanned in a half circle about the nurses' station, which was bathed in a well of white light. Behind the counter, a nurse in a blue smock, hair caught in a blue cap, was flipping through the papers on a clipboard. She looked up and gave him a smile of recognition. *Ah, the Indian priest.*

"You'll find Morningside in there, Father." She gestured toward the second door.

He thanked her and, slipping the compact out of his shirt pocket, went into the room. Darryl was propped upright in the high, narrow bed, eyes closed, face blanched and drawn, a clear plastic tube jammed into his throat. Other tubes ran from a steel pole next to the bed into his arms, which lay at his sides like thin, brown logs. His chest rose and fell under the white sheet, the sound of his breathing as forced as the push-pull of a bellows.

Father John dipped his fingers into the sacred oil and, praying silently, made the sign of the cross on the man's eyelids, nose, mouth, and hands.

When he had finished, he said, "May God have mercy on you, Darryl."

"Amen." The woman's voice came from behind.

Father John glanced around. Dr. Emily Jordan, a tall, middle-aged woman with blond hair that brushed the shoulders of her white smock, stood in the doorway. "Can I have a word with you, Father?" she said.

He followed her out to the nurses' station. She turned and, leaning back against the counter, hugging a clipboard against her chest, looked up at him. "I'm puzzled, Father," she began. "There's no sign of a bacterial infection. It looks like an allergic reaction. There's acute swelling in the ventricular folds within the larynx. He's not responding to the intravenous steroids. The tracheotomy is keeping him alive now, but . . ." She shook her head. "If we knew what he might have ingested, we may be able to find an antidote. I've talked to Darryl's grandmother. She said he's never had an allergic reaction before. She has no idea what might have caused this. What can you tell me, Father? You know the Arapaho culture. Have they started using some new plant or herb in the ceremonies?"

Father John shook his head. "Not that I've heard."

The doctor drew in a long breath and did a half turn toward Darryl's room. "I'm going to lose him, Father. I don't like losing a patient, especially when I don't understand the reason." She faced him again. "I did a search of the medical literature on unexplained allergic reactions. Thirty years ago, there was a similar case on the reservation. Another Arapaho. Leon Whiteman."

"What happened to him?"

Dr. Jordan closed her eyes a moment. "The man was found dead at his home. Cause of death? Asphyxia due to acute swelling within the larynx. Look . . ." She lifted a hand, as if to detain him, although he hadn't moved. "Darryl's grandmother also said she never knew Whiteman. She was living in Oklahoma at the time, and the Whiteman family left the reservation before she moved here. But somebody on the rez must remember the man. Whoever it is might know what caused Whiteman's reaction. If we can find the cause, Father, we might be able to help Darryl." She paused. "It's our only hope."

Father John drove north through the fog and sputtering traffic toward the apartment building where Vicky Holden lived. They'd worked on dozens of cases together: adoptions, divorces, DUIs. He, the mission priest—the Indian priest, people called him—and Vicky, the Arapaho lawyer. She'd grown up on the reservation. The people, the culture—they were part of her. If anyone would know how to help Darryl, it would be Vicky.

Inside the lobby, Father John leaned on the button next to her name. A mixture of cigarette smoke and wet wool lingered in the air. From somewhere inside the building came a faint vibrating noise.

Then the familiar voice: "Who is it?"

He bent toward the speaker. "John O'Malley."

There was a half second of silence before a buzzer sounded over his head. He opened the inner door, took the stairs two at a time, and hurried down the second-floor hallway. Vicky was standing outside the door at the far end—a slight figure in a blue sweater and khaki-colored slacks, with shoulder-length black hair that gleamed under the ceiling light.

"What's going on?" she said, motioning him inside to the sofa. She sat down beside him. The yellowish light from the table lamp cut through the afternoon grayness.

"Darryl Morningside's in the hospital," Father John said. "The doctor thinks he's had an allergic reaction. He's dying."

Vicky let out a gasp. "How's Cindy taking it?"

"You know her?"

"She came to see me a couple weeks ago. Darryl wanted a divorce and she needed a lawyer. She was devastated. I agreed to represent her. And then . . ." Vicky shook her head. "Last week Cindy called and said she wouldn't be needing a lawyer, after all. I figured she and Darryl were getting back together."

"I don't think so." Father John told her what the young man's grandmother had said. "Listen, Vicky," he said, hurrying on. "Thirty years ago, there was a similar case on the reservation. An Arapaho named Leon Whiteman died from an unexplained allergic reaction. The doctor thinks someone on the rez might know the cause. Maybe some plant or herb . . ."

The idea hung in the air between them a moment. Then Vicky got to her feet and walked around the sofa to the window. She pulled the slats of the blinds apart and stared out into the fog. "I was only a kid at the time," she said, "but I remember when Whiteman died. The moccasin telegraph was filled with gossip. Everybody was talking about his death, but . . ." She glanced back at him. "When the kids walked in, the adults stopped talking. That's how we knew it was bad."

"What did you think happened?" Father John stood up and went to her.

Vicky was staring out the window again. The fog was rolling over the flat-roofed building across the street. Quarter-sized snowflakes stuck to the window. "The kids gossiped, too," she said finally. "They said that Leon's wife, Albertine—we all knew her, a skinny, crabby woman who used to glare at us at the tribal get-togethers." She drew in a long breath. "The kids said that Albertine killed her husband."

"How, Vicky? How did she do it?" The doctor could be right, Father John was thinking. Both Darryl and Whiteman could have reacted to the same poisonous plant.

Vicky turned toward him. "Josie Yellow Calf would remember. She's never forgotten anything."

Of course, Father John was thinking. Eighty-some years old, with a sharp wisdom about her, Josie was respected by everyone, even the other grandmothers. He said, "I'll go see her right away."

"I'll go with you," Vicky said.

Vicky wondered whether Josie was home, the little house looked so dark and quiet in the fog and blowing snow. Father John guided the pickup through the snowdrifts in the yard and stopped a few feet from the ice-crusted stoop at the front door.

Vicky hesitated a moment, reluctant to abandon the warmth of the pickup, but Father John was already out, walking around the pickup, ducking into the storm, his cowboy hat pulled low. She let herself out her door and, clutching her coat collar at her throat, followed him up the steps to the stoop. The sound of his hand rapping the door splintered in the cold. Flecks of snow clung to the shoulders of his jacket.

A couple of seconds passed. Vicky exchanged a glance with the man beside her. Josie could be waiting out the storm at the home of one of her children. They should have called first.

There was a squealing sound. The door was inching open. Peering around the edge out of the dimness inside was Josie Yellow Calf, a tiny woman with two thick braids of gray hair that hung down the front of her red sweater. The narrow eyes darted about: Vicky, Father John, Vicky again. Slowly the old woman's lined face softened in recognition.

"Get yourselves in here out of the cold," she commanded, yanking the door wide open and motioning them into the small living room. She closed the door and, reaching up, began brushing the snow off Father John's jacket. Flakes fluttered over the vinyl floor like white ash.

"We have to talk to you, Grandmother." Vicky shrugged out of her own coat and laid it over the back of a chair.

"Yes, yes," the old woman said. Nodding, brushing. A tangle of gray hair worked loose from one of the braids and fell across her cheek as she helped Father John out of his jacket. "I didn't suppose you come all the way out here in a blizzard to drink coffee with an old lady. Sit down." Josie tossed her head toward the sofa. She walked over and turned on the table lamp, sending a flare of light into the center of the room. Then she turned toward the kitchen. "You need some coffee to warm your bones."

"Let me help you, Grandmother." Vicky started after her.

Josie swung around. "I said, sit down, Granddaughter."

Vicky walked over to the sofa and dropped down beside Father John. From the kitchen came the muffled sound of the old woman's footsteps on the hard floor and the clank of pottery.

After a few moments, Josie was back, handing out two mugs of coffee with steam curling over the brims. Vicky took a sip, savoring the warmth that began to spread inside her.

"Tell me about the worry that's sitting on your shoulders like crows."

Josie settled herself in a recliner, smoothed her dress over her lap, and clasped her hands. She took up only half the seat, like a small doll leaning against the armrest. The edge of the light fell over her face.

"It's about Darryl Morningside," Father John began. He had both hands wrapped around his coffee mug.

"I hear Darryl's real sick." The old woman nodded.

"His larynx is closing, Grandmother. Just like Leon Whiteman's."

Something moved behind the old woman's black eyes, as if a chink of memory had fallen loose. "Leon," she said. "He wasn't a bad sort."

"What happened to him, Grandmother?" Vicky shifted forward. "I remember the gossip."

"You were just a kid," Josie said, brushing back the loose strand of hair and tucking it into the braid. "But kids always know, don't they?"

"I remember people saying Albertine killed her husband. How, Grandmother? Did she use some kind of poison?"

"Poison!" Josie laid her head back against the chair and laughed. "Albertine Whiteman didn't need poison," she said finally. "That woman was the devil."

"What are you saying, Grandmother?" Now Father John leaned toward the old woman.

"She had spiritual power, Albertine. Power to do good for the people, but all she thought about was herself. She didn't ever think about the people. Just herself. Got mad at Leon and used her power to get revenge. She thought that was gonna solve all her problems." The old woman gave a little laugh and rolled her head along the back of the recliner.

Vicky took a long sip of coffee, but the warmth inside her had turned to ice. She was beginning to understand. The jumble of old stories, parts left untold, the whispering voices of the elders, the wordless sorrow in their eyes: all falling into place now. *Albertine had used her power for evil.*

She said, "Albertine put a curse on her husband."

Josie kept her gaze steady, her face frozen in acknowledgment. "She made his larynx close up. Doctors might've helped him if she'd taken him to the hospital. But she didn't. She just waited for him to die. Said she come home and found him. You think that wife of Darryl's got spiritual power? You think she put a curse on the boy?"

"I don't know," Vicky heard herself saying. She didn't want to believe in curses—what doctor would believe a curse had caused Darryl's larynx to swell? She glanced sideways at Father John, who was leaning forward, taking a drink of coffee. Did he believe? Maybe, she thought. There were people who received the gift of spiritual power. He had received his own. Spiritual power was always given to help others, but sometimes . . .

"Darryl wanted a divorce," she said, "and Cindy was very upset."

Josie was quiet a moment. Finally she said, "Moccasin telegraph says the girl's part Arapaho, one of them city Indians. Who are her people?"

Vicky finished her coffee and set the mug on the floor next to her boots, taking a minute to pull from her memory everything Cindy had told her about herself. "Her father was Cheyenne," she began. "Jim Red Feather. Her mother was Arapaho. I don't know her mother's name."

The old woman exhaled a long breath, like steam whistling from a kettle. "Ah. I heard Virginia married a Cheyenne in Denver."

"Virginia?" Father John said.

"I can see that girl yet. Fourteen years old, she was, thin as a stick with long black hair and eyes that stared at you but didn't see nothing. She never cried, not one tear, when her daddy died. She knew. Oh, she knew, all right, what her mother had done."

"Wait a minute, Grandmother," Father John said. "Are you saying that Cindy is Albertine Whiteman's granddaughter?"

Josie nodded. "She could've learned the curse. It could've been passed down to her mother. Her mother could've given it to her."

Vicky lifted her head toward the window behind the old woman. Outside the snow was still falling through the thick, gray light. "What about the spiritual power?" she said.

"Albertine was blessed with the power to do good. Maybe Cindy got the same blessing." The old woman's voice sounded far away. "Albertine chose evil. Now Cindy's gone and done like her grandmother."

"How can we help Darryl?" Father John said.

Josie shook her head. "Cindy's the only one can help him. She put the curse on him. She's the one has to take it away."

"She's going back to Denver." Father John got to his feet. "We've got to catch her before she gets on the bus."

Vicky held his eyes a moment. He *did* believe. She said, "Cindy won't take the curse away. She's angry and hurt. All she can think about is revenge."

"There's something else she better think about," Josie said, pushing herself out of the recliner. "Let's get over to the bus station."

The station looked like a brown cube dropped into the middle of the snow-covered parking lot. Black exhaust belched out of the blue and silver bus parked at the entrance. Father John caught the word DENVER in the destination slot above the windshield. A group of people—they all looked alike, bundled in coats and hoods—were getting on board. He stopped a few feet away and scanned the faces. Cindy wasn't there, and he could see that several passengers were still making their way out of the station.

They got out of the pickup and threaded their way past the passengers, Father John holding one of Josie's arms, Vicky the other. The waiting room was hot and smelled of stale food. Behind the ticket counter, the agent sat hunched over the book opened in front of him.

On the far side of the waiting room, Cindy was shrugging into a jacket, fixing a black bag over one shoulder, her gaze on the windows and the bus beyond. She reached down, grabbed the handle of the roll-on at her feet, and started pulling it toward the door. The wheels rattled over the hard floor.

"Hello, Cindy," Father John said.

The girl stopped. She looked at Father John, then swung her gaze to the old woman. A mixture of fear and comprehension bubbled beneath her expression. "What're you doing here?" she said.

"You come sit down." Josie reached out, took the girl's hand, and led her to the bench beneath the windows.

"I gotta catch my bus."

"We want to talk to you, Cindy," Father John said. He and Vicky followed them over to the bench.

"I don't need no priest. I don't need no lawyer, either."

"You're going to need a lawyer when Darryl dies," Vicky said. "You could face a murder charge."

"Murder?" There was a spasm of laughter. "You're all crazy." The girl had perched on the edge of the bench, keeping her eyes averted from the old woman beside her.

Father John sat down on the other side. "We know about the curse," he said. "Darryl's still alive. It's not too late. You must take the curse away."

"Don't tell me you believe that Indian crap about curses." Cindy was watching the door where the last passenger had stepped outside. "Look, I gotta go." She jumped to her feet and gripped the handle of the roll-on. "Cops sure as hell ain't gonna believe Darryl got himself murdered by a curse," she said. "There ain't a white judge or jury in this world that's gonna believe it. I don't care what you say; they ain't gonna believe you."

Father John exchanged a glance with Vicky. The girl was right; they both knew it. There was no place for curses—Indian superstition—in the world of law and rationality.

"It don't matter what white people think." Josie set one hand on the roll-on, as if to hold it in place. "What matters is, the spirits gave you a gift. You was blessed. You gotta use your gift to help people. You gotta send goodness into the world, not evil."

"I don't know what you're talking about."

"Oh, you know, all right," Josie said. "You send goodness into the world, it comes back on you. You send out evil, it's gonna come back on you, just like it did on Albertine."

Cindy jerked the roll-on free. "My grandmother died in a car accident. Could happen to anybody."

"One year after your granddaddy died of the throat sickness, Albertine's car went off the road, but it wasn't the accident killed her. You know that, don't you, Cindy?" The old woman hurried on. "It was the evil that come back and killed her. The car went into the river. Real shallow river, but the water came up and got in her throat and cut off all her air, so she couldn't breathe no more. Just like Leon couldn't breathe no more after she put the curse on him. You want the evil coming back on you, Cindy? You wanna die like your grandmother? All your air cut off?"

"Stop it!" The girl swung around and faced the old woman. "You don't know what Darryl did to me. Stood up in front of the judge and said he took me for his wife. Said he was gonna love and cherish me forever and ever, and three weeks later, he says to me, 'I don't want you no more.' 'Don't want me!' I said. 'Where'm I supposed to go? What'm I supposed to do? Nobody's gonna want me now, if you throw me away.' He says, 'I don't care. Get outta my life,' so I think, Jesus, now I need a lawyer. But then I think, I don't need no lawyer, and I don't need Darryl, and he was gonna pay for the lies that come outta his throat. I got the power, all right, just like Grandmother, and she give the curses to my mama, and Mama give 'em to me."

The front door opened and a gust of cold air blew across the waiting room. The driver leaned inside. "Last call for the Denver bus," he shouted.

"It's not too late." Father John got to his feet. "Call the evil back, Cindy."

Vicky said, "If you won't take the curse away for Darryl's sake, Cindy, you'd better do it for your own."

The driver had disappeared. From outside came the muffled sound of the bus motor turning over.

The girl stood motionless, staring into the gray light of the waiting room. Finally she leaned over, pulled open the zipper on the roll-on, and began tossing out items: tee shirts, jeans, sneakers trailing over the floor. Finally she held something solid in her hands.

She sat down and placed the object in her lap. It looked like a gourd, Father John thought, except that the rounded end was smooth and painted like a doll, with black hair around the forehead, black eyes and nostrils, and pinkish, scowling lips. The neck of the gourd was long and wrapped with a leather thong. Cindy stared at the gourd a moment, then looked around at Josie.

"Go on," the old woman said.

The girl set both hands over the gourd, leaned into the wall again, and closed her eyes. Her lips began moving silently; her arms and hands seemed to go limp. Finally, she opened her eyes and cupped the head of the gourd in her left hand. With her right hand, she began unwrapping the leather thong.

Father John watched the thong falling over the girl's lap, like a brown snake uncoiling itself. He thought he detected—Dear God, could it be true? The painted face seemed to relax, as if the gourd itself could now breathe. The girl was shivering. Tears, like silver threads, were running down her face, which seemed softer, relaxed, as if the mask had slipped away.

Father John took her hand. "You're free now, Cindy," he said.

"I'm happy to report that our patient's doing fine." Dr. Jordan had stepped out of Darryl's room just as Father John and Vicky were about to enter. Through the doorway, Father John could see the young man sitting up in bed, laughing and gesturing with one hand toward his grandmother, who had pushed her chair so close the white sheet draped over her lap. And yet, Father John thought, there was something different about the young man, as if he'd been traveling in a foreign place and was marked by the experience.

"A couple hours ago," the doctor went on, not trying to disguise the relief in her voice, "Darryl woke up and indicated that he wanted the tube taken out. And, indeed, the swelling in his larynx has gone down. It appears the steroids have started to work, after all. I want to keep him overnight to be sure he's going to be okay, but I suspect he'll be home tomorrow."

"That's good news," Father John said.

The doctor was quiet a moment, as if she were trying to grasp some other idea. Finally she said—shifting her gaze from Father John to Vicky—"It wasn't an allergy, was it?"

Father John shook his head.

"I see." Her tone indicated that she didn't see at all. "No infection and no allergy." She shrugged. "I suppose it doesn't matter. Darryl's recovering, and that's all that counts."

"That's all that counts," Father John said, but the doctor had already spun around and was hurrying down the corridor.

"She wouldn't believe you if you told her," Vicky said.

"She knows." He smiled at the Arapaho woman beside him. "It's an Indian matter. She doesn't expect to understand. Come on," he said, ushering her into the room. "Let's go see Darryl."

Bad Heart

The Third Commandment:
Thou shalt not take my name in vain.

From inside the apartment came the muffled sound of a ringing phone. Vicky Holden balanced the bag of groceries against the wall and dug inside her purse for the key. She'd heard the ringing the minute she'd stepped off the elevator. She'd hurried down the corridor to her apartment at the far end, the sound growing louder, more distinct. Then the ringing had stopped. Now it was starting up again.

"Hold on," she said out loud. She jammed the key into the lock and turned the knob. Gripping her purse and the grocery bag in one arm, she plunged across the living room toward the desk and lifted the receiver. A can toppled out of the bag and rolled over the carpet, clinking against the leg of the coffee table.

"Hello," she said as she struggled to right the rest of the groceries on the desk. She set her purse down and flipped on the little lamp that beamed a puddle of light over the brown paper bag.

"Is this Vicky Holden, the lawyer?" She couldn't place the man's voice, yet there was something familiar about it, something unsettling, with a hint of intimacy that made her think the caller must be someone she knew.

"Yes," she said. She could hear the hesitancy in her own voice. The caller was probably an Arapaho looking for a lawyer, picked up on a DUI or an assault, calling from the Fremont County jail, his one desperate call. Vicky was accustomed to such calls. They came during the day at her law office in Lander at the southern edge of the Wind River Reservation. Sometimes they came in the middle of the night. She was the only Arapaho attorney in the area.

"This is Warden Ransom from the state penitentiary."

Vicky dropped onto the chair in front of the desk and stared into the shadows falling through the living room. Beyond the sofa, lights from outside flickered across the window in the wind. The bag of groceries toppled sideways, spilling oranges and a loaf of bread onto the desktop.

"What is it?"she asked. Two or three of her clients had been sentenced to the penitentiary in the last couple of years. The best she'd been able to manage for them were reduced sentences. The warden had never called her before.

"Seems like you'd want to hear about Lonny Hereford." The voice waited a beat, then hurried on. "You remember Lonny, don't you?"

"Yes, of course." Something wasn't right. Lonny Hereford had never been her client. Vicky felt her fingers tighten around the receiver. Her thoughts raced back three years. Lonny Hereford hunched over the grave of his wife, Muriel, at the St. Francis Mission cemetery, loud gusts of grief erupting from his throat as the coffin disappeared into the earth, everybody pressing around, patting the man's shoulders. Even members of Muriel's family, sad-eyed and solicitous, gathered around Lonny in an invisible harness of agreement. A horrible accident. Slipped and fell down the basement steps in the house the couple had been renting in Riverton, hit her head wrong on the concrete floor. Nobody could live through that, and Lonny was so broken up. Kept swearing to God that he wished it could've been him, and everybody in the family had believed him.

"Yeah, thought you wouldn't forget Lonny. He told me himself that you and that mission priest on the reservation, Father John O'Malley, I think he said, was responsible for putting him behind bars."

Vicky didn't say anything for a moment. The morning she'd read about Muriel's death in the newspaper, she'd gone to the detective in charge of the investigation and told him how Muriel had come to her office two days earlier. Vicky could still see the woman, not much more than a teenager, with long black hair and thin, hunched shoulders, hesitating at the door, fingers kneading the flowery red bag clasped to her chest. She'd moved inside, slowly, eyes scanning the office as if she expected something to jump out at her, and perched on a side chair. She wanted to divorce Lonny, she'd said, her voice small and whispery. She'd had enough, all the drinking and raging and knocking her around. She'd gone to Father John and told him the same thing. He was the one who said, "Muriel, for your own sake, you have to leave him."

Later, at the trial, Father John had testified for the prosecution; then Vicky had followed him to the witness stand. It had been unusual. Most of the time, they were on the side of the defense—priest and attorney— but it was Muriel who had come to them, scared and defenseless. Vicky remembered how Lonny Hereford sat with his chair tilted onto the back legs, chin dropped into his chest, black braids trailing down the front of his blue shirt, the squinting, black eyes never leaving her.

"What's this all about?"

"Got to thinking how you'd want to be the first to know, seeing how Lonny might have some scores to settle." The voice on the other end had shifted into a lower, more intimate range. "About four hours ago, Lonny up and said his good-byes to the old Gray House. Still haven't figured out how he escaped, but he sure left everybody here shaking our heads at the man's genius. You wouldn't be alone, now, would you?"

God. Vicky held the receiver away and stared at the black, inert plastic. On the other end was Lonny Hereford—the strange, partly familiar voice, the intimate, insidious tone. Bad Heart, the people called him after the trial. Arapahos were called Good Hearts in the Old Time, for their generosity and even tempers, but a man who pushed his wife down a steep flight of stairs onto a concrete floor—that man was no longer one of the people. The man could be outside her apartment building now, looking up at the dim light glowing in the window. The realization sent a cold spasm down her spine. Lonny Hereford, who'd twisted his head around after he'd been sentenced and the guards were guiding him toward the door—the narrow eyes searching the courtroom until they'd locked on her. *You're gonna pay,* he'd shouted. *I swear to God.*

Vicky slid the receiver back to her ear. "Thank you for letting me know, Warden," she said, playing the game, keeping her voice calm and confident, the courtroom voice she always summoned to camouflage the tremors running through her. "I guess it's fortunate that I'm not alone now that my boyfriend lives here." She glanced around the shadows. She didn't have a boyfriend. "We're having friends in for dinner tonight. We'll certainly keep our eyes out for any sign of Lonny."

"You do that." Was there a trace of disappointment in the tone, or was she only trying to assure herself that she'd convinced him? There was a click, followed by the electronic buzzing noise.

Vicky got to her feet and moved to the window. She tugged at the cords, guiding the shades down over the glass pane until all that was visible of the streetlamp was a faint circle of light glowing like the aftermath of an explosion. She made her way around the apartment, conscious of the sound of her own footsteps muffled in the carpet, and closed all the shades. Then she retraced her steps and flipped on the overhead lights. A white, preternatural light flooded around her, giving the apartment the surreal feel of a nightmare.

The doors. God, she'd forgotten the doors. She lunged for the corridor door and shot the bolt, then ran into the kitchen and checked the locks on the door to the back hall. She leaned against the counter and made herself take a deep breath. Maybe she was overreacting, doing exactly what Bad Heart hoped. He could be making his way back to his cell now, congratulating himself on the fact that Vicky Holden—*Bitch*, he'd shouted at her as the guards had pushed him through the courtroom door—wouldn't be getting much sleep tonight.

She went back to the desk and called the Riverton Police Department. The receiver was still warm and slightly moist in her hand. Two rings, three. Finally a woman came on the line. Vicky gave her name and asked to speak to Matt Hover, the detective who had handled the investigation into Muriel's death.

"Hold on," the woman said. "I'll see if he's still on duty."

A long moment passed. Then, a man's voice: "Vicky, you must've heard the news."

"Then it's true?"

"The warden thinks the bastard hid inside one of the supply trucks while he was unloading it. Rode the truck out of the prison grounds."

"He just called me."

"What!"

"He claimed to be Warden Ransom. He wanted to know if I was alone."

"I'm notifying the Lander police. They'll send a car over to your place. You're going to have an officer camped at your front door until we get Lonny Hereford back where he belongs."

"Look, Matt," Vicky said. "I may have convinced him that I'm not alone. Lonny could head for the mission first."

"Just like Hereford to go looking for revenge on you and Father O'Malley. I'll notify the Wind River police. They'll get a car over to the mission."

Vicky thanked the man and pressed the off button. She felt the tightness in her chest, the quick, shallow gulps of breath. She dialed the number for St. Francis Mission and listened to the sound of a phone ringing across the reservation. Pick up. Pick up.

"This is Father O'Malley. Please leave your name and number and I'll return your call."

Vicky waited for the beep, her fingers tapping out a nervous, staccato rhythm on the edge of the desk. John O'Malley wasn't at the mission. That was good. She left the message that Lonny Hereford had escaped. "Be careful, John," she said.

She dropped the receiver into the cradle, a new thought creeping like a shadow in the back of her mind. Bad Heart could be at the mission waiting, hiding somewhere on the grounds. There were so many buildings, so many nooks and crannies. A police cruiser might drive right past the man. Bad Heart could lunge out of the darkness before John O'Malley had gotten the message.

Vicky picked up her purse and headed back out into the corridor.

Father John O'Malley stood at the door in Eagle Hall and shook hands with members of the parish council as they filed outside. Brown, knobby hands of four elders in blue jeans and plaid shirts, with hunched shoulders and gray braids falling from beneath the cowboy hats pushed back on their heads. The work-roughened hands of Don and Beatrice Gray Wolf, both in their late forties, about his age. They seemed older. And Lucia Running Horse, a grandmother with long gray hair swept back from a wrinkled brown face and a small hand with a grip of steel.

"Good meeting, Father," the old woman said.

Father John waited until the council members had climbed inside the old pickups parked at angles in front of the hall as if they'd dropped out of the sky. One by one, the engines choked into life, emitting little clouds of black exhaust. Then the pickups swung into a procession out onto Circle Drive and headed into the tunnel of cottonwoods that led to Seventeen-Mile Road, taillights flickering like fireflies in the darkness at the far edges of the mission grounds.

Father John went back inside. It *had* been a good meeting, he thought. The elders and grandmothers were accustomed to making decisions, and the people trusted them. They were good hearts. He walked through the hall, straightening the chairs. A gust of wind caught the door and thumped it against the wall. He threw a final glance around the hall, turned off the lights, and stepped outside, pulling the door after him. Then he plunged across the mission grounds toward the residence.

The lights around Circle Drive swayed on their poles in the sharp and erratic gusts of wind that swept over the grounds. Even the church steeple, white against the darkness, seemed to be swaying. For a half second, the lights snapped off, then flickered on again. The evening was warm with the faintest odors of cattle and horses in the air and stars glittering in a sky that looked like an inverted black bowl. Father John crossed the drive and bounded up three steps to the concrete stoop in front of the residence. He reached for the doorknob and stopped. Someone was there in the shadows behind him. He could feel eyes boring like a laser into his back.

He swung around. Nothing but shadows and light shimmying in the gusts. Except for the whoosh of the wind and the howling of a coyote out on the prairie, it was quiet. The only vehicle on the grounds was his own pickup, a dark hulk nosed against the curb. His assistant, Father George Reinhold, had left for a meeting in Casper this morning and wouldn't be back until tomorrow.

Father John turned back, opened the door, and stepped into the entry hall. Probably an animal skulking by, he told himself. Coyote, fox, raccoon—they all came out in the evenings. He shut the door, turned on the table lamp, and walked down the hall to the kitchen. He flipped on the overhead light. Walks-On, his three-legged golden retriever, was crouched low on his rug in the far corner, eyes fixed on the back door. A low guttural sound rumbled in the dog's throat.

"Hey, buddy." Father John walked over, bent down, and patted the furry head. "It's okay," he said. He wondered whether that were true. Usually Walks-On met him at the front door, stuffing a wet muzzle into his hand before darting back to the kitchen and waiting at the door, wagging his tail.

"Ready to go out?" Father John straightened up, stepped around the end of the counter, and opened the door. The dog leapt forward, skitter-ing across the vinyl floor into the back porch, barking into the quiet.

"Take it easy," he said, moving past the animal. He opened the outside door that led to a short flight of wooden steps into the backyard. Walks-On darted down, head lowered, his single rear leg spinning to keep up. He was growling now, growling and barking.

Father John followed the dog down into the yard. Something was wrong, off-kilter. He'd sensed it on the walk over from Eagle Hall, the almost imperceptible change in the atmosphere that had made him sud-denly aware of his surroundings—the light from the overhead poles stut-tering into the darkness, the shadows wavering over the buildings, and the unmistakable sense that someone was there.

Now, in the dim light from the kitchen window, he looked around the yard. Nothing out of the ordinary. The dog was still barking as he dashed along the rear of the house. He stopped to sniff at a basement window before crashing through the bushes to get to the next window. The wind was knocking a cottonwood branch against the side of the house, and the clack-clack punctuated the noise the dog was making.

Probably a wild animal, Father John told himself again. A fox bedded down for the night in the shelter of the bushes, until Walks-On had plunged down the steps, raising a ruckus, and chased the animal off. The dog stopped barking and trotted over.

Father John patted the dog's head. Then Walks-On darted away and started running around the yard, his usual evening exercise. Father John went back up to the kitchen and poured out a mug of the coffee, black and thick with grounds, left over from dinner. He'd just started back down the hall for his study when the phone started to ring. The jangling noise swelled into the quiet.

He hurried past the door that led to the basement and crossed into the study. Setting the coffee mug at the edge of the stacks of papers that toppled over his desk, he reached for the phone. The tiny message light was blinking red. Someone must have called while he was at the meeting.

"Father O'Malley," he said into the receiver.

"This is Molly Redman, Father."

"What's going on?" Streaks of light from outside scribbled across the window behind the desk. Father John walked around, nudged the leather chair back with his boot, and sat down. He turned the switch on the desk lamp and pulled a yellow pad out from one of the stacks.

"Ethan's up to his old tricks again. Drinkin' and makin' trouble."

Father John rummaged in the desk drawer for a pen, then stopped. He sat very still. Someone was outside the window: a presence behind him as real as the aroma of coffee wafting over the desk. He could *feel* someone watching him.

He swiveled around, pitched himself to his feet, and leaned close to the window. No sign of anyone outside. Nothing but the branches moving in the wind and the dim light fading into darkness at the edge of the grounds. But someone had been there a moment ago. Someone had been looking through the window; he was certain of it.

"Last night Ethan—"

"Listen, Molly," Father John cut in. "Someone's here now," he said. "Suppose you come to the mission first thing tomorrow morning."

The woman started to protest—he could hear the reluctance in her voice. "I'm sorry, Molly," he said. "We'll have to talk tomorrow." Before the woman could say anything else, he hung up.

A few feet below where he was standing, Father John could hear the scrape of footsteps across a hard floor, followed by a thud. Whoever was in the basement had stumbled against something. The dog must have heard the noise because he started barking again, an explosive sound that burst through the house.

Father John went out into the entry. Keeping his gaze locked on the basement door, he stayed close to the wall, conscious of the sound of floorboards creaking under his boots. He moved past the door and pressed his shoulder against the frame next to the hinges. He could sense the atmosphere begin to shift as the footsteps came up the stairs and moved into the space on the other side of the door. His eyes were on the knob now, waiting for it to turn.

* * *

Vicky stared into the cone of headlights that pushed into the darkness on Rendezvous Road, barely aware of the shadows rushing past outside. Ten minutes ago, as she'd slowed through the one-street town of Hudson at the southern boundary of the reservation, she'd tried St. Francis Mission again, jamming the cell against her ear and willing the intermittent buzzing noise to stop.

The answering machine had picked up. "This is Father O'Malley . . ."

She'd hit the end button, tossed the cell across the seat, and, pressing down hard on the accelerator, drove onto the reservation, unable to shake the image from her mind: John O'Malley getting out of the pickup, walking across the grounds, starting up the sidewalk to the residence. And Lonny Hereford—Bad Heart—lunging out of the dark. Somewhere between the prison and the mission, the man could have gotten ahold of a weapon. A gun or a knife. Lonny would know how to get a weapon.

She had to warn John O'Malley. No telling how long it might take for a police car to arrive. Twenty, thirty minutes. It depended on where the car was. Nothing was close on the reservation; everything was surrounded by miles and miles of empty space.

Vicky turned right onto Seventeen-Mile Road, holding the accelerator to the floor, the speedometer needle jumping at eighty. Two miles. Three miles. Ahead the lighted sign loomed through the darkness. St. Francis Mission. She let up on the accelerator and made another right into the tunnel of cottonwoods that led to the mission grounds. A gust of wind swept through the trees, and for a moment, she had the odd, disconcerting sense that the tunnel itself was shifting around her.

She swung onto Circle Drive. Over in the trees, at the edge of the headlights, there was . . . the glint of metal. Vicky hit the brake pedal and skidded to a stop. She shifted into reverse and started backing up, turning the wheel until the headlights framed a pickup wedged among the trees. *Hidden*. Lonny Hereford was already here.

Vicky swallowed hard at the dry knot in her throat, shifted back into forward, and shot around Circle Drive. Of course Lonny had stolen the pickup. It was probably the first thing he'd done after breaking out of prison. Stolen the pickup and headed for the reservation. She could hear the man's voice on the telephone: *Seeing how Lonny might have some scores to settle . . .*

The knob started turning, then stopped. A half second passed before the knob moved again, as if whoever was on the other side had considered the possibility that Father John could be waiting and had decided what to do. The door cracked open, then began moving into the hall. The hinges squealed like a small, trapped animal. Past the edge, Father John could see the tip of a man's boot, the green pants leg, the brown fist gripping a knife. The steel blade shimmered in the light of the hall lamp.

Come on. Come on. A few more inches. Father John clenched his muscles, ready to throw his weight against the door and jam whoever was behind it into the frame.

Then it happened: A sharp knock on the front door, the sound of the door crashing open against the entry wall, and Vicky's voice: "John? Where are you?"

"Go back!" Father John yelled.

The man lunged past the basement door and swung around, jabbing the knife into the air. Father John ducked away, then grabbed at the man's arm and pushed it back. Lonny Hereford. The realization came like a flash of light in the darkness that Father John hardly had time to register. Lonny plowed into him, ramming his forearm across his throat. Father John gasped for breath. He could see the glint of the knife blade below his jaw. Bringing his fist up, he sunk it into the other man's soft belly, then pounded against his chest. The weight against his throat seemed to release, and Father John braced himself against the wall and swung hard at the man's arm. The knife clanked onto the floor.

"Just you and me, Priest," the man shouted. He was breathing hard, the brown face contorted into a grotesque mask. Strips of black hair fell over the narrowed eyes. Fists bunched, he started moving forward.

Beyond the man's shoulders, Father John glimpsed the movement of shadow and light. There was the sharp crack of metal on bone. Lonny Hereford froze, the grotesque mask suddenly wiped away, and in its place appeared the fixed features of surprise. Then the man started crumbling, and Father John saw Vicky standing behind him. Both hands gripped the twisted shaft of the hall lamp. She started to raise the lamp again over Lonny's head, but the man was down, the bulky frame folded onto the floor.

Father John reached over Lonny and grabbed Vicky by the shoulders. "It's okay," he said. "You took care of him." Then he took the lamp out of Vicky's hands, unpeeling her fingers to get it loose.

"Are you all right?" she asked. Her voice was shaky, and her eyes were lit as if she had a fever.

Father John nodded. He wasn't sure. He felt a stab of pain with each breath, and his knuckles, he realized, were trickling blood. He crouched down and placed a finger on Lonny's carotid artery. The skin felt hot, the pulse strong. "He'll be okay."

Father John pulled himself upright. "Thanks," he said, watching her, trying to make sure that she was okay. "You have a pretty good arm. Great timing, too. What brought you here?"

"A lucky guess." She was smiling at him, her voice steadier.

"I'm going to call the police." Father John started down the hall. Through the front door, he saw the dark police cruiser slide alongside the curb, the kaleidoscope of red, blue, and yellow lights flashing over the roof.

"Looks like they're here," Vicky said.

Day of Rest

The Fourth Commandment:

Remember to keep holy the Sabbath Day.

"Good sermon this morning, Father."

"Glad you approve." Father John O'Malley took Nathan Bird-song's brown, outstretched hand. It had the firm strength of dried leather. He patted the Arapaho on the shoulder and reached for the next hand as parishioners spilled through the double doors of the church and out into the warm sun bathing the grounds of St. Francis Mission on the Wind River Reservation. Several others pressed into the half circle of Arapahos clustered on the sidewalk, waiting patiently to shake the pastor's hand and say a few kind words about this Sunday's sermon—even those he'd caught nodding off—before they headed around the corner of the church toward doughnuts and coffee in Eagle Hall.

It was a good ten minutes before Father John had greeted the last congregant. He bounded up the concrete steps of the stoop that passed for a porch in front of the white stucco church and stopped. Someone was watching him. He could feel the eyes piercing his back like a laser beam. He swung around, expecting to see someone who had been waiting to speak to him. Someone he'd failed to notice.

There was no one. The mission grounds might have been deserted, except for the pickups and cars parked around Circle Drive and the nearly imperceptible undercurrent of voices floating from Eagle Hall. Around the drive, the sun bounced and glittered across the priest's redbrick residence, the gray stone museum, and the yellow stucco administration building. It glistened in the water shooting out of the sprinkler on the grasses in the center of the drive.

Father John shrugged and turned back just as the church door sprang open and Leonard Bizzel stepped outside. The Arapaho had been the caretaker at St. Francis for so long that nobody remembered when he'd taken the job, only that he was part of the mission, much like the cottonwoods sheltering the old buildings. He was a big man, probably in his fifties now, judging by the gray running through his black hair, with the rounded, powerful shoulders and confident black eyes of a younger man. Every morning, Leonard assisted Father John at Mass, and on Sundays, he took special care to tidy up the sacristy, making sure that the prayer books, altar linens, and chalice were placed in the appropriate cabinets for the following week. When he finished, Leonard usually ducked out the sacristy door in back and headed to Eagle Hall.

"Been lookin' for you, Father," the Arapaho said. "Everything's picked up and put away. You comin' to Eagle Hall?" He started down the steps.

"See you there," Father John called after the man. The women in the parish handled the coffee and doughnuts on Sunday mornings, but Father John knew that Leonard would be hovering about like a raven, ready to swoop down at the first sign of an emergency—spilled coffee, upset plate of doughnuts, somebody looking for a folding chair on which to sit down.

Father John let himself inside the church and headed down the aisle, starting to shrug out of his chasuble as he went. The church was small—a chapel, really. Leonard had turned out the overhead lights and snuffed the candles. The air felt cool in the dim light that filtered through the stained glass windows and spattered red, blue, and yellow blotches over the wood pews. The altar ahead was almost lost in shadow, the red votive light flickering in front of the tabernacle that resembled a miniature tipi. Traces of gray smoke curled around the ceiling, and the faintest whiff of smoke mingled with the lingering smells of perspiration and perfume. A sense of serenity and eternity seemed to fill the vacant space.

The door opened behind him, sending a blast of hot air into the coolness. Father John turned around as the door thudded shut. The smallest tremor ran through the old wood floor. A large man faced him from the shadows, and for a moment, Father John felt again the laser beam piercing into him.

"Can I help you?" he said, tossing the chasuble over a pew.

The man was holding what looked like a paper bag. Leaning sideways, he stretched his free hand toward the door and clicked the bolt into place. Then he lurched forward until he emerged into the dim light, traces of red and yellow flitting over a brown face hardened like granite. "Looks like nobody's here 'cept you and me, Priest," he said. His fingers rattled the paper bag.

"What's going on, Kenny?" Father John kept his voice calm, but he could feel his muscles tense. Kenny Yellow Plume was a drunk and a troublemaker. Father John started back down the aisle, removing his stole and the white alb. He set the vestments on another pew, freer now, wearing just his blue jeans and plaid shirt. The smell of alcohol floated toward him.

"Don't try to bullshit me, Priest," the Indian shouted. He was swaying from one foot to the other, as if he couldn't make a solid connection with the floor. Then, in a lower tone, more menacing, he said, "Melba left me, like you tol' her. Took the kids and walked out. I can't find her nowhere. Yesterday some clown knocks on the door and hands me papers that say she's divorcing me. That Arapaho lawyer, Vicky Holden, wrote out the papers, made 'em all legal and final, like there's no more talkin', no more putting things back together for me and Melba. Ten years of being together thrown out like garbage."

Father John stopped a couple of feet from the man. The stench of whiskey was so strong that he had to breathe through his mouth. He said, "Melba couldn't take your drinking anymore, Kenny."

"That what you tol' her? 'Melba, you can't take his drinkin'. You gotta take the kids and get out.'"

The man started pulling at the paper bag, hands shaking. Finally he yanked out a small, metallic pistol, letting the bag flutter to the floor. Father John could see down the barrel of the gun, an immense black tunnel.

"You don't need a gun, Kenny," he said, surprised by the steadiness of his tone, the focused, relaxed feeling that came over him, as if all of his energies had turned to the gun. He had to make an effort to pull his eyes from the barrel. "Put it away, and we can sit down and talk."

"You done enough talkin'." Kenny's face cracked into a half smile, half sneer. "Melba's gone, and I got me a couple scores to settle. Sit down." The gun jerked toward the last pew.

Father John moved sideways, backed into the pew, and dropped onto the hard wooden seat. His left knee cracked against the pew ahead. "What are you going to do, Kenny?" he said. "Shoot me?"

"You got about twenty minutes, my guess." The Indian didn't take his eyes away—the laser eyes—while he shifted the gun into his right hand and tugged with the left at an even smaller object in the pocket of the blue denim shirt plastered with sweat against his chest. He withdrew a cell phone and flipped it open with his thumb. There was a half second when the laser eyes shifted to the phone as his thumb hit a couple of keys. Father John felt his muscles tighten again. He was about to spring forward when the laser eyes returned and the gun bobbed back toward him.

"Don't move," the Indian shouted. He lifted the phone to his left ear, his boots still fighting for a purchase on the floor.

Father John stared at the black tunnel, aware of the silence pressing around them and the shades of mottled light flickering over the pews and the floor. It was hard to imagine—fifty feet away, beyond the walls of two buildings, parishioners were laughing, drinking coffee, munching doughnuts; kids were shouting and playing tag around the tables and chairs. They might have been on another planet.

He was alone with Kenny Yellow Plume, a man who intended to kill him.

Vicky Holden had just poured a mug of fresh coffee and was about to settle into the sofa with the Sunday newspaper when the telephone rang. She threw a glance at the phone on the desk against the wall. The window was open and a warm breeze billowed the sheer curtains into the living room. The carpet and walls were striped with sunshine. The phone rang again. She wasn't expecting any calls. The answering machine can take the message, she told herself. And yet, the ringing had already disrupted the quiet morning she'd been looking forward to. There was something unnerving about an unanswered phone. The call could be an emergency, someone arrested last night on a DUI or domestic disturbance or—who knew what? Someone sitting at the Fremont County jail in need of a lawyer.

She set the mug on the coffee table, crossed the room, and picked up the receiver. "Vicky Holden," she said. She held her breath. She could almost feel the malevolence at the other end. The response was slow in coming. For a couple of seconds, there was nothing but the sound of breathing. Finally, a man's voice said, "You got twenty minutes to get over to the mission." The words slurred into one another, the words of a drunk.

"Who is this?" Vicky felt her hand tightening over the plastic receiver.

"Twenty minutes, if you want to see the priest alive."

She knew who the caller was now. It wasn't the voice that she recognized—she couldn't remember ever speaking to Kenny Yellow Plume. It was the anger, the craziness, washing through the slurred words. What was it Melba had said? *You don't know him, Vicky. He starts drinking and he gets crazy. No telling what he might do.* And Vicky had said, *You have to leave him, Melba. For your sake and the sake of the kids. That's what Father John told me,* the woman had replied. Vicky could still see her slumped against the back of the chair, small, almost like a child. She took up only half of the chair. Mopping at her eyes with a tissue, strings of black hair hanging over her thin shoulders.

"Where are you, Kenny?" Vicky struggled to sound calm and rational, as if she were examining a witness in the courtroom, as if she were in control. She was playing for time, she knew, trying to pull her thoughts together, searching for the right words. She could feel the blood pounding in her ears. The man had been served the divorce papers yesterday. He'd gone berserk, just as Melba had predicted, which was the reason Vicky had made certain that Melba and the kids were safe at a friend's house in Casper before she'd had the papers delivered.

"Me and the priest are havin' a little party in the church, just waitin' for you. You better be knocking on the front door in twenty minutes, or the priest's gonna accidentally get shot dead."

"I can't get to the mission in twenty minutes." Vicky could hear the note of panic sounding in her voice.

"Well, you better get goin', lady, 'cuz that's all you got."

"Listen to me, Kenny," Vicky began, but she was speaking into a dead line. The buzzing noise pulsed in her ear.

She tapped out *69 and, keeping her eyes on the red numbers in the readout, scrambled for a pen in the drawer and jotted the numbers across the corner of the top sheet of papers stacked next to the phone. She ripped off the corner and stuffed it into the pocket of her blue jeans. Then she grabbed her bag and ran out the door of the apartment. Two minutes later she was down the flight of stairs and jamming the key into the ignition of her Jeep. She pressed down on the accelerator and glanced at her watch as the Jeep squealed out of the parking lot ahead of a sedan that swerved and honked behind her. Eighteen minutes left.

My God, Father John thought. The minute Vicky walked through the door, Kenny would start shooting. He intended to kill both of them at the same time, before the sound of gunshots brought people stampeding into the church.

He kept his eyes on the Indian. The man needed a drink. Father John knew the signs: the sweat-glistened forehead, the widening circles of perspiration at his armpits. His hand was shaking so that the gun swung like a pendulum. He weaved back and forth, as unsteady as a broken branch in the wind. He'd just clicked off the cell and stuffed it back into his shirt pocket, but the laser eyes kept darting toward the door, as if Vicky might knock at any moment.

Father John shifted forward. Somehow, he had to get the gun before Vicky arrived. He said, "You don't want to shoot anybody." It was the counselor's voice that came back to him in the quiet of the church— smooth, confident, and consoling.

The Indian regarded him from beneath drooping eyelids, the gun still jumping in front of his belt buckle. "Wasn't for you and that lawyer, everything would've been okay. I had me a wife." His voice quivered, and for a second, Father John thought the man might burst into tears. "Two kids, the house. So me and Melba had some problems. What right you got to go poking into what's none of your business? I ain't got nothing to go on for, but I ain't dying alone."

So that was it, Father John thought. After he killed them, he intended to kill himself. "You know what day it is, Kenny?" He didn't wait for an answer. "Today is the Sabbath."

The Indian dipped his head and blinked hard, as if he were trying to grasp hold of something in the dimness.

Father John pushed on: "It's the day of rest, Kenny. The day to let go of everything that's bothering you, all the heavy burdens. Let them go for today. Tomorrow you can come to the mission, and we'll sit down and talk. You know that Melba doesn't want to divorce you. She wants you to stop drinking."

Father John inched his way to the end of the pew and started to get to his feet. "Give me the gun, Kenny. We can figure things out tomorrow."

A look of comprehension began to settle in the laser eyes. "You think

I don't know what you're up to? Bullshittin' me? You're full of bullshit, you and that lawyer."

"If you go into a rehab program . . ."

"Shut up! Shut up! I don't wanna hear no more words." The pistol started bucking up and down, and Father John dropped back onto the pew. "Words, words, that's all you got. Melba ain't never coming back." The Indian threw a glance at the door. "That lawyer don't get here in three minutes, you're gonna be dead."

Vicky could see the parked cars and pickups flashing through the stand of cottonwoods as she turned into St. Francis Mission. It might have been an ordinary Sunday, sunshine stippling the grounds, a warm breeze rustling the leaves in the branches. A mixture of relief and alarm washed over her. The mission wasn't deserted; there were people still having coffee in Eagle Hall. And yet, if anyone tried to enter the church, Kenny would start shooting. And the minute she stepped through the door, she knew, she and John O'Malley could both be dead.

She'd realized the truth of it back on Rendezvous Road, the brush and sunflowers in the ditches blurring past. She'd yanked her cell out of her bag and started to punch in 911, then dropped the cell into her lap. She could picture the police cars speeding into the mission, the uniforms rushing up the steps of the church. She could hear the gunshots. She pushed the next picture into the shadows of her mind: John O'Malley crumpling to the floor. She was still a couple of miles away—checking her watch. God. Only three minutes—when she knew what she had to do.

She drove past the church, turned into the alley, and slid to a stop behind the bumper of a pickup. Grabbing the cell, she slammed out of the Jeep. A group of kids were playing on the stoop in front of Eagle Hall. She brushed past and let herself through the door. The sound of voices hung in a haze of coffee smells. Little groups of people sat at the tables scattered about, while several women fussed over the empty plates and Styrofoam cups on the table against the wall on the left.

"Have you seen Leonard?" Vicky said, her eyes roaming over the crowded hall, aware only that someone was standing inside the door.

"Over there." It was a man's voice. A bulky arm shot past her in the direction of the far corner.

Vicky started around the tables, barely registering the startled looks on the faces that turned up as she passed. She was in blue jeans and a tee shirt. She didn't remember combing her hair this morning; she hadn't put on makeup. God, she must look a mess. Someone called, "Hey, Vicky." She dodged the hand reaching for hers and kept going, her gaze fixed on the back of Leonard's plaid shirt. The man was folding a chair. He stacked it against a pile of chairs in the corner.

"Leonard," she said, coming up behind him. He swung around, then reared back a little, as if the breeze had just blown her through the door. He started to say something, but she cut him off. "There's an emergency. Kenny Yellow Plume has a gun on Father John over in the church."

"What?" The man's face froze in disbelief. "I was just thinking about going over to see if Father John needed help with something."

"We don't have any time." Vicky hurried on. "We've got to get some men and get over there. Kenny called me almost twenty minutes ago. He's threatening to kill Father John."

Leonard started past her, and she grabbed his arm. "I think Kenny locked the front door. He told me to knock."

"Don't worry. I got the keys."

"What about the back door, in case he locked that, too?"

"The back door?" He tossed her a sideways glance. "Yeah, I can unlock it. Let's go."

He pushed past her, and Vicky followed the man across the hall, weaving around the tables, dodging the knots of people. Leonard pulled up at one of the tables, leaned down, and said something to Nathan Birdsong, then kept going. Behind her, Vicky could hear the scrape of Nathan's boots. A couple more stops, and two other men jumped up. They were a little crowd by the time they got out the door and started for the church, boots scuffling the gravel.

"We'll bust through the door and take Kenny down," Leonard said.

"No!" Vicky shouted. She fumbled for the scrap of paper in her pocket and started tapping out Kenny's number on her cell. "We have to distract him first."

The ringing phone seemed to startle the man, Father John thought. Kenny Yellow Plume rolled his eyes around the church, as if the phone might be in one of the pews. Finally he reached up and tugged the cell out of his shirt pocket.

"Yeah?" he said, still gripping the gun. An absent look came into his expression, and Father John braced one hand on the pew ahead and watched Kenny's expression dissolve into a half smile.

"Well, the lawyer lady finally got here," the Indian said, snapping the phone shut and plugging it back into his pocket. "Won't be long now, Priest. She's waiting outside the door." He began moving backward, a slow, unsteady gait. Two feet, three feet, until he'd covered the space between the pew and the door. He was still pointing the gun. Father John watched the black tunnel of the barrel bobbing and weaving at his chest.

Kenny reached around with his free hand and turned the bolt. The metallic click echoed in the stillness.

"Here I am, Kenny." Vicky's voice came from the front of the church.

The Indian's head spun sideways, and for a split second, the pistol pointed down the aisle. Father John sprang out of the pew and slammed into the man, grabbing his arm and pushing it upward as the pistol dropped down and skittered over the floor. The double doors burst open and a blur of blue jeans, brown arms, and fists swarmed over Kenny Yellow Plume. The air was filled with the sounds of shouting and grunting. Father John lunged for the pistol and wrapped his fist around the handle.

When he looked around, Kenny was belly-down on the floor. Two men were straddling the outstretched legs, while Leonard and Nathan Birdsong were yanking Kenny's arms behind his back. Someone had produced a belt, which Leonard set about circling around Kenny's arms. He jammed the end into the buckle and pulled hard as Kenny thumped his head against the floor, a sustained howl erupting from his throat.

Father John glanced around. Vicky was coming down the aisle, a cell phone pressed against one ear. She stopped beside him and slipped the phone into her jeans pocket. "Police are on the way," she said.

They stood outside on the sun-washed stoop as two uniformed officers led Kenny Yellow Plume toward the three white cars with Wind River Police stamped in blue letters on the sides. Groups of parishioners stood around the church, worry and shock stamped in their expressions. A few minutes earlier, the police cars had screamed into the mission and a phalanx of officers had come through the opened doors of the church. Now two of the officers pushed Kenny into the backseat of a car. In a moment, engines growled into life and the cars started around Circle Drive. Father John caught a glimpse of Kenny Yellow Plume, black head bobbing over his chest, and he realized that the Indian was weeping.

"Well, he's not gonna be causing any more trouble for a while," Leonard said. Nathan and the other two men grunted in agreement. They were still breathing hard, gulping at the hot air as if they couldn't get enough.

"You took a huge risk. All of you," Father John said, but he kept his eyes on Vicky. He couldn't shake the image of what might have happened if Kenny had fired down the aisle.

"We were just following instructions," Leonard said. "Vicky said she'd distract the guy, so you could jump him and get the gun. We waited for the commotion inside before we came busting in."

"I figured that you would only need a split second," Vicky said.

Father John was quiet a moment; then he said, almost to himself, "I wasn't able to talk Kenny out of the gun." He turned away.

"He'd made up his mind to kill us both," Vicky said.

Father John was aware of the warm pressure of Vicky's hand on his arm as he stared across the grounds, past the sunshine dancing in the sprinkling water and past the stands of cottonwoods, until, finally, the last police car had disappeared.

Honor

The Fifth Commandment:
Honor thy father and thy mother.

"The boy's dead."

"What?" Father John O'Malley pressed the receiver against his ear, wondering whether he had misunderstood the faint, raspy voice on the other end of the line. A pale, wavy light from the streetlamps around St. Francis Mission filtered through the window, streaking the walls and carpet in the front hall of the priest's residence. Blackness bunched up at the far end. The old house sighed and creaked with the oncoming night. Only a few minutes ago, the clock over the mantel in the living room had chimed ten o'clock.

The man at the other end of the line said nothing. Father John could hear the stifled sobs, the quick, jagged breathing. "Who is this?" he said, struggling for a gentle, reassuring tone.

"This here's Randolph Whitebird," the voice managed after a moment. "Scottie's been shot, Father." The sobs started again, unconcealed now, long and scraping, like the tearing of canvas.

Father John waited. Then, still the gentle tone: "Where are you?"

"Over here at Scottie's place." A forced control came into the man's voice. "He got himself a house on Route Two. Everybody's here—police and Scottie's girlfriend. She's the girl found him." The voice cracked on the word *girl*. "Her folks just showed up."

Father John said, "I'll be right over."

The sky was a field of stars sparkling in the blackness as Father John drove west across the Wind River Reservation. As he wheeled the Toyota pickup into a sharp right onto Route Two, his headlights flashed over the white shingles of the little house. Light blazed out of the front windows, illuminating the scrubbed patch of dirt that served as a yard. A strip of yellow police tape wrapped around stakes driven into the ground formed a half circle in front of the concrete steps that led to the stoop. People gathered in groups outside the tape, shadows moving in and out of the pale streams of light.

Parked at the edge of the road was a line of vehicles: A couple of BIA police cars, the red Jeep that Ted Gianelli, the local FBI agent, drove, and the white van Father O'Malley had seen at other death scenes: the coroner's wagon. Father John parked behind the wagon.

As he started across the bare dirt yard, he spotted Gianelli coming toward him. A big man, with the rounded shoulders and thick neck and the long, graceful strides of the linebacker he had once been. The light pouring out of the house shone in his dark hair and cast his face in shadow. "What happened?" Father John asked when the agent was still a few feet away.

"Scott Whitebird took a slug in the back of the head, execution style." The agent glanced back toward the house, and for a moment, light glinted in his deep-set eyes. "Seen too many homicides like this. Always mixed up with drugs. Coroner thinks he's been dead about two hours, which puts time of death at about eight thirty. Neighbor says he saw the roommate's truck peeling out of the yard around then. Girlfriend walked in about nine and found the body. Called her dad right away, and he called the BIA police." Another glance backward, this time in the direction of the clot of people on the other side of the yard. "Tammy Dotson. You know her?"

Father John shook his head. The name huddled somewhere in his memory, but he couldn't pull it free. He followed the agent's glance. The girl huddled in the center of the group, a childlike look about her in the shadowy light. Head bent forward, long, black hair clumped around the shoulders of her white tee shirt, she stared at the ground, oblivious to the man and woman on either side of her, arms looped around her waist. Probably her parents, Father John thought. The woman was an older version of the girl herself—the same downward bent of the head, the same black hair flaring over her shoulders. The man wore a white cowboy hat that sat back on his head, as if it had settled into its most natural perch. He was tall—the two women came barely to his shoulder—and he stood with shoulders squared, squinting downward at the yellow tape flapping in the breeze, the people flowing back and forth between groups, stamping their feet, nodding, murmuring into the hushed quiet.

"You know the way the moccasin telegraph works," the agent went on. "Scott's dad and the rest of the Whitebird family got here in about twenty minutes." Gianelli cleared his throat, as if to clear away a minor nuisance. "No weapon around. Killer most likely took it, but we're checking anyway. Couple of BIA officers are combing the area down by the creek in back of the house. "

The front door swung open and a man stepped backward onto the stoop, pulling the end of a gurney, white sheet trailing over the sides. The man started down the steps and the gurney bumped after him, guided by an attendant at the other end.

"Go ahead." Gianelli nodded. Father John stepped across the tape and walked over to the gurney. One of the attendants gave him a weary, here-we-go-again-another-homicide smile. Father John pulled back the white sheet, exposing the face of a young man, with black hair falling loosely over a high forehead, a finely sculpted nose and cheekbones, full mouth turned upward in a half smile of surprise, and eyes closed, almost peaceful in death. Father John made the sign of the cross over the still body. "May God receive you into your eternal home, Scottie, and look not upon your sins, but upon all the good you brought into the world. May you be at peace in His everlasting love."

As Father John stepped aside, the gurney started rattling over the hard earth toward the coroner's wagon, an attendant still at each end. Randolph Whitebird appeared out of the shadows. Leaping across the yellow tape, he started after the gurney. "My boy," he shouted. "Don't take my boy away."

Father John hurried over and set one hand on the man's arm. "Take it easy," he said. The man jerked backward, stumbling sideways, then seemed to catch an uneasy balance, as if he were unsure of the planes beneath his feet shifting into a new and strange alignment. His eyes were opened wide, startled and relieved at the same time. "You blessed Scottie, Father?"

Father John nodded.

"Tammy found him," the man said. "Just sitting there in front of the TV, blood everywhere. Poor girl." He threw his head back toward the people still in the same place near the house. "They was gonna get married. Tammy loved him, too. She's in bad shock, what with the fed asking a lot of questions. Good thing her folks're here to be some comfort. Girl's never gonna get over this, walkin' in and seeing him like that." The man's voice cracked; low sobs started to thunder out of his chest. He raised a clenched fist to his mouth, as if to stop the noise. Moisture ran along his cheeks and trailed over his knuckles. Father John patted his shoulder, at a loss for the right words. Words were so inadequate.

Suddenly Randolph reared backward and, looking out to the road, shouted: "He's not gonna get away with it. Not gonna get away with killing my boy."

"Who?" Father John asked, not really startled at the abrupt shift in the man's emotions.

Randolph slowly brought his eyes back, as if he couldn't comprehend the question. "That roommate of Scottie's. Who else?"

"Gianelli thinks drugs might have been involved. Could that be true?"

"Drugs!" The man turned halfway around, his boots kicking at the dirt. "The fed's wrong. Scottie didn't have no truck with drugs. It's his roommate, no-good drunk, that did it. That's why he's not around. He took off. He's hidin' somewhere, so the cops can't find him. But I'm gonna find him. I'm gonna find him, Father, and I'm gonna kill him."

Father John gripped the man's shoulders with both hands. He stared into his eyes. "No, you won't, Randolph. You're not going to do anything like that. You're going to let the fed and the police handle Scott's killer." He could feel the man's muscles begin to relax, the sobs gathering somewhere deep inside. After a moment, he said, "Who's the roommate?"

"Larson Bell." The man spit out the words.

Father John was quiet. A picture took shape in his mind: The Alcoholics Anonymous meetings two or three months ago at the mission; the long, thin face, the dark eyes wise beyond the man's twenty-some years; the studied way he rose to his feet and took in the faces turned to him; the gentle, quiet voice: *I'm Larson. I'm an alcoholic.*

It was not the picture of a murderer, but who knew? Who ever knew? Larson Bell was an alcoholic, and alcoholics . . . Well, Father John was one himself. Recovering, today at least, by the grace of God, but still an alcoholic. Larson Bell was in serious trouble. The police were looking for him, but Father John had a pretty good idea of where to find him. He decided to talk to the young man first, before the police picked him up, before Randolph Whitebird found him.

The cloud of smoke hung low and moist around the booths inside the Buffalo Bar, which occupied a narrow slot between the trailer court and a warehouse on Highway 26, just outside the reservation boundary.

Father John set the door in place behind him and squinted into the smoke and the dim light. The odors of whiskey and beer floated around him, stinging his nose and cheeks like a thousand invisible bees. A shout of derision from the poolroom on the other side of a wide archway broke through the hushed conversations. Five or six men straddled the stools in front of the bar at the far end; most of the booths were occupied by small groups of men and women—Indians all. White folks in the area had their own places.

Father John started toward the bar. The voices trailed off into a hushed, surprised silence. Suddenly, a thin, wiry man rose out of the far booth and started toward him. "What're you doin' here, Father?" Larson Bell made no effort to disguise the astonishment in his voice.

"Looking for you," Father John said.

The thin face crumbled in apprehension. He took a step backward, drawing his forces together, as if to ward off a blow. "Oh, God," he managed. "Something's happened. It's my dad, isn't it? His heart? Is it Mom? Something's happened to Mom?"

Father John took hold of the man's arm. "It's not your folks, Larson."

The man's sigh came like an explosion, sudden and jerky, leaving a little cloud of distilled beer in the air between them. Father John tried not to breathe it in, wanting to breathe it in. "Let's go outside," he said.

Larson Bell kept one hand on the hood of the Toyota pickup, as if to steady himself, even though he seemed mildly sober, Father John thought. Two or three beers, at the most. "It's Scott," he said. "Someone shot him this evening."

"Scott?" The young man blinked his eyes and leaned farther toward the hood. "No." He shook his head. "Scott's at home. He's okay."

"It's true, Larson. I'm sorry."

The young man was quiet, staring out across the highway. After a moment, Father John said, "When did you last see him?"

"I don't know." Larson brought his eyes back to Father John's. "I left the house maybe eight, eight thirty. Scott was watchin' some dumb show on TV. Tried to get him to come along, you know, shoot some pool." He gave a little wave toward the bar. "Scott's been—what d'ya call it—preoccupied lately, what with that girlfriend of his. She takes up most of his time." Now the young man raised his eyes and began searching the sky. "Used to take up most of his time. Jesus, I can't believe he's dead."

Father John didn't say anything. He'd been watching the young man, searching for the signs—the quick blinks, the imperceptible trembles. He knew when people were lying; it was so transparent, once you understood what to look for. Larson Bell was telling the truth, but that didn't keep him from being in a lot of trouble. He had been at the house about the time Scott Whitebird was murdered. Father John said, "The police are looking for you. They want to ask you some questions."

"Looking for me? Why? I don't know nothing. I didn't even know he was dead 'til you come here. They think I killed Scott? Jesus, Father. You gotta tell 'em. I'd never killed nobody."

"Oh, man." Larson turned his hand into a fist and thumped the hood. "That's enough to send Tammy over."

"What're you talking about?" There was the lonely wail of a siren somewhere in the darkness down the highway.

Larson shrugged. "My opinion, she's got a whole lotta problems, but Scott was hung up on her, you know what I mean? Didn't wanna hear nothing bad about her. Said all she needed was some help, and he was the one that could help her."

The girl's image worked its way into Father John's mind: head bent forward, eyes fixed on the ground, her mother and father holding her close. "The fed thinks Scott's death was about drugs."

"Drugs? Scott?" Larson gave his head a furious shake. "Get real, Father."

"What about Tammy? Were drugs one of her problems?"

Larson stepped back from the Toyota. He turned sideways and stared at the brown siding on the Buffalo Bar for a long moment. Then he looked back. "I don't know for sure, Father. I asked Scott once. He said no way was she using drugs anymore. He said her problems come from her situation. Soon's they got married, she was gonna be out of that situation for good."

"What situation? Some job? Kids she was hanging around with? What?" Nothing was making sense.

Larson looked out toward the highway. The sirens had risen to a furious pitch. Slowly he brought his gaze back, and Father John saw the raw look of fear transforming his expression. "It's her mom and dad," he said. "Scott said he had to do whatever it took to get Tammy away from her mom and dad. He said they were killing her."

The sirens welled behind them as a police car swung into the parking lot. Father John blinked into the headlights sweeping over the pickup, past the front of the bar. Suddenly, the sirens shut off, leaving only the soft shush of the breeze moving over the asphalt. Two policemen jumped out of the car. "You Larson Bell?" one of them called.

The young man gave a little nod, stepping back, stumbling against the bumper of the Toyota. The muscles in his face constricted in fear. For a moment, Father John feared he would turn and run. "It's going to be okay," he said quietly.

"Where were you tonight?" the other cop asked.

"Here." The word was choked, almost inaudible. Father John could see the young man's Adam's apple bobbing under his skin. "Here," he said again, louder this time.

"FBI agent wants to ask you some questions," the first officer said. "We'd like you to come along with no trouble."

Larson swung his head and shoulders around, his eyes locked on Father John's. "I didn't have nothing to do with Scott's death," Larson said, a pleading tone.

Father John nodded, but they both knew Larson was a primary suspect. He laid an opened hand on the young man's shoulder. He could feel the tenseness beneath the ridges of the corduroy jacket—the muscles of a mountain lion ready to spring. "I'm going to call a lawyer. You don't have to say anything without a lawyer present."

Larson drew in a long breath. The squared shoulders dropped, and he stuffed his hands into the pockets of his jacket. "Okay," he said, starting toward the police car.

Father John watched the two officers hustle the young man into the backseat, slam the door, and lower themselves into the front. The car was already rolling when the doors shut, and then it shot out onto the highway, sending back a spray of gravel that peppered Father John's face. He fished a quarter out of the pocket of his blue jeans and walked over to the pay phone that hung lopsidedly from the wall close to the bar entrance. He pushed the coin into the slot and punched in the number for Vicky Holden.

It was still early in the morning when Father John wheeled the Toyota to the curb in front of the redbrick building on Lander's Main Street. The sun bored through the back of his cotton shirt as he hurried up the outside steps to the one-lawyer, second-floor office. The secretary glanced up from behind the desk in the far corner, a confident look in her eyes, as if she had known he would arrive. "She's been waiting for you," she said, giving a little nod toward the opened door to the private office.

Father John rapped on the doorframe as he walked into the small office. Vicky sat behind an oak desk, her dark eyes watching as he settled into a barrel-shaped chair on the other side. Her black hair was pulled back and fastened somehow. She was wearing a blue blouse that made a little V at her neck where a silver necklace showed. He had known her for almost five years now. They had worked together on more cases—more divorces and accidents, more murders—than he wanted to think about. She was the lawyer, he the priest. Usually they were both necessary.

"You look about the way I feel." She gave him a slow, knowing smile.

Father John rubbed his hand across his chin, wondering whether he had remembered to shave this morning. He'd been up most of the night, sitting at his desk in the study, sipping on coffee that turned lukewarm, wondering whether the phone would ring, wondering about Larson, trying to make the pieces fit into some logical explanation. He realized Vicky had also been up most of the night.

"How's Larson," he said.

Vicky didn't answer for a moment. Then: "Larson's in a lot of trouble. The fed has a witness who swears Larson was at the house about the time Scott was murdered. And the police found a revolver down by the creek. They're pretty sure it's the murder weapon. It was in a brown paper bag with a pair of gloves. If the fed traces that gun to Larson, he'll be charged with first-degree murder so fast it will make his head spin around."

"Larson didn't kill Scott."

Vicky raised her chin, regarding him a moment. "What makes you think so?"

"I talked to Larson. He said Scott was alive, watching TV, when he left the house. I believe him."

"You believe him," she said. "Well, that's sure to carry a lot of weight in a courtroom." She gave him a half smile. "Gianelli's working on the drug angle. He's convinced Larson shot Scott over drugs. He asked Larson a lot of questions about drugs last night, but Larson insisted he didn't have anything to do with drugs, and neither did Scott. The problem . . ." She hesitated.

"What's the problem," Father John said.

"Tammy says Scott was dealing."

Father John got to his feet and walked over to the window. A truck crawled below on Main Street, and as he watched it slide to a stop at the light, he wondered why Tammy would want Gianelli to believe Scott was a drug dealer. He could feel Vicky's eyes on him, and he turned to face her. "What do you know about the girl?"

Vicky let out a long breath. "She has a penchant for getting mixed up with the wrong people. About a year ago, she was picked up for selling cocaine." Vicky shrugged. "Her parents called me."

Father John stepped back to the chair and sat down. "What happened?" he asked.

"Nothing," she said. "There wasn't any evidence, except for the story of some drugged-out kid the BIA police had picked up. The kid tried to buy himself out of trouble by implicating Tammy. She wasn't even charged. But I had the feeling she was on coke herself—not selling it, just using it. Somebody else was supplying her." Vicky pulled her eyes away, remembering. "In my opinion, she was a good kid. Just fallen in with a bad crowd. Maybe . . ." Another hesitation. "Maybe the fed's right. Maybe Scott was her supplier." She locked eyes with him again. "I suggested to her parents that they get her some help."

Father John leaned forward and tapped a finger on the edge of the desk. "Larson said Scott was trying to help her."

"Help her? The drug supplier trying to help her get off of drugs?"

"Help her get away from her parents."

Vicky gave a little laugh. "That's ridiculous. Arapaho families are close, John, very close. No parent wants to lose contact with a child, and I can't imagine any kid wanting to break with her parents."

"He said they were going to kill her."

"What?" Vicky jumped to her feet. "They came the minute she called them last night. They stayed with her all night. Last year they called me when she was in trouble. They love Tammy."

Father John stood up and walked back to the window. This was what had bothered him during the night—the nagging feeling that something was wrong, something didn't fit—but now, like a perfect syllogism developing in the far reaches of his mind, it was beginning to make sense. He looked at Vicky. "Suppose Tammy's parents are the drug dealers."

He expected her to argue, to protest that he didn't know what he was talking about. Instead, Vicky stood at the desk, gripping the edge, her knuckles turning white. "Last year I tried to get Tammy to tell me where she was getting her cocaine. She said she could never tell. If she had been charged, John, she might have gone to prison, but she would never have given up her parents. She would never have wanted to break with her parents. She would have wanted to protect them. She would have done whatever it takes . . ." Vicky flinched, as to ward off the force of the truth. Neither of them spoke for a moment, and then she said, "If Scott knew what her parents were doing, he might have threatened to go to the police."

"He told Larson he would do whatever it took to save her," Father John said.

"But she didn't want to be saved, John. They were her parents. She couldn't allow Scott to destroy them."

"She must have gone to the house and waited until she saw Larson drive away. Then she went inside. Scott was sitting in front of the TV. He probably never saw her before she shot him."

Vicky closed her eyes. She swayed slightly, as if a gust of wind had broken through the office. "Execution style," she said, the words barely audible. She opened her eyes and sank down onto her chair. "All we have is conjecture, John. A theory about a girl terrified of losing her family. We have no proof."

"We have to talk to Gianelli." Father John started across the office.

"And tell him what?" Vicky swung around the desk and sprinted ahead, blocking the door. "He'll laugh us out of his office, unless . . ."

"What?" Father John could almost see the idea forming behind her eyes.

"Suppose Tammy used her father's gun."

"You said the police can't trace the gun."

"That doesn't mean it doesn't belong to her father. It would have been the easiest way for her to get ahold of a weapon. It's possible, John. And if that's the case, she just may confess."

"Why would she do that? She killed a man to protect her parents." Suddenly Father John understood. He drew in a long breath; then: "Tammy will keep protecting them."

"Exactly," Vicky said.

* * *

The door stood open, creaking into the wind that swooped over the stoop. Father John could see the shadows lying like a blanket over a corner of the living room, spilling like blood on the dark carpet, the plaid sofa against the near wall. He glanced at Vicky waiting beside him on the stoop. In her eyes, he saw his own concern. The girl wasn't home.

From inside somewhere came the scuff of footsteps, and then the girl stepped out from the shadows—small and waiflike in blue jeans and a brown tee shirt that hung loosely over her hips. Her face looked thin and drawn, too small for the frizzed black hair that hung over her forehead and draped around her shoulders. Under the dark complexion was a hint of paleness. She was rubbing her hands together, as if to warm them. Her eyes were wide and blank. "If you're lookin' for the fed, him and a couple cops are out back talkin' private to my folks."

Father John realized she must have been in the back of the house, probably watching her parents out the window. "We'd like to talk to you," he said.

The girl was rubbing her hands furiously now, as if she were mashing something hard between her palms. "I don't need a priest." She looked at Vicky. "I don't need a lawyer, either."

"The fed knows who killed Scott," Vicky said.

The girl began stepping backward. "Larson did it." There was a tentativeness in the girl's voice. "They got into it over some stuff, so Larson killed him."

"Larson didn't kill Scott," Father John said. He followed Vicky inside. A faint, musty odor permeated the room, as if the doors and windows hadn't been thrown open in a long time.

"The police found the gun," Vicky said. "That's why the fed's talking to your father now."

The girl stopped rubbing her hands together. A look of comprehension spread slowly over the thin face; her breath came in short bursts. "No," she said, backing up, stumbling, dropping onto the sofa. "My dad didn't have nothin' to do with it."

Father John said, "Your father may be arrested, Tammy. Perhaps your mother, too, if the fed thinks she was involved. They could both stand trial for murder."

"No. No. It's crazy." Tammy shook her head, staring into the shadows across the room. Her eyes seemed to go in and out of focus.

"Why did your parents want Scott dead?" Vicky asked, a quiet, assured courtroom voice.

"They didn't do it," the girl shouted. "Just 'cause the police found some old pistol, that don't mean it's Dad's." Her voice cracked like that of an adolescent boy's. She raised both hands and began pulling at her hair, tangling her fingers in the frizz. "My parents don't know nothing about it. They didn't know what Scott was gonna do." She stopped, her eyes darting about the room. "Scott's the one wanted them dead. Worse than dead. He wanted them in prison. He was gonna tell the police a lotta stuff was nobody's business. He was gonna ruin everything, ruin our family. He's the one that . . ." Another pause, longer this time, filled with the words still unspoken, the truth.

Tammy looked at Father John, and then at Vicky. "He was the one that made me do it." She lifted her hair and piled it on top of her head in great clumps of curls that cascaded over her face as her hands fell. She began to sob. Behind the strands of hair, moisture glistened on the thin cheeks. Finally, she said, "The gun's been around here forever; somebody give it to Dad a long time ago. I never thought the police was gonna think it was his."

Suddenly the girl's head snapped up. She pulled her hair away from her face and, fixing her eyes on the opened door, began struggling to her feet. "Mommy! Daddy!" she cried, stumbling forward.

Father John glanced around. Standing just inside the door were a broad-shouldered man in jeans and a plaid shirt and a reed-thin woman with the same black, frizzed hair, the same blank eyes as Tammy's. Their expressions were frozen in stunned disbelief. Ted Gianelli stood next to the couple, and behind them on the stoop were two uniformed police officers.

The girl pushed between Father John and Vicky and crumpled against her mother. Her father reached around, enfolding both mother and daughter in his arms. "Oh, God, oh, God," he kept repeating.

Gianelli brushed the girl's shoulder with his fingertips. "Tammy—," he said softly, "I'm placing you under arrest for the murder of Scott . . ."

Her mother pulled the girl closer, running one hand over her hair, patting her back. She might have been soothing a fretful child. Looking at her husband, she said: "What have we done, Donald? What have we done?"

Dead End

The Sixth Commandment:
Thou shalt do no murder.

Father John O'Malley felt his jaw muscles clench. He'd known it was serious when he saw the police car racing around the bend on Seventeen-Mile Road, sirens screeching. He'd turned after it down Bull Bear Road, a narrow, gravelly stub that ran into a dead end on the banks of the Wind River. Someone might need a priest, he'd thought; maybe one of his Arapaho parishioners at St. Francis Mission.

Now he stopped the Toyota pickup behind the three police cars blocking the road, red and blue lights blinking on the roofs, radios crackling. Several police officers and a young woman huddled near the ditch, eyes turned downslope at the brown truck. Its grill jutted upward into the August sun.

"What happened?" Father John called as he slammed out of the pickup. Art Banner, chief of the Bureau of Indian Affairs police on the Wind River Reservation, was sidling past the police cars toward him.

"Got us a shooting." The chief gave a quick nod toward the truck. "Amos Starbird's inside with a bullet in his head. Neighbor lady got home from work about five thirty and seen his truck in the ditch. You know him?"

Father John knew him: a breed—half-Arapaho, half-white—with a quick temper and a grudge as big as the outdoors. He seldom came around the mission. It was Amos' wife, Nancy, who shuffled their two little boys into the front pew every Sunday for ten-o'clock Mass.

Pulling the brim of his cowboy hat against the sun, Father John started toward the truck. On the other side of the ditch, the parched plains crept into the cloudless blue sky; the wild grasses and stalks of sunflowers rode sideways in the hot, steady breeze. He slid down the gravelly slope, aware of the policemen and the young woman watching from above.

Inside the truck, Amos Starbird curled over the steering wheel, head a mass of gray, bloody matter, shirt black with blood. Father John reached one hand through the opened window and made the sign of the cross over the body. "Lord have mercy on his soul," he prayed out loud. "Grant him peace."

As Father John climbed back, the chief said, "Must've just happened." A tentativeness in the words, as if he were testing them. "Most likely Amos was comin' home from work. Been working at Hank's Garage over in Riverton. Somebody might've followed him." The chief glanced across the flat expanse of sun-splashed plains toward Seventeen-Mile Road in the distance. "Amos could've turned down here to get away, not thinkin' it was a dead end. I sure hope . . ." He let the thought trail off a moment.

". . . hope Nancy didn't have anything to do with this. We had a few too many domestic disturbance calls out at their place."

Father John regarded the police chief a moment. So the rumors on the moccasin telegraph—the reservation's grapevine—were true. Still, it was hard to imagine Nancy Starbird pulling out a gun, slamming back the trigger, and sending a bullet into her husband's head. Yet he'd heard enough confessions to know what human beings might do, might be driven to do.

"No telling what might've got into Nancy." The chief was shaking his head. "She's part of that Echo Hawk Clan lives up in Squirrel Canyon in that compound of theirs. They go their own ways. Stick to themselves, like Arapaho clans used to live in the Old Time. Anyway, the fed's gonna have to sort it out." He glanced down the empty road—an expectant look, as if a vehicle might materialize out of the hazy heat.

Father John nodded. Murder on an Indian reservation fell under FBI jurisdiction. But that didn't mean Banner wouldn't help with the investigation. "Anyone see anything?" he asked.

The chief waved toward the three small houses hunkered down among the cottonwoods where the road dead-ended. "My boys already knocked on the doors. Nobody home this afternoon 'til she got here." He shot a glance toward the woman talking with one of the police officers. "The fed's gonna be outta luck for witnesses."

The telephone jangled into the quiet as Vicky Holden stuffed into her briefcase the legal papers she wanted to review at home tonight. Her secretary had already left. The answering machine could take the call, she told herself, snapping the lock. She picked up the briefcase and started around the desk as the phone emitted another jangle. She stopped, swung around, and lifted the receiver. "Vicky Holden here," she said, struggling to mask her irritation.

"You that Arapaho lawyer?" It was a woman's voice, not one she recognized.

"Yes."

"You gotta get over to Nancy Starbird's place."

Vicky felt her heart sink. When was it—three weeks ago?—she'd filed Nancy's divorce papers and gotten the restraining order against Amos. "Is Nancy all right?" She held her breath.

"Amos got killed."

A wave of relief washed over Vicky: Nancy was okay, and whatever had happened to Amos—God help her for thinking it—he had it coming.

"You better get to Nancy's place," the caller said.

* * *

The sun bulged orange-red over the Wind River Mountains, shooting red, orange, and pink flares through the blue sky as Vicky left the Bronco behind a line of pickups at the side of Willow Road. The small green house stood in the middle of a bare dirt yard with an old pickup on one side. Lined up across the yard like guards were about a dozen men: plaid shirts and blue jeans, black braids hanging from beneath cowboy hats. There were the little nods, the flick of eyebrows, the slanted eyes on her as she hurried past. A medley of hushed conversations floated outside through the screened door. The entire Echo Hawk Clan was here, Vicky thought as she rapped on the thin frame.

The screened door swung outward, and Nancy stood in the opening, two black braids spilling down a thin chest, a bruise purpling the side of her face. Wordlessly, she reached for Vicky's hand, and Vicky followed her into the small living room crowded with young women, grandmothers, and elders. The smell of fresh coffee seeped into the air. Across the room, sitting in a circle of elders, was Father John O'Malley. She caught his eyes a moment before turning to Nancy. "Tell me what happened," she said.

"Somebody shot Amos." Nancy sank back against the doorjamb, eyes puddling with tears. Vicky was about to put her arms around Nancy when a puffy-faced woman with narrow, dark eyes and a cap of gray hair stepped between them. Edna Echo Hawk, the clan matriarch, began cradling Nancy. "Now, now, we're gonna take care of you and the kids," she said.

Suddenly Vicky was aware of the tall, redheaded white man beside her. Father John was always present, she thought, when someone needed him. Glancing up, she asked, "When did it happen?"

"About five thirty. Out on Bull Bear Road," Father John said. His voice was soft.

Vicky felt a little chill course through her. Nancy's trips to the emergency room, the disturbance calls—enough for her to finally seek a divorce, a restraining order. And now the bruise on Nancy's face. What had she decided to do next?

"I got real worried when Amos didn't get home," Nancy was saying.

"What?" Vicky stared at the young woman.

"I was gonna tell you, Vicky," she began in a thin, childlike voice. "We got everything patched up, Amos and me. He come back home last week. He promised we was all gonna move up to the compound with the clan, so things was goin' real good."

"Real good?" Vicky heard the sharpness in her tone. "He hit you again."

"We told her not to get back with that no-good husband of hers," the grandmother said. "What good's that restraining order when he kept comin' round anyway? He'd tell her anything, and she'd believe him." Turning toward Nancy, she said, "He wasn't never gonna bring you up to the compound, 'cause he knew he couldn't kick you and the kids around up there. No way was we gonna let him."

Just like in the Old Time, Vicky was thinking, when the family clans lived together—clung together—following the buffalo across the plains, setting up tipis along the streams, the warriors always standing guard, protecting the women and children. But Nancy didn't live in Squirrel Canyon with the rest of the clan. She and Amos were *Kono'utose'i Oi*—modern people. They had their own home, their own little family. Except Nancy had no one to protect her and the kids. Only herself.

"Was anyone else here this afternoon?" Father John asked Nancy. In his eyes, Vicky saw the reflection of her own worry.

The young woman shook her head. "The boys was playing over with LuAnn Runner's kids." She paused, eyes darting between Father John and Vicky. "What d'ya think? I went out to Bull Bear Road and shot Amos just 'cause he hit me again?"

"Don't talk crazy," the grandmother said. "Mary Wilson come over for coffee this afternoon."

Surprise and confusion crept into Nancy's face. "Mary Wilson wasn't here."

"Course she was. What're you talkin' about? She was here all the time that no-good husband of yours was gettin' himself shot." Locking eyes now with Vicky, the old woman said, "Mary Wilson'll tell everybody so."

"Look, Nancy," Vicky said, a lawyer tone, "don't talk to anyone—the police or the fed—without calling me. Do you understand?"

Father John and Vicky walked past Nancy's clansmen—her brothers and cousins—silently holding their line in the dirt yard. The sky glowed orange with the fading sunset; the air was still hot. When they reached the Bronco, Vicky said, "As soon as the fed learns about the divorce filing, the restraining order, the emergency room visits, Nancy will be facing a murder charge. Who had more reason to kill Amos? Obviously the clan thinks she killed him. That's why they called me. That's why Edna Echo Hawk is insisting she has an alibi."

Father John was quiet a moment. Then, taking Vicky's arm and leading her past the Bronco to the Toyota, he said, "Let's go have a talk with Mary Wilson."

Father John had knocked a second time on the front door when an old woman with thin shoulders hunched inside a pink cotton dress appeared around the corner of the white frame house. "Vicky? Father John? You lookin' for me?" Mary Wilson clutched a black bag to her sunken chest.

Father John began explaining that they'd come about Amos Starbird.

Yes. Yes. Mary Wilson nodded. She'd heard about Amos. She was on her way over to Nancy's now, poor girl, even though the whole clan was most likely there looking after her and the kids, but you never know, she might help fix some food, or . . .

"Grandmother," Vicky said, using the Arapaho term of respect. "Did you go to Nancy's this afternoon?"

Worry and confusion mingled in the old woman's face. "Maybe I should've stopped in, like she asked me, but . . ."

"Who asked you?" Father John said.

"Well, I didn't ask who was calling, just one of Nancy's grandmothers wanting me to check on her. I figured Amos was acting up again." Disapproval flashed in Mary Wilson's eyes. "So I drove over about four thirty and seen Nancy out in the side yard by that old pickup her clan give her. Looked like she was fixin' to go somewhere, so I come on back home."

They watched Mary Wilson's old Chevy pull onto the road, jerking forward in a blue cloud of exhaust, before they got back into the Toyota. "Nancy had all the time in the world," Vicky said, a sense of dread as heavy as a buffalo robe pressing down on her. "She grabbed one of Amos' guns and drove across Seventeen-Mile Road to meet him. He must have seen her. Probably had a good idea what she had in mind, so he turned off on Bull Bear Road. She followed him to the dead end, shot him, threw the gun into a ditch somewhere, and drove back home before anybody could show up with the bad news. Oh, God, John." She drew in a long breath. "Tell me I'm wrong."

Vicky saw the little vein pulsing in his temple, recognized the look that always came into his eyes as he searched for the faulty proposition, the hole in the logic. Wheeling the Toyota into the center of the road, he said, "We don't know when Amos left the garage."

The low-slung building sat on an apron of cement at the eastern edge of Riverton. Black letters spelled HA K'S on a plate glass window in front. Father John drew up next to the opened garage door. In the dim interior, he could make out the shadowy hulk of a truck. As he and Vicky climbed out of the Toyota, a stoop-shouldered man in overalls came around the edge of the door, hands crumpling a red, grease-streaked rag. "Closed up," he said.

Father John introduced himself, then Vicky, and the man nodded, a grudging recognition: Indian priest, Indian lawyer lady. Stuffing the rag into a back pocket, he said, "What can I do for ya?"

"We'd like to talk to you about Amos Starbird," Father John said.

"Yeah? What about him?"

"Amos is dead," Vicky said. "Somebody shot him this afternoon."

The man shifted his gaze a moment to Vicky. "No great loss to the world."

"Where were you this afternoon about five thirty?" Vicky asked. She was grasping, she knew, looking for someone else with a motive to kill Amos.

"You ain't the police. Nobody's business where I might've been."

"The FBI agent will want to know," Father John said.

The man eyed Father John for a long moment, considering. "Right here," he said.

"When did Amos leave?"

Leaning sideways, the man shot a wad of spit across the pavement. "How'd I know? I was on the dolly under that truck." He waved a bony hand toward the shadowy interior. "Phone rung, and next thing I know, Amos says he's gotta get home. Guess that wife of his must've called."

There was an eagerness to the way people moved across the sun-baked cemetery at St. Francis Mission toward the pickups parked in the drive, Father John thought, as if no one wanted to linger at the grave of Amos Starbird. Members of the Echo Hawk Clan were already piling into the beds of old pickups and sliding three and four together onto the front seats.

Father John said another prayer over the grave before following the last of the crowd across the cemetery. He saw Vicky leaning against the door of the Toyota, squinting into the sun. "Nancy's no longer a suspect," she said when he reached her.

He drew in a long breath, feeling a sense of relief. He'd spent the past three days dreading the phone call, the news that Nancy Starbird had been arrested for murder.

Doors slammed; an engine backfired; a rust-smeared pickup wheeled past, tires crunching the gravel. Vicky waited; then: "The coroner's report says Amos was probably killed about four thirty, at least an hour before his body was found. Mary Wilson swears she saw Nancy in her yard about four thirty. According to the fed, there was only one call to Hank's Garage all afternoon. It was made from a pay phone at Ethete at exactly four o'clock. Amos left right away. In twenty minutes, he would've been at the bend on Seventeen-Mile Road where somebody was waiting, so he turned down Bull Bear Road—a dead end."

Father John glanced at the slowly moving pickups, the little clouds of dust clumping in the hot air. "Somebody wanted to make sure Nancy wouldn't take the blame," he said.

Vicky nodded. "Whoever called Mary Wilson used the same pay phone at Ethete."

Father John wasn't surprised. "Where will the investigation go from here?"

Turning her gaze at some point behind him, Vicky said, "The fed still has other leads. Amos got in his share of bar fights and he owed money to a few people in town. But . . ." She paused, keeping her eyes on the distances. "The fed will never solve this case. He doesn't know the old Arapaho ways."

Father John followed her gaze past the dirt-mounded graves, plastic flowers drooping in the heat, toward the line of pickups snaking around the curved drive and out onto Seventeen-Mile Road, carrying the elders and grandmothers, the women and the warriors of the Echo Hawk Clan.

He felt the soft pressure of Vicky's hand on his arm. "It was all of them, John," she whispered. "All of them."

"I know," he said.

Hole in the Wall

The Seventh Commandment:
Thou shalt commit no adultery.

Vicky Holden sensed another presence in the office. She looked up from the legal brief on her desk. Bertie Eagle Cloud stood in the doorway, black hair falling around the shoulders of her white tee shirt, worn blue jeans stretched tight around thick thighs. She raised her arm. In her hand was a black pistol.

"Bertie!" Vicky sat motionless, her breath caught in her chest. From outside came the muffled hum of late-afternoon traffic on Main Street in Lander, the sharp retort of an engine backfiring.

"I shot Ralph." The arm began to waver. Falling, falling, the nose of the pistol dropping toward the carpet.

"Let me have the gun." Vicky slowly rose to her feet and crossed the small office. Reaching down, she slipped the cold, hard metal from the woman's hand. "Come sit down," she said, guiding Bertie to a barrel-shaped chair in front of the desk.

She walked around the desk and set the gun inside the center drawer before sinking into her own chair. Clasping her hands to still the trembling, she leaned toward the other woman. A client, of sorts. Last year she had helped Bertie negotiate a new lease for her convenience store at Ethete on the Wind River Reservation. Just a month ago, Vicky had run into Bertie and Ralph at the Ethete powwow. They sat together watching the dances—an Arapaho couple sliding into middle age.

Bertie said, "I give Ralph fair warning. I tol' him, 'You take up with that whore again, I'm gonna kill you.'" She rearranged herself in the chair and folded her arms across the heaving chest. "He can't have some other wife. He ain't some great chief in the Old Time. He's got one wife for twenty years now, and that's me. Well, he goes off with that whore Liz Redman anyway. I didn't have no other choice."

Vicky was quiet. Outside, the traffic sounds seemed far away; the golden light of sunset glowed in the window. "Is Ralph dead?" She heard the hushed sound of her own voice.

"I missed the bastard." Bertie's head tilted in an angle of defiance. "I should've grabbed Ralph's rifle instead of that pistol. I can shoot the thirty-ought-six. I got an elk with it last month. It would've hit Ralph, instead of putting a hole in the wall. Next time I'm gonna use the rifle."

Vicky lifted herself out of the chair, walked over, and perched on the vacant chair next to Bertie. "Listen to me. There's not going to be a next time."

Something changed behind the woman's narrow eyes. "I thought you was gonna understand, Vicky. I don't got a choice. He took up with that woman again. I got every right . . ."

"Not to kill him." Vicky emphasized each word. "Whatever Ralph has done, it's not worth spending the rest of your life in prison."

The woman let her gaze roam around the office. "Next time I'm gonna use the rifle."

Vicky drew in a long breath. Bertie had just confessed to a crime of assault with a deadly weapon. "I must advise you to turn yourself in to the police," she said. "I'll go with you."

"If I'd found the thirty-ought-six, that bastard wouldn't still be walkin' around."

"If you turn yourself in, it will go easier for you," Vicky said. "Maybe Ralph won't press charges."

Bertie laid both hands on the armrests, propelled herself upright, and started for the door. "I think I remember where he put it."

"No, Bertie!" Vicky got to her feet. The woman was already through the waiting room, flinging open the door.

Vicky ran after her. "Wait," she called as the woman hurried along the outside corridor that led to the second-floor offices. She turned into the stairway. The clip-clop of footsteps echoed against the wood walls. And then she was on the street below, arms swinging, thick legs pumping toward the black pickup at the curb.

"No, Bertie," Vicky shouted over the railing, as the woman folded herself behind the steering wheel. Another moment, and the pickup pulled into traffic, engine growling, blue exhaust bursting from the tailpipe.

Vicky knew with a cold certainty that Bertie Eagle Cloud intended to finish the job she had started. She had to warn Ralph.

She ran back to her desk and flipped through the Rolodex until she found the couple's listing. Then she picked up the receiver and punched in the number. The electronic ringing buzzed in her ear. There was no answer. Ralph was probably at Liz Redman's house. She tapped out the number for information. One, two, three rings before the operator came on the line. "Sorry." The voice sounded bored. "No listing for Liz Redman."

Vicky slammed down the receiver. She would have to warn Ralph herself. But Liz Redman lived near the Wind River on the eastern edge of the reservation—an hour's drive away. By the time she got there, it might be too late.

She lifted the receiver again and called the Bureau of Indian Affairs police on the Wind River Reservation. Another operator, and finally the familiar rumble of the police chief's voice. "Art Banner here."

"It's Vicky," she said, her mind searching for the words that would protect a client, yet notify the chief of an imminent danger. She said, "Bertie Eagle Cloud just left my office and . . ."

The chief cut in: "So that's where she's been. My boys been lookin' all over the rez last couple hours."

Vicky was quiet a moment. Ralph must have already pressed charges. "What's this about, Art?"

A long intake of breath sounded over the line. Finally, the chief said, "Ralph Eagle Cloud's dead."

"Dead." The word sank into the office quiet like a boulder falling to the bottom of a lake. Her mind replayed the slow-motion image: Bertie retreating down the corridor, sliding into the pickup, on the way to kill a man already dead.

"What happened?" she managed.

"Got himself shot over at his girlfriend's place, damn fool," the chief said. "We got an anonymous call somebody heard a gunshot at the house. Couple of my boys checked it out, and there was Ralph on the living room sofa with a thirty-ought-six slug in his chest. The girlfriend was standing there in some kind of shock. Still holding on to the rifle."

Vicky shook her head, trying to fit the pieces together. "He was shot with a rifle?"

"Wouldn't surprise me if it turns out to be his own gun. My boys held the girlfriend until the FBI agent got there. He took her into custody on suspicion of murder. We went to the convenience store to give Bertie the bad news. Clerk said she didn't come in today. Didn't find her at the house, either."

"She's on the way home now," Vicky said.

The chief drew in another long breath. "Sure gonna be tough on Bertie. Ralph might've fooled around some, but he wasn't a bad sort. I'm gonna ask Father John to drive out to Plunkett Road and give her the bad news."

Vicky said, "Bertie's a client. I'll drive over, too."

She started to hang up when the chief said, "What was on your mind?"

"It's not important."

Father John O'Malley wheeled the Toyota pickup onto Plunkett Road, a narrow strip of gravel snaking through the open plains of the Wind River Reservation. A cloud of dust rose ahead, and out of the dust appeared a light brown Bronco, metal trim glinting in the sun. A sense of relief washed over him. He was usually the sole bearer of heartbreaking news— the part of his job as pastor at St. Francis Mission that he never got used to. But it looked as if Vicky Holden was also on her way to see Bertie Eagle Cloud.

He followed the Bronco into the dirt yard that sprawled in front of a yellow cubelike house, the only sign of human habitation he'd seen for miles. A white propane tank stood at one side on spindly legs, and nearby, a rusty pickup sloped into the dirt. He let himself out and walked over to Vicky, who was standing at the door of the Bronco.

"How did you hear?" he asked.

"Banner."

They walked across the yard to the house. The front door was ajar, and he rapped on the thin wood. From inside came a thud, like that of a cabinet hitting the floor. Father John pushed the door open a few inches. "Bertie?"

Another thud. He glanced at Vicky. "Stay here."

He stepped into the small living room. A sofa, two chairs, and television console stood mutely along the walls. There was no one around.

The thuds started again, hard and rhythmic, like the beat of a drum. He walked into the kitchen and down a hallway, following the sounds to a bedroom. Clothing and papers tumbled over the bed and dresser and crept across the floor. Bertie stood in the closet, her back to him, several large boxes at her feet. She yanked a stretch of shirts and dresses off hangers and tossed them behind her into the room. Then she reached up and tugged at a cardboard box on the top shelf, white tee shirt stretching around rolls of flesh. The box crashed to the floor.

"Bertie!" Father John said. "What are you doing?"

The woman swung around and glared at him. "Why'd you come here?" Her gaze shifted sideways, and he realized Vicky had come down the hall and was standing behind him.

"I told you, Vicky." Bertie stepped over the boxes, shaking a fist. "I'm gonna find that rifle. I got my rights. You bringing Father John round ain't gonna change my mind."

"It's not what you think," Vicky said. Her voice was gentle.

Father John stepped across the room and took Bertie's hand. "Let's go into the living room and sit down, Bertie. We have bad news."

The woman tilted her head and fixed him for a moment with clear, steady eyes. Then she shouldered past and disappeared through the door. Father John and Vicky followed her into the living room.

"So, let's have it." Bertie plopped onto the middle cushion of the sofa. Vicky sat down beside her.

Father John pulled over a straight-backed chair and sat facing them. "I'm sorry, Bertie," he began—it was never easy—"Ralph is dead."

"Dead!" The woman's mouth gaped open, formed around the word. She turned to Vicky. "That bastard can't be dead."

Vicky nodded slowly. "The police found him this afternoon at Liz Redman's house. He was shot. Liz has been arrested."

"No!" Bertie was shaking her head. The black hair swung around like a veil. "What right's that whore got to shoot him? I got the right. I should've finished him off when I had the chance. If I'd've found the rifle instead of that pistol, I could've done it. I wouldn't've put no hole in the wall."

"Sshh," Vicky said, patting the woman's hand. She might have been trying to soothe a child. "Ralph's dead, Bertie. Let it be."

Father John was quiet. He saw the picture: at some point Bertie had tried to shoot Ralph with a pistol, and Vicky knew about it.

Suddenly Bertie was working her way off the sofa, heaving herself upright. "I wanna see that bastard."

Father John stood up and reached out one hand, steadying her. "You may not want to do that."

The woman brushed past him. "I'm goin' to that whore's house."

The wooden house might have been dropped onto the flat stretch of plains—a collection of boards with streaks of faded white paint and a roof that sloped over the small front stoop. Yellow police tape stretched around the perimeter of the dirt yard. Parked on the graveled road in front were a couple of four-wheel drives and two white Bureau of Indian Affairs police cars. Father John parked behind the last car. In the rearview mirror, he saw the Bronco sliding to a stop. The passenger door swung open and, in a half second, Bertie had stepped over the tape and was grinding her way toward the porch.

Father John let himself out and waited as Vicky came around the Bronco. "Bertie's in shock," Vicky said. "She rambled on and on all the way over here. She never shut up."

Suddenly Bertie's voice split the air: "I got my rights. I'm the wife." Chief Banner stood on the stoop blocking her way.

Vicky hurried up the steps. "Come on, Art. You know she has the right to see her husband."

"She may have the right, Vicky, but it might not be best."

Father John joined them. "We've already gone over this," he said.

The chief shrugged and led the way into a small living room crowded with uniformed policemen and several men dressed in slacks and dark sport coats. There was a hush of conversations. Ted Gianelli, the local FBI agent, huddled with a group in front of the sofa pushed against the opposite wall. A photographer bent down; light flashed through the room. As he stepped aside, Father John saw the body slumped over the edge of the sofa.

Bertie lurched forward. "He's dead!" It was a scream. "He's really dead."

Gianelli stepped over to the woman. He wore a dark blue sport coat and gray, wrinkled slacks. The red tie draped down the center of his white shirt looked like a streak of blood. "You've seen him, Bertie. Let's go outside and let the lab technicians finish their job." He took her arm—an unsuccessful attempt to turn her around.

Bertie jerked away. "That whore shot him."

Gianelli drew in a long breath. "Liz says she found Ralph when she got home from work. The rifle was next to the sofa. Says that's all she remembers. But the police found her standing over him with the rifle in hand. Looks like she fired twice. One shot missed and blew a hole in the wall."

For the first time, Father John saw the broken wallboard, the dark hole boring into the wall above the sofa. He glanced at Vicky. She was staring at the wall.

Banner spoke up. "My boys found two rifle cartridges on the floor. Crime boys dug a thirty-ought-six slug out of the wall."

Vicky glanced from the chief to the FBI agent. "What are you saying? That the same gun hit both Ralph and the wall?"

Both men nodded. "Thirty-ought-six," Gianelli said.

The murmur of conversations over by the sofa punctuated the quiet. Father John saw the look of shock and comprehension cross Vicky's face, and he understood.

"I told Ralph he was gonna get shot some day," Bertie was saying, "but he kept whorin' around."

"Don't say anything else." Vicky's tone was sharp.

Bertie reared back. She stared at Vicky a moment, then wheeled toward Father John. A frantic look came into her eyes, like the look in the eyes of an animal searching for a way out of a trap. "He shouldn't've done that to me, Father. You understand, don't you?" She started backing toward the door. The room grew quiet.

"Listen to Vicky," Father John said. "You have the right not to say anything."

The woman threw back her head and gave out a laugh edged with hysteria. "Nobody understands," she said, backing up, laughing. "Ralph deserved to die, and that whore deserves to go to prison forever." She drew in a shuddering breath. "I left the rifle for her. I waited at the gas station 'til I seen her comin' home; then I called the police. She picked up the rifle, like I knew she'd do, and the police come walkin' in. It worked just like I planned."

"Bertie, for God's sake, stop talking," Vicky said.

Chief Banner moved behind Bertie, blocking the door, and Gianelli stepped in front. "Bertie Eagle Cloud," he said. "I'm placing you under arrest for the murder of your husband."

Nobody's Going to Cry

The Eighth Commandment:
Thou shalt not steal.

She'd left Lander thirty minutes ago for the eight-o'clock appointment at the Arapaho tribal offices in Ethete twenty miles inside the Wind River Reservation. It should have allowed plenty of time, and Vicky Holden liked to be on time. A compulsion from the ten years she'd spent going to school and practicing law in Denver. Highway 287 had been a clear shot north with only a few pickups and sedans in the oncoming lane, Arapahos heading to jobs in town, sun glinting on windshields and bumpers. The morning air was light and suffused with gold. It would be another hot day. The wind knocked against the Jeep and flattened the wild grasses in the open fields on both sides of the highway.

It was after she'd turned right and gone about a mile on Blue Sky Highway that she regretted not having left earlier. Blocking the road ahead were four police cars, an ambulance, and two SUVs. The blue and red lights flashing on the roof of a police car looked faded in the sunlight. Vicky tapped on the brake and slowed alongside the Wind River police officer holding up one hand like a traffic cop. She recognized Howie Thunder. The wind plastered his gray uniform shirt to his chest.

Vicky rolled down her window. "What's going on?"

"Better turn around, Vicky. Go back to 287."

Vicky glanced past him. Milling about were other uniformed officers as well as a couple of sheriff's detectives in blue jeans, light-colored shirts, and cowboy hats. Beyond the vehicles she could see the brown pickup sloped into the ditch, the wheels on the driver's side clinging to the section of dirt that bordered the asphalt. The slightest jar, she was thinking, and the pickup would turn over. Inside, an Indian slumped over the steering wheel, clumps of black hair falling over his face. A broad-shouldered man in a cowboy hat climbed out of the ditch behind the pickup. Ted Gianelli, the local FBI agent, looked like the other cops in civvies. The wind was blowing the fronts of his tan leather vest away from his white shirt.

"What happened, Howie?" she said, looking up at the officer still outside her door. She'd known Howie and his wife, Myrna, since they were kids. They'd gone to school together at St. Francis Mission.

"Police business," he said, squinting in the sun. He was about six feet tall and looked in shape, with a flat stomach and muscular brown arms that hung beneath the short sleeves of his uniform shirt.

"Since when does the fed handle traffic accidents?" Vicky got out of the Jeep into the warm air. She had to hold her hair back in the wind.

The man shrugged and glanced back at the pickup. "Since bullets put a drug dealer into the ditch," he said. "Anonymous call came in at seven this morning. Said somebody was dead inside a pickup. I got here first. Fed thinks it must've happened in the middle of the night. Jose Montecon. You heard of him?"

Vicky nodded. There had been numerous articles in the *Gazette* about the Mexican drug ring that had moved onto the Wind River Reservation. Montecon was identified as the leader, but he'd hooked up with a local partner, Ernest Redbird. The news had made her feel sick to her stomach. She knew the Redbird family. Sylvia, Ernest's sister, had raised him after their parents had been killed in an automobile accident. Both Redbird and Montecon had been indicted by a federal grand jury, but they'd fled the area before they could be arrested.

"We got a tip last week Montecon was back," Howie was saying. "Word on the rez is that Redbird made off with a lot of his money, and Montecon was after him. We figured Montecon must've thought Redbird was here. Otherwise, why would he take the risk of coming back? Every law enforcement agency in the area has had an alert out for both of them." He clenched his hands into fists and threw another glance at the pickup. "Looks like Redbird found Montecon before Montecon found him."

"How do you know that?" Vicky could hear the tightness in her voice.

She was grasping for some other explanation, she knew. There could be dozens of people on the rez who would like to see the drug dealer shot.

Another thought hit her. Sylvia had been through a lot trying to help Ernest get off drugs. Every time he got clean, Montecon showed up and got him hooked again. And Sylvia knew how to handle a gun. She could bring down an elk with a single shot. Oh, my God, Vicky thought.

She tried to concentrate on what Howie was saying, something about it being a deliberate killing. "Redbird shot out the rear right tire," he said, shaking his head. "Waited for the pickup to skid to a stop and drove alongside. Made sure he had a clear aim before he shot Montecon in the face. You ask me, he wanted that bastard to be looking at him when he pulled the trigger so he knew who done it. He saw the chance to take over the drug ring, cut out Montecon, and run it himself."

"Any evidence? What about the gun?" She was going to have to talk to Sylvia right away, Vicky was thinking. Prepare her for the fact that the police would be looking for Ernest in connection with a murder. And sooner or later, they may start looking at her.

Howie let out a cough of laughter. "Whatever gun he used, he dropped into a well by now. It'll never be found. Redbird's the one with the motive," he went on, squinting into the distance. "Makes the most sense. One drug dealer cutting out another. Happens all the time. Both of 'em are bastards. Ruined a lot of folks' lives here. Got kids on meth—kids! Jesus Christ, Vicky, he got a lot of adults hooked, too. Nobody's going to cry over Montecon."

* * *

"Bull crap what those cops say about Ernest." Sylvia Redbird peered into an empty pack of cigarettes, then rolled it into a ball and tossed it onto the table next to her chair. She was a large woman with black hair pulled back from a leathery face and tied into a ponytail, and roughened hands the size of a man's. She wore blue jeans, red tee shirt, and dust-covered hiking boots.

"They framed him, made it look like he was guilty so him and Montecon both got indicted. What was he supposed to do? Hang around and let them cops arrest him? He had to take off."

"The police think he came back," Vicky said. "They think he killed Montecon."

The woman let out a noise that sounded like the howl of a coyote.

"Ernest? Kill somebody?" She threw up one of her big hands. "Okay, okay. Maybe there was a time when Ernest could've done something crazy like that. Montecon was a slimeball—that's a fact. Sucked the life outta everybody he knew. Got Ernest hooked on meth, then kept raising the price on him. Forced him to start dealing, get more customers on the rez. That's the truth, Vicky. No way Ernest would've starting selling meth if he wasn't forced."

"Where is he?"

Sylvia shrugged. "How would I know?"

"The court might go easier on him if he surrendered."

"Like hell. He'd go to prison for dealing drugs. They throw in a murder charge, he'll be locked up the rest of his life." Sylvia folded her arms across her broad waist. "I'm telling you, Ernest's clean now. Went to the mission and talked things over with Father John." She gave another shrug and looked away. For a moment Vicky thought she would jump to her feet and end the conversation.

"Father John would have suggested he turn himself in," Vicky said.

It was a moment before Sylvia responded. "How do you know?"

"I know Father John." Oh, she knew him well—John O'Malley, the pastor at St. Francis Mission. They'd worked together for six years—priest and lawyer. There had been so many divorces, accidents, adoptions, DUIs, assaults, even homicides that had drawn them together, she felt as if she could recite word by word what Father John would have told Ernest Redbird.

"Went to rehab, got himself together," Sylvia said, turning the topic back to Ernest. She moved her eyes to some point across the room. "Got himself a nice girlfriend. He's done with the rez and all the problems. Making a new life for himself somewhere else. He's not coming back. Let it be."

"The police think Montecon was looking for him, and that Ernest found Montecon first."

The woman leapt from her chair. "Can't they leave him alone? Montecon's put him through enough hell. Hell, I tell you! He's free now. Somebody else shot that bastard, not Ernest. Let the cops go find the real killer."

Vicky got to her feet. She dug through her purse and handed the other woman her business card. "Ernest is going to need a lawyer," she said. She was thinking that Sylvia Redbird might also need a lawyer.

Howie Thunder stood in the doorway of the tri-level house with faded, yellowish siding. The door had swung open before Father John had gotten out of the pickup. The Arapaho had the look of a general awaiting the arrival of his troops, arms rigid at the sides of his gray uniform. Yet, there was something removed and vacant about him, as if part of him were somewhere else. Forty minutes ago, he'd called the mission. "Can you come over, Father? Need to talk."

Father John had told the Arapaho he was on the way. He'd been half expecting the call since he'd heard the news on the radio this morning: Jose Montecon, indicted leader of a drug ring on the reservation, had been found shot to death on Blue Sky Highway. The police reported he'd been killed sometime in the middle of the night. The responding officer was Howie Thunder. Ironic that Howie was the one to find the drug dealer's body. Three weeks ago, Father John had spent most of the day helping Howie and Myrna get their teenaged daughter, Patsy, into another rehab center. Father John walked across the strip of bare dirt that lay between the pickup and the wooden stoop in front of the house. A hot gust of wind swept across the open fields, pressing his shirt against his skin.

"How're you doing?" he said.

Howie was backing into the house, tossing his head, beckoning Father John to follow. "Thanks for coming by," he said. "I can't get her calmed down."

"Her?" Father John had assumed Howie wanted to talk about finding Montecon's body, but it was probably Patsy he was worried about, or possibly Myrna. He stood inside the door a second, letting his eyes adjust from the brightness outside. Curtains were drawn across the front window, leaving only a faint outline of light at the edges. The sofa and chairs looked like black shadows. Thin streaks of sunlight from the kitchen in back ran like water across a corner of the vinyl floor. The light winked in the metallic frames of three photos arranged on a table next to the sofa. A door leading to bedrooms on the right was closed. He could hear the faint, intermittent sound of weeping.

"Myrna's in there . . ." Howie nodded toward the closed door. "Can't get her to stop crying." He let out a sharp sob.

"Sit down," Father John said. He took hold of Howie's arm and guided him through the shadows to the sofa. Then he pulled up a wooden chair and sat down across from him. "Tell me what's going on."

The Arapaho seemed to be gathering his thoughts. Finally he said, "Day before yesterday, Patsy overdosed. Meth and alcohol." He dropped his head into his hands and sobbed out loud. Tears glistened between his brown fingers. After a moment, he said, "Just got out of rehab, was doing real good. This time, we thought . . ." He let the rest of it trail off.

"You thought she'd make it." Father John set a hand on the man's shoulder. Beneath the hard seams of the uniform shirt, he could feel the trembling that ran past the man's skin and muscles, into his bones. From somewhere in the house, beyond the closed door, came the quiet, rhythmic noise of weeping.

"Montecon and that other slimeball, Redbird, must've gotten hold of her again. Got her back on meth. Seventeen years old is all she is, Father." The words came in jerky monosyllables. "Two days ago Myrna answers the phone. Patsy's boyfriend says she can't wake up. Can't wake up? Myrna says. She thought Patsy spent the night with her girlfriend. Myrna calls me right away. I was just finishing up patrol. I notify the dispatcher, and the ambulance has Patsy in the emergency room before Myrna and me got there. Docs say she's in a coma. Maybe she'll come out, maybe not. They don't know."

Howie dropped his head and stared down at his hands clasped in his lap. The moisture dropping from his cheeks made little black tracks across the front of his gray shirt. "We stayed with her all day, all night, and most of yesterday, watching that plastic tube drip fluids into her to keep her from dying. I held her hand. It was cold, Father, cold as death. We seen her eyelids move once in a while, like she was trying to open them, trying to come back. That's how we knew our little girl was still alive."

Howie lifted his palms against his face and wiped away the moisture. Then he reached around the armrest and picked up one of the metallic-framed photographs. "There she is, last year before they got her on meth," he said, holding out the photo, staring down the length of his arms, as if the girl herself had moved out of reach. "So much life in her. She's so pretty."

"Yes, she is." Even in the shadows, the girl's eyes shone with light. Black, curly hair hung loosely about a face that still had the soft, unformed look of a child. Father John could feel his own muscles tense. Meth and alcohol were a lethal combination.

"She's an artist," Howie said, tossing his head one way, then the other.

For the first time, Father John noticed the small paintings arranged on the walls. There was a picture of the golden brown prairie rolling into blue mountains, another picture of a cluster of white tipis with dark shadows flung over the prairie, and one of a black horse grazing in the pasture.

"I took her out to the pasture the day she painted it," Howie said, nodding toward the painting. "Rigged up some branches to set her easel on. Fourteen years old, she was. She said that horse was so beautiful, she wanted to capture him forever. She painted most of the day, and when I came back for her, she'd captured that stallion. There he was on the canvas, true as life. It's gonna kill Myrna, if . . ."

"Try to have hope," Father John said.

"I brought Myrna home yesterday. Fixed her a little dinner, but she couldn't eat. Finally got her to sleep—God, she was exhausted. So was I, but I had to go out on patrol. We were shorthanded, and we had a tip Montecon was on the rez looking for Redbird. Redbird got to him first. Shot him in the head this morning. The bastard deserved to die. Redbird's gonna get what he deserves, too. Gonna be sitting in prison the rest of his stinking life. Soon's my shift ended, I took Myrna back to the hospital. Nothing had changed." Howie pushed himself off the sofa. "Will you talk to her?" he said. "I'm awful worried about her." He raised a palm, then made his way around the sofa and opened the door. His boots made a clacking noise in the hallway. In a moment he was back. "She says come on in."

Father John followed the Indian down the darkened hallway and into a small bedroom. Myrna was propped up on the bed, facing the opposite wall, her expression as rigid as the wood headboard she leaned against. She was dressed in blue jeans and a tee shirt, her face red and puffy, her black hair flung across the pillows around her. Clumps of tissues lay on the floor beside the bed. A faint light glowed in the closed curtains, giving the room the feel of twilight.

"I'm so sorry about Patsy," Father John said, perching on the chair that Howie had pushed behind him. "She's in God's hands, Myrna. Try to believe God is taking care of her."

"She's gonna die." Myrna turned her head toward him—a slow, robotic movement.

"Patsy's gonna live." Howie leaned over and ran his hand over his wife's forehead, as if she were a patient with a delusional fever. "That scum that got her on the stuff is dead. The other druggie killed him. They won't be hurting her again. She's gonna get on with her life."

The woman swallowed hard, then leaned into the pillows and went back to focusing on some point across the room. Another painting, Father John realized, another picture of the black stallion.

"Let's pray together," he said. "Our Father, Who art in heaven . . ." Howie's voice joined his own. Then, after a moment, the timid, frightened voice of Myrna.

Father John hurried through the front door of the administration building and nearly collided with Vicky on the concrete stoop. "Whoa!" he said. "I wasn't expecting you."

"It's a bad time. I'll call you later." She turned toward the steps. The sunlight glistened in the black hair brushing the shoulders of her blue blouse.

"Hold on," he said. Vicky never came to the mission unless something important had come up. "Is everything okay?"

Vicky turned back and locked eyes with him. "I wanted to thank you for advising Ernest Redbird to turn himself in. He surrendered to the police in Denver yesterday." She gave a little wave, letting her hand drift in the space between them. "Somebody's probably waiting for a priest."

"Howie Thunder," he said. "His daughter's taken a turn for the worse. I'm on my way to the hospital."

"Oh, my God. Poor Myrna and Howie. I'll ride along, if it's okay."

Of course it was okay, Father John thought, conscious of her presence next to him in the pickup. They'd worked together on a lot of cases, more than he wanted to think about. He hated the homicides, suicides, and arrests—the tragedies—they'd been involved in, yet he couldn't bring himself to regret the time they'd spent together.

"Ernest has been cleared of any connection to Montecon's death," she was saying. Father John glanced over. Vicky kept her eyes straight ahead, her profile backlit by the sunshine flaring in the passenger window. "He was at a party in Denver with his girlfriend until two in the morning the day of the murder. At least fifty people saw him. Nine o'clock in the morning, he showed up at a day-care center to drop off his girlfriend's little boy. There's no way he could have been on the reservation around six."

Father John glanced over at her again. "Six? The newspapers and radio said Montecon was killed in the middle of the night."

Vicky met his eyes for a brief moment. "That's what the FBI and the police thought at first, but the coroner determined that Montecon had only been dead about an hour before Howie got there. Ernest still faces charges for dealing drugs. He's being transported here from Denver."

"The coroner's certain about the time of death?" Father John gripped the steering wheel hard. Something about this latest piece of news made him uncomfortable.

"About six, the autopsy said. Even without a murder charge, everyone's clamoring for Ernest's head. I intend to ask for a change of venue. He doesn't stand a chance of a fair trial close to the rez. Too many families have been hurt by the meth that Montecon brought here. A local jury won't want to hear how Montecon forced Ernest to sell the drugs. How he was an addict, out of control, doing what he had to do to get his own drugs. He's sorry for what he did. He's cleaned up his life, John. I think he deserves a break." Father John turned right into the parking lot of Riverton Memorial Hospital, the time of Montecon's death still running through his mind. Before the autopsy report, everyone had believed Montecon had been killed in the middle of the night.

Everyone, he was thinking, with the exception of Howie Thunder. *Shot him in the head this morning*, Howie had said.

Death invaded the hospital corridor like an invisible gas. It fell over the sloping shoulders of the doctor in green scrubs coming through the metal swinging doors and two white-clad nurses hovering over papers inside a glass-enclosed cubicle. Vicky was aware of the synchronized rhythm of her footsteps with Father John's on the hard vinyl floor.

"The family's with her," the receptionist at the desk outside the intensive care unit had told them. "They're having a ceremony. You can go back." Father John stopped outside an opened door, and Vicky stepped past into the small room crowded with people—a blur of brown faces and black hair, blue denim shirts and blue jeans propped against the tan walls and perched on the windowsill. The odor of sage filled the air, pushing back the scent of death. She moved to the side to make room for Father John. Patsy Thunder lay on the narrow bed, face turned upward, eyes closed. The thin contours of her body rose against the white blanket pulled up to her shoulders. Myrna and Howie occupied two chairs at the side of the bed.

Will Standing Bear, one of the elders, stood at the foot. His gray hair was pulled back into a ponytail, his face skull-like beneath the wrinkled brown skin. Slowly he lifted a metal pan over the dead girl. A faint trail of smoke from the burning sage drifted around the edges of the pan. *"Hevedathuwin nenaidenu jethaujene,"* he prayed in Arapaho. *"Hethete hevedathuwin nehathe Ichjevaneatha haeain ichjeve."*

Vicky felt the words falling over her like a cool rain. She understood the meaning; she'd heard the prayer so often. *Your soul will live forever. Your soul goes to God to our home on high.*

When he'd finished the prayers, he lowered the pan and set a lid on top. The cuffs of his blue shirt stood out from the thin, knobby wrists. Someone pulled a chair around and he dropped down onto the seat, not taking his eyes from the dead girl. The room went quiet, except for the sounds of breathing. After several minutes, the elder stood up. Leaning over, he patted Myrna's shoulder, then Howie's. Then he nodded at Vicky and Father John as he made his way out into the corridor. The others started stirring about the room. One by one they leaned toward the couple and whispered condolences before following the elder through the door.

"She's with the ancestors now," Howie said, after they had all left. Myrna let out a little sob and curled toward the bed, dropping her head onto the edge.

"I'm so sorry," Vicky said, aware of Father John's words blending with her own.

Howie got to his feet and turned toward them. "She had hopes and dreams. She was gonna be a great artist, show her pictures in big museums. She was gonna get married and have lots of kids like she wanted. He stole all that from her. Stole all that." His voice trailed off. He stared past them, and in that moment Vicky saw something move behind the black eyes, almost like the shadow of the images that the man himself was watching.

She stepped back and leaned against the doorframe. The edge bit hard into her back. Let it not be true, she thought.

Howie continued talking, his words measured and deliberate, like a slow-motion rerun of the tape playing nonstop in his head. "Stole her life," he said.

The words filled the room like physical objects, as real as the chairs or the bed of the dead girl. "Stole her from us, stole everything. He deserved to die."

Father John placed a hand on the man's arm, and it was then that Vicky knew it was true. "God have mercy on you, Howie," he said.

"Bless our little girl, Father," Howie said, turning slowly toward the bed. "It's too late for me."

The Woman Who Climbed to the Sky

The Ninth Commandment:
Thou shalt not covet thy neighbor's wife.

Vicky Holden followed the gray-uniformed guard through the cell block of the Fremont County jail. The crash of a steel door behind her echoed off the cement-block walls and metal bars on either side of the corridor. The air was thick with odors of sweat and disinfectant. Someone was shouting above the jumble of radio and TV noise that pressed around her. Who was it—which client?—who said that the worst part about being in jail was the noise?

The guard stopped at a closed door on the right and leaned forward, peering for a moment through the small window. "Sure you wanna go in alone? He's one mad Indian."

Vicky swallowed back the impulse to admit the truth. She didn't especially like the idea of being alone in the consultation room with Phillip Blindy. The Arapaho had a reputation on the Wind River Reservation for being a hothead, somebody you walked across the road to avoid. Once, he took a wrench to a customer who didn't like the way Phillip had repaired his truck. Now he'd been indicted in the shooting death of James Moon.

Midmorning yesterday, the telephone had rung at her one-woman law office in Lander. "Vicky?" The federal magistrate's voice. "Indian named Phillip Blindy needs a defense. You're on the case, Counselor." She'd been half expecting the call. The only Arapaho lawyer in the area—why wouldn't the magistrate appoint her?

She'd spent the rest of the day and most of the night going over the charging documents and grand jury transcript, a knot of futility tightening inside her. There was a witness who'd seen the two men fighting outside Phillip's garage about an hour before Moon was shot on Cedar Butte Road. The murder weapon was found next to the body—a .22-caliber pistol registered to Phillip. He admitted he was involved with Moon's wife, Gloria, and, to make matters worse, he had no alibi.

Vicky said she'd be fine alone with Phillip.

The guard lifted a bushy eyebrow, regarded her for a moment with renewed interest, then jammed a key into the lock. "We got him handcuffed," he said, pushing the door open. "Press the button if you need me."

She stepped past the guard's protruding stomach and set her briefcase on the metal table in the center of a small room that smelled of oranges and baloney, as if somebody had eaten lunch there not long ago. A large red button projected from the wall on the side of the table where she sat down. The door clanged shut, sending a ripple of noise through the quiet.

Across the table, a muscular man about six feet tall stood with his back to her, forehead pressed against the square, mesh-covered window. His black hair was tied into a ponytail that bisected the back of his orange jail jumpsuit.

"About time you got here," he said, turning away from the view of the sheriff's cars lined up in a row in the parking lot. The dark eyes narrowed in accusation as he swayed forward, wrists cuffed in front, arms pulled into a V. "You know what it's like? Locked up in hell?"

"Sit down, Phillip." Vicky waited while the man kicked at the chair across from her until it was far enough out that he could slide onto the seat. The handcuffs clanked against the metal table.

"I'll need your story," she said, unzipping her briefcase. She withdrew a yellow legal pad and pen.

The Indian was quiet a moment—head tilted back, eyes fixed on the ceiling. The fluorescent light spilled over the wide brown face, the clenched jaw. "Moon got what was comin' to him," he said, lowering his gaze to her. "Somebody shot his sorry ass."

Vicky took a deep breath. "Whoever killed him used your pistol."

"It got stole out of the garage."

"Did you report it stolen?"

"How'd I know it was gone?" Phillip shifted forward, scraping the handcuffs over the table. "I kept it under the counter for emergencies, some warrior coming in and eyeing the cash register. Haven't been any emergencies lately."

"Who knew about the gun?"

He shrugged. "Everybody on the rez. What's the good of protection, nobody knows you got it?"

Vicky made a quick note: *pistol stolen from garage.* Then she said, "You were having an affair with Moon's wife, right?"

The man kept his gaze steady. "Wasn't no secret. She's a good woman, Gloria. Traditional, you know what I mean?"

Vicky nodded and he went on: "Been learning the stories from Regina Old Bear. Someday Gloria's gonna be a storyteller herself, so she can pass on the Arapaho Way to the younger generation." The brown, bulky arms slid forward on the handcuffs. He kept his eyes locked on hers. "All me and Gloria wants is a little happiness. She's been trying to get a divorce, but that bastard Moon was fighting her. Wouldn't let her go."

Vicky swallowed hard. There it was—the motive. She could hear the prosecutor's voice in her head: *The only way Phillip Blindy could have Gloria Moon was if James Moon was dead.*

"What about the afternoon of the murder?" Vicky said. "Martin Greasy saw . . ."

"Yeah, well, he don't know . . ."

"What, Phillip? What doesn't he know?" Vicky could hear the hope in her voice. Maybe the prosecution's key witness had missed something.

The Indian threw another glance at the ceiling. "He don't know how scared Gloria was when she come running into the garage. Said Moon was gonna kill her. Next thing I know, Moon's wheeling his truck in behind Gloria's Honda. He comes stomping inside, screaming like a wounded bull. 'Told you to stay away from this SOB.' He grabs Gloria, pulls her outside, and starts slapping her around."

"What did you do?" Vicky held her breath. It was like watching the first act of a play when you knew the final act was murder.

"What d'ya think?" The handcuffs pounded the table. Vicky could feel the vibration in her chest, like the aftermath of a drumbeat. "I run outside and pull him off her. The bastard turns on me and throws a sucker punch to the gut, and I go down on all fours."

"What about Gloria?"

"She's outta there. I seen the Honda driving off and Moon's truck peeling out after her. I seen Greasy's truck parked across the road. He's watching everything."

Vicky wrote: *Greasy saw Moon assault wife.* Then she said, "According to Greasy, Gloria and Moon drove off about ten minutes before three. You went back into the garage, then left a few minutes later. You know what that means, don't you? The prosecution will argue you went back to get your gun. Then you followed Moon, forced him onto Cedar Butte Road, and shot him." She watched the Indian's face for some sign that what she'd said was true—the tiniest nod, the faintest twitch. There was nothing.

She hurried on: "The prosecution will also say you intended to bury the body, so it would look like Moon disappeared. You started to dig a hole next to the road, but something happened. A car coming, maybe. So you drove off in a hurry . . ."

"Yeah, and I'm stupid enough to leave my gun there." Blindy let out a loud guffaw, an explosion of breath. "And I'm gonna hang around to bury that bastard? You look in my toolbox. You'll see my shovel's busted. What'd I use to dig a hole? A stick?"

He leaned back, the self-mockery in his expression edging toward despair. "Like I told the fed that come around asking questions, I went back inside to lock up. Then I drove straight over to Gloria's place. She never showed, so I went driving around the rez looking for her. After a while I went home, thinking maybe she went to my place." He shook his head. "Moon'd kill her for sure, he found her there. Pretty soon she calls, says she drove right to Regina Old Bear's. Should've figured she'd go there to get some comfort from the stories."

Vicky sat back, aware of the jail sounds coming from far away, the smell of perspiration, like fear, in the man across from her. She could imagine the prosecutor's summation—she could write it herself: *Blindy wants us to believe he spent an hour just driving around. No one saw him. No one talked to him until four o'clock when Gloria finally got ahold of him. Where was he, ladies and gentlemen of the jury? Out on Cedar Butte Road shooting James Moon.*

Vicky felt a sense of hopelessness pouring through her like a cold rain. She had nothing—Phillip's story; that was all. The prosecutor would demolish it in five minutes. And yet, and yet . . . the story rang true. Why would a killer leave the murder weapon at the scene, unless the killer wanted to frame Phillip Blindy?

She said, "I believe you, Phillip." God help us both, she was thinking as she stuffed the tablet and pen into her briefcase and started to her feet. The door opened behind her, and a wave of air—not fresh, just different— floated into the room.

"Father O'Malley waiting to see you, Blindy," the guard said.

The Indian jumped to his feet, as if a lifeline had been tossed out that he meant to grab. In his eyes, Vicky saw a surge of hope that matched her own. She and the pastor of St. Francis Mission had worked on many cases together. He was logical—relentlessly logical. If anyone could find the missing piece of logic in the evidence against Phillip Blindy, it would be John O'Malley.

"I'll be in touch," she told the Indian. She brushed past the guard and hurried down the corridor to the lobby.

"How's he doing?" Father John was just outside the double security doors—tall and redheaded, in the usual blue jeans and plaid shirt, slapping his tan cowboy hat against one leg. He looked out of breath, worried, as if he'd been called to the scene of an accident.

"He's scared," she said. She stopped herself from adding: *So am I.* "He wants to talk to you. I'll be waiting outside."

Thirty minutes later, Vicky spotted Father John coming out of the glass-fronted entrance. She got out of her Bronco, where she'd been going over the grand jury transcripts once again, and hurried across the parking lot. The hot asphalt grabbed at her heels; the sun burned through the back of her suit jacket. "What do you think?" she said when she reached him.

"He's innocent, Vicky."

"The evidence says otherwise." An engine turned over. A car backed out of a slot and drove past, emitting a blast of gray exhaust.

"Phillip's not the only one with a motive," Father John said after a moment. "Gloria Moon also had a motive . . ."

Vicky cut in: "She has an airtight alibi, John. Regina Old Bear says Gloria came to her house at three, ten minutes after she'd left the garage. Regina's spent her life memorizing the old stories and telling them exactly as they've always been told. She tells the truth. She wouldn't lie for anyone."

Father John glanced at some point across the parking lot. After a moment, he brought his eyes to hers. "Phillip's worried about Gloria. He says she's so upset, she's been staying with Regina since the murder. Why don't we drive over and have a talk with them?"

* * *

The house was painted pink, fading to gray. The woman in the doorway looked bent and ancient, wearing a blue dress that brushed the top of her white moccasins, clasping a red shawl about her shoulders. Her hair was almost white, pulled back from a narrow, creased face with wide-set black eyes and a thin slash of a mouth. Pinned in one side of her hair was a tiny black feather—her only jewelry.

"Well, Father John and Vicky, come in, come in." Regina Old Bear swung the door back and motioned them inside.

Vicky felt as if she'd stepped into the Old Time. The oblong living room resembled the interior of a tipi on the plains. Thick buffalo robes and Indian blankets were draped over the low couches that surrounded a faded Indian rug. On a small table near the door—a place of honor—was a buffalo skull, painted sky blue and decorated in red and yellow lines and circles, Arapaho symbols for life and the people. Everything in the room was old and worn. Nothing hinted of the present.

"We got company," Regina Old Bear called down a hallway on the other side of the table. Then she dropped onto a couch and waved them to another: "Make yourselves comfortable," she said.

Vicky sat down on a cushion covered with a scratchy wool blanket. Father John perched next to her. "How have you been, Grandmother," he said, using the term of respect for the old woman.

"Real worried about Gloria. She's been in a state." Regina Old Bear shook her head. "Terrible thing, James getting murdered. It's good Gloria's learning the stories. They're gonna make her strong. You know"—she nodded toward Vicky—"stories about the girl who became a bear, and the man who sharpened his foot, and the woman who climbed to the sky."

Vicky felt as if Regina Old Bear had hurled a stone and hit her in the chest. She gasped for breath. Out of the corner of her eye, she saw Father John shift forward, his posture suddenly rigid with understanding.

"And married Moon," she managed.

Somewhere in the house, a door slammed shut. There was the shush of footsteps coming down the hall, then Gloria standing in the doorway. Still in her twenties, Vicky guessed, a trim figure in tight blue jeans and a short, white tee shirt that exposed her navel. There was a mixture of hardness and vulnerability in the finely sculptured features, the black hair parted in the middle and draping over her shoulders, the narrow eyes as dark as river stones.

"What are you doing here?" she said.

"We want to talk to you about Phillip." Father John got to his feet. "He's charged with a murder he didn't commit."

"If that's what he told you, he's lying," Gloria said.

"Grandmother says you've been learning the stories," Vicky began, selecting the words. "She says you know 'The Woman Who Climbed to the Sky.'"

Did she imagine it? The almost imperceptible flinch in the young woman's cheeks?

"Gloria got that story down just right." Regina Old Bear rearranged herself on the couch, patting her blue dress over the bony knobs of her knees. "The woman was unhappy, married to Moon. She wanted to come back to her people on earth. But Moon said no. He said he'd kill her if she left."

"She left anyway." Vicky kept her eyes on Gloria. "The woman took a stick."

Vicky hesitated, Phillip's words burning in her mind: *What'd I use to dig a hole? A stick?* "She dug a hole in the sky. Then she looped a line over the stick, set the stick over the hole, and swung down to earth on the line. Remember the rest, Gloria?"

The young woman didn't say anything, and Vicky went on: "Moon killed her, just as he'd said. He threw a boulder down and crushed her."

Gloria jerked sideways, knocking against the edge of the table. The buffalo skull skidded over the top, and she grabbed at it and set it upright.

For a long moment, there were only the sounds of breathing—in and out—in the room. Finally Father John said, "You wanted to change the story, didn't you, Gloria?"

"I don't know what you're talking about." A note of hysteria worked into the woman's voice.

"You can't change the stories." Regina Old Bear set both hands on the edge of the couch and leaned forward. "Gloria's gotta pass 'em on truthfully, like she learned them."

Father John pushed on: "The story meant a lot to you, Gloria."

"It's your favorite," the old woman said. "You been telling me how you know the woman."

"Grandmother, don't . . ."

"You understand her, 'cause she's like you." Something new—a tightness—had come into the old woman's voice.

Gloria swung around and opened the door. "Why don't you get out, Vicky. You, too, Father. All you care about is Phillip. You don't know anything about me."

Vicky stood up. "If you hadn't taken a stick and dug the hole, Gloria, Phillip would have paid for a murder he didn't commit. But you wanted to leave a sign that the story could turn out differently. The woman didn't have to die. Moon died instead."

"You're crazy, both of you." Gloria was shouting now. "I tell you, Phillip killed my husband."

"That's what you'd hoped would happen," Vicky said. "Phillip has a quick temper, and he was in love with you. You arranged the meeting at the garage, knowing your husband would rush over and start a fight. You were counting on Phillip going for the gun and shooting him. But he didn't. Instead, they got into a fistfight outside."

Vicky stopped. It was clear now. She could almost see the story unfolding. "You had to change your plans. You ran back inside and got the gun while they were fighting. Then you drove to Cedar Butte Road, knowing James would be right behind you. When he got out of his truck, you shot him."

Gloria let out a scream of laughter. "You can't prove anything."

Father John said, "Not true, Gloria. How did James know when to come to the garage, unless you called him? There'll be a record of your call. And I suspect Martin Greasy, when he thinks about it, will remember that you ran back into the garage before you drove off."

"I got a witness," Gloria said, turning toward the old woman. "Grandmother knows I got here at three o'clock. Tell them, Grandmother."

"How can you know, Grandmother?" Vicky said. "I don't see any clocks here. You don't wear a watch."

"Of course there are clocks . . ." Gloria began.

"I don't need clocks." The old woman pushed herself off the couch and walked stiff-legged over to Gloria. "Sun comes up, I know the day's started. Sun's high in the sky, day's half over. Sun drops behind the mountains, I know night's coming on. That's all I need to know."

"Please, Grandmother . . ." Gloria swallowed back the rest of the plea.

"You come rushing in here, said your husband and Phillip got in a fight, said it was three o'clock. I believed you was telling a true story, but you changed the time, just like you wanted to change the story." The old woman drew herself upright in a rictus of rage. "You forgot the ending, Gloria. The woman gave birth to a son before she died. He grew up in her village. He was called *Hiiciiisisa*, Moon-child. He was brave and strong, like his mother. He lived a hundred years and taught the people good things—only good things."

Regina Old Bear grabbed Gloria by the shoulders and pulled her forward. She looked small in the old woman's grasp, limp as a rag doll. "The woman brought goodness to her people, you hear me, Gloria? Not murder."

Gloria slumped forward, hands clawing behind her at the table, the buffalo skull, and for a moment, Vicky thought she would crumble to the floor.

"He wouldn't let me go, Grandmother." She was sobbing, shoulders heaving inside the old woman's grasp. "He was just like Moon. He was gonna kill me. I had to change the story."

Regina Old Bear stared at her a long moment, then wrapped her arms around her and pulled her close. The sound of sobs, muffled and intermittent, drifted into the silence.

"She's going to need a good lawyer," Father John said.

Vicky felt the pressure of his hand on her shoulder.

She drew in a long breath. "As soon as I get Phillip's case dismissed," she said, "I'll be available."

Whirlwind Woman

The Tenth Commandment:
Thou shalt not covet thy neighbor's goods.

Hospitals. Nursing homes. Hospice centers. They had a sameness about them, Vicky thought. The same vinyl floors gleaming under fluorescent ceiling lights, mop marks visible in the wax; the same dust motes floating in columns of sunshine that shot into the middle of the seating areas; the same odors of disinfectant mingling with the smells of half-dead roses on a stand somewhere. She signed in on the register that the gray-haired woman in the dark blue business suit pushed across the counter toward her. Under Patient, she wrote, *Anna Running Fast*.

"Vicky Holden?" the woman said, her eyes on the register. "Are you family?"

"Granddaughter," Vicky said.

The woman looked up, skepticism pinging in her gaze. The name on the white plastic badge shimmering on her lapel was Alice Berkel. She said, "We didn't realize that Mrs. Running Fast had any granddaughters."

Vicky kept her own expression immobile, her gaze steady. She didn't say anything. There was no explaining to a white woman the complicated relationships of the Arapahos, relationships that had nothing to do with blood ties. Anna had been her grandmother's friend. She and her family had lived down the road from her grandparents' ranch. Another friend, Mamie Yellow Bird, had lived across the road. They'd gone back and forth, the three families, visiting and eating and looking after one another's kids and grandkids. She could still see herself, a small brown child, tugging on one of the women's skirts, staring up into warm brown eyes, saying, "Grandmother. Grandmother." She would keep tugging until either Anna or Mamie would scoop her up, prop her on one hip, and nuzzle her neck. "My, you are a persistent little girl," Anna would usually say.

And now Anna was dying. Another patient at Riverton Memorial moved to the hospice floor where only family members were allowed to visit.

Vicky knew the white woman was waiting for some explanation, some proof, perhaps—birth certificate, marriage license—that would give her the right to a final visit with Anna Running Fast. There was no proof, nothing but tradition and the way things were on the Wind River Reservation. She remained silent, knowing she could outwait the woman. Silence made white people nervous.

Finally, the woman shrugged. "Room three twenty-two. I must ask you not to stay too long. She has to save her strength."

Save her strength? Vicky was thinking, but she didn't say it. For dying? She turned toward the corridor.

"Her other granddaughter's with her now."

Vicky looked back.

"You know, Tammy," the woman said, as if to reassure herself that she hadn't allowed two non-family members into Anna Running Fast's room.

Vicky gave a little nod and started down the corridor, past the closed doors on either side that muffled the whispered voices and the labored breathing of the dying. She tried to place Tammy. Anna's only child, Justice, had been killed in an accident out in the oil fields twenty years ago, two months after the heart attack that had killed his father. She'd been left with only her grandson, Jackie, who, as far as Vicky knew, hadn't come around the reservation in years. Tammy could be another family friend close enough to call Anna Grandmother. Or maybe Jackie had gotten married. Odd, Anna hadn't said anything about Jackie getting married, even though she talked about him nonstop, hardly catching a breath, every time Vicky had visited her: Jackie was in Nashville trying to get into the music business; Jackie had gone to Arizona, a real good job on a ranch; Jackie had moved to Las Vegas to deal blackjack. Jackie was smart. He could do anything he set his mind to.

Vicky was about to knock on the door with the bronze numerals 322 canted slightly to one side. She stopped; her hand hung motionless in the air. The smell of disinfectant was pure and undiluted, emanating up from the floor and out from the walls. From the other side of the door came the sound of a woman's voice, high-pitched and quick, followed by notes of laughter that rang up the scale and dissolved into a sharp squealing noise.

Vicky rapped once, then opened the door and stepped into a room that would have been bare without the small chest under the window and the metal-rimmed hospital bed that jutted into the center. Leaning over the bed, smoothing the white blanket that covered the sticklike contours of Anna's body, was a woman who might have been in her thirties or forties; it was hard to tell. She was as slim as a boy, with narrow hips and stovepipe legs wrapped in tight blue jeans and the outline of breast buds beneath the front of a red tee shirt. She swiveled toward Vicky, her lips a red O of surprise in her powdery white face. She had dark eyes outlined in black, thin black eyebrows, and coal-black hair cut short with little black spikes that crawled down her forehead.

"You're Tammy?" Vicky said.

"Yeah, that's me." She went back to smoothing the blanket. "Been lookin' after my grandma today."

Vicky went to the other side of the bed. Anna appeared to be asleep, her face as quiet and peaceful as a mask of brown pottery. Yet there was the faintest twitch in her eyelids, as if she were making an effort to keep them closed. Her hair looked like thin strands of gray silk spread over the white pillow. "How is she today?"

"Oh, she's doin' great. I mean, as great as you can expect in the circumstances. Been sort of unconscious most the time, but I been talkin' to her, telling her jokes and stories about me and Jackie traveling around, all the places we seen and the things we done, you know, just in case she can hear. 'Cause you know what they say."

"What do they say?"

"How people in comas, they can still hear you. They know everything that's goin' on. It's just they can't talk. So how're you related?"

Vicky looked at the woman on the other side of the bed. "She's my grandmother."

The red lips formed another O; her forehead creased into a frown, the black eyebrows darting toward each other. "Jackie never said nothing about a sister or a cousin or whatever. He's alone, he told me, except for me and him. Only relation on the rez is Grandma Anna."

"Grandmother," Vicky said.

"Yeah, whatever." Tammy shrugged.

"You must be Jackie's wife."

"One and only. Tammy Running Fast." She flung her hand across the bed and flexed her fingers. They looked bony and raw, the nails bitten down over reddened knobs.

"Vicky Holden." She took hold of the outstretched hand for a moment; she could feel the quivering energy beneath the roughened palm. "Is Jackie here?"

"I been tellin' Grandma he's on the way. I think it makes her happy, Jackie being her only grandson and all. Stopped off in Rawlins to see a guy about some money he owes him. Frigging Internet, can't trust nobody. Jackie sold the guy a real nice harness and never got a check. He was gonna pay the creep a surprise visit, you know, collect what he's got coming. Told me to take the U-Haul—it's got all our stuff—and go on to Grandma's house, 'cause we're gonna be living here now. So I drove to the rez this morning, unloaded a couple boxes, then come to town to see how Grandma's doin'. Jackie'll be here any minute now."

She drew in her lips and took a breath as if she were sucking air through a straw. "How'd you say you and Jackie was related?"

Vicky laid her hand over Anna's. She had the sense that, somewhere deep inside, Anna was taking in everything. The old woman's fingers fluttered beneath her own. "I told you," Vicky said.

The door swung open and Alice Berkel stepped into the room. She held on to the edge of the door and closed it behind her, keeping her gaze on Tammy. "Mrs. Running Fast?" she said, her voice leaking sympathy. "Would you step outside a moment?"

Tammy crossed her arms and tilted her head back, as if she were weighing her options. "What's it about?"

"Father John O'Malley, the priest from St. Francis Mission, would like to speak with you. I've told him you're here."

"What's he want me for?"

"Please . . ." Alice Berkel nodded toward the bed. Keeping her voice low, she said, "He's waiting in my office." Then she opened the door. The silence of the corridor floated into the room.

Tammy let her arms fall to her sides. She moved slowly along the bed and walked past the woman, who stepped behind her and pulled the door shut.

A soft, raspy sound came from the bed.

"What is it, Grandmother?" Vicky leaned closer.

The old woman was struggling to lift her head; her eyes were wide-open, staring across the room. For a moment, her thin lips worked around soundless words, as if she were savoring the taste of them. "Jackie," she said. "Jackie. Jackie."

"His wife says he'll be here soon," Vicky said. She eased Grandmother Anna's head back into the pillow.

"*Neyo:xe't!*" What sounded like a guffaw bubbled up from the old woman's chest.

"Shhh," Vicky said, trying to pull the meaning of the word from her memory. Something to do with the wind, but it made no sense. There were so many stories that her own grandmother and Grandmother Anna and Grandmother Mamie used to tell in Arapaho when Vicky was a child. The ancient language had washed over her, caressing her, and somehow she'd understood the stories. They had always made sense.

She clasped Anna's hand and held it lightly in her own, half afraid that the birdlike bones might snap. "Don't upset yourself," she whispered.

A scream, like the high, shrill sound of an animal caught in the steel jaws of a trap, came from the direction of the lobby. Vicky felt Anna's hand stiffen inside her own. "I'll go see what's happened," she said, trying for a neutral tone that concealed her own misgivings. She let herself into the corridor, closed the door, and hurried toward the lobby.

The chair behind the counter was vacant, swung sideways as if Alice Berkel had gotten up in a hurry. The phone started to ring. Vicky half expected the woman to burst past the door behind the counter, but the door remained closed. The noise of the phone mingled with the muffled sound of sobbing.

Vicky stepped around the counter and rapped on the door. The sobbing stopped, and in its place came the measured rhythm of footsteps. Then the door opened, and standing in front of her was Father John, more than six feet tall with reddish hair and blue eyes and the look about him of sadness and compassion that she had often seen him wear.

"I'm afraid it's bad news," he said, nodding her into the office. Tammy was hunched forward in one of the side chairs in front of the desk, her dark head cradled in her hands. The white woman stood behind her, patting and caressing her shoulder with the confidence of someone accustomed to consoling the grieving.

"Jackie?" Vicky said.

"He was found dead this morning on the highway about twenty miles south of town," Father John said. "His truck ran off the road."

"I never should've let Jackie go see that guy alone." Tammy lifted her head and twisted around in the chair, looking from Father John to Vicky. Black mascara tears ran down her cheeks. "I should've gone with him. I wanted to go, but he was real worried about Grandma. Told me to go on and tell her how we was gonna be living here now and how we was gonna take real good care of her house. But I should've . . ."

"You mustn't blame yourself," Alice Berkel said, smoothing the red tee shirt over Tammy's shoulder.

"You don't understand." Tammy shrugged away from the woman's hand and locked eyes with Vicky. "That guy must've followed him," she said, a pleading tone now. "He run him off the road and killed him. I bet he made sure he got his money out of the truck before he took off."

"Jackie's truck was forced off the road?" Vicky dropped onto the chair next to Tammy.

It was Father John's voice behind her: "He was shot in the head."

"My God!" Vicky said. "Why would anyone do that?"

"I told you. That guy in Rawlins tried to rip us off." Tammy curled back over herself and dropped her face into her hands.

The room was quiet a moment. Then Father John said, "The sheriff will want to talk to you." He kept his voice low and steady.

"Me?" Tammy's head snapped back. She squared her shoulders. "What do I know? I told you, I should've been there, but I wasn't."

"He'll want to know about the man in Rawlins. Name. Address. Any other information you can give him."

Tammy squeezed her eyes shut and started sobbing again. Her thin chest rose and fell in spasms beneath the red tee shirt. It was a moment before she took the tissue that Alice Berkel held out to her and began swabbing at her cheeks. "It was Jackie's deal." She was staring straight ahead across the desk. "He was the one sold the harness. I didn't have no part of it."

"The sheriff will still need your statement," Vicky said. "It could help him find the man."

Tammy took a moment before she started nodding, the way she might have nodded at the inevitability of a thunderstorm moving in. "It's gonna kill Grandma," she said.

"We think it's best not to tell her." Alice Berkel glanced over Tammy's head at Vicky. "I've explained to Father John that Mrs. Running Fast is in and out of consciousness, and she's very weak. She's hoping to see her grandson again before she dies. I'm sure the family would agree that there isn't any reason to rob her of hope in the little time she has left."

Vicky nodded. She couldn't shake the feeling that, somehow, Grandmother Anna already knew.

The call came about eight o'clock that evening. Vicky had just finished some Chinese takeout at the kitchen counter in her apartment in Lander when the phone started ringing over the music of Clint Black on the CD player. She turned down the volume and lifted the receiver, some part of her knowing what she was about to hear. She could feel her stomach muscles clench, and for a moment, she thought she might be sick.

"Ms. Holden?" It was Alice Berkel's voice, as steady as a recording. "I'm so sorry to have to tell you that your grandmother passed away a few minutes ago." She paused. "Ms. Holden?" she said again when Vicky didn't say anything.

"Was anyone with her?" Vicky walked around the counter and sat down at the dining table. It was so sad to die alone. She should have stayed longer with Grandmother Anna, but she and Father John had been concerned about Tammy. They had walked her outside and offered to drive her to Grandmother's house. She'd insisted that she was fine. Down the elevator, through the lobby, and across the parking lot to the U-Haul truck, wiping at her tears the whole time. She needed some time; that was all. She wanted to be alone.

Vicky had gone back to Grandmother Anna's room, and Father John had come with her. But Grandmother Anna had seemed to be asleep.

She'd looked peaceful, and they hadn't wanted to disturb her. They'd shut the door quietly and left her alone.

"Mrs. Running Fast didn't die alone." The voice at the other end of the line cut into Vicky's thoughts. She felt the wave of relief rush over her like a warm gust of wind.

"Fortunately, her other granddaughter was with her."

"Tammy?"

"She returned shortly after you left. Said she wanted to stay with her grandmother. But when Mrs. Running Fast's heart gave out, well . . . it was more than the poor girl could take. She came running into the office crying. Collapsed in the chair. Naturally the nurses went immediately into Mrs. Running Fast's room. They confirmed that she was gone. Tammy was inconsolable. Such a shock, losing her husband and her grandmother in the same day!"

"Where is she now?"

"She ran out of here a little while ago. She really shouldn't be alone in the state she's in." A long sigh came down the line. "I can't imagine where she might have gone to."

"Don't worry. I'll find her," Vicky said. Then, before she hung up, she asked the woman to call the elder Will Standing Bear and Father John and ask them to bless Grandmother Anna's body. Five minutes later she was in her Jeep driving north to the reservation.

Plunkett Road ran straight ahead, disappearing into the darkness beyond the yellow sweep of headlights. The lights in Grandmother Anna's house glowed in the distance, like the beacon of a lighthouse rising over the dark sea of the plains. Vicky slowed as she neared the turnoff. Parked in the bare dirt yard was the U-Haul truck. Then she saw the faint light winking in the windows of the house across the road. She drove ahead a few yards, turned right, and bounced across the dirt to the little rectangular house with white siding and a wooden stoop with sloping steps at the front door.

It was several seconds before Grandmother Mamie cracked the door about an inch and peered out. "Vicky!" she said, hauling the door back into the shadows of the living room. Light flickered from a mute TV somewhere. "I was hoping you'd come."

Vicky stepped inside. She was surprised at the strength and determination in Grandmother Mamie's thin arms as they wrapped around her and drew her close, the way they had drawn her close when she was a child. She held on for a long time before she let her go. "Phone's been ringing for an hour," she said. Her voice was raspy, as if she'd been crying. "Everybody's talking about how Jackie got killed and how Anna's gone now."

"I'll miss her," Vicky said. The truth of it struck her like an unexpected blow. She would miss the past filled with people like her own grandparents and Grandmother Anna and Grandmother Mamie. It was as if part of her own life were slipping away. She blinked back the moisture thickening in her eyes.

"I saw her just yesterday," Grandmother Mamie said. She was as small and slight as ever, with the same silvery hair framing her narrow face, the same pinpricks of light in her brown eyes. "That white woman at the counter wanted to know if I was family," she went on. "Yeah, Anna and me are sisters, I told her. Only she was never gonna understand the Arapaho Way, so I didn't say anything else. She let me see her. It was the last time."

Mamie started to cry then, long, choking sobs that shook her narrow shoulders. Vicky put her arm around the old woman and led her past the TV to the sofa. She waited while Mamie pulled a tissue out of the pocket of her blouse and dabbed at her eyes. When she leaned back against the cushion, Vicky asked whether Anna had ever mentioned Jackie's wife.

For a long moment, Mamie stared at the two vacant chairs across the room. Finally she said, "We had a real good visit before she had to go into the hospital. Spent all afternoon sitting here talking. She told me Jackie got mixed up with some white woman named Tammy. Kept following her around the country. They were always on the move, that woman and Jackie after her. Gonna hit it big here, there, and everywhere.

Never lightin' anywhere, just running, running to the next big deal. Suited Jackie just fine, 'cause he never liked staying in one place anyway. But Tammy was worse than him. He couldn't keep up with her, Anna said. Like trying to keep up with a whirlwind."

"*Neyo:xe't*," Vicky said, remembering now. "It means whirlwind."

"You remember the story?" Grandmother Mamie turned toward Vicky. Her dark eyes danced with surprise and even a hint of joy. "Whirlwind was always running, running, and the man that loved her went running after her. Until . . ." Her features became rigid. She raised her hand and covered her mouth, as if she wanted to stop the rest of it.

"She killed him," Vicky said. And Grandmother Anna had sensed the truth of it, she was thinking.

"It's only a story," Mamie said. She was waving her hand, pushing the story away. "One of the old stories."

Vicky took a moment before she said, "Did Anna mention why Jackie and Tammy decided to come back to the rez to live?"

"Where'd you get that idea?"

"Tammy told me they planned to live in Anna's house. She's there now. The U-Haul is parked in the yard."

The old woman looked back at the chairs across the room. "Anna told me she wrote Jackie a long letter." She was speaking slowly, as if she were listening in on the conversation from an afternoon two weeks ago and repeating it word for word. "Told him that after she was gone, the house was gonna be his. She was hoping he might be ready to come home and settle down, give up all that runnin' around. She told him her time was getting close. Three days later, they put her in the hospital. Next thing I heard, they moved her to the hospice floor so she could die."

Mamie closed her eyes and sank back against the sofa. "Jackie called her up in the hospital," she said. "Told her he didn't want the house. Couldn't see him and Tammy settling down in one place. Just about broke Anna's heart, the idea of him never coming back to the rez. Surprised me when I heard him and that woman had decided to come visit. Too bad Jackie never got there. She would've died happy." She started crying again, a soft gur-gling noise that ran through the gnarled fingers pressed to her mouth.

Vicky put her arm around Mamie's shoulders. She could feel the fragile bones pressing through the thin fabric of her dress, and something else: the almost physical sense of grief. She'd sensed it in Anna that afternoon, she realized. In the frail, knobby hand had been the fluttering of grief for her grandson.

And now . . . With Jackie dead, Grandmother Anna's house and all the contents would go to his wife. It wasn't much—a small house with a leaking roof and a cracked stoop; an old sofa and chairs with springs pushing through the fabric; two or three small tables and the kitchen table where Anna had rolled flour into fry bread; a couple of sagging beds. But it was something.

Vicky waited until Mamie seemed calmer, as if she were beginning to settle into a kind of acceptance. She'd lifted the old woman's feet onto an ottoman, refilled the glass of water on the table next to the sofa, and told her to try to rest. She should call her if she needed anything. Yes, yes, Granddaughter. Mamie had smiled up at her, already half-asleep.

A white ball of light shone in the darkness ahead and gradually dissolved into two headlights riding high—the headlights of a pickup. Vicky slowed down and turned into the yard in front of Grandmother Anna's house, the headlights flickering in the rearview mirror. She parked next to the U-Haul truck, and the pickup pulled in alongside her.

Father John was coming around the hood by the time she'd gathered her bag from the passenger seat and gotten out. She slammed the door shut. The air was warm and clear, the stars bright overhead. It didn't sur-prise her that he was here. He would want to make sure that Tammy was all right.

"I think Tammy shot her husband and pushed his car off the road," Vicky said.

"What?" Father John moved closer and leaned toward her. "What makes you think that?" he said, but in the way that he said it, she sensed that he'd been wondering whether it might be true.

"Grandmother Anna tried to tell me." Vicky took a gulp of air to stop the sob forming in her throat. "She whispered whirlwind to me in Arapaho. *Neyo:xe't.* It refers to one of the old stories where a man follows a whirlwind woman everywhere, until she finally kills him."

Father John turned toward the little house set back in the shadows. Light shone in the two front windows and leaked around the edges of the door. "The house would have been Jackie's," he said, and she could see that he was starting to put everything together.

"Jackie didn't want it. He had no intention of moving back to the reservation."

The door juddered open; Tammy peered around the edge, her thin figure backlit by the light inside. "Who's out there?" she called.

"Father John and Vicky," Father John said. They walked over to the stoop and started up the steps. "Are you all right?"

"Yeah, I'm okay." She flung the door back. "Guess you can come in."

"You've had a hard day," Vicky said as they stepped inside. There was a pile of cardboard boxes in the center of the room. The top box was open; the sleeves of what looked like a man's plaid shirt hung over the flaps. "What are your plans now?"

"Plans?" This seemed to take her by surprise. She stepped backward around the pile of boxes and sat down in the middle of the sofa. "Guess I'll be taking off," she said, "soon's I get my money outta the house."

"What about the funerals?" Father John said.

"Oh, yeah. After Jackie and Grandma get buried and everything's settled."

Vicky took the worn upholstered chair next to the sofa, and Father John pulled over a wood chair and sat down. "What makes you think the house is yours?" Vicky said.

"Oh, I get it." Tammy crossed one jeans-wrapped leg over the other and squeezed her hands together on top of her thigh. "You're looking to get a piece of it, but I'm on to you. I asked Grandma if you was a blood relative, and she shook her head. I seen her shaking her head. That's how I know her only blood relative was Jackie, and now that he's dead, it's just me, Jackie's wife."

"You'll have to prove that," Vicky said.

"What're you talking about?"

"Do you have a marriage certificate?" Father John said.

She smiled at this, as if she'd anticipated the strongest argument. "We didn't need no certificate to prove we was married. We was man and wife in the Arapaho Way—that's what Jackie said. And the Arapaho Way is what counts on the rez."

"But not in court," Vicky said.

"What're you talkin' about?"

"All your actions were for nothing," Vicky said. "You murdered Jackie for nothing."

"You don't have no proof," Tammy said, and Vicky marveled at the calmness in her voice, like the calmness in the eye of a storm. "The guy in Rawlins . . ."

"The sheriff has already gotten a warrant to compare the dents and paint marks on Jackie's car with the U-Haul," Vicky said. She was guessing that was the case, probing for a way to break through the invisible shield the woman had pulled around her. "He'll find a perfect match, won't he?"

At this, Tammy jumped to her feet. She swiveled her head about, glancing between Vicky and Father John. "What do you know about it? Who the hell are you to judge me? I never had nothin'. I been lookin' all my life for what other people got. Some security, isn't that what rich folks call it? Security? So I don't have to dig in a Dumpster for enough scraps to keep alive. Sleep in an alley with the rats crawling over me. You know what that's like? I'm worn-out traveling around, looking for a score so me and Jackie'd both have some security. That fool, he got security dropped into his lap, and he says, 'No way am I gonna live on the rez. The tribe can take the stupid house!' That's what he was gonna do. Sign over the deed to this house and all the stuff." She swung her arms in a half circle, taking it all in. "All he had to do was sell it all. Sell it! Then we'd have our stake. We'd get some security, but he said no. He didn't want nothing to do with it. He didn't give me no choice."

"So you packed your things in a U-Haul and started for the reservation," Vicky said. "You knew he'd come after you. He always followed you. You were close to the rez by the time he caught up. Were you waiting for him at the side of the highway? As soon as he pulled up, you got in his car and shot him. Then you pushed the car down the embankment."

"Shut up!" Tammy was swinging her arms about again.

Father John stood up. "Take it easy," he said, but she was stomping around now, circling the pile of boxes, like an animal circling the blown-in debris in a cage.

She knocked the top box to the floor, stooped over, and pulled out a pistol. "I'm getting out of here," she said.

"Don't make things harder for yourself," Vicky said. "The court will appoint a lawyer who will get you the best deal possible."

"Give me your keys." She pointed the pistol at Father John. "Your keys!" she shouted.

Father John pulled a ring of keys out of his jeans pocket and tossed it across the boxes. She caught the keys in midair and turned to Vicky. "You're next," she said.

Vicky unzipped the outside pocket of her bag, extracted her key holder, and set it in the hand stretched toward her.

"I'm gonna have to shoot both of you." Tammy waved the gun back and forth. "Shoot you and be done with it. I'll be in Nebraska before anybody finds you."

"Then what will you do?" Father John said.

"Just keep going," she said, prowling past the boxes like a cat. She reached the door and yanked it open without taking her eyes from them. "Keep on runnin', like before. I can run forever." She gripped the gun in both hands and pointed it at Vicky's chest.

"Don't be a fool," Vicky said. She tried to keep her voice steady; she felt as if she were looking down an endless black pipe. "You could be lucky enough to get twenty years. If you kill us, you'll get the death penalty."

Tammy seemed to think about this for a moment. Then she walked back into the room, yanked the phone off a table, and pulled the cord from the wall. Vicky held her breath, waiting for her to demand her bag with the cell phone inside. But Tammy went back to the opened door. "You stay here for one hour. Hear me? One hour!" she said, backing out onto the stoop. "You leave sooner, and I swear, I'll come back and kill you." She reached inside and pulled the door shut. It was a moment before an engine rumbled into life followed by the sound of tires crunching the dirt, then the heavy noise of the U-Haul driving away.

Vicky felt herself starting to breathe again, but her legs had turned to liquid. She sank back into the chair and fumbled with her bag, aware of Father John's eyes on her. Finally she managed to pull out her cell phone. She pressed the keys for the Wind River police, gave the operator her name, and said that the woman who called herself Tammy Running Fast had just confessed to her and Father O'Malley that she had killed Jackie Running Fast. She was driving a U-Haul truck on Plunkett Road.

Vicky closed the phone lid and glanced up at Father John. "How long before the police stop a U-Haul on the reservation?" she said.

"Ten minutes," he said. "We'd better report what happened. Come on, I'll take you to the sheriff's office."

"Are you planning to walk me there?"

"I'm planning to hot-wire the pickup," he said.

Stories from Beyond

Yellow Roses

She had wondered how long it would be before someone came to tell her what to do. It had required two weeks. Two weeks to the day that the horse-drawn cart had carried the plank coffin down Larimer Street and out onto the gold and red hills that wrapped around the settlement. The men had dug a hole in the hard earth, lowered the coffin inside, and shoveled the sandy dirt on top. She had grasped Little Mary's hand and followed the small crowd of mourners to the cabin on Larimer Street that she and Jed had moved into only a month before.

Now Tom Holt sat on the other side of the plank table that Jed had nailed and glued together a week or so before he had died. The coughing had been so bad he'd had to stop and catch his breath every few minutes. When she'd washed their clothes in the tub outside, she had found blood on the rag he used to cover his mouth.

"Have you thought on what you will do, Mrs. Salton?" Tom Holt looked uncomfortable. Forehead creased like an accordion, eyebrows drawn together in a bushy line. He had deep-set brown eyes that surveyed the chinked logs in the walls and the hard dirt floor.

"You may call me Mary Ann," she said, trying to put him at ease. She gathered Little Mary onto her lap. Fitting that Tom Holt was the one delegated, she thought. She had half expected old Mrs. Ericson with the stone-carved face and the gray hair tightened into a knot on top of her head. But it was Holt who had guided the wagon train safely across the plains into the gold region. Only two families in the train—the Ericsons and the Saltons, and all the rest single men bragging about how they were going to strike it rich, go back home, and live like kings. They had all pitched canvas tents in the tent city not far from Larimer Street, but that was only temporary. In a few days, most of the single men had started for the mountains, and Jed had gone out looking for a suitable cabin where they could pass the winter.

"Nothing else I've been thinking on," she said. The door stood open, allowing the early October warmth to flow inside. She was aware of the carts and wagons passing outside, the sound of metal wheels grinding into the dirt street and the footsteps pounding the wood sidewalk. "I'm afraid I don't have a plan."

"In that case, Mrs. Salton—Mary Ann—may I suggest . . ." Holt cleared his throat, making a loud, strangling noise.

Mary Ann felt her heart beating in her ears. Now Captain Holt would tell her what to do, just as Papa had always told her exactly what she should do.

"Next few days," Holt said, "I expect to organize the last train for the States before winter sets in. Number of men coming down from the mountains. Tired of standing in the creeks all day, freezing themselves, for a few nuggets and a lot of fool's gold. They're wanting to go back. It'll be best for you and the child to join the train."

"I see," Mary Ann said. They had passed the go-backs on the way out here—shoulders hunched in discouragement, mouths set in bitter lines, poorer than when they had started out. She and Jed had watched them pick up some of the leavings along the trail—heavy pieces of furniture that folks had pulled out of the wagons for fear the oxen would collapse before they got to the Denver settlement. Jed had set out her mother's mahogany desk and the organ he had loved to play. She wondered whether some of the go-backs had picked them up. She had never thought she would be one of the go-backs.

She brushed her lips against Little Mary's silky yellow hair. Such a docile child, holding on to a cloth doll. Not yet four years old, but listening to the man across from them with such calm acceptance that, it seemed, she grasped the way her future was now changed. How easily they would mold her at Madame Sylvestre's school in St. Louis into a proper young lady who spoke French and knew how to make lace. She would grow into a pinched and placid woman, like her grandmother, who took her pleasure every afternoon at the front window, watching the world pass by.

"This was our dream, Jed's and mine," Mary Ann said. They had wanted something different for their child. A new land with new ways. Even on the trail, the women had worked alongside the men. She had loved striding next to the wagon, the swinging movement of her legs and arms, the blue sky all around, and Little Mary running ahead.

"I'm sorry for your loss," Holt said. "But respectable women alone don't belong in a rough, uncivilized place like this. Indians everywhere. Never know when a fight with the Indians might break out."

He glanced about the cabin, and Mary Ann followed his gaze. More like a store than a home, she'd thought when Jed had let her through the front door. Dark log walls, pieces of chink falling onto the dirt floor. He'd given one of the go-backs eighty dollars for the cabin and its contents— an iron stove in the narrow room attached to the back and the iron safe that took up one corner of the front room. Too heavy to move out, the safe claimed its space, squat and ugly, an unwelcome guest. The only safe in the settlement, Jed had told her, as if that would make it more acceptable.

Next to the safe was the barrel packed with sacks of flour, sugar, salt and hardtack, winter clothing, quilts and good china, everything she'd brought across the plains to make their new home. There had been no time to unpack. Jed was already in the last sickness by the time they had moved in. They'd laid the feather mattress and blanket on the dirt floor, and she had set about nursing him as best she could.

"The Indians seem friendly enough," she said. She'd seen the Arapaho village at the confluence of Cherry Creek and the South Platte. She'd heard that the chief—Left Hand was his name—and some of his warriors had attended the play at the Apollo Theatre down the street. After the play, he'd jumped onto the stage and given a speech in English. Told the gold seekers to take their gold and go home. Once, when Jed had felt up to it, they had walked to a racetrack outside the settlement and watched the Arapahos and gold seekers race their ponies. The Arapahos had won. Every day on Larimer Street, Arapahos traded buffalo robes for tobacco, coffee, sugar, and whiskey that the gold seekers had brought.

"Friendly enough so far," Holt said. "But hostiles have attacked outlying ranches, killed innocent families. I hear Governor Evans is real worried that a full-scale war's gonna erupt. Like I say, this is no place for a lady and a little girl. Lots of desperate men on Larimer Street. Get drunk on Taos lightning and shoot up the place."

That was true, she thought. There was a night when gunshots had rattled the paper that passed for glass in the windows. Sick as he was, Jed had pulled her and Little Mary close, shielding them with his own body. But Jed was gone now.

She looked over at the two tiny yellow rosebushes, still in the porcelain cups, that she had set on top of the safe. She had brought three roses from St. Louis, sparing her own drinking water to keep them alive. One was planted on Jed's grave. She meant to plant the others in front of the cabin before she had to go back.

"Best be ready in the next few days," Holt said, getting to his feet. He worked the brim of his hat through his fingers. "I'm waiting for a family of go-backs with room in their wagon. Figure you'd be more comfortable with another woman around. Wouldn't surprise me none if the Ericson family decided to leave. Old man didn't have any luck in Gregory Gulch."

Little Mary scooted off her lap as Mary Ann started to get up. The stern image of Mrs. Ericson ordering her about on the crossing was almost more than she could bear. She could feel the freedom that she and Jed had hoped for slipping away. She would return to her parents' home a failure, just as Papa had predicted. *Craziest notion I ever heard, traipsing across the plains thinking you're gonna find gold,* he'd said when she had told him that she and Jed and Little Mary would be leaving Westport in the next wagon train. *Nothing but Indians, buffalo, and desperados out there. You belong here with your own kind of people.*

Mary Ann thanked Tom Holt for his trouble and showed him to the door. A warm breeze stirred up little clouds of dust along the street. The rolling hills in the distance had turned magenta in the afternoon sun. On the horizon, the mountain peaks, streaked with snow, floated into the blue sky. She could hear Jed's voice: *All that land and sky, Mary Ann. There's opportunity waiting for us like we never could've dreamed.*

She watched Tom Holt make his way down the sidewalk, the long, rangy figure dodging the groups of men milling about, until he stepped into the street and disappeared in the pile of wagons and carts. Then she put on her bonnet. She tied on Little Mary's bonnet.

"Where we goin', Mama?" The child was looking up at her, the pink face so trusting and sweet and hopeful. Oh, how Madame Sylvestre would change all that.

"Out for a good walk," Mary Ann said, taking the child's hand and leading her outside. Wagons clattered past, wheels kicking out sprays of dust. The air was thick with the smells of horse droppings. The sun burned through her gingham dress. They made their way through the groups of men standing about. Past two fine hotels, the Pacific House and the Broadwell House, past the drugstore and the news and periodical shop, past saloons and billiard halls and a barber shop. Some of the men tipped their slouch hats. The widow Salton.

Mary Ann tightened her hand around Little Mary's. What was there in such a place for a widow and her child? How could she earn their keep when all she knew was French and lace making? She might start a school, except there was only a handful of children in town and few families. She might take in laundry and sewing, she supposed, but most likely it would give them only a small pittance. This was a place of gold seekers. How could she traipse into the mountains and pan for gold like the men, with Little Mary to care for?

They turned into the confectionary shop. Mary Ann found two pennies in her skirt pocket, and Litle Mary selected a peppermint stick, which she sucked loudly as they continued down Larimer Street, weaving through the knots of men. Wagons clanked past, and sounds of laughter erupted from the saloon in Apollo Hall. Several men were lined up in front of the Eldorado eating house on the corner. Rough and uncivilized, Tom Holt had said, and yet Denver City seemed a place of energy and possibility. They would walk every day, she decided, until they had to leave. She would memorize every detail. She never wanted to forget.

They reached the dry bed of Cherry Creek and were about to start back when Mary Ann saw what looked like a crowd of prospectors bunched in front of the two-story plank building that stood in the middle of the creek bed. A sign that said Rocky Mountain News stretched across the top of the peaked roof. Wagons were rolling in, prospectors jumping out and joining the crowd. Each man gripped a drawstring canvas bag.

She walked the child a little way down E Street until she was close enough to make out the sign on the side of the building: Assay Office, Byers & Shermer. In an instant she understood why Jed had paid out so much of their funds for the cabin. Too ill by then to follow the creeks into the mountains panning for gold, he had searched for another way to earn their living. Then he'd met the go-back looking for somebody to take the cabin and its contents off his hands, and in the cabin was a safe.

She started back, pulling Little Mary along, something opening up inside her, like a rose turning to the sun. "We must hurry," she told the child. Little Mary started skipping, as if she felt it, too, a new possibility.

Inside the cabin, she dropped to her knees in front of the dull green safe. The door held fast. Somehow she would have to work out the combination. She leaned in close—she'd seen Papa do this at the safe in the back room of his store countless times. She turned the knob slowly, listening for the tiny clicking sound. Ah, there it was.

She kept turning the knob. Another sound, then another. Still the door didn't open. She sat back on her heels, stung by the sharp sense of defeat, and closed her eyes a moment. She could almost feel the bounce of the wagon and smell the perspiration pouring off the oxen. She looked around at Little Mary, dancing her doll across the tabletop.

She got to her feet and went over to the small chest of Jed's things that she kept next to the mattress. Inside was Jed's second best shirt, the one he wore every day. She had seen that he wore his best shirt for burial. She set the few items of clothing on top of the bed and lifted out a mahogany box. She opened the lid and stared at Jed's revolver, memories tumbling through her head. They had walked along the bed of Cherry Creek a half mile or so from town, she and Jed and Little Mary, and Jed coughing so bad. He had placed the revolver in her hand. "You must learn to shoot," he'd said. "Ladies here must know such things."

She set the mahogany box to one side and drew out the canvas-backed ledger book. The lined pages contained the accounts of their life together, recorded in Jed's precise handwriting. The pay he had earned in Papa's store, the costs of household items and food. The last entry was for September 16, 1860. $80. Cabin and contents.

Beneath the entry was a series of numbers separated by dashes. She went back to the safe and turned the knob according to the numbers. The door sprang open. She clasped the ledger book to her chest, conscious of the salty tears stinging her eyes. "Thank you, Jed," she whispered.

It didn't take long—not more than twenty minutes, she reckoned—to tear four empty pages from the back of the ledger book, then tear them again into narrow strips, the size of a calling card back in St. Louis. She copied down the same words on each strip:

KEEP YOUR GOLD SAFE!
THE ONLY SAFE IN DENVER CITY
LARIMER STREET
PROPRIETOR: MARY ANN SALTON

She put the strips of paper in her pocket and tied Little Mary's bonnet under her chin. "We're going for another walk," she said, guiding the child into the street. Little Mary skipped ahead, trailing her doll along the sidewalk, giggling in the afternoon sun.

Mary Ann recognized Captain Holt's footsteps on the sidewalk before she opened the door. Outside, the yellow rosebushes were beginning to stand tall. The captain studied them a moment before he removed his hat and stepped inside.

"What's all this?" he said, looking about the cabin. She had hammered pegs into the log walls and hung the clothing that had been in the bottom of the barrel. A good linen cloth covered the table, and another linen cloth was draped over the top of the barrel. The wood carton that she'd found on the street made a satisfactory cabinet for the good china. She had made another doll from scraps of fabric in the barrel, but Little Mary seemed happier running and playing on the sidewalk. The child had insisted upon helping her plant the roses.

"We've been settling in, Captain," she said.

"Settling in? The wagon train leaves day after tomorrow. I must warn you, there's snow already in the mountains. Winter is coming soon. Won't be any other trains going back. Mrs. Ericson has been kind enough to make room for you and the child in their wagon. She says to tell you, however, that you must leave behind your personal possessions."

"I thank you for your trouble, and please thank Mrs. Ericson for her kind offer," Mary Ann said. She felt the tip of her tongue scraping the back of her teeth. "We won't be going back. This is our home now."

"Heard about your scheme, renting space in that safe of yours." Holt nodded toward the corner of the room occupied by the iron safe. The bushy eyebrows pulled together. "Don't see how that's gonna bring in enough to keep you alive."

"I'll be using some of my earnings to grubstake my most reputable clients," she said. "Just as I am sure my husband had planned to do.

Little Mary and I will have a share in whatever gold my clients find. Other clients are wanting to join me in the investments. I'll take an even larger share for putting the ventures together. There are great possibilities here, Captain. Little Mary and I would be sorry to leave them behind."

Holt let out a loud guffaw. "At the mercy of the flotsam and jetsam out there?" He stepped sideways and waved through the opened door at the wagons passing, the groups of men sauntering along the wooden sidewalk. "They could burst in here and rob you blind."

Mary Ann moved toward the barrel, lifted the linen cloth, and brought out Jed's revolver. "I hardly think that will be a matter of concern," she said.

St. Elmo in Winter

"St. Elmo oughta be up ahead somewhere," Liam shouted over one shoulder. His voice was muffled in the canyon, almost lost in the wind whispering in the pine trees and the swoosh of snow falling from the branches. He hunched forward over his cross-country skis, knees slightly bent, and stared at the GPS cushioned in the palms of his black ski mitts. He'd planted his skis across the trail. "Another half mile," he said. Then he looked back. "Think you can make it?"

Charlie dug both ski poles into the snow and pushed another few feet up the steep incline. Half a mile? They might as well be going to the moon. She flashed Liam the most reassuring smile she could muster. The temperature must have dropped fifteen degrees in the last ten minutes. Her fingers felt like icicles inside her gloves. The cold was seeping past her scarf and crawling around inside her jacket. It was starting to snow. They hadn't seen any other skiers on the trail in more than an hour. Probably the other skiers had already turned back. But she and Liam had set out this morning for the old ghost town of St. Elmo, and she didn't want to admit that the steep trail, the falling temperatures, and a little snow were more than she could handle.

"You have to see St. Elmo in winter," Liam had told her—what, a thousand times? "It's just like it was in the 1880s. All the shops and houses up and down Main Street are the same. The wooden sidewalks are still there, and the log railings where they used to hitch the horses."

"And how would you know St. Elmo looks the same?" She could never resist teasing Liam about his ongoing love affair with Colorado history. It rivaled his affair with her, she sometimes thought, and she wondered which he would choose, if he had to choose between them. A graduate student in physics, in love with history! "You're in the wrong field," she'd told him, but had he taken up history, she never would have met him. He'd been her instructor in physics lab class. She guessed she probably wasn't the first student who had fallen in love with Liam Hollings, with his black curly hair and green eyes, and when he wore his cowboy hat and boots, he looked as if he'd stepped out of the Old West. There were times—when he was lost in a novel about the Old West or one of those grainy cowboy and Indian films—that, she thought, he wished he had lived back then.

"We could drive to St. Elmo next summer," she'd suggested. But Liam had gone on about how St. Elmo in the summer just wasn't the same. It was perfect in the winter, so isolated and still in the snow, like one of those miniature towns in a snow globe or a little town under a Christmas tree. He'd gone to St. Elmo many times, summer and winter. Winter was best.

Liam smiled at her now as Charlie dug her poles in hard and pulled alongside him. There was a light dusting of snow across his backpack and shoulders, and snowflakes were popping out like ice crystals on the sleeves of her own jacket. She edged her skis to keep from slipping backward and tried to catch her breath. She could hear her heart pounding. The freezing air stung her lungs. The world had been blue and white and golden when they'd started out, the sun blazing in a clear blue sky, the snow on the ground glistening so white it had stung her eyes. The sun had disappeared some time ago, and now the sky looked like a sheet of lead pressing down. The snow on the trail had turned gray.

"Looks like a few flurries; that's all." Liam shrugged the snow off his shoulders. "The storm isn't forecast until tonight." He threw a glance up the trail. "See the fork ahead?" he said, but even as he spoke, the gray sky seemed to drop down and envelop the fork. "St. Elmo's just a short distance on the right. We have plenty of time to see the place before we have to ski back down."

They were staying at a cabin at Mount Princeton at the foot of Chalk Creek Canyon, and the thought of the fireplace and the way the warmth of the fire last night had spread into the small living room and the red firelight had licked at the log walls sent a shiver down Charlie's spine. Even if they were to start back now, it would take the rest of the afternoon to reach the cabin. Her legs and arms felt numb with the cold.

"Ready?" Liam said, but he was already skiing up the trail, poles pounding the snow.

Charlie started after him. It felt better to move, loosen her muscles, get the blood flowing. She could see her breath floating ahead in gray puffs. Liam was right, she told herself. He was always right. He knew Chalk Creek Canyon, all the old gold mines and mining camps, all the ghost towns. He'd hiked and skied the trails with his grandfather when he was a kid, filling up on stories that his grandfather told about the way things used to be. And Liam had been hiking and skiing to ghost towns ever since.

"We'll follow the old railroad bed up the canyon," he'd told her this morning, a map of the area spread on the table in front of them, their coffee mugs holding down two corners. "The Denver South Park and Pacific ran up Chalk Creek Canyon to the gold mines. Four or five trains a day, imagine, and every one of them stopped at St. Elmo. Passengers coming and going, all kinds of freight being loaded and unloaded. The depot was like Grand Central Station. St. Elmo was the biggest town in the area in the boom days of the 1880s and 1890s. Miners and railroaders lived there. Ranchers came into town on the weekends. There were boardinghouses, all kinds of stores—merchandise and hardware—a livery and fire station, the town hall where dances were held every Saturday night. Saloons and gambling parlors and whorehouses. Then the mines played out. The trains kept running for a while, but pretty soon there wasn't much reason to go up Chalk Creek Canyon. The tracks were finally pulled up in 1926. The few folks still living in St. Elmo just walked out the front doors and left everything the way it was."

"I get the picture," she'd told him, and she'd even admitted that St. Elmo would be something to see, a town that had stayed on in the canyon when everything else had left. Mines shut down, tracks pulled up, people gone away.

"We'll have to watch ourselves on the trail," Liam had said. "It's not very wide. The old narrow-gauge trains didn't need much room."

Now Charlie planted her poles as hard as she could and tried to ski faster. Still Liam seemed farther and farther ahead, a gray splotch moving up the trail carved into the mountainside. The dark shadows of pine trees, boulders, and gray snow covered the slope that loomed over the south side of the narrow railroad bed. On the north side was the sheer drop-off into the canyon several hundred feet below. Charlie tried to stay close to the left, but the snow was getting heavier, blowing across the trail and stinging her face. She had to keep her head down, her chin tucked inside the folds of her scarf. Her face felt like ice. Her goggles were fogging. It was hard to make out where she was on the trail. She concentrated on staying close to the line of trees. If she swerved too far to the right, tipped her skis over the edge, she could tumble into the canyon before she knew what had happened. No one would ever find her. She could taste the panic beginning to rise inside her, like the burning aftermath of a spicy dinner.

She couldn't see Liam! The realization took her breath away. "Liam!" she shouted, but it was only the sound of her own voice that echoed in the silence of the falling snow. She made herself ski faster, digging the poles in hard to pull herself along. The snow cracked like ice beneath her skis, and the driving snow crusted on the front of her jacket and ski pants. She shouted again: "Liam, wait up!"

She'd reached the fork in the trail, she realized. It had to be the fork because directly ahead were the dark shapes of trees looming out of the snow. She was in a whiteout, nearly blinded by the whiteness everywhere: air, sky, ground. She felt disoriented, slightly dizzy, and she had to lean forward on her poles a moment to regain her equilibrium. The storm predicted for tonight, when she and Liam had planned to be back at the cabin cooking steaks on the little grill in the kitchen and roasting potatoes in the fireplace and sipping hot wine—that storm was here now. Weather forecasts seldom got it right about the mountains: sunny and beautiful one moment, a blizzard the next. She could barely make out the branches of the fork. St. Elmo on the right, Liam had said.

She headed to the right, still trying to stay with the line of trees, using their dark shadows as a guide. St. Elmo had to be close by. Houses and other buildings were still there, Liam had said. He was probably already in town looking for someplace where they could get in out of the storm. He'd come back for her. He wouldn't leave her alone out here. "Liam!" she shouted again, hearing the panic rippling through the echo that came back to her.

The trail was getting steeper, and that was almost funny, because she couldn't see that she was climbing higher. But she felt the tightness in her chest, the strain in her calf muscles. Only the grooves in the base of her skis kept her from slipping backward. Exhaustion pulled at her, as if iron weights had attached themselves to her legs and arms. Her backpack felt like a hundred pounds. The cold had worked its way into her bones. She tried to flex her fingers, but they were numb. You could die in a storm like this—that was a fact—just lie down in the snow and go to sleep. She had to keep moving. Every few minutes, she heard someone shouting for Liam, and she realized that she was shouting and that she had settled into a weird rhythm: Ski, ski, shout. Ski, ski, shout.

And then she was skiing downhill. She started telemarking to slow herself. Gradually the dark shadows of the trees gave way to another shadow coming toward her. She blinked hard to bring the shadow into focus: a rectangular building of some kind, snow clinging to the sloped roof and bunching beneath the windows. A cabin! She'd skied down into St. Elmo, but where were the other cabins and houses? The main street with vacant shops? The town hall and the saloons? She called out again. "Liam, Liam! Where are you?"

Nothing but the hush of the falling snow and the shush of her skis as she turned left off the trail and headed for the shadow. A log cabin, she could see now, slanted to one side, as if it had followed the slope of the mountain, with a little porch at the front almost buried in the snow. She got to the porch before she stepped out of her skis. Then she picked them up so they wouldn't get lost in the snow and, struggling with the skis and poles, stomped across the porch. Her boots made a soft, thudding noise in the snow. She tried the doorknob, but when it didn't turn, she threw herself against the door. It creaked open, and she stumbled into the darkness inside, dragging the skis and poles with her, knocking her backpack against the frame.

The cabin was as cold as the outdoors, but it was a different kind of cold, like the cold in a freezer, compacted and still. She was shaking with the cold. She managed to swing her backpack off her shoulders; then she removed her gloves and began rummaging in the backpack for the emergency kit that she always carried on a cross-country ski outing. Her fingers were frozen claws, her hands refusing to work. Finally she managed to drag out the kit. She let the backpack drop to the floor and concentrated all of her energies on the kit. It was a moment before she found the flashlight. Still shaking, she shone the dim light around the little room. The light beam flitted over the plank floor, jumped across the clumps of paper wallboard peeling off the log walls.

This was it, then, a one-room cabin, and yet, what more did miners need? They had never planned to stay in the West, Liam had said. A place where they could eat and sleep and stay warm in the storm was all they needed until they hit the big lode of gold. Then they planned to go back East and live like kings.

But here was something: a fireplace built out of stone, no wider than
a column set into the far corner. And she could see she wasn't the first to
seek shelter in the one-room cabin. Someone had been here in the last
few days, judging by the trace of ashes in the fireplace and the two small
logs stacked next to the hearth.

She set the flashlight on the floor and started digging in the kit for
matches. She always carried matches; where were the matches? The beam
from the flashlight made a starry pattern of light on the plank floor. Then
her fingers closed on the narrow matchbook. Five matches inside, but
that would be enough, if she were careful. She realized that the possibility of getting warm—the fireplace and logs and now the matches—had
rolled over her, obliterated every other thought, even that of Liam. But
if she could get warm, she told herself—if she could just not be so cold—
she would go back onto the trail and look for him.

She began ripping off pieces of the paper wallboard, tearing at it with
raw, frozen hands. The wallboard came off in chunks, brittle and hard.
She built a pile in the fireplace and went back for more, moving through
the dim beam of light patterning the floor, trying to ignore the tired-
ness that dragged at her. Then she laid the logs on top of the wallboard,
just the way Liam had stacked logs on top of crumpled newspaper to build
the fire at the cabin last night. She crouched next to the fireplace and
struck a match. It flickered a second, but before she could get it to the
wallboard, it went out. She leaned in closer and held the matchbook next
to the wallboard. Her hands were still shaking. She tried to steady them
before she lit the second match. This time the wallboard caught on fire.
Another moment and the logs started burning.

Charlie crawled over to the flashlight and turned it off. The little cabin
shimmered in the firelight, and the air was filled with the crackling sound
of fire. Inside her backpack, she found the folded plastic cloth that she
and Liam had spread in the snow about halfway to St. Elmo, when the
sun was still shining. They'd sat on the cloth and eaten nuts and dried
fruit and shared a bottle of water and turned their faces to the sun. She
crawled back to the fireplace, smoothed the cloth on the floor in front of

the hearth, and lay down, hugging herself. The warmth leapt out and caressed her tingling face and hands. A few minutes was all she needed. Then she would find Liam and bring him to the cabin. Liam would know how to get more logs, and they could wait out the storm and stay warm.

Liam, Liam, where are you?

Charlie awoke in the freezing cold. Coming through the darkness was the faint sound of laughter and music. It took a moment to get her bearings. At first she thought she was in the cabin at Mount Princeton, but why was it so cold? Liam must have let the fire die down. Then it came to her, like an arctic blast of wind, that she was in an abandoned log cabin in a ghost town, and the fire had burned out, and she was alone. Except that she wasn't alone. Outside somewhere, somebody was having a party!

She managed to get to her feet, her legs and arms as numb and heavy as logs. She struggled into her backpack and gathered up the skis and poles. She hadn't meant to fall asleep. Liam was out there somewhere looking for her, but now there were other people around. Someone could have seen him. She could get other skiers to help her find him.

Charlie stepped out onto the porch and stopped. It was night, and the sky was light and clear. The blizzard had worn itself out, leaving little flurries of snow swirling in the air. Main Street in St. Elmo stretched ahead in the moonlight that flooded the snowy ground. Wooden sidewalks ran up and down the street in front of the buildings—houses and stores shouldering one another, painted blue, red, and yellow. She could see the black lettering painted on the front windows. There were boot tracks in the snow on the sidewalks. Snow drifted over the roofs and piled behind the second-story false fronts.

Amber lights glowed in the windows, and in a nearby house, she could see a woman seated at a dressing table brushing her hair. Outside, a horse was hitched to a small sleigh. The music and laughter were coming from the building about halfway down the street, lights shining in the front window. The saloon, Charlie thought. Everything was just as Liam had described it, a little town in a snow globe, a little town beneath a Christmas tree.

Two men came out of a shop and hurried along the sidewalk. One of them called out to someone on the other side of the street. Charlie hadn't noticed anyone else, but now she saw there were a lot of people walking along the sidewalks. Most were men, but there were a few women, and the women wore long dresses that swept over the snow.

Charlie swallowed hard. Her mouth had gone dry, and she could feel the cold working its way back inside her. There was a party going on, all right, a party that she and Liam had known nothing about when they had set off for St. Elmo. Some historical society must have scheduled a get-together in the old ghost town and people had brought clothes from the 1880s. Somebody had even driven a horse and sleigh up the trail. There were societies like that, Liam had said, people who dressed up like mountain men and went to rendezvous, just like the mountain men in the 1800s, and people who dressed up like cavalry and Indians and staged mock battles on old battlegrounds. Liam would be furious, she thought, when he saw all the people here. He had wanted St. Elmo in winter just for the two of them.

Charlie stepped into her skis and started down Main Street. There were tracks everywhere made by hooves and wheels and sleigh runners. The gathering, whatever it was, had been going on for some time. She expected the tracks to be frozen, but the snow was soft, glinting like diamonds in the moonlight, and her skis glided through them. "Hello!" she called to several men wearing long black coats and brimmed hats. They stood in a little circle in front of a shop with a false front and black letters that spelled Tobacco painted on the window. "Can you help me?" But they ignored her and kept on talking, one of them puffing on a cigar, another throwing back his head and laughing into the night sky, as if no one saw her, as if she didn't exist.

"Hello! Hello there!" Charlie called out to a couple walking arm in arm along the sidewalk, but they kept walking. "Hello!" she called to two men heading into the shop with letters that spelled Hardware on the window. The door shut behind them, and she skied toward two other men farther down the street, standing on the sidewalk, heads dipped in conversation. Still no response, as if she weren't there. It was as if the people attending the gathering had decided to ignore anything—or anyone—from the present.

The music was louder. A tinny-sounding piano pounded out a ragtime piece that burst out of the saloon and floated down Main Street every time someone opened the door. Above the door, St. Elmo Saloon was painted in red letters across the false, second-story front. Charlie took a diagonal route across the street. She left her skis propped against the hitching log at the edge of the sidewalk. Farther up the street a black horse was tied to another log. She walked over to the front window of the saloon. It was crowded inside, women in brightly colored, shiny dresses that sloped off their shoulders, with ruffles at their ankles that showed off their high-heeled shoes; men in dark suits with white shirts and black string ties, some with cowboy hats pushed back on their heads.

Across the room, a line of men stood shoulder to shoulder in front of the bar, but Charlie watched the line break up and the men turn around as a tall woman in a blue dress, with blond hair stacked on top of her head, walked over. There were a half dozen round tables set about where men were laying down cards on the green baize tabletops. A shiny-dressed woman perched on the lap of one of the cardplayers.

It was then that she spotted Liam. The black-haired man with the mustache—he'd always wanted to grow a mustache—and the redheaded woman in a green dress leaning over his shoulder, brushing her face against his. Several cards lay facedown in front of him. Deftly he lifted the corner of one card, then tossed some gold coins toward the coins stacked in the middle of the table. The dealer dealt out a round of cards, and then it seemed to be over. Liam reached out both hands, circled the stacks of coins and pulled them toward him. He handed some coins to the woman. Grasping his chin with one hand, she turned his face toward her. She kissed him on the lips.

Charlie pressed her face against the freezing window and tried to blink back the tears that had made the saloon seem watery and unreal. At first the tears felt warm on her cheeks, but then they turned to ice. Still she couldn't take her eyes away from the black-haired man with the mustache, staring at the new round of cards that had been dealt, pushing a small stack of coins into the center of the table. It was Liam, and yet it was not Liam. The truth hit her like a sledgehammer: The Liam that she knew and loved was dead.

The saloon door opened and two men spilled outside and walked past. Charlie made herself move away from the window. She walked over to the edge of the sidewalk where the men stood looking up and down Main Street, as if they were expecting someone. She reached out and tried to take hold of one of the men's arms, but the sleeve of his jacket dissolved in her grasp. There was nothing but air. She could hear the rumble of a train, the shrill sound of the whistle, and the swooshing noise of steam coming closer. They had pulled up the tracks in 1926, Liam had said.

Later, Charlie barely remembered stepping into her skis and heading back down Main Street, past the lights in the windows and the people walking about. Barely remembered the freezing cold and the blizzard starting up again and the snow driving against her face as she skied up the incline past the little cabin and started downhill toward the fork in the trail. She remembered only skiing as fast as she could, the music and laughter receding into the night behind her and the words pounding in her head: *Get away from here. Get away from here.*

"Can you hear me?"

A man's voice cut through the blackness, and Charlie tried to fight her way upward into consciousness. She blinked into the bright spotlight shining somewhere above her. The face of a man with a knitted ski cap pulled low on his head was coming closer, and she struggled to bring him into focus. Snow was everywhere: snow on her jacket and gloves, snow piled over her legs. She was buried in snow. She tried to sit up, aware of the strength in the hands pressing on her shoulders.

"Better lie still until we make sure you don't have any broken bones," the man said. Then he shouted: "Over here! We found the woman off the trail."

Other men were stomping through the snow, and a woman, too, and then all of them were hovering over her, brushing the snow from her jacket and pants. She could barely feel the hands moving over her arms and legs. It was as if they were moving over stone.

"Can you tell us what happened?" The man's voice again. "Did you fall?"

"I don't know," she said. "It was snowing. I was so cold."

"Maybe she just lay down," the woman said.

"What about your friend, Liam Hollings?" The man's face came into focus now: a prominent nose and flushed cheeks. Light eyes peering at her from beneath the cliff of his forehead.

"Liam," Charlie said, feeling the softness of his name on her lips.

"Any idea where he might be? When did you last see him? Did he fall off the trail?"

Charlie closed her eyes. She and Liam were skiing up the trail together, the old railroad bed. *We'll have to watch ourselves. The old narrow-gauge trains didn't need much room.* She could feel the tears starting again as she looked at the man. "He got ahead of me. Somewhere around the fork. I couldn't see him."

"Trail gets real narrow in that area," the man said. "Not much room for mistakes." He dropped his head into the hush that moved over them. Charlie could hear the soft thud of snow falling off a branch and the quiet sound of her own weeping. Then the man said, "We're going to move you onto the snowmobile. An ambulance is waiting in Mount Princeton to take you to the hospital in Salida."

Already the strong hands were sliding her out of the snow.

"You're lucky you didn't get any farther off the trail." The woman's voice came from somewhere behind. "Another foot and you would have rolled into the canyon. We never would have found you."

The Salida Journal

The search for missing skier Liam Hollings has been called off after two weeks, according to a spokesman at the Chaffee County Sheriff's Department. Hollings, 29, and Charlie Lambert, 26, graduate students in physics at the University of Colorado, had set out the morning of January 6 on a cross-country skiing trip along the abandoned railroad bed in Chalk Creek Canyon. When they didn't return that evening to Mount Princeton, where they had rented a cabin, the manager notified the sheriff. The county search and rescue team located Lambert around 10 p.m. about a mile from the abandoned town of St. Elmo, but the team has been unable to find any sign of Hollings.

"The extreme winter weather, with deep snows and freezing temperatures, makes it highly unlikely that Hollings can be found alive," the spokesman said. "The skiers were on a very steep and narrow expert trail. The rescue team believes that Hollings became disoriented in a blizzard and may have skied off the trail into the canyon."

Lambert was evacuated to Salida Community Hospital where she was treated for hypothermia, frostbite, and exhaustion before being released last week. She could not be located for comment.

Otto's Sons

"Robert's come home." Otto Hunting Bear stood in the doorway, leaning on a knobby walking stick carved from a branch. He was bronze-skinned and whipcord thin, with buzz-top gray hair, and a worn, weathered look that made him seem older than his seventy years.

Father John got to his feet and motioned him into the office. "Nice to see you, Grandfather," he said, using the polite Arapaho term for addressing an older man. "I heard the good news," he said as Otto lowered himself into a side chair that Father John kept for visitors. Outside St. Francis Mission was quiet, except for the undertow of the wind and the small tapping of a cottonwood branch against the front window. Beyond the mission were the open, brown stretches of the Wind River Reservation. If he put his finger on a map, the reservation looked like a small rectangular block in the center of Wyoming, but that was only because Wyoming itself was so big. It took the best part of an hour to drive anywhere on the rez.

"You must be very happy," Father John said.

"Happy? Happy don't touch it." A smile creased the old man's face, light bouncing in his eyes. "Walked into the living room two weeks ago, like he'd been gone a couple hours. Just stood there, hands in his jeans pockets, that stupid smile he used to get on his face when he was little and got himself into trouble. That was Robert. He could pretty much smile his way out of anything with Mame. 'Hi, Dad,' he says. 'You're lookin' good,' like I wasn't busted up with two hips the doctor give me and a back that don't hold me straight. Wonder I didn't have a heart attack. I couldn't even speak. I got outta my chair, went over, and hugged him so hard, I like to squeezed the breath outta him. 'Take it easy, Dad,' he said, but I couldn't let go. All I could think was, My son was dead and now he's alive. He's come back."

"How's he doing?" Father John resumed his seat behind the desk.

"Okay, I guess." Otto gave a forced shrug and piled his hands on top of the walking stick. "Hard work fitting in again after all them years." He shook his head and stared into the middle of the office. "Twelve years, and not a word, no sign he was walking the earth. Nothing but the big, empty space he left behind the day he packed his bag and drove off. I'll never forget that old wreck of a pickup that he won off some guy in a poker game bumping across the yard and heading down the road, trailing black smoke. 'Gotta get off the rez,' he'd told me. 'Nothing for me here.' Mame and me didn't know where he went, what he was up to. After five, six years, we started thinking our boy was dead. Tried to convince ourselves there wasn't no reason to keep hoping, but it was tough. Wore her out, worrying about Robert and what become of him. She got thinner and thinner until she was nothing but a skeleton in a bag of skin before she died. Only thing that kept her hanging on long as she did was our other boy. Tom was still with us. He's a good boy."

Father John took a moment. He could sense the unspoken words hanging in the air like mist: the good son, the one who had stayed home, helped his father on the ranch, branded the cattle, loaded the trucks and drove to market, bred and cared for the horses, watched his mother die and looked after his father, witnessing his father's love poured out to his brother. He waited for the old man to go on, and when he didn't, Father John said, "Want to talk about it, Otto?"

"I was thinking we'd be a family again," Otto said, trying to staunch the cracking in his voice. Moisture pooled in his eyes, and he wiped it away with the pads of his fingers, surreptitiously, as if he were brushing away a mosquito. "Mame's gone, but ever since Robert got back, I been feeling like her spirit's with us, like she knows our boys are back on the ranch. Robert's real sorry for staying away. Spent time in prison in Colorado. Got mixed up with a bad sort and did time for breaking and entering, assault. That's why he never got in touch. He was too ashamed, and to tell the truth, if Mame had known, it would've killed her even sooner. But all that's past now. Robert got his life turned around. Even got himself a son down in Denver. Wants to bring him home soon's he can work it out with the boy's mother. Bring the boy home to the ranch." Otto waved one hand in a wide arc. "Things are like Mame and me always dreamed they'd be. Our boys running the ranch together. I turned the deed over to them last week, one of those quit claims that Rap lawyer helped me with. Equal shares for each of 'em."

Father John set his elbows on the armrests and looked at the old man over the tipi he made with his fingers. Surely Vicky Holden would have suggested he might want to go slowly, give Tom time to adjust. Before his brother's return, Tom would have inherited the entire ranch. "How's Tom taking it?" he said.

"I thought he was gonna be real happy. Ranch is big enough for him and Robert. It's easier running a spread if you got somebody alongside you that loves it much as you do. Only Tom don't like it." Otto laid his head back, gulped in some air, and exhaled slowly, as if he were exhaling cigarette smoke. "He hates Robert," he said, and Father John could hear the pain in the old man's words. "Don't want him around. Yesterday I heard him tell Robert, 'Go on back to whatever hole you crawled out from. We got along fine without you. We don't need you.'" He ran his knuckles over his eyelids again and stared up at the ceiling a moment before he said, "Trouble is, I need both my boys."

"How about Robert? What did he say?"

"Nothing. Looked real sad. Glanced over and seen me in the hallway. Give me a little smile, like he wanted to encourage me and make me think Tom was gonna change his mind sooner or later."

"Maybe he will, Otto."

"You don't know my boys." The old man spoke out of the corner of his mouth. "They're stubborn as mules. Clamp their minds shut like traps. Take a crowbar to pry them open." He shifted sideways a little as if to readjust the weight on his hips. His expression was filled with desperation. "You think you could talk to Tom, Father?" he said. "Might be you could get his mind open."

The ranch sprawled across acres of sun-dried plains that rolled on a gentle upslope into the stunted pines and rocks of the Wind River range. The Toyota pickup shuddered as Father John tapped on the brake pedal and drove through the opened gate with Hunting Bear Ranch carved on the overhead post. The skies were alive: the sun, a great orange ball, riding over the mountain peaks; orange, magenta, and purple flames shooting across the western horizon. The air was bright and intense. He drove down a narrow dirt road, squinting past the visor, swerving to avoid the potholes and slowing almost to a crawl over a section of washboard. The road dead-ended in a Y. On the left was the ranch house, two stories of blue siding and a sloping front porch huddled under a canopy of cottonwoods, white blossoms blazing against the orange sky. He took the road that branched right and led directly to the double doors of the rawboard barn ahead. The doors were closed. Everything about the place looked deserted.

"Best time to see Tom alone will be around seven," Otto had said. "He'll be in the barn like usual, pitching hay for the horses. I got a meeting over at the senior center, so Tom won't think we was expecting company. It'll be like you were in the area and dropped by."

Father John veered off the dirt road and parked alongside the barn. A gust of wind sent a tumbleweed skittering past the front of the Toyota. There was no sign of any other vehicle, and he wondered whether Tom had finished the chores and gone up to the house. The pickup door made a loud thwack when he shut it. He walked over to the front of the barn and waited. If Tom was inside and wanted company, he'd come through the doors. It was polite to wait, not hammer on the doors and push himself on anyone. If Tom didn't show in two or three minutes, he'd get back into the pickup, drive off, and return tomorrow. It was the Arapaho Way.

The door on the right flew open a couple of feet and stopped, as if the wind had pushed against it, then caught and held it. A man bolted through the opening. Tall and broad-hipped, black cowboy hat, dun-colored jacket, jeans—a blur dashing down the front of the barn and darting around the corner.

"Hey!" Father John ran after him, but when he reached the corner, the man was already racing across the pasture. He leapt over a gulley without breaking stride, the black hat bobbing against the orange horizon, the dun-colored jacket flashing green in the brightness. He was like a cartoon character, fading into the plains until he was lost altogether in the fringe of trees that bordered the far side of the pasture. It had all happened so fast, a matter of seconds. There was nothing distinctive about the man. The cowboy hat, jacket, and jeans—almost every man on the rez dressed the same. He could be anybody, Father John realized. He hadn't seen the man's face.

Father John swung around and walked to the door that juddered in the wind. An icy sense of foreboding gripped him like a steel vise. He jammed the door hard against the side of the barn and stepped inside. "Tom," he called. "You in here?" The inside of the barn seemed pitch-dark. It took a moment for his eyes to adjust to the dim light that glowed in a bank of windows beneath the ceiling and shone past the bales of hay stacked overhead. "Tom!" he shouted.

There was no sound except for the quiet shuffling of the horses in the stalls and a muffled snorting noise that mingled with the drip-drip-drip of a water pipe somewhere. He took several steps across the dirt floor, taking in the whole place: the tack hanging on the walls, the horse blankets draped over benches, the tools arranged above a workbench, the bin of loose hay, the faucet over the metal tub half-filled with water. A neat, tidy barn, a working barn that someone took pride in.

He moved deeper inside, the foreboding changing into a certainty. He could hear his heart thumping. He knew what he would find before he spotted the body of a man facedown, legs bent at odd angles, as if he had fallen in midstride, arms flung ahead to fight off his attacker. Next to the body was a pitchfork, stone gray, inert and yet as menacing as an instrument from hell.

Father John dropped onto his knees. Part of the man's face was pressed into the dirt, but Father John could see who he was. He laid a finger on the man's carotid artery. There was no pulse. Blood had puddled in the deep gash that ran down the side of his head, and there was a dark wetness glistening along the edge of the pitchfork. "God have mercy," he said, making the sign of the cross over the body of Tom Hunting Bear. "God have mercy."

He got to his feet, dug in the pocket of his jacket for his cell, and tapped out 911.

"My boy Tom's dead." The old man's voice was strangled with grief, barely audible, as if the words had made their own way down the line without any effort on his part.

"I'm so sorry," Vicky said. She leaned into her desk and pressed the receiver against her ear. The moccasin telegraph had been zinging all morning: Tom Hunting Bear killed last night in the barn. Robert must've done it. Never should've come back, that man. Always was trouble.

"Robert's all I got left now," Otto said. "They're gonna try to take him away. You know the fed?"

Vicky said yes, she knew FBI agent Ted Gianelli.

"Knocked on the door this morning. It wasn't much after dawn. Told Robert to get dressed. He was taking him in for questioning. Questioning? Robert didn't have nothing to do with Tom getting killed. Somebody else done it. We got cowboys coming by all the time looking for work. Sometimes they're desperate. Haven't landed a job in months. Things have been tough on ranchers in the area. Some of 'em are barely holding on, so they're not hiring. Since Robert got back, we don't need any extra hands. Could've made a guy real mad when Tom told him that, could have sent him over the edge. The fed says it looked like Tom put up a fight for his life until the guy got hold of the pitchfork and hit him in the head. But it wasn't Robert. He wouldn't've done that."

Otto stopped for a moment, cleared his throat, and made a couple of stabs at beginning again before he managed to say that Tom and Robert had gotten into a couple of fights. "We was still adjusting, working things out," he said.

"A couple of fights?" Vicky said. "Where?"

She could hear the slow, deliberate exhalation at the other end. She held her own breath and waited for the old man to go on. It didn't look good for Robert Hunting Bear. She could have listed the reasons Gianelli had for questioning him. Robert had disappeared for twelve years, while Tom had stayed and helped his father run the ranch. Still, Otto had insisted upon deeding the ranch to both sons. Now, with Tom dead, the ranch would be Robert's. That could be construed as a motive as big as the side of a barn. Even Otto admitted his sons weren't getting along. They had gotten into fights. There were probably witnesses. Gianelli had all the elements of a strong circumstantial case against Robert Hunting Bear.

"The casino parking lot." Otto's voice was a whisper. "Last week, I sent Tom over to the casino to get his brother home before he lost half the ranch on the tables. Tom did like I said. He was a good son. He asked Robert politely to leave, but Robert was a hothead. He threw a punch, the security guards took 'em both outside, and . . ." He smothered a sob. "I guess they fought it out pretty hard. Took four guards to separate 'em. Guards told 'em to get off the property and not come back."

"Anybody call the police?"

"Nah. I guess the guards figured it was a family beef." The old man's voice dissolved into sobs a moment before he cleared his throat and said, "None of it means anything. They was brothers, and sooner or later, brothers come together. Just needed a little time, that's all. Please, Vicky, you gotta help Robert. He's all I got in the world."

Vicky parked in the asphalt lot that abutted the dark brick building with Wind River Law Enforcement plastered across the front in tall, black letters. A row of white BIA police cars stood at the back of the lot. She let herself into the closet-sized reception room and waited until the gray-uniformed officer behind the glass window looked up. Before she could say that she represented Robert Hunting Bear, the officer was on his feet, as if he had been expecting her. In an instant the inside door swung open, and the officer nodded her into the hollow, concrete-walled corridor that led to the tribal jail on the right and the BIA police headquarters on the left. She could have found her own way to the conference room, but that would have broken the rules. She followed her escort down the corridor past rows of closed doors that faced one another like silent guards. A phone rang over the scraping noise of their footsteps. He opened one of the doors, and she brushed past him into a windowless room that might have been an underground cavern lit with white fluorescent lights. The local fed, Ted Gianelli, sat on the far side of the long metal table across from a thick-necked Indian with wiry, black hair that fell into the collar of his red plaid shirt.

"I believe your lawyer has arrived," Gianelli said, holding her gaze.

Robert Hunting Bear shifted in his chair and glanced up at her. "Lawyer?" he said.

"Your father has retained me," she told him.

"I don't need any lawyer. I'm not responsible for what happened to Tom."

"Any evidence that implicates my client?" Vicky looked past Robert to the man with black, gray-streaked hair, methodically closing a notepad, as if he were folding a piece of laundry.

"Your client has motive and no alibi," Gianelli said, finally lifting his eyes to hers.

"There could be others with motive. Any fingerprints on the pitchfork?"

"Tom's."

"The killer would have worn gloves, wouldn't he? You're telling me you don't have any physical evidence against my client. Nothing with which to press charges. We're leaving." She nodded to Robert, who shoved his chair back and scooped up the black cowboy hat and folded jacket from the chair next to him.

"We have a witness," Gianelli said.

"A witness?" This was the first she had heard about a witness. "My client can't possibly be placed at the barn when his brother was killed, since he wasn't there," she managed, hoping it was true.

"Father O'Malley saw the killer run away." Vicky felt her heart jump. She sucked a breath through her teeth. John O'Malley would be a reliable witness. Whatever he said, the fed, the U.S. attorney, the judge, everyone, would believe. It would be impossible to discredit testimony from the pastor at St. Francis Mission. "Are you saying he has ID'd my client?"

"Not exactly."

"Not exactly!" She could feel the tension begin to drain away. "That means you don't have jack. We're out of here." She motioned Robert toward the door.

Vicky turned the ignition and listened to the Jeep spurt into life. Then she drove out of the parking lot, eager to put as much distance as possible between her client and the cold, implacability of the brick building dedicated to law enforcement. The large, dark figure of Robert Hunting Bear hovered in her peripheral vision, filling the passenger seat with enormous jeans-clad knees that jutted against the dashboard, shoulders that rose beneath the dun-colored jacket, and pawlike hands he kept clasped in his lap. He kept his black cowboy hat pulled low and stared out the window as she slowed through Fort Washakie, then turned south onto the highway and clamped down hard on the accelerator.

"Who did Father John see?" she said.

"I wouldn't know."

"You weren't there?"

"That's what you told the fed."

"I can't help you unless you level with me." Vicky glanced over at the man. He kept his face turned to the window, and it struck her that she was looking at a man whose identity she was certain of, and yet she could never testify that Robert Hunting Bear was in her Jeep if she didn't see his face. She wondered how much of the fleeing man John O'Malley had actually seen. She pushed on: "The fed knows the ranch will go to you. He knows about the fight at the casino. He's going to build a strong, circumstantial case against you. Defendants are convicted every day on circumstantial evidence. If you and Tom got into another fight at the barn, if you picked up the pitchfork to protect yourself, you need to tell me now."

He turned his head and she could feel the laser heat of his eyes boring into her. "What? And go back to prison? I'm never goin' back. I got my life straightened out. I got me a kid to think about now. I'm gonna run the ranch, take care of my father, and bring my kid here. His mother will be okay with it. Her boyfriend don't want my kid around anyway." He exhaled as if he had been holding his breath for a long time. "I'm sorry about Tom. I thought we'd be ranching together, me and my brother, the way it was supposed to be. I never wanted nothing bad to happen to him."

"So it wasn't you Father John saw at the barn," Vicky said.

Robert Hunting Bear went back to staring out the passenger window.

Otto was slumped in a recliner, ragged boots with torn stitching protruding into the living room. The house had filled with Arapahos—relatives, neighbors, elders who had spent their lives, like Otto, running ranches, brigades of grandmothers who arrived whenever someone died, wearing faces of practiced sympathy, carrying casseroles and cakes. People jammed themselves into the living room, spilled into the kitchen and down the hallway. The odors of coffee and fried bread and hot stew drifted through the low buzz of conversations. Father John perched on the edge of an ottoman in front of the recliner and sipped at the mug of coffee someone had handed him.

"Robert's all I got left," Otto said. That was how it had been all afternoon, spurts of conversation that alternated with long periods of silence while the man wandered through his own thoughts. But now it seemed a torrent of words had worked their way up into his throat and were about to burst out. "I lost him once, but he came back. Never thought I'd lose Tom. He was always here with me. It looks like now I've lost both my sons."

"Vicky will do her best to bring Robert home," Father John said. He had already tried to assure the old man, but it was obvious that his assurances hadn't cut through Otto's fear. "Could I get you some more coffee?" he said.

The old man blinked at him as if he were trying to comprehend something so normal, so ordinary as coffee in the enormity of his loss. He gave a half nod. Father John had set his own mug on the lamp table and gotten to his feet when the front door opened. Beyond the Arapahos circling about, he watched Vicky Holden step inside. She glanced around the living room, her expression unreadable, yet fixed with determination. She caught his eye for a moment; then her gaze flashed to Otto in the recliner. She started over, and the crowd seemed to fall to the sides making a straight path across the linoleum floor. Conversations died back, like the wind lying down, and Father John realized that all the eyes were turned on the big Indian who had just come into the house, as if he had waited outside a moment before following Vicky.

He stayed a few feet behind her, moving through the living room without acknowledging anyone, his gaze on his father. He was probably in his thirties, but he could have been twenty years older, with a roughened face etched with experience and pain, and hooded, sad eyes. He wore blue jeans and a dun-colored jacket that swung open from a red plaid shirt. His black cowboy hat sat back from a strip of black hair that looked shiny and sweat-plastered to the top of his forehead.

He stepped past Vicky and leaned over the recliner and placed his father's hands between his own.

"Gianelli said you saw the killer," Vicky said. She was standing close to Father John, her back to the people in the living room, who stayed quiet and watchful. He could see the deep reservoir of dread in her eyes.

He glanced at the big man hovering over the recliner, still holding Otto's hands in his own, saying something in a tone that was intimate and confidential. The front of the dun-colored jacket folded over the old man's arm.

Father John looked back at Vicky. "I saw a man run out of the barn," he said. "I'm afraid I can't identify him. I never saw his face."

An Incident in Aspen

"Stay awhile."

Bunny shivered at the tips of Derrick's fingers playing down her spine. She snuggled against him another moment, then swung out of bed. Party noises floated up from outside, drunken ski bums singing and shouting, girls squealing like rabbits. The condo was stacked in a complex of wood buildings so far out of Aspen she'd had to ask Derrick for directions the first time he'd invited her here after a day on the slopes.

"Sloan's at the house," she said, rummaging for her own clothes in the litter of dirty clothes, ski boots, porno DVDs, cigarette butts, and plastic containers crusted with moldy food. "The slopes closed two hours ago. He'll wonder where I am."

"So? The old man's never heard of après ski?" Derrick pushed himself up on his elbow. She could feel his eyes, black as concentrated night, following her. Panties on the chair, bra on the floor, turtleneck on the desk, ski pants flung against the closet door. She dressed quickly. Today had been a perfect ski day, but nearly every day this season had been crisp and sunny with crystal-blue skies, the kind of days Aspen was famous for. She and Sloan had arrived in February, and now it was the end of March. Another week or so, she knew, they would have Parker fly them in the jet to the house on the Costa del Sol for a few weeks' vacation, before the hot weather set in there. Then they would jet to the main house in Long Island before returning to Aspen. She wondered whether Derrick Fitzsimmons would still be instructing for the ski school. She finished dressing, shook out her sandy hair, and perched on the edge of a debris-laden chair to pull on her boots.

"You can't go back to him, Bunny."

"We're having fun, aren't we?" She zipped up the boots.

"I want more than fun. I want you, Bunny. All I think about is you and him together. I can't stand it anymore."

"My point, Derrick, is that this season has been fantastic. Can't we just leave it at that?"

"You don't love him," Derrick said. He had gotten up, pulled on some jeans, and dropped onto the side of the bed. "You love me, and I'm crazy for you. If you don't tell him, I will."

Bunny squeezed her eyes shut against the image of Derrick Fitzsimmons, all black hair and cocky attitude, bursting into the office Sloan kept in the center of Aspen, like some demented, half-stoned ski instructor, demanding that Sloan release her.

"What we have is all there is." She sounded like a schoolteacher, she thought, admonishing an unruly adolescent student.

"Tell him you don't love him anymore. You want a divorce."

"Impossible," Bunny said. Drums had started pounding outside, and the noise reverberated off the walls. Through the window, she could see the big yellow caterpillars grooming the slopes, headlights flickering in the dusk. "You don't understand how things are." She picked her jacket off the floor, shrugged into it, and walked over to the door.

"Well, why don't you explain it to me, since I'm so dumb . . ."

"I never said that."

"You sure as hell treat me like a half-wit. I told you, we'll have a sweet life together."

Bunny took hold of the doorknob and looked back at the man with black hair bristling on his chest and a ridge of knees poking through the tears in his jeans. "What kind of a future do you imagine for us?"

"Are you kidding me?" Derrick jumped up and began doing squats, bending, rising, as flexible as a lion. "Ski every day the whole season. Every damn day."

"And when the season ends? Do I get to help you clear the slopes, haul out the fallen trees?"

"Only for a month or so, then we head west and spend five months rafting the Grand Canyon. Every night, sleeping out under the stars, and you haven't seen stars 'til you've been in the Grand Canyon. Fuck all night long. You know anything sweeter?"

He walked over and clasped both of her hands in his. "Tell Sloan tonight. You've put it off long enough."

"And move in here with you?" She yanked herself free and flicked her fingers at the cluttered room.

"I was thinking I'd move in with you," Derrick said.

The simplicity of his thought processes was so transparent, it was comical. Bunny zipped up her jacket and started to open the door when Derrick's grip on her arm pulled her back into the room. "Let him wait," he said. "I'd do anything for you, Bunny. Tell me what to do! I'll break the news to Sloan myself. He might take it better coming from, you know, the other man."

"No divorce. Do you understand?" Bunny heard herself shouting.

"What the hell is it? Money? You're one of the richest bitches in Aspen. What do you need his money for?"

God, Sloan would be stomping through the house, hollering for her, wondering where she was. She tried to marshal her thoughts into a logical order that Derrick Fitzsimmons could comprehend. "Sloan and I are the perfect couple. Harvey Sloan Pearl from Jefferson, Mississippi, with a software startup in his garage that sold for a billion dollars. Can you comprehend that kind of money, Derrick? How does that compare to the hundred-dollar tips the really big spenders lay on you?"

"We don't need his money." Derrick had loosened his grip on her arm. "You got enough."

"Even a billion dollars doesn't buy respect, which is why Sloan married Charlotte Amelia Buntsler, Bunny to her friends, descendant of the Old New York Buntslers who once owned half of Manhattan, but lost their fortune in the great stock market crash of 1929. You've heard of that, I presume?" She hurried on. "Now he holds membership in the best New York clubs, the best golf courses around the world, and I get to come along."

Pinpricks of comprehension lit Derrick's eyes. "You telling me you signed a prenup?" He let out a cough of laughter. "What're you gonna be stuck with? Twenty, thirty million? Christ, we can live like royalty. Fly around in your jet. 'Oh, Jeeves,'" he said, slipping into a falsetto. "'Bring the jet around. There's a good boy.'"

Bunny leaned against the door, feeling a little weak with the effort of trying to make him understand. The image of Tanya Kendricks flashed in front of her. Two months ago, Clifford Kendricks, boy wonder of handheld media devices, had filed for divorce, and now a For Sale sign stood in front of Tanya's house. She had also signed a prenup, but the poor little Las Vegas showgirl hadn't really understood what it meant. She'd be lucky to walk away with enough money to remain in Aspen, most likely in some dingy condominium down valley. A virtual charity case, and Bunny had adopted her, including her in social events when she had been left off the invitation list, something that had never happened when Tanya was married to the boy wonder. At least at the proper kind of social event, Tanya might snag another billionaire.

"So, how much?" Derrick said.

Bunny tried to focus on the question. "How much would I get?" Such impertinence! He was like a bloodhound. Was there nothing that would send him off the trail?

"Ten million," she told him.

Derrick's jaw actually dropped; his tongue lolled over his lips. "You crack me up," he said. "Poor little rich girl, only worth ten million. We can live forever on ten million."

"No Aspen house," she said. "No houses in Spain and Long Island. No jet or personal pilot. Ten million for the rest of my life. I'd be broke in three years."

Derrick started pacing, kicking at the clothes and other debris on the floor. He toed a fat ski glove and arced it against a wall. Then he swung toward her. "Tell me what to do," he said. "I'll do anything you say."

Bunny tried for a smile that conveyed the impossibility of the situation. Then she opened the door and hurried along the outside corridor into the drunken noise and the pounding drums and the heavy, wet snow that had started to fall.

The lights of Aspen glowed through the dusk and snow fog as Bunny drove the BMW up the winding, mountain road, past the hulking stone-and-wood houses that belonged to the right people. Lights had flicked on inside most of the houses, but some remained dark. People who dropped in to Aspen for a week or two of skiing before jetting off to milder climates. Tanya seemed to be at home; the Mercedes parked in front, lights in the upstairs windows, the outdoor lights marking the snow-scraped sidewalk next to the For Sale sign. She gripped the wheel hard to guide the BMW out of a skid. She could never be like Tanya.

No sign of Sloan's Audi in the driveway at the house, but he might have parked in the garage next to the guesthouse in back. She hurried up the front steps, jammed her key into the lock, and stepped into the entry of polished wood floors, floating steel stairway, and balconies with steel railings overhead. Bauhaus and Frank Lloyd Wright mixed together, was the way Sloan had explained his idea of a dream home in Aspen. The furniture was custom-made; leather chairs and sofas slung onto steel frames, steel and glass tables, floor lamps that might have been left behind by aliens. The lights that suffused the entry and the great room beyond reflected in the floor-to-ceiling windows that looked out onto the mountainside. Snow weighed down the pine branches and, far below, headlights floated through the valley. She turned to disarm the security system, then remembered it wasn't working. The repairman had assured Sloan the necessary part would be delivered by the end of the week.

She flipped on the bolt. Still she would be more comfortable when the system was up again. There had been several house break-ins in the neighborhood this season. She tried not to think about how easily the burglars had disarmed the security systems.

"Sloan!" she called, removing her ski jacket and trailing it behind her through the great room and the kitchen, her boots tapping out a sharp rhythm. "Are you here?"

The sound of her own voice reverberated around the glass, wood, and steel surfaces. She checked both her cell and the house phone for voice messages. There were none.

An hour later, she had showered, slipped on the black cashmere dress that Sloan always said complemented her figure. And that was funny. Derrick would have said, "Hot! Baby. Hot!" She pulled on her long, black suede boots with the five-inch heels, fastened the gold beads around her neck, and finished applying her makeup and brushing out her hair. Still no sign of Sloan. What was it he had said at breakfast? Something about a meeting on a possible investment? They would be late for the gallery opening, unfashionably late. Even more annoying, she would have to go alone, which made it look as if she were . . . *single*, and therefore the prey of every divorced, former CEO on the prowl. Let Tanya have them!

Tanya. She glanced out the window at the road coming up the mountain. Sloan's Audi was nowhere in sight. Then she called Tanya and listened to Tanya's cell ringing somewhere in the house down the mountain. When voice mail didn't come on, Bunny tried the house phone. Still no answer, and yet Tanya was home. She had seen the lights on and the Mercedes parked in front. Probably depressed, and who wouldn't be with that For Sale sign in the yard?

Bunny shrugged into her mink coat and headed outside to the BMW.

She would stop at Tanya's on the way down the mountain. Even if she had to wait thirty minutes for Tanya to get dressed, it would still be better than going alone.

She drove around the curve onto Tanya's property and stopped next to the Mercedes. She might be the Good Samaritan, she thought, rescuing a friend from the fate the boy wonder had consigned her to. She picked her way across the sheen of snow that lay over the sidewalk and the porch, lifted the bronze knocker, and clacked it against the plate. She leaned into the door, expecting to hear the familiar rap of footsteps. Nothing but silence inside. She knocked again, struggling to banish the scenarios that flitted into her mind: Tanya upstairs, sunk into a bathtub of blood. Passed out on the bed next to empty prescription bottles. Because, she realized, that was what she might be tempted to do. She knocked again, and this time, footsteps padded down the stairs and across the entry.

The door flung open, and Tanya stood in front of her. Blond hair mussed, lipstick smeared, white hands shaking as she cinched up the pink peignoir that stopped at midthigh. She wore frowsy blue slippers, the kind you'd expect to see on a bleached blonde with a cigarette dangling from her mouth in Derrick's complex.

"Everything okay?" Bunny asked. Tanya looked startled, half-sick even.

"What are you doing here?" she said.

"Sloan is tied up in a meeting, so I came to take you to the art opening. Come on, get dressed. You'll be my date."

"Who is it, honey?"

Sloan's voice came from the top of the stairs and slapped at Bunny with the force of an avalanche rumbling down the mountain. Bunny wasn't sure how she had gotten inside, but she realized she was standing in the middle of the entry surrounded by slabs of tile as blue as an aquarium, watching her husband coming down the curved stairway, looping a belt around the fluffy white robe he wore.

"This is awkward," he said, moving in close beside Tanya.

Bunny felt as if she were floating near the ceiling, looking down on the bald spot in her husband's head and the rumpled hair of her own personal charity project. Sloan looked tense, wound as tight as steel, a sense of dread coming off him like perspiration, as if he expected her to make a scene, the kind a Las Vegas showgirl might make: scream and shout and burst into tears, pick up the crystal vase on the table and smash it into his face. But she was Charlotte Amelia Buntsler, trained to handle every situation with the appropriate decorum, which was why he had married her. She dug her heels into the tile to steady herself and said, "I had no idea you and Tanya were having a little afternoon affair."

"You misunderstand." For the first time, she saw how old and worn-out Sloan looked, features craggier, nose bigger and redder. She wondered why she hadn't noticed the gray hairs that stood straight up in his eyebrows. Tanya was at least twenty years younger. It was all perfectly clear: middle-aged man sliding downhill; beautiful, available, and desperate divorcée.

Bunny tried to focus on what he was saying, something about how Tanya and he loved each other. "I've asked her to be my wife," he said.

The words jammed in Bunny's throat. Finally she forced them out: "How inconvenient that you already have a wife."

"I've intended to tell you for some time," he said. Tanya snuggled close, staring up at him with doelike eyes. "There wasn't a good time. Chester's in LA until the end of the week." Bunny tried to keep herself from sliding onto the floor. Chester Aaronson, the town's best lawyer, especially skilled in handling divorces. He prided himself on the fact that none of his clients' prenups had ever been broken. "When he returns, I intend to have him draw up the divorce papers."

"This is a mistake," Bunny managed. "You and I were meant for each other. Tanya's"—she nodded at the complacent young woman beside her husband—"just a passing phase. Women like her come and go, but you and I are parts of a whole. Bunny and Sloan. All of our crowd will tell you that is the truth."

"There's no mistake," Sloan said. He leaned down and kissed the top of Tanya's head. "I'm afraid you will have to accept reality."

Bunny struggled with another smile to show that she remained calm. "I'll see you later at home," she said, listing sideways. Then she yanked open the door, stepped outside, and closed the door quietly, appropriately, behind her. She had to lean on the railing to keep from sliding down the steps and sprawling facedown in Tanya Kendricks' front yard next to the For Sale sign.

Bunny huddled in the corner of the window seat and watched Derrick saunter toward the entrance to the condo, bowlegged, shoulders swinging about. The elevator clanked and bumped to the second floor, and Derrick plunged through the door. He flinched, and lobbed his head about, as if he were trying to clear his line of vision and convince himself that she was in the window seat.

"We have to talk," she said.

"Oh, Christ! You think I haven't heard that breakup line a million times?" He lunged for what served as the kitchen and grabbed a bottle of beer out of the miniature fridge. "Don't tell me we can't make things work out," he said, turning toward her and lifting the bottle in a salute. "Because it's a lie. You know how I feel about you."

Bunny nodded toward a plastic chair draped with jeans and shirts and damp-smelling towels. "Sit down," she said. She waited until Derrick had tipped the items onto the floor and settled into the chair before she told him that Sloan wanted a divorce.

"What!" Beer foam sloshed over the rim of the bottle. "Why didn't you tell me, instead of giving me a heart attack?"

"I've explained why a divorce would never work."

"You want me to talk to him? Convince him to cut you in for a bigger slice? You tell me what you want, and I'm all over it."

"I want you to kill my husband."

Derrick's head snapped backward, his eyes widening. "Kill him? You want me to kill him?" He gave a shout of laughter.

"There's no other way." Bunny kept her voice quiet, certain.

He took a moment; then he said, "You're not kidding, are you?"

"I've thought it through carefully," she said.

"In what, ten minutes?"

Bunny turned sideways and looked out the window at the lights shining in the windows across the way, the streetlights washing over the snow on the road. The mountain itself was a black mass; the caterpillars had finished for the night. After stumbling away from Tanya's, Bunny had spent two hours driving through the old Aspen neighborhoods and up the winding roads into the mountain suburbs. Around and around she had driven, going over every possible detail.

Only one problem was left.

"Have you told anyone about us?" she said.

Derrick chugged the last of the beer, set the bottle on the floor, and pushed himself out of the chair. He started patrolling the room, kicking at the litter on the floor. Finally he turned toward her. "You said it was our little secret. Mrs. Sloan Pearl getting it on with her ski instructor, didn't want her high-and-mighty friends to know."

Bunny felt a wave of relief wash through her. He hadn't told anyone, because he hadn't wanted it to end. "This will be our little secret, too," she said. "First thing tomorrow morning, I'll have Sloan's pilot fly me to Denver. Sloan will figure I'm upset over the possibility of divorce. He'll expect me to go shopping. Tomorrow night . . ."

"Tomorrow night?" Derrick waved a hand back and forth between them like a flag. "Oh, no. I have to think about this."

"We'll have everything, Derrick. Any hot sports car you want, our own yacht, our own private jet, our own pilot on call. We'll spend months at the house in Spain on the Mediterranean. We'll fly to the house in Long Island, and we'll come back here for ski season. You can ski every day. No more instructing! If you get bored, we'll go to Switzerland or France to ski. Anything you want, Derrick, we'll do."

Derrick stopped moving about the room. He planted his hands against the wall and leaned forward, the knobs of his spine bursting through the back of his shirt. For a couple seconds, he didn't say anything. The party noise from another condo sounded muffled and far away, the sound of a CD like the dull drone of a plane passing overhead.

"Chile?" he said.

"What?"

"I always wanted to ski in Chile."

She had him then, she knew. Derrick Fitzsimmons wanted all of it; he had always wanted what the wealthy skiers on the slopes had. She went over the details of the plan: It had to happen tomorrow night, before the security system was repaired. Otherwise he would have to disable the system somehow, and that could be a problem. And it had to happen before Sloan's lawyer had any idea that Sloan wanted a divorce. Derrick would park down the mountain and hike up to the house through the trees. He should tie towels over his boots to obscure the markings on the soles. Was that clear? He would break through the basement window at the back of the house. It had to look like a break-in because there had been several in the neighborhood. By three a.m. Sloan would be in his usual sleeping-pill-induced coma. No matter where he might go earlier, Sloan liked sleeping in his own bed. Once inside the house, Derrick would take the back steps to the second floor. The master bedroom suite was on the right. He would use the large, bronze candlestick holder above the fireplace.

Derrick looked up at that. "Christ, Bunny!"

"It will be fast, a few blows. Be sure to remove the money from his wallet on the dresser, but don't take anything else that could connect you to the . . ." She stopped. "Incident," she finished.

"Christ!" he said again.

"The cleaning lady will arrive in the morning and find him." Bunny got up and went over to Derrick. She ran her hands along the hard knobs of his spine. "Remember," she said, "we'll have everything."

Sunshine flooded the Palace Arms at the Brown Palace Hotel. The velvet burgundy draperies, pulled to the sides and secured with golden rope. The tables, set with crisp, white linens and heavy silver flatware and vases of fresh roses. Not a vacant seat in the restaurant. Bunny settled back and sipped at the steaming coffee in the white porcelain cup. Beyond the windows, the morning traffic crawled down Seventeenth Street and serious-looking business types hurried along the sidewalk. Yesterday had been perfect: the boutiques in Cherry Creek, the Denver Country Club for lunch, the fine jewelry shops where she had treated herself to a diamond pendant and a Piaget watch; Sloan would expect no less. A peaceful night in the penthouse suite of the Brown Palace.

She spotted the pair of burly suits walking past the window outside. Everything was going as she planned. The two police detectives had come to inform Mrs. Sloan Pearl that she was now a grieving widow. They came through the restaurant door, went over to the blond, willowy hostess with the Hermès scarf arranged around the neck of her blue dress, and huddled for a moment around her desk, voices as subdued as water trickling over rocks. In a moment, the hostess came walking over. "I'm sorry to bother you, Mrs. Pearl," she said, "but the two gentlemen from the Denver Police Department wish to have a word with you."

Bunny hesitated for an appropriate moment before she said, "Send them over."

"Mrs. Pearl?" The cop with the round, reddish face and Marine-style haircut stood on the other side of the table and held out a badge wallet. "Detective Garrity, DPD," he said. "My partner, Detective Simson." He gave a backward toss of his head toward the man hovering at his shoulder. "I'm afraid we have some very bad news for you."

"Bad news?" Bunny said. "I don't understand."

"The hostess has made a private room available," Garrity said. "Follow us, please."

The room was located at the far end of the restaurant, all low, leather chairs, dark wood tables, and Oriental carpets, with sunlight refracted in the mullioned windows. Bunny had felt the eyes looking up from Eggs Benedict and waffles and coffee and following the progress across the restaurant of the stylish, beautiful woman and the two men who might as well have had neon lights blinking Cops on their backs. Highly embarrassing, and hardly part of her plans, but inconsequential next to a billion dollars. She had stepped into the room and perched on the edge of the leather chair nearest the door.

"What is it?" she asked again. She could hear her voice, breathless and filled with trepidation, as if she were prepared to break into tears at any moment.

The two detectives occupied the chairs on the other side of a small table. "I'm afraid your husband . . ." Garrity began.

"My husband! Oh, God, something's happened to Sloan? Tell me it's not true! Please, tell me he's all right."

The detective took his time, rubbing a knuckle around the edge of his chin, before he said, "Mr. Pearl is fine. He was not harmed."

"Not harmed?" Bunny sank against the back of the chair and dropped her face into her hands, aware of a warm flush of shock and surprise moving through her. "Oh, thank God," she said, wishing the chair might swallow her. "What exactly happened?" She clasped her hands in her lap now to steady herself.

"I'm afraid there was a break-in at your home last night," Garrity said. "A man by the name of Derrick Fitzsimmons . . ."

Bunny forced herself to look up. Her face burned, as if the cop had slapped her. "Derrick, my ski instructor?"

"I'm sorry to have to tell you that he broke into your house and bludgeoned to death a young woman, Tanya Kendricks, who happened to be there. Mr. Pearl was in the bathroom when he heard the commotion. He grabbed a pistol he keeps in a bathroom drawer and confronted the perpetrator. Unfortunately, the Kendricks woman had been killed instantly. Mr. Pearl held the perpetrator at gunpoint until the Aspen police arrived."

"My God," Bunny said. She pressed both hands over her eyes for a long moment, feeling the moisture warm her palm. All the carefully thought-out details, smashed. She had tried to think of everything. She had even thought of the pistol, but Sloan was sure to have been in his nightly coma when Derrick arrived. She had never thought Sloan would bring his tart home for the night, not with the cleaning lady expected first thing in the morning. Sloan was nothing if not scrupulous about complying with the proper social norms she had taught him.

"How perfectly dreadful," she said in the most cultivated voice she could muster. "I must go to my husband at once."

"We've already asked the doorman to summon your pilot," the first cop said.

Bunny sat close to Sloan, thigh against thigh, hands entangled, and waited for the Aspen detective to scribble in his notepad. The guesthouse was quiet, except for the ticking of a branch against the living room window and the stuttering noise of voices from outside where police officers, forensics people, photographers, and journalists were stomping about. Yellow police tape had been strung around the main house. The minute Bunny had swung the BMW into the driveway, an officer had materialized and directed her to the guesthouse in back. Sloan was waiting in the living room, and she had flung herself into his arms, surprised at the salty taste of the tears stinging her face.

"I'm sorry, Bunny." She had felt his breath moving in her hair. "I made a terrible mistake." Then he had introduced Detective Peterson, the big-shouldered man with the shiny bald head waiting across the room. "You know Chester," Sloan said, nodding toward the short, blocklike man against the wall, in gray suit, pink shirt, and cowboy boots. Then he led her around the coffee table to the overstuffed cream-colored sofa. "The detective would like a few words with you," he said.

Chester stepped forward, lowering his head toward her. "You are under no legal obligation to answer any questions," he said.

"I wish to cooperate in any way I can," Bunny said, giving him a dismissive wave. The lawyer moved back to the wall, head still bowed, hands clasped across his chest.

Detective Peterson had dropped down on a chair across from the sofa. He turned his attention for a moment to the tape player whirring on the table before regarding Bunny out of small, watery blue eyes. "I regret to have to ask these questions, Mrs. Pearl," he said, finally, "but we have a statement from Derrick Fitzsimmons to the effect that you arranged for him to kill your husband. He claims that you made all the plans."

"Preposterous," Bunny said, squeezing Sloan's hand. "Derrick was my ski instructor. I skied with him several days a week. I can't imagine . . ."

"Were you lovers, Mrs. Pearl? Did you promise to marry him?"

Bunny leaned against Sloan's shoulder. His breathing was quick and raspy, as if he were struggling for air. Everything depended on whether Sloan believed her, but why wouldn't he? No one knew about her and Derrick. There were no rumors or gossip about them. She had never mentioned Derrick to any of her friends, and Derrick had been equally discreet. "I believe I understand," she said. "Derrick developed a crush on me in the last few weeks, inviting me to join him for drinks after the lifts closed, complimenting me, pawing at me. Naturally I rebuffed him and insisted our relationship remain strictly professional."

"How did he take your rejection?"

"It disturbed him," Bunny said. "I didn't want to think about the fantasies he was entertaining. His behavior became more and more annoying. Standing too close, placing his hand on my arm or my back, as if he could make me change my mind. I informed him of my intention to hire another instructor."

Detective Peterson went back to scribbling. After a moment, he said, "It's possible you were the intended victim."

"Oh, my." Bunny was grateful for the weight of Sloan's arm slipping around her shoulders, keeping her anchored in place. The scenario had shifted so fast, she felt dizzy and confused. And yet, she realized that this new scenario gave Derrick a more plausible motive to commit murder than his assertion that the wife of Sloan Pearl had wanted him dead. In that instant, she knew she was free. No police detective or district attorney in Aspen would take the word of a ski instructor over the word of a billionaire's wife, a prominent New York socialite.

"One more matter to clear up." The detective flicked a glance at her.

"Fitzsimmons claims you told him the security system was disabled. How else would he have known?"

Chester lunged forward. "No need to say anything else, Bunny."

Sloan put up one hand. "I'll handle this," he said. "It's clear the man is a liar. No doubt he came prepared to disable the system himself, which is what occurred in the other burglaries in the neighborhood. He is using the fact that our system happened to be down in his attempt to incriminate my wife. The man is shameless."

Detective Peterson nodded; then he pocketed the tape recorder and notepad and got to his feet. He would send over the statements for their signatures later, he said. He planned to walk Derrick Fitzsimmons through the crime scene to confirm his path in the house, and he hoped that wouldn't inconvenience them. Naturally he understood the couple had long-standing plans to leave for Spain this evening, but they would be expected to return to testify at the trial.

"Naturally," Sloan had said, following the big detective and the lawyer across the room and ushering them out the door. Then he turned slowly to Bunny. There was such bright relief in his eyes that she clamped her hand over her mouth to keep from laughing. After a moment, he cleared his throat. "At Tanya's house, my dear," he said, "you conducted yourself like the lady you are. I knew then I had made a terrible mistake. I intended to break it off with her before you returned from Denver. Can you ever forgive me?"

Bunny felt the SUV shiver as the driver thumped the luggage into the back. The car had arrived precisely at six p.m., as Sloan had ordered. They had packed only a few personal items, but after all, they kept the appropriate wardrobes in each house. The tailgate slammed and the driver hurried around. A blast of icy air mixed with flakes of snow invaded the SUV as he climbed behind the wheel. Sloan had taken hold of her gloved hand and was holding on tight, as if she were a lifeline of some sort. The engine coughed into life as they started bouncing down the driveway next to the house. A line of police vehicles was parked in front. What nuisance and inconvenience, she thought. Such scandal. She was grateful to be leaving. She sat straight, facing the road that wound down the mountainside past Tanya's house, past the trees on the right that Derrick had climbed through last night, Sloan's profile floating beside her, the granite jaw and bulbous nose, the eyes trained ahead.

Another police car crawled up the road, and the driver guided the SUV over to make room. Bunny forced herself not to look at the occupant in the backseat as the car passed, and yet, there was the slightest glimpse of the tousled black hair, the red-rimmed dark eyes in the handsome face with features carved in the mountain winds and baked in the snow glare of the sun. She could feel Derrick looking at her, and then, as quickly as he had appeared in her life, he was gone, snow from the rear wheels of the police car flecking her window. She thought he might have waved, but she couldn't be sure.

Molly Brown
and Cleopatra's Diamond

{ A Novella }

"Welcome to the Brown Palace, Mrs. Brown." The doorman extended a black-gloved hand. Specks of snow glistened on the dark shoulders of his uniform and speckled the top of his cap. Molly Brown took his hand and stepped down from the buggy, as the pair of horses whinnied, stamped their hooves, and blew gusts of steam into the frigid evening air. Bells jangled on the other buggies passing along Tremont Street.

"Good evening, Mr. Brown," the doorman said, as J.J. alighted beside her. Through her silver fox cape, Molly could feel the pressure of J.J.'s hand on her arm, guiding her toward the glass revolving door. Other doormen doffed their caps, and she and J.J. stepped into a vestibule of marble floors and bronze elevators and electricity-lit sconces that sent tongues of light flickering over the mahogany walls.

"They think we own the place," Molly said. The idea made her suppress a little giggle. Two years ago, in 1894, the only thing they had owned was a two-room bungalow—not much more than a shack—in Leadville. Then J.J. had tunneled into a vast deposit of gold in the Little Jonny Mine, and the Brown family—she and J.J. and the children, Helen and

Lawrence—had packed their belongings, ridden the train to Denver, and moved into a mansion on Pennsylvania Avenue on Capitol Hill, Denver's best neighborhood.

How many times since had she corrected some well-meaning new acquaintance who blurted out: "Brown? Oh, you must be the Browns of the Brown Palace!"

"I'm afraid not." Molly had learned to lift her chin in an attempt to dismiss the matter. She had no intention of being linked to old Henry Cordes Brown, despite the fact that he was among the Old Guard that had arrived in the 1860s, when Denver was nothing but a collection of tents, cabins, and dusty roads filled with gold seekers desperate to find fortunes. Old Henry had built the Brown Palace in 1892 and promptly gone broke, which hardly left him a member in good standing in society.

The finest of the Old Guard—the Sacred 36, they called themselves— ruled Denver society, and never mind that J.J., sitting on a lake of gold, could buy and sell most of them. Never mind that he had purchased other gold and silver mines across Colorado and Arizona, Nevada and California, and enough real estate, including hotels, to assemble his own town. Never mind all of that. Molly and J. J. Brown were considered newcomers, interlopers sniffing outside the golden fence that surrounded the Sacred 36.

Except that tonight, the Sacred 36 was coming to them.

Molly slipped free of J.J.'s hand steering her left toward the bronze elevators and moved straight ahead into the spacious lobby filled with men in black tuxedos and women in shimmering gowns, strolling the Turkish carpets and reclining in plush chairs arranged around potted artificial trees. The domed ceiling soared overhead, six stories high. Suspended from the ceiling was a crystal chandelier that, Molly guessed, would fill most of the two-room shack in Leadville. Light from the chandelier danced and gleamed in the rows of brass balconies overlooking the lobby.

The muted conversations and the rustling of taffeta gowns seemed to fade into the paneled walls as Molly led J.J. across the far end of the lobby to the winding stairway. She gave a little nod to some of the guests as she passed. Louise Hill—Mrs. Crawford Hill, ruler of the Sacred 36—was surrounded by a knot of other society women, all of them leaning toward Louise, gulping in her every word. She wore a lavender dress that trailed over the carpet, her chestnut-brown hair piled high and fastened with diamond pins that flitted like fireflies when she moved her head.

Molly could feel the eyes boring into the back of her fox cape as she and J.J. started up the stairs, J.J.'s hand firm on the small of her back. Oh, they were a fine-looking couple, she knew. J.J., tall and broad-shouldered, with red hair oil-slicked into place, every inch the gentleman in his cashmere top coat and tailored black tuxedo, and the confidence about him of a man who had made his own fortune. J.J. had never been a common miner. He was a mining engineer, and when nobody believed that the mountains around Leadville—the silver city—would disgorge anything other than silver or lead, J.J. had believed otherwise. He had recognized the signs that gold could also be found, and he figured out how to get to it.

Molly glanced over one shoulder and gave him a smile. She looked her best, she knew. The blue lace dress complemented her blue eyes and her own red hair was swept up and wound even higher than Louise Hill's. She had worn the aquamarine necklace that J.J. had given her their first Christmas in Denver. Oh, how she had screamed with delight when she opened the red velvet box and saw the enormous blue gems winking in their gold setting. That evening she and J.J. and the children had taken a sleigh ride through the streets of Capitol Hill, laughing at the snow that blew in their faces and exclaiming at the fine mansions, light blazing in the windows, that loomed around them. She had worn the aquamarine necklace.

At the top of the stairway, Molly linked her arm in J.J.'s and slowed their pace as they strolled along the brass balcony to give everyone in the lobby below a clear view of their progress toward the ballroom. Not until she and J.J. had inspected the ballroom and the dinner table settings and greeted the guests of honor would the maître d' invite the other guests to ascend the stairs. She and J.J. were the hosts, and just as she had expected, no one in the Sacred 36 had turned down the invitation from the J. J. Browns to dine with Prince Alexander Orlovsky and his daughter, Princess Katerina, of St. Petersburg, with the royal blood of tzars coursing in their veins.

"His friends call him Sasha," Alice Beltran had written on the ivory sheet with the golden crown of the Plaza Hotel engraved at the top. Such a lovely woman, Alice, the kind Molly had dreamed of befriending even when she lived in Leadville, and she and Alice had gravitated toward each other that weekend last fall when they had each settled their children into the boarding school in Connecticut. Alice was living at the Plaza while her husband, George, made arrangements for their residence in St. Petersburg, where he was about to take up the duties of Ambassador to Russia.

"Sasha has spent such a grand time in New York," Alice had written. "As you know, Molly, royalty must associate with the best people. For that reason, my dear friend, I entrust the prince and his lovely daughter to you and J.J. for their stay in Denver. I know you will introduce them to the right sort. You can reach the prince at the Palmer House in Chicago until next week when he and Princess Katerina will embark by train to Denver."

Molly had fled down the second-floor corridor of the mansion and flung open the paneled door to J.J.'s study. "Royalty is coming to Denver!" she announced, waving the note in the air.

J.J. had lifted his head from the pile of papers he was hunched over at the rolltop desk. "Royalty?" he said, blinking up at her. "We don't know any royalty."

"Oh, but we will." Molly crossed the study and let the note drop on top of the papers. "Alice Beltran, wife of our Ambassador to Russia—remember, I told you about her?—has entrusted a Russian prince and his daughter to us. It is our duty to see that they meet the right people."

"Hold on just one minute, Mol." J.J. pushed his chair back and stared up at her with that supercilious grin that meant he was enjoying himself. "The right people haven't exactly taken us to their hearts," he said, amusement leaking out of his voice. The fact was that J.J. didn't care a fig about the right people and the Sacred 36, which he called a bunch of self-appointed old biddies and their trained-pony husbands. J.J. had his mines, an expanding business empire, and a thousand employees, more than enough to keep him occupied without any concern for the Sacred 36.

"But that's the point." Molly heard the exasperation in her voice. "This is our chance to be accepted. We must give a dinner at the Brown Palace. There must be an orchestra and dancing. What a stroke of luck! No one in society will turn down the opportunity to meet Russian royalty!" She had whirled about the study, letting the skirt of her morning dress swing out in a circle as if it were the blue lace dress that she already knew she would wear to the gala event. "They arrive next week," she said, gripping the top of J.J.'s chair to stop the room from spinning. "So little time to plan a grand evening."

"I'm sure you'll manage." J.J. pedaled his chair back to the desk and waved a hand over the papers in the sign that she knew well. She could do whatever she wished. Back in Leadville, after he had discovered more gold than they could ever spend, he had told her, "Enjoy yourself, Mol, and don't forget the name of the bank."

Molly flung herself into the plans. It was like preparing for a military campaign, she thought, an assault on the Sacred 36. Nothing could be left to chance, nothing left undone. She sent a telegram to Prince Orlov-sky telling him of the gala event she and J.J. would host, and received a reply that same evening. The prince and princess would be honored to be their guests. She ordered engraved invitations with golden ribbons tied about the envelopes and had them hand-delivered to the mansions of Capitol Hill. She spent hours on the arrangements at the Brown Palace, selecting the menu of ducks' eggs, quail and roasted venison, parsleyed potatoes and squash, hothouse tomatoes and chocolate tarts accompanied by Champagne and the best French wines. She herself selected the cream-colored Irish linen tablecloths, the embroidered napkins, and the center-pieces of lilies, roses, and chrysanthemums, all coordinated with the candles that would flicker about the ballroom.

The arrangements in hand, she sent a handwritten note to Polly Pry, editor of the *Tattler*, Denver's gossip sheet, announcing that Mr. and Mrs. J. J. Brown would host a gala dinner at the Brown Palace Hotel to introduce Prince Orlovsky and his daughter, Princess Katerina, of St. Petersburg, Russia, to the finest of Denver society.

She waited four days for the responses. They arrived almost at the same time, and she had understood. The initial victory in her campaign to storm the gates of Denver society was hers. The ruler of the Sacred 36 had given the approval that sent her entire battalion into retreat. Louise Hill could not resist a Russian prince and princess.

Just as they reached the entrance to the ballroom, Molly spotted a tall, thin-looking man at the far end of the corridor, hovering near the stairs to the third floor. He was dressed in black, with a pale, gaunt face and a short black beard that emphasized the tight line of his mouth. "Who could that be?" she said.

"A hotel guest, Mol," J.J. said, but she noticed that he had barely glanced down the corridor.

"I wonder why he looks familiar," Molly went on. "He doesn't seem to belong here."

"Some might have said the same about us not so long ago." J.J. squeezed her hand and steered her toward the double walnut doors that swung open before them. They stepped past a pair of doormen into a ballroom that took her breath away. Silver and china settings gleaming, ivory cloths draping the tables and bunching about the parquet floor, flower centerpieces perfuming the air, and soft candlelight suffusing everything. The ceiling floated two stories overhead with crystal chandeliers that dangled on brass chains. A brass balcony encircled the ballroom, like the balconies above the lobby. Burgundy velvet draperies had been pulled back, and the lights of Denver shone like diamonds in the dark windows. Over in the far corner, the orchestra was tuning up, violins and violas screeching softly.

"A fine job you've done, Mol." J.J.'s voice was close to her ear. "Rivals anything in St. Petersburg, I'd say."

Molly tried for her best smile, but she still felt the sting from Louise

Hill's remark in the *Tattler* not long after the Browns had moved to Denver. A remark aimed at her, Molly knew, like the first fusillade in a battle. "Two things mark the finest people," Louise had stated. "They have money and they know how to use it." Well, this evening, Louise Hill would see for herself that the J. J. Browns knew how to use their money.

"Where are they?" Molly said, glancing about the room. The prince and princess were to arrive on the afternoon train, but what if there had been a delay? And all of the Sacred 36 waiting in the lobby? She could feel her heart begin to sink.

"Now, Mol. You shouldn't be worrying," J.J. said.

"Ah, Mr. and Mrs. Brown!" The maître d' in a white jacket with a red carnation in the lapel broke from a group of waiters and hurried over. "May I take your wraps?" he said. Molly allowed the fox cape to drop into his arms, then waited while J.J. shrugged out of the top coat. After handing the wraps to a doorman, the maître d' said, "The prince has asked that I show you into the anteroom. Please follow me."

"Thank you," J.J. said, and Molly felt her knees go weak with relief. She was grateful for J.J.'s hand on her arm, steering her across the ballroom in the direction of the man in the white jacket.

They entered a large sitting room, with damask chairs, sofas, and marble lamp tables arranged around Turkish carpets. Light glowed through the silk lampshades. Seated on a red sofa was a thin-looking man with silver hair and a matching goatee, dressed in dark trousers and a gray jacket buttoned up to the black cravat at his neck. Beside him was a young woman in a white dress studded with beads that reflected the color of the sofa. She had black hair, pinned back into rolls, with tiny ringlets that framed her oval-shaped face and emphasized her long, graceful neck. Suspended from the gold chain at her neck was a large black gemstone that glinted in the lamplight.

"Our charming hosts have arrived, Kitty." The man lifted himself to a height of six feet or more and came forward, one hand outstretched.

Molly started to curtsy. "Your Highness," she murmured as the prince started pumping J.J.'s hand.

"Prince Orlovsky," he said, "but you must call me Sasha. And you must be J. J. Brown, while this lovely woman"—he turned toward Molly, who was frozen in a half curtsy—"must be your wife. May I call you Molly?" He dropped J.J.'s hand and leaned toward her. His eyes were the light blue of a mountain lake in the morning. "We are grateful to you for taking such poor pilgrims as ourselves under your wing and arranging this magnificent evening with the finest of Denver society. May I present my daughter, Princess Katerina," he said, sweeping one hand toward the young woman.

"Your Highness." Molly sank into the curtsy that she had practiced, following the instructions in the book she had read on the proper etiquette for greeting royalty.

The princess remained posed on the sofa in a half turn that showed off the black gem at her throat. She gave a slight smile and lowered her eyes in what struck Molly as an attempt to appear more modest and younger than she most certainly was. The pale powder on her face barely covered the blemishes or the fine lines cut into her forehead.

Molly turned back to the prince, who, despite the silver hair, hardly seemed old enough to be the father of a woman at least thirty years old, three years older than Molly herself. An image of her own pa, John Tobin, gray-haired and bent, flitted before her eyes, but surely there could be no comparison. Pa had spent his youth and strength at hard manual labor, hardly the life of this Russian prince.

"Everything is prepared, Your Highness," she said. "The guests are assembled in the lobby waiting to be summoned." She hoped she hadn't betrayed the delight she felt at having kept the Sacred 36 waiting.

"Then we must proceed." Prince Orlovsky stepped backward and held out his hand to the princess, who lifted herself from the sofa. "Allow us to follow you," he said, shoulders straight and head high, as if he were about to set off in a military parade.

Molly felt J.J. tuck her hand under his arm as they made their way into the ballroom. A long red Turkish carpet had been unrolled just inside the double doors to mark the reception area. J.J. led her to the far end, and the prince and his daughter assumed places next to them. Molly could hear the buzz of conversations on the other side of the doors, the faint shuffling of footsteps. She had to swallow back the laughter threatening to erupt in her throat. All the beautiful people of Denver who had looked the other way whenever their carriages passed on the avenues were about to step through the doors and come face-to-face with Mr. and Mrs. J. J. Brown. And she, Molly Brown from Hannibal, Missouri, lately of Leadville, would have the honor of presenting each guest to a Russian prince and princess.

The instant J.J. nodded to the doormen, the double doors opened, and the guests pressed forward, Louise Hill in the lead, followed by her husband, a slight-looking man, stoop-shouldered inside the black tuxedo jacket, black hair combed over the bald top of his head and a black handlebar mustache drooping around his mouth.

Louise set a white-gloved hand inside J.J.'s. "So delightful to see you," she said. Retrieving her hand, she glided toward Molly, leaving Crawford to shake hands with J.J. and slap him on the back.

"Good show, old man," Crawford said, and Molly could hear in his tone the mixture of admiration and contempt that men whose fathers had made great fortunes, but were incapable of such feats themselves, reserved for a man like J.J.

"Such a lovely party, Molly dear," Louise was saying, as if they were the oldest of friends. Her gaze drifted upward to Prince Orlovsky. "You must present me to your guests."

"May I present Mr. and Mrs. Crawford Hill," Molly said, waving her own gloved hand toward the royal guests. She held her head high, allowing Louise a full view of the aquamarine necklace and savoring the sense of accomplishment that poured over her. "Prince Alexander Orlovsky and his daughter, Princess Katerina, of St. Petersburg."

"A delight, Your Highnesses," Louise said, bowing the pile of stiffened chestnut hair toward the prince's chest and swooping into an unsteady curtsy. "Such an honor to welcome you and your lovely daughter to Denver." Her gaze swooped upward again, fastening on the black diamond shimmering in the hollow of Princess Katerina's throat. "My, what a beautiful gem," she said, as if the words had burst forth, breaking the boundary of propriety, before she could stop herself. The faintest trace of a blush blossomed in her cheeks. She turned back to the prince. "I hope you and your lovely daughter will be our guests during your stay in Denver," she said.

"It would be our pleasure." The prince nodded toward his daughter, who gave him a fixed smile before turning the same smile on Louise. "You must speak with Mrs. Brown," the prince went on. "She has graciously agreed to oversee our social engagements in your fine city."

"Oh, yes, of course." The smile on Louise's face was etched in ice as she moved along the Turkish carpet and waited while Crawford pumped the prince's hand and bowed to the princess. Then Louise lifted a glass of Champagne from the tray that one of the waiters held and promenaded across the ballroom floor toward the tables, Crawford hovering behind her.

Other familiar faces were coming along the reception line now, all the lovely people who dined and danced at the Crawford Hills' and were on the invitation list every year for the Christmas ball that the Hills hosted at the Denver Country Club. Mr. and Mrs. Harry Tammen, Mr. and Mrs. Henry McCallister, Mr. and Mrs. Claude Boettcher. The women lovely in silks and organzas and jewels, the men puffed up, shoulders back in the attempt, Molly thought, to appear as royal as the guests beside her. "May I present . . ." she said, over and over, not missing a beat. She had memorized the names of the Sacred 36, and soon, she was certain, her own name, along with J.J.'s, would be added to the list. The Sacred 38. Except that it would mean nothing to J.J. She tried not to laugh at the thought that most likely she would have to remind him from time to time that they were on the list.

Several couples still waited inside the door when Molly started to present Mr. and Mrs. David Moffat. Out of the corner of her eye, she glimpsed a dark figure moving like a shadow along the railing of the balcony overhead. She glanced up just as a man dressed in black with a black mask across his upper face drew a long-barreled revolver from inside his jacket, leaned over the railing, and trained the gun on Prince Orlovsky.

"Get down!" Molly screamed. The crack of a gunshot burst the air as she threw herself against the prince, pushing him backward, conscious of the princess caught in the tangle and J.J.'s weight pressing against all of them as they crashed onto the Turkish carpet.

"Stay down, Mol," J.J. shouted, the weight of his arm heavy against her head, pushing her cheek against the carpet. Across the floor was a blur of patent leather shoes and satin high heels and the swirling silk hems of the many-colored gowns. The sounds of women screaming and men shouting mixed with dissonant noises coming from the direction of the orchestra. She could imagine the musicians scrambling around the instruments and ducking to the floor.

"There he goes!" It was J.J.'s voice, and Molly managed to pull herself free and look up. The man in black was running along the balcony, weaving back and forth, as if he expected someone to shoot at him. He yanked open a door and plunged into the upstairs corridor, letting the door slam shut behind him.

"Are you all right, Mol?" J.J. said.

"Yes, I think so." Molly managed to sit up. She turned toward Prince Orlovsky and his daughter, who were trying to right themselves. "Are you hurt?" she said.

"I believe he has missed his target," the prince said, pushing himself to his feet. He leaned forward, set his hands on his daughter's shoulders, and pulled her upright. "Thank heaven, we have survived another assassination attempt," he said.

"By thunder! He can't get away with this." J.J. was on his feet, heading toward the double doors. "I'm going after him," he shouted.

"No!" Molly spun around and tried to grab his arm, but J.J. twisted away, flung open the doors, and ran out of the ballroom. The two doormen plunged after him. She glanced around, expecting the other men to follow, but the beautiful people of Denver stood like statues, fixed in a tableau, gripping Champagne glasses, faces as pale as the linen tablecloths.

In the next instant, as if the tableau had ended, the guests began swaying and stumbling about. A woman emitted a sharp scream; other women began sobbing. Louise Hill laid one arm across her forehead and swooned into the arms of her husband. Some of the men had started waving and shouting at the waiters hovering in the corner. "Wraps! Wraps! Bring our wraps!"

Molly tried to fight off the panic rising in her chest. The gala dinner she had planned was dissolving into pandemonium. She tried to concentrate on what the prince was saying, something about adjourning to the anteroom.

"Oh, but the evening must go on," she said.

"Yes, yes," the prince said, and in that moment, he seemed to become aware of the guests flowing toward the doors, the waiters scurrying about with wraps piled in their arms. Pulling himself to his royal height, he stepped to the middle of the Turkish carpet, which allowed the best view of the ballroom, and clapped his hands. Everyone stood in place, wraps hanging off their shoulders.

"My dear people of Denver." The prince spoke in a royal stentorian voice accustomed to obedience. "It appears that the troubles of my own country have followed me to your beautiful city. My daughter and I wish to apologize for this most unfortunate intrusion, but I assure you that the intruder will be apprehended. With Mr. Brown in pursuit"—the prince glanced at Molly—"I expect the culprit is already in hand. I beg you to allow the evening to continue. Please enjoy the dinner and music that Mrs. Brown has arranged. Princess Katerina and I will join you shortly." The prince then took the arm of his daughter and led her toward the door to the anteroom.

A second passed, then another. Molly felt her breath lumped in her throat. Finally the guests started moving about, pulling off the wraps and coats that dropped onto the waiters' arms and making their way around the tables, glancing down at the place cards. One by one they began to take their chairs. Molly walked over to the maître d'—his face as pale as that of the guests—and instructed him to serve dinner immediately. Then she crossed the ballroom, nodding and smiling, as if the evening were going as planned. The orchestra was in disarray; half of the musicians had pulled on their coats, the instruments already stored in cases. "You've been hired for the evening," she told the conductor. "I expect you to perform. Play something lively. A Strauss waltz."

"Yes, madam," the conductor said as she swung about and headed back toward the ballroom entrance. She was beginning to feel slightly ill—the most important evening of her life, and all of her plans tossed about like so much confetti thrown across the ballroom. Oh, Polly Pry would have the story for tomorrow's *Tattler*. Everyone in Denver would be talking about the assassin who interrupted the gala dinner party hosted by Mr. and Mrs. J. J. Brown.

She reached the double doors that still hung open, the way J.J. had left them, stepped out into the corridor, and glanced toward the place where she had spotted the man with black hair in a black suit, half expecting him to materialize. It was the same man, she was certain, who had shot at Prince Orlovsky. Despite the mask, she had recognized the tight, thin line of the man's mouth, the short, stubbly beard. She forced herself to walk over to the railing and look down into the lobby where uniformed policemen and men in dark suits were hurrying about, barking orders as they shouldered past groups of hotel guests that huddled close together. The clerk at the reception desk was shouting into the crank telephone, his voice rising in waves of alarm. A phalanx of policemen burst into the vestibule, leaving the revolving door spinning like an empty carousel as they rushed toward the elevators. Molly pressed her fist against her mouth to keep from being sick. Somewhere in the dark streets beyond the spinning door, J.J. was chasing an assassin with a gun.

She turned back toward the ballroom just as the maître d' came through the doors. "I've been looking for you, Mrs. Brown," he said. "The prince has asked to see you."

Molly hurried back inside, down the Turkish carpet to the door to the anteroom, taking in the guests seated at the tables as she went, the waiters bobbing about with plates of food. She rapped at the door. Odors of pungent spices and roast venison stung her eyes, and strains of "The Emperor's Waltz" rolled through the ballroom.

A long moment passed, and Molly was about to rap again when the door opened. Prince Orlovsky stood before her, silver hair combed back, and nothing in his demeanor that suggested the ordeal that had taken place only minutes before, except for the cravat slightly askew at his neck.

"Molly, dear. Thank you for coming," he said, ushering her inside. The dim lamplight flickered over the Turkish carpets and sofa where Princess Katerina reclined, as if she had folded in a fainting spell. The black diamond lay slantwise against the base of her throat.

"Should I summon a doctor," Molly said, wringing her hands, hoping it would not be necessary. She had barely managed to salvage the evening, and now this—the princess collapsed in the anteroom!

The prince made a clicking noise with his tongue. "This unfortunate incident has sent her heart racing, I'm afraid," he said, "but she'll be well in a moment." He pressed a hand on Molly's elbow and steered her toward two chairs on either side of a small, gilt-edged table. "I'm afraid I owe you an explanation," he said.

"It certainly isn't necessary." Molly sat on the chair he indicated, trying not to give any sign that, indeed, it was necessary. An assassin at her gala event! What if he had shot a Russian prince? How would she have held up her head in Denver? An image of the crowded, dusty streets of Leadville burned into her mind. The J. J. Browns would have been forced to move back to Leadville.

"Oh, but it is," the prince said, perching on the edge of the chair across from her. "I'm afraid this is all my fault. I should have anticipated that Baron Pavlovich"—he let the name hang between them as he extracted a monogrammed handkerchief from a pocket and wiped at his brow—"would dispatch the same scoundrel to Denver who tried to assassinate me in New York. Fortunately, as happened this evening, the man failed. I have you to thank for screaming and pushing me out of the line of fire. The sound of your scream must have caused him to miss his mark. I thank you from the bottom of my heart, dear lady."

"I saw him lurking in the corridor when we arrived," Molly said. "Something about him seemed familiar."

"Really?" The prince took a moment to fold the handkerchief and slip it back inside his pocket. "Perhaps all ruffians look the same. The man has followed me from Russia, sent by my estate manager, Baron Mikhail Pavlovich."

"But why, Your Highness?"

"Please, call me Sasha."

"Why would anyone want you dead?" Molly drew in her breath, then added, "Sasha."

"A very simple reason," the prince said. "He intends to take possession of my estate. Oh, it is a beautiful estate, spread over one hundred thousand acres near Tsarkoe Selo. From the grand staircase in front of the palace, one has an unobstructed view of the Gulf of Finland. It is my hope that you and J.J. will one day be my guests. But first I must retrieve my estate from Baron Pavlovich, a scoundrel more evil than all the devils of hell."

Prince Orlovsky shifted his weight about and stared for a long moment at the reclining princess, worry and sadness mingling in his expression. Finally he turned back. Leaning forward, he said, "My poor Kitty has suffered with bad health since she was a child." His voice was low and confidential. "We were forced to spend the last two years in Baden-Baden so that she could take the waters for her heart congestion. Foolishly, I trusted my estate manager, Baron Pavlovich, to handle my affairs. He did so by stealing the income and neglecting to pay the expenses. As a result my estate is now in debtor's court and will be auctioned next month to the highest bidder."

"How dreadful," Molly said.

"That is not the worst." The prince shook his head and lifted his gaze to the ceiling. "A favorite servant, who served my father before me, has telegrammed me that the baron himself has arranged to place the highest bid. He intends to purchase my estate with the monies he has stolen from me! My only hope is to borrow enough money in the United States to pay the debts so that the estate will be released from debtor's court before the auction can take place. The Baron intends to see that I do not succeed."

"Whatever can we do to help? J.J. and I . . ." Molly glanced back at the door, half expecting J.J. to bound into the room. "My husband is still pursuing the assassin," she managed, her throat dry with anxiety. "I do hope he is safe."

"Your husband is a brave man," the prince said. "I am sure he will return safely. You and J.J. have already done much to come to our aid. There is nothing more we could ask."

"But your estate?"

"Never fear. I have great hopes that the bankers I have arranged to see tomorrow will loan us the necessary funds, even though, I'm sorry to say, the banks in New York and Chicago turned down my request." He leaned forward and clasped his hands on top of the gilt-edged table. The polished surface reflected his image like a cloudy mirror. "The fact is, my child and I are destitute. All that is left is the black diamond that you see Kitty wearing, her only legacy from her mother who died in childbirth. My dear wife was born in Paris, the great-granddaughter of Napoleon, and the black diamond was passed down through the family. Napoleon himself found the diamond in the ruins of Cleopatra's palace in Alexandria. There are records that prove the queen herself wore the diamond. Naturally, Napoleon presented the diamond to his own queen, Josephine."

Molly found her gaze wandering over to the sofa where Princess Katerina was now seated upright, a pale hand pressed over her heart. The black diamond lay against her throat, larger and more beautiful, Molly thought, than any gem she had ever seen.

The prince seemed to have followed her gaze. "Some believe that black diamonds are the stars of night," he said. "They do not come from the earth, like other diamonds, but fall out of the sky. So you see, my poor girl's legacy is very rare and valuable. She insisted that we offer the diamond to the banks for collateral. Naturally I refused, but my poor girl kept insisting until I acquiesced. Alas"—the prince shook his head and pulled at the tip of his silver goatee—"the bankers still refused. What would they do with a black diamond? they said. Who would take it off their hands? And for what price? No. No. It was too much for the parched imagination of Wall Street and State Street bankers."

"But here in Colorado . . ."

"Yes!" Molly felt the prince place her hand between his palms. "In Colorado, men of finance understand the value of minerals. Why, the mountains are filled with gold and silver and all types of gems."

"My necklace is from the aquamarine mine on Mount Antero," Molly said.

The prince freed her hand, sat back, and smiled at her. "Then you understand why I have every hope of success when I meet with the Seventeenth Street bankers tomorrow."

"Several bankers are here this evening," Molly said. "Mr. David Moffat and Mr. George Kassler."

"Yes, yes." The prince put up the palm of one hand. "But we must not allow business matters to interfere with the lovely evening you have planned. Tomorrow will be time enough . . ."

The door to the corridor crashed open. Molly swung around as J.J. strode across the room. She jumped up and fell against his chest, gratitude surging inside her. "You're all right?" she said.

J.J. said something about failing to apprehend the culprit, but Molly barely heard the words. She had stepped back and was studying his face, which had never seemed more handsome, trying to reassure herself that he was, in fact, all right. "We went up and down the streets around the hotel," he said, "but there was no sign of him. The police suspect that he never left the hotel. They are searching every room now."

"We know the culprit did not return to the ballroom, and he certainly isn't here," the prince said. "I do hope the police will not cause any more disturbance for your guests."

J.J. lifted one hand, as if to halt any concern the prince might have. "I'll inform the police that these rooms are clear."

"But the assassin is still on the loose." Molly heard the alarm sounding in her voice. She turned to the prince. "He knows where to find you.

He could wait until after the dinner, then come to your suite. You must not stay at the hotel. You and the princess must stay with us."

"Molly's right," J.J. said. "You will be safe in our home. It's unlikely that the culprit would guess your whereabouts."

"Assassin," Molly said, looking up at J.J. "He was sent from Russia to kill the prince by a villain who intends to take control of the prince's estate. He will stop at nothing." She looked back at the prince. "You must stay with us."

"You're very kind." Prince Orlovsky removed his handkerchief again and patted the dots of perspiration that had blossomed on his forehead. "My daughter and I would welcome a secure night's rest. We have meetings scheduled tomorrow at three banks," he said.

"His Highness must arrange the finances to retrieve his estate," Molly said, waving away the explanation. Any mention of finances could prompt endless questions from J.J. that would only keep the royal guests from rejoining the gala event. She hurried on: "It's settled, then. You and Princess Katerina will come to our home tonight. Tomorrow evening we shall have a small soiree with a few important guests to celebrate what will certainly be a successful arrangement with the banks."

Prince Orlovsky dipped his head in a graceful bow, lifted Molly's hand, and brushed his lips over the top. "You are too kind," he said. "Everything your friend Mrs. Beltran said about you has proved to be true."

"I suggest we return to the party," J.J. said.

"Well, Mol, you have quite a success on your hands." J.J. opened the glass door on the mahogany console in the parlor. Light from the Tiffany lamp on top of the grand piano reflected the red wallpaper, casting a suffused red glow over the room. The wall clock chimed twice. J.J. lifted a crystal decanter half-filled with amber liquid. "Sherry?" he said. He poured the liquid into two crystal goblets.

Molly dropped onto a leather chair, took the goblet he handed to her, and allowed herself to drift with the sense of peace that always came over her in the formal parlor. She had dreamed of such a room all of her life, it seemed. The marble fireplace with the carved wood mantel, the blue horsehair sofa, the grand piano made of inlaid wood, the fine oil paintings and white marble statues—all like a fairy tale. Beyond the paneled doors that J.J. had slid open, she could see the vestibule with lamplight dancing in the stained glass windows and shining in the polished wood of the staircase. From outside came the muffled clip-clop sounds of a buggy. J.J. had sent the driver, Stanton, back to the Brown Palace Hotel with the buggy for the prince and princess. They should arrive at any moment. She held her breath, expecting the sounds to stop, but they continued, fading into a muffled noise at the end of the avenue. She could hear the upstairs maid moving about, readying the guest rooms.

Apart from the dreadful appearance of an assassin, the evening had matched her dreams. Why, the beautiful people of Denver had practically lined up for a turn on the dance floor with royalty. And the prince, so handsome and attentive to the women—he had danced with her twice! Not wanting to monopolize his attention, Molly herself had led him over to Louise Hill, whose eyes had followed them on the dance floor with such longing that Molly felt she could do no less. The princess had been even more popular, unable to sit out a dance. A waltz was still playing when David Moffat of the First National Bank had tapped J.J.'s shoulder and taken the princess into his arms. For a woman with a fluttering heart, the princess could have been mistaken for the heartiest woman in the ballroom.

J.J. took the leather chair on the other side of the parlor and sipped at his sherry. "What does the prince propose to offer the banks as collateral?" he said.

Molly gave a little shout of laughter. Usually they enjoyed reminiscing about a social evening—the occasional function at the Denver Country Club or the Miners' Club—fixing the memory in their minds. And yet the question was so like J.J., his mind always on business. She took another sip of sherry, then asked whether he had noticed the black diamond Princess Katerina wore.

"How could I miss it? Everyone was admiring it. I overheard Louise Hill ask about it."

"The diamond is all they have left," Molly said. "It's the princess's only legacy from her mother, but she insists that her father offer it to the banks."

J.J. tipped back the crystal goblet and drained the last of his sherry. "And if the banks refuse . . ." He set the glass on the side table. "Would you like the diamond, Molly?"

"What?" Molly shifted forward, spilling drops of sherry on the armrest. "Cleopatra herself wore the diamond," she said. "Napoleon presented it to Josephine. There is nothing else like it in the world."

"I would have to do some research, determine the worth of such a gem, and have it authenticated by a certified gemologist."

Molly smiled over the rim of her goblet. J.J. would drive a hard bargain, she knew. He would not pay a penny more than the diamond was worth. But he would still pay a fortune.

"We'll have to see what the bankers say first," J.J. said, lifting himself to his feet. He went back to the console, refilled his sherry glass, and took out his pocket watch. "I wonder what's keeping our royal guests?" he said.

"Our luck is holding, Alex." Kitty stopped pacing the length of the anteroom and stared down at the man seated on the leather sofa. She smoothed the front of her white beaded dress, making a point of ignoring the man in the black suit who slouched in a corner chair. "I don't want to think what we would have done if Molly hadn't offered her home. We can't afford ten minutes in this fancy hotel, thanks to that poker game in Chicago. I told you to walk away before you left all our money on the table."

"Well, isn't that the goose's behind!" The man in the black suit shifted forward, as if he were about to deliver an oration. "Royalty is off to a fine mansion with feather beds, and just where am I to take my lodgings?"

"The same miserable hovel where we found you," Kitty said. She turned her back to the man and looked down at Alex.

"We can't relax yet," she said. "The ladies still have to take the bait. You could have done a better job of playing your role. Russian royalty, indeed. Baden-Baden for the waters. Estate overlooking the Bay of Finland. Destitute, no less. Well, that part was true."

"You forget that I played Hamlet in Stratford." Alex combed his fingers through his silver hair, then pulled at his silver goatee.

Kitty let out a bark of laughter. "You refer to the soliloquy you delivered uninvited at the Stratford pub? As I recall, the patrons shouted you down."

"For pity's sake, Kitty." Alex threw a glance at the man seated in the corner. "No actor could have played the role better. I had Molly Brown and that dreadful Mrs. Hill in the palm of my hand. After I told them about the black diamond, they couldn't keep their eyes off that piece of glass you're wearing. Edwin Booth couldn't have done a better job of convincing the audience of the ghost of Elsinore."

"All the same, you haven't closed the deal."

"Tomorrow, pet. Tomorrow and tomorrow and tomorrow."

"Well, I want my payment now." The man in the black suit jumped to his feet. "I played my part, and I played it damn well. Just like John Wilkes Booth, Edwin's brother—isn't that what you said? Shoot from a balcony, but use a prop gun with wax bullets, not like Booth. We don't want to kill anybody—isn't that what you said? Make your escape into the corridor and take the door to the anteroom. Stay hidden in the cabinet. All make-believe, you said, a grand production for an audience of swells."

He took a couple of steps forward. "I'm fed up with your strutting around this fancy hotel, wining and dining with the likes of them out there"—he swept a hand in the direction of the ballroom—"while I'm hiding in the cabinet holding my breath that the police don't come bursting in. Give me what's owed, and I'll be on my way."

"You forget our agreement," Alex said.

Kitty interrupted. "Let me deal with this." She faced the man in the black suit. "You will be paid after we collect our money. Not before."

The man swung around a table and came toward her, stopping so close that Kitty could smell the sour mixture of perspiration and tobacco that rolled off him. The flickering lamplight reflected in his black eyes. She forced herself to hold her place. She would not be intimidated by Edward Alsop, a broken-down actor they had found in a squalid boardinghouse after they spoke to the manager at the Orpheum Theater about hiring an actor for a private performance.

"Now," he said. "I want my money now. Or maybe I'll help myself to your precious black diamond that's nothing but a worthless piece of glass. You won't be able to palm it off onto any suckers if I take hold of it."

"You wouldn't do that." Alex jumped to his feet with more alacrity than Kitty had seen in the five years they had been traveling around Europe, bilking rich Americans with one scheme or another. Investing in Congo gold. Wyoming diamond mines. Buckingham Palace, to help out the old queen who couldn't let her subjects know that she was broke.

"You think not?" Edward Alsop started to reach for the piece of glass dangling from the gold chain on Kitty's neck just as Alex planted a fist against his jaw that sent the man sprawling across the table.

"Get out," Kitty said. She was behind the sofa, barely aware of how she had gotten there. An impulsive movement, she realized, that overcame all the years on the boards, playing one inane minor role after another, waiting for the big chance that never came. She gripped the piece of glass, aware of the edges cutting into her palm. The black diamond scheme was their way out of all of it—the drafty, musty theaters in a hundred towns she didn't want to remember, the crummy boardinghouses and cold puddings and moldy chops. They had been in a dank pub, sipping warm beer, when Alex—in a stroke of brilliance, she had to admit—hit on the black diamond scheme. They had found a glass blower in Chelsea who produced a dozen pieces of black glass. Tomorrow they would sell the sixth piece. They were sure to sell the seventh in San Francisco. Then back to Europe. Amsterdam, perhaps. Copenhagen, Berlin, Madrid. The trick was to keep moving. Never return to the same city.

Edward Alsop had managed to roll sideways off the table and was staggering to his feet, keeping a wary eye on Alex, who stood over him, fist raised. Then he began backing up, crashing against the edge of a chair and righting himself before he stumbled over to the cabinet. He yanked open the door and pulled out the black cloak they had purchased in New York to give Alex the authentic look of a Russian prince.

"No policeman's gonna stop me in this, aye?" Alsop said. "They're still crawling over this hotel, but they're gonna see a fine gentleman exiting the front door. You got one hour, understand?"

"What are you talking about?" Alex started toward the man, but Edward put up his hand.

"What're you gonna do? Beat me to death in this fine hotel? That won't look so good for a Russian prince, now, will it? Think of the headlines. 'Prince Murders Poor Actor.' Some reporter gets nosy and starts asking questions and the word is out. Prince Orlovsky is nothing but an imposter from across the pond, never seen St. Petersburg. What's more, his daughter isn't any princess. She isn't even his daughter. Oh, my. All your grand plans broken into pieces of glass. One hour, that's all you have to give me what's due. I'll be taking myself to a fine hotel. The Oxford will suit. I'll be having a glass of wine in the bar. There's an alley right outside. I'll expect to meet you there in one hour."

"Be reasonable," Alex said. He stood his place, but Kitty knew he had backed off. "We'll come to your lodging and pay you tomorrow. Surely you can wait one day."

Edward snapped up the cloak and pulled the collar about his ears. He was right, Kitty thought. He did look the part of a gentleman. "If I do not see you in one hour, I will come to the fine mansion on Pennsylvania Avenue and inform Mr. J. J. Brown of the rapscallions under his roof. Do I make myself clear?" The man turned around and opened the door, allowing the cloak to sweep about in a half circle as he made his grand exit. The door slammed behind him.

Kitty let out a burst of air. "We have to take care of him," she said.

"He's calling our bluff." Alex waved at the door as if he were swatting a fly. He walked over to the cabinet and started dragging out the suitcases. "The buggy should be here any moment."

"Did you hear me?" Kitty walked over and planted herself next to him. "He'll ruin everything."

Alex pulled himself up straight and took hold of her hands. "Let me worry about Edward Alsop."

"Oh, yes! Like you worried about that giant-headed idiot in London that missed the shot and nearly killed you, then threatened to call the bobbies if you didn't pay double, which he maintained he had earned since he hadn't killed you?" She yanked herself free, pulled a dark cape off a hook in the cabinet, and threw it about her shoulders. Leaning over, she opened a valise and withdrew a small, pink satin bag. She undid the clasp, took out an ivory-handled pistol, and examined it a moment. "I'll take care of Edward the same way I took care of that idiot." She slipped the pistol back into the bag, stretched out her hand, and said, "I'll need coins for taxis."

Alex rummaged in his trouser pockets and dropped several coins into her hand. "Whatever shall I say when the buggy arrives?" A plaintive, defeated note had come into his voice.

"I am a Russian princess, you fool. The driver will expect to be kept waiting!"

The clock had chimed three times before Molly heard the clip-clop sounds halt on the avenue. She rushed over to the window, pulled back the drapery, and watched the buggy draw up in front of the house. The prince stepped down first and held out his hand to steady the princess as she came down the steps. Molly could see the suitcases piled in the back, and Stanton, huddled on the bench, bent over with the cold, a muffler wrapped around his neck, the reins caught in his gloved hands. She stepped back and poked J.J., who was snoring in his chair. "They've arrived," she said, feeling slightly giddy at the thought of a Russian prince and princess staying in her home.

The guests were fatigued, pleading not to be regarded as impolite but longing to retire. Princess Katerina—"Her heart, you know," said her father—looking pale and drawn. Mary Mulligan, the maid, showed them to the guest rooms on the second floor, and Stanton made three trips up the back stairs with the suitcases. There was the noise of rummaging about, suitcases thumping the floor, and doors closing until, finally, the sounds subsided into the drifting nighttime peacefulness of the mansion, and Molly and J.J. climbed the stairs and fell asleep in their own bedroom.

The royal guests had already departed when Molly came downstairs the next morning and found J.J. in the dining room, intent on the *Rocky Mountain News* and sipping at his coffee. "Eager to be at the First National Bank when the doors open," he explained. "Stanton drove them in the buggy."

Molly went to the sideboard, poured a cup of coffee, and slid a pastry onto a plate. She settled across from J.J. "Did you hear anything last night?" she said.

"Wind knocking against the windows, I suspect." J.J. folded the newspaper to an inside page and kept reading.

"I thought I heard footsteps in the corridor," Molly said.

"Oh?" J.J. looked up. "Perhaps the princess felt unwell and her father went to check on her." He looked sideways, studying the light filtering through the stained glass window. "She seemed to be feeling okay this morning."

Molly had just gotten up to pour a second cup of coffee when the buggy rumbled up the drive to the carriage house in back. J.J. got to his feet and announced that he intended to spend the morning doing research in the Miners' Club library. He leaned across the table, winked at her, and disappeared into the hallway. A few minutes later, the buggy rolled back down the drive, sending little vibrations across the wood floor. She heard the front door open and slam shut, followed by the sound of the horses clopping into Pennsylvania Avenue.

She threw herself into preparations for the evening's soiree. So much to do, and so little time! She made a list of the members of the Sacred 36 that she intended to invite, with Mr. and Mrs. Crawford Hill at the top. Any society event of importance had to include Louise Hill. No more than five couples, Molly thought—an intimate soiree with the prince and princess—but the list quickly expanded to ten couples, then fifteen. She drew a line below the last names—Mr. and Mrs. David Moffat—then set about writing the invitations on fine linen stationary with the intertwined initials MB embossed at the top. As soon as the buggy returned, she instructed Stanton to deliver the invitations to each mansion.

Then she called Mary to the upstairs sitting room and went over everything that needed to be done: furniture dusted and floors mopped, silver platters set out, the best Irish lace tablecloth draped over the dining room table, fresh flowers everywhere.

An hour later Molly went downstairs to the entry where the crank telephone was mounted on the wall and placed a call to the best caterer in Denver. She had to shout over the static and repeat herself to order the evening's menu: Deviled eggs, not shriveled eggs. No. No. Not lamb capers. Lamb kabobs. Strawberry tarts, not candied hearts. She felt her jaw clench as she hung up. Candied hearts and lamb capers and shriveled eggs, indeed!

Molly stood in front of the fireplace, her arm linked in J.J.'s, and surveyed the small crowd of guests. Beautiful women in shimmering gowns and men in tailored suits moving back and forth between the front parlor, drawing room, and dining room, candlelight flickering on the red wallpaper, Chopin wafting from the symphonia and the catering staff nodding and bowing as they offered silver platters of hors d'oeuvres. And in the center of it all, Louise Hill herself, chestnut hair piled high, diamond earrings sparkling, wearing the black-and-white striped gown that the *Tattler* had called the "Frenchiest thing in Denver." She had engaged the prince in conversation some time ago, and he still seemed enchanted, leaning in close, not taking his gaze from her, throwing back his head from time to time to emit a strained laugh at something she had said.

Molly stood on tiptoes so that her lips brushed J.J.'s ear. "My dear," she said, "we have finally made it."

"Made it?" J.J. pulled away and smiled down at her. "Don't you know, Molly, we made it two years ago?"

"But all this," she said, waving toward the guests. "I never dreamed . . ."

"Of course you did. You always dreamed."

Molly smiled. Oh, J.J. had always understood. From the very first, when she had agreed to step out with him in Leadville. He had called for her in a wagon, and she had sent him away until he could call in a carriage.

She went back to surveying her guests and tried to ignore the uneasy feeling that pricked her skin like the bubbly Champagne spilling over her. The soiree was supposed to be a celebration, but she was afraid that the prince's efforts to borrow funds had not met with success. An hour before the guests were due to arrive, a messenger had brought regrets from Mr. and Mrs. David Moffat and Mr. and Mrs. George Kassler, the bankers. Fifteen minutes later, the royal guests had returned to the mansion, a pinched look about the prince's face, a grayish cast to the silver hair and goatee. He had begged her pardon. He and the princess—"Her heart, I fear"—required time to rest before the evening festivities. He had placed an arm on his daughter's shoulders and guided her up the stairs, and for the next thirty minutes Molly had heard the floorboards crackling overhead as her guests, instead of resting, had paced about.

She had found J.J. in his study poring over a thick mining book that she guessed he had borrowed from the Miners' Club library. "I believe the prince has been disappointed," she said.

J.J. had slammed the book shut, sat back in his chair, and clasped his hands over his chest. The gold chain of his watch shone against his blue waistcoat. "The black diamond is worth no more than fifteen thousand," he said. "Hardly enough collateral for a loan large enough to rescue a Russian estate, I suspect."

Molly sank into the black leather chair next to the desk. "The diamond is all they have," she said. "What will they do?"

"I'm afraid his plight can't be helped," J.J. said. "I'll offer him fifteen thousand. I doubt it will do much good."

Molly had remained in the chair for several moments. She could hear the caterers bustling about in the kitchen downstairs, the noise of cabinets opening and closing, china and silver clanking together. Finally she had gotten up and gone to the bedroom to dress in the new red gown the dressmaker had delivered that afternoon—the most beautiful gown she owned. She had surveyed herself in the full-length mirror, imagining the way the black diamond would sit just above the lacy neckline.

Now it seemed as if the conversation between the prince and Louise had settled into a more serious vein. Princess Katerina and Crawford Hill had joined them, four heads bent together, brows furrowed, voices lowered to whispers. Molly threw a glance about the drawing room. Louise had a way of dominating any gathering. If she was glad, the other guests were glad. If she disapproved, if she became bored, if she was worried—well, she set the tone. The soiree could succeed or fail on her whim.

Molly had just let go of J.J.'s arm and started toward the little group when Prince Orlovsky rang a spoon against the flute of Champagne he was holding. "Please, everyone," he said. "May I have a moment?" He waited until the buzz of conversations died back and heads swiveled about, eyes fastening on him. He lifted the flute. "Here's to our hosts, Molly and J. J. Brown, who have bestowed their generous hospitality on Princess Katerina and myself."

"Hear, hear!" A chorus of voices sounded over the crystal flutes clinking together.

"May I add a personal note," the prince said. "You have been very kind to interest yourselves in the misfortune that my daughter and I have suffered at the hands of an unscrupulous manager who intends to take possession of the Orlovsky estate that has been in my family for five centuries."

Several women gasped at this, and even Louise's eyes had gone wide for an instant, Molly was sure. Compared to five centuries, the estates of everyone at the soiree were practically brand-new. J.J. had discovered gold in the Little Jonny Mine two years ago, and most of the other estates were built only a decade or so earlier, after some ancestor had struck a rich vein of silver or gold. Even the oldest estate—that of Crawford and Louise

Hill—dated back only thirty years to when Crawford's father had built a string of smelters to take advantage of the ore pouring out of the mountains. Prince Orlovsky represented real money, so old that nobody remembered where it had come from, and all of the trappings and sophistication and cultured society that Louise Hill and everyone else in the room, including herself, Molly realized, longed to be part of. Everyone except J.J.

Molly tried to focus her attention on what the prince was saying, something about the expectations that he and his dear daughter had counted on having been dashed. "The bankers in this fair city," the prince said, "hold the same opinion as the bankers in New York and Chicago. They are unwilling to accept this beautiful and rare black diamond"—he reached out and stroked the gem at the base of his daughter's neck—"as collateral for the loan we need to save the estate. We shall depart for San Francisco tomorrow in the hope that the banks of that fair city will grasp the opportunity we offer."

"But if they do not?" Alarm sounded in Louise's voice.

"Ah." The prince spread his hands in a gesture of despair. The princess let her head drop until Molly could see the fine line of gray roots at the crown of her black hair. "I cannot bear to think about such a circumstance. A diamond worn by Cleopatra herself! Warmed by the palm of Napoleon's hand. Touched by the lovely Josephine's chest. Surely someone will see the value . . ."

Behind her, Molly heard J.J. clear his throat. "If I may . . ."

Louise Hill interrupted. "Your Highness," she said, moving even closer to the prince. She held her head at least an inch higher. "May I be so bold as to say that my husband and I have concluded that the fine people in Denver society could never allow you to endure another disappointment as you endured today. We apologize for the bankers who do not realize the historical importance of your daughter's diamond. Would twenty-five thousand dollars suit your needs?"

"My dear Louise!" Astonishment and relief mingled in the prince's expression. "Am I to hope . . . ?"

"More than hope," Louise said. "I would be honored if you would allow me to assist you and your lovely daughter by purchasing the diamond."

Everyone seemed to start speaking at once. The guests might have broken into a dance the way they were turning about, nodding and exclaiming. Through the cacophony of noise and excitement, Molly heard J.J. clearing his throat again. She squeezed his hand, fearing that he would make a higher offer, an affront that Louise Hill would never forgive. There would never be an invitation to the annual Christmas party at the Denver Country Club, never an invitation to the summer garden parties at the Hill mansion where women in white linen dresses and floppy hats and men in sand-colored linen suits played croquet. "Let her have it," she whispered.

J.J. turned to her. "She pays too much," he said, his voice so low that Molly had to lean close to catch the words. She had been wrong. J.J. had no intention of bidding higher. He had intended to inform Louise of the diamond's value.

"I must let her know the truth," J.J. said.

Molly shook her head. "She will be the only one in Denver to have Cleopatra's black diamond. Let her pay what it is worth to her."

"Indeed, you do us a great honor." The prince's voice rose over the other voices that had subsided into the droning noise of bumblebees.

"Then you will come to my home first thing tomorrow, and we will settle the matter," Louise said.

Molly found herself running a finger over her bare neck. She could have worn the aquamarine necklace, or even one of the diamonds that lay cushioned in black velvet cases in her bedroom chiffonier, but it had seemed as if only the black diamond belonged with the red gown.

The mansion seemed unusually quiet, not even the sound of buggies on the avenue, when Molly arose the next morning. By the time she had bathed in the warm water that Mary had drawn, put on her best morning dress, fixed her hair into a bun, and come down the stairs, every sign of the soiree had been whisked away. Trays of leftover food, Champagne flutes with golden liquid winking in the bottoms, linen napkins and tablecloths—all disappeared. Furniture dusted. Floors mopped. Everything in place, as if thirty guests had not milled about, munching on deviled eggs and lamb kabobs and getting tipsy on Champagne. Some of them, in any case, including Louise Hill, although part of her lurching about and giggling could be attributed to the fact that the black diamond was about to be hers. Both Molly and J.J. had made a point of joining Crawford in ignoring his wife's exuberance.

Molly found J.J. at his usual place at the dining table, the newspaper folded to one side of his cup and saucer. "Good morning," she said, sweeping past to the sideboard where Mary had set out the usual tray of pastries.

"I don't know what this town is coming to," J.J. said. She suspected he hadn't looked up from the paper.

"Have our royal guests breakfasted?" Molly poured herself a cup of coffee.

"Another murder. Seems like there's a new one every week." J.J. glanced up as Molly set the saucer and cup on the table. "Guests?" he said. "They left early. Stanton drove them. I daresay they were eager to complete the arrangements with Mrs. Hill before she had time to come to her senses."

He went back to perusing the newspaper. "An actor this time, poor fellow," he said.

Molly turned back to the sideboard and set a lemon pastry on a small plate. "I'm sure all of Denver society will be talking about the soiree," she said. "Everyone who wasn't invited will be quite envious, especially DiPazza McAllister. She expects to be invited everywhere Louise Hill goes."

"Murdered in the alley behind the Oxford Hotel."

"What?" Molly dropped the plate. The pastry slid to the carpet. "DiPazza McAllister murdered behind the Oxford Hotel?"

J.J. dragged his chair around and stared up at her. "Have you not been listening? An actor was murdered."

"Oh, of course. How dreadful." Molly picked up the pastry and set it at the far end of the sideboard. Then she helped herself to another pastry and turned back to the table. She was about to sit down when she saw the black-and-white sketch of a man's face near the top of the newspaper. She perched on the chair. "May I see the paper, please?"

"No need to worry yourself," J.J. said, but Molly had already pulled the newspaper across the table. She stared at the sketch, then lifted the paper and studied the slant of the black eyes, the arrogance in the thin mouth, the black, stubbly beard.

"I know that man," she said.

"Have we seen him in a performance?"

"The performance of his life!" Molly set the newspaper down. But they must have seen him in a theater performance, she realized. It explained why he had looked familiar. She felt slightly dizzy, as if the room were turning with the thoughts jamming her mind.

"I don't understand . . ."

Molly interrupted. "He's the assassin who tried to kill Prince Orlovsky."

J.J. was on his feet now, holding the newspaper close to his face. "How can you be sure? The assassin wore a mask."

"He was the same man I saw in the corridor," Molly said, feeling more and more certain. She jabbed a finger onto the sketch of the man's face. "I'll never forget the hateful look in his eyes behind that mask he wore, and the way his lips were locked shut. That is the assassin."

J.J. tossed the newspaper into the center of the table. He jammed his hands into his trouser pockets and started pacing up and down along the sideboard. "Good heavens," he said. "The assassin was only an actor! Hired to play a role, no doubt, and easy to dispense with after the performance." He stopped pacing and fixed his eyes on Molly. "Come to think of it, I did hear footsteps last night in the corridor. Prince Orlovsky and his daughter, indeed! She is no daughter. He has been visiting her room the last two nights. Cleopatra's diamond, indeed. Why, it is no more than a piece of glass! What a story the so-called prince concocted. An unscrupulous villain trying to steal his estate! Why, we are the ones who have been taken in by an unscrupulous villain and his accomplices." He threw a glance over his shoulder toward the closed door to the kitchen. "Mary!" he shouted.

In a second, the maid pushed through the swinging door, toweling soapy suds on her hands. "Yes, Mr. Brown?" she said.

"When did the guests depart?"

The young woman's forehead accordioned. "Best part of an hour ago, I would say. Stanton brought their suitcases down the back steps . . ."

"They left with their suitcases?" Molly started to her feet, upsetting the cup of coffee. She was barely aware of the black liquid blossoming through the white tablecloth. "They must intend to take the train for San Francisco as soon as they . . ." She stopped herself. No sense in informing Mary that Mrs. Crawford Hill was about to be bilked of twenty-five thousand dollars by guests in the home of Mr. and Mrs. Brown. Bad enough that it was about to happen. Even worse would be the gossip among all the servants on Capitol Hill. No one in Denver society would speak to them again. There would be nothing to do except return to Leadville. She felt as if the mansion itself were crashing around her, the plaster and pillars, the polished staircase and the gold-tinted ceiling—all falling on her head.

"Tell Stanton to bring the carriage immediately," J.J. said. He waited until Mary had disappeared into the kitchen and the door had stopped swinging, then drew his pocket watch from his waistcoat. "Seven minutes past ten. The westbound train leaves at eleven. We must telephone the police."

"Oh, no!" Molly said, unable to conceal the panic in her voice. Louise Hill would never forgive her for bringing the police to her door and turning her into a public spectacle. "We must stop the scoundrels before they can take Louise's money."

Five minutes later they were hurtling down the avenue, horses galloping, Stanton shouting and snapping the whip, and Molly tossing between J.J. and the hard knobs on the buggy door. Everything had happened so fast: J.J. pulling on his overcoat, swinging the cloak over her shoulders, and she still in her morning dress. There had been no time to find her gloves or scarf, and the cold bit at her hands and worked its way past the cloak into the thin bodice of her dress.

The buggy plunged to a stop in front of the Hill mansion, and Molly had to grab hold of J.J.'s arm to keep from hitting the floor. The door flung open. J.J. jumped out, then leaned in and pulled her after him. She stepped into a pile of ice and snow that invaded her slippers, but there was no time to stop and shake out the snow. J.J. was practically dragging her past the black iron gates and up the curving sidewalk.

"Our only hope is that we have arrived in time," J.J. said, lifting the brass knocker and letting it drop against the door. He banged the knocker again, then started pounding with his fist.

From inside came the hurried tap of footsteps on a hard surface. The door opened a few inches and the round, reddish face of a young woman with a white cap stuck on top of a mass of brown curls jutted into the opening. "Yes?" she said in a voice imbued with all the confidence that came from serving the likes of Mr. and Mrs. Crawford Hill.

"Mr. and Mrs. J. J. Brown to see Mrs. Hill," J.J. said.

"Come in, please." The maid pulled the door back, and Molly stepped into the spacious vestibule with gilded mirrors and fresh flowers in crystal vases on the mahogany tables arranged around the black-and-white-checkered marble floor. Rows of massive closed doors lined the wall on the left, formidable barriers, Molly thought, to the inner sanctum of the Hill mansion. A stairway on the right led upward to a landing that bowed over the vestibule—large enough, Molly had heard, to accommodate the orchestras that played for the balls at the Hill mansion.

"I'll see if Mrs. Hill is receiving other guests," the maid said, sinking into a half curtsy before hurrying to the closed doors. She rapped once before sliding one of the doors far enough into the wall pocket to slip through the opening. Then she slid it back into place, but not before Molly caught a slice of the drawing room, with an overstuffed sofa and small tables on spindly bronze legs and an array of palm trees in blue and white Chinese vases.

"Other guests," Molly said. "They must still be here."

"Then we're in luck." J.J. studied the face of his pocket watch. "Thirty minutes before the train departs. We can detain them long enough to prevent them from making it."

The door slid open again and the maid stepped into the entry. "Terribly sorry," she said. "Mrs. Hill is not receiving at the moment. She suggests you return during her regular calling hours on Tuesday and Thursday afternoons."

"The hell she isn't receiving!" Molly shouldered past J.J. and the maid and rammed the door open.

"Please, madam!" the maid said, as Molly strode into the drawing room, conscious of J.J. looming behind her, every muscle and sinew in her body prepared to confront the tall, silver-haired, and goateed phony prince and his paramour with the piece of black glass at her throat.

But Louise Hill was alone, surrounded by overstuffed sofas and chairs and tables draped with velvet cloths with fringe six inches deep and the pale light of an overcast day seeping through the wall of glass doors that led to the veranda outdoors. "What is the meaning of this?" she said, rising from a deep-cushioned chair, hands clasped over her stomach in the pose of an empress. She wore a yellow dress with puffed sleeves and a pleated skirt. Dangling from the golden chain at her throat was the large piece of black glass.

"Oh, we are too late," Molly said.

"I never receive in the mornings."

"We came to purchase the black diamond," J.J. said. Molly felt a wave of warmth and gratitude washing over her at J.J.'s ingenious plan. Louise Hill would never know she had been bilked by a pair of scoundrels— scoundrels introduced by the Browns.

"Purchase Cleopatra's diamond?" Louise lifted her hand and wrapped her fingers around the glass. "Surely you had the chance to purchase it from the prince, but I trumped your plans, did I not? You missed your opportunity and now you actually believe . . ."

"Twenty-six thousand," J.J. said, pulling from the inside pocket of his coat the leather wallet that contained a stack of empty bank drafts. "I believe you paid twenty-five thousand. A very nice profit, I say."

Louise turned toward Molly, the muscles in her jaw working silently for a moment before she said, "Really, Mrs. Brown! You and your husband go too far!"

"Thirty thousand," J.J. said. "There's no time to dicker."

"No time to dicker!" Louise stepped back as if she had been struck. Saliva bubbled at the corners of her mouth. "Who are you?" she said, spitting little specks of moisture. "Nothing but a common Leadville miner who got lucky and struck gold. And you . . ." She turned to Molly. "The worst kind of parvenu. You really thought you could use a charming prince and princess, who obviously know nothing of your background, to pave your way into the society of cultured people? Let me inform you of a sacred fact—certain things cannot be purchased with all of your gold."

"We must go," J.J. said. Molly felt his hand pressed on her arm, turning her toward the door. J.J. slid the door open, and the maid jumped backward, emitting a little giggle. She scurried across the entry to the entrance and opened the door.

Molly was about to step outside when she yanked herself free, walked back across the marble floor, and leaned past the sliding door that still stood open. Louise Hill looked frozen in place, a red flush moving up her neck and into her cheeks, eyes widened with insult and rage.

"You must have the black diamond appraised by a good gemologist," Molly said. "I'm sure you know one."

Long lines of carriages and wagons were drawn up in front of the Denver Union Station, an imposing block of gray granite, arched paned windows, and black tiled roof. People hurried between the carriages and the station, banging through the tall black doors, a kaleidoscope of Denver

society, Molly thought. Men in fine black top coats and silk hats escort-
ing women in fur coats and long dresses that swept over the little piles of
snow. Other men in frayed plaid jackets and women in thin, patched coats
with scarves around their necks, struggling with piles of suitcases and
toddlers running about. The whistle of a train cut through the shouting
voices and the whine of horses and the thud of wagons heaped with bag-
gage. Great clouds of steam rose into the air from the tracks on the other
side of the station.

"Stop here," J.J. instructed, and Stanton reined in the horses in the
middle of the street alongside the line of carriages and wagons. "We must
hurry," J.J. said, as Molly took his hand and jumped from the buggy. She
sprinted after him, darting between the back of a carriage and the horses
harnessed to a wagon, in and out of the groups of people and through the
black double doors into the vast marbled expanse of Union Station, with
rows of oak benches lined in front of black-grilled windows where men
in green shade caps dispensed tickets. Crowds of people stood about or
claimed spaces on the benches, suitcases piled beside them.

Molly hurried alongside J.J. to the large black-and-white notice board
under the sign that read Departures. She scanned the list of cities and
times: Fort Worth, 11:15, track 3. Chicago, 11:05, track 2. San Francisco,
10:52, track 1.

"It's leaving early!" Molly heard herself shout over the deep voice on
the public address system: "All aboard for San Francisco."

J.J. swung about and started running and Molly ran after him, ignoring the hard knot in her chest, the hot bursts of her own breath. She
slipped on the marble floor, flung out both hands to right herself against
a stack of suitcases, and ran on toward the entrance to the tunnel that led
under the station to the tracks in back. Above the entrance was the sign
that said Tracks 1, 2, and 3.

She could see J.J. sprinting ahead through the crowds moving along
the tunnel. She flung back her head and ran all out after him, bumping
against the passengers, sending a woman in a feathered hat reeling against
the stone wall. Molly was right behind J.J. as they ran out of the tunnel

and into the pale light of the platform. A few passengers were still boarding the train, the conductor stationed next to the steps, but most of the passengers were on board, judging by the faces pressed against the windows and the white handkerchiefs fluttering good-bye.

"All aboard," the conductor shouted. The locomotive let out a long whistle, and steam rolled back along the train and bunched like fog around the wheels. It was then that the man with the silver hair and silver goatee and the black-haired woman darted out of the tunnel and hurtled toward the conductor, bumping suitcases across the platform.

"There they are!" Molly ran toward the couple. "Stop! Stop!" she shouted.

J.J. darted past and grabbed the prince's arm hard, Molly guessed, by the grimace of pain that flashed above the silver goatee. "Do as she says," J.J. said.

"We'll miss our train." The black-haired woman let go of the suitcase she was hauling and started to dodge past as Molly reached for her arm.

"You aren't going anywhere," Molly said, spinning her around. "Not with Mrs. Hill's money."

"This is outrageous!" the woman said, her cheeks reddened in rage. "We made a legitimate business arrangement."

"With an illegitimate stone," J.J. said, "worth no more than a few pennies."

"All aboard," the conductor called again.

"Give us the money," Molly said, holding on tight as the woman struggled to tug free.

"Conductor!" The silver-haired man yanked himself sideways and lifted one arm in the direction of the train. "We are being detained against our will," he shouted.

J.J. kept hold of the man's other arm. "Summon the police," he shouted.

"The police?" the woman said. "For god sakes, Alex, I can't go back to jail. Give them the bloody envelope."

"Is there a problem, gentlemen?" Molly realized the conductor had materialized beside them, a blur of navy blue uniform and gold buttons.

"No problem," said the man. "We'll be boarding soon."

"We've boarded all the other passengers, sir," the conductor said. "Do come along."

"Try to understand," the man said, turning toward J.J. "Everything I told you is true. I must reclaim my estate."

"Oh, please, Alex," the woman said. "The game is up. The blasted train's gonna leave without us." She leaned over, opened the lid on a small valise, and lifted out a brown envelope. She shoved it at Molly.

"Hold on," J.J. said, still gripping the man's arm. "Make sure it's all there." Molly had to pry the envelope open with one hand. She heard herself gasp. Inside was a stack of greenbacks in one-thousand-dollar denominations. She hadn't seen so many greenbacks since the day in Leadville when J.J. had come home with a grip stuffed with greenbacks. They had danced around the little house, tossing money in the air, laughing at the way it fluttered over the furniture like snowflakes.

"You have the money," the man said. "Now unhand us, sir."

"Police!" J.J. shouted.

"We will not abide this!" The black-haired woman started twisting about, an arm flailing toward Molly, who tightened her grip on the woman's other arm. Out of the corner of her eye, she could see the trio of policemen running down the platform. She managed to secure the brown envelope in the waistband of her dress and close her cloak before the policemen slid to a stop, brandishing black nightsticks.

"What's the trouble?" The officer with captain's bars on his jacket faced J.J.

"Arrest this man and woman." J.J. hadn't relinquished his grip on the man's arm, and Molly found herself stumbling across the platform as the woman pitched herself in the direction of the train that was bucking and screeching forward. Still she held on and managed to drag the woman back.

"They accosted you, sir?"

"They murdered the actor in the alley behind the Oxford Hotel," J.J. said.

"A serious charge," the policeman said, but the other policemen moved in closer, blocking any chance for the couple to escape.

"If you check their suitcases, you will no doubt find the murder weapon," J.J. said. "I'm J. J. Brown, and what I have told you is fact."

"Oh, yes, Mr. Brown. I recognize your name." For a moment, Molly thought the policeman might bow before them. "Arrest this couple," he said, turning to the other officers. The woman let out the high shriek of a trapped mountain lion and flailed about until the policeman gripped both of her arms behind her back and clamped handcuffs about her wrists. But the man stood like a statue, or a prince, Molly thought, faced with the inevitable, scarcely moving, except to extend both hands for the handcuffs that might have been snapped onto someone else. His gaze followed the train moving out of the station, whistle blowing and steam and smoke rolling back along the empty track.

"May I ask your connection to this pair," the officer said as the other policemen picked up the suitcases and nudged the couple toward the tunnel.

J.J. took a moment, reaching inside his coat pocket, then extended his hand to the officer, who grasped it as if they were the oldest of friends. "All the evidence you need will be in the suitcases," J.J. said. "My wife and I do not wish to be publicly associated with this affair. I'm sure you understand."

"Certainly, sir. Certainly." The officer started backing away, fumbling at the flap on his jacket pocket and slipping something inside. He spun about and hurried after the other policemen and their prisoners.

Molly wrapped her arm around J.J.'s and leaned against him. The bulk of the envelope pressed against her stomach. "How much did you give him?" she said.

"Enough to keep us out of the police record," J.J. said. "And the newspapers."

Another policeman must have directed the buggy to move on because it was stopped a half block down from the entrance to Union Station. Molly gripped J.J.'s arm as they skirted the snow and ice on the pavement, darted past the line of buggies and wagons, and crawled onto the cold leather seats. "Mrs. Hill's home," J.J. said.

The same round-faced maid with arrogance etched into the set of her mouth opened the mansion's door. "I have been instructed to tell you that Mrs. Hill will not receive you," she said. "Now or ever."

J.J. pushed the door open, giving the girl no choice except to back into the vestibule as they stepped inside. Molly held up the brown envelope. "Tell Mrs. Hill we are returning her property."

The maid hesitated a moment, throwing several glances toward the closed wood doors, eyes wide with a mixture of indecision and fright. Finally she seemed to brace herself, pulling herself up to her full height of five and one-half feet, her black-laced shoes tapping out a deliberate rhythm on the marble floor as she approached the door. She pushed it open, stepped inside, and slid the door shut. A second passed, followed by the angry sounds of scolding and belittling over the muffled sounds of sobbing. Finally the door slid open and the girl emerged, face reddened and eyes glistening. "She'll see you," she sobbed, then ran toward the back of the house.

Molly flung her cloak back on her shoulders and walked into the drawing room, J.J.'s footsteps clacking behind her. Louise stood ramrod straight, framed in the light from the windows overlooking the veranda, the rolls of her hair slightly askew, arms hanging at her sides.

"I demand to know the meaning of this further intrusion," she said.

Molly took a direct route across the Oriental carpet between a pair of leather sofas. She held out the envelope. "This belongs to you," she said, certain that Louise Hill recognized the envelope by the way she had fastened her gaze on it.

"I don't understand," Louise said.

"It's yours." Molly thrust the envelope toward the other woman, who finally reached out and took it. "We saw the prince and princess at Union Station. He wasn't able to keep the money, so he gave it to us. We are returning it."

"We have an agreement . . ." Louise began. She was sputtering, the gray eyes flitting back and forth, as if she could pluck the words off the velvet cloths that draped the tables or the smooth cushions of the leather sofas. "How dare you make your own arrangement with the prince! I have purchased Cleopatra's diamond. He has no right to sell it to you. He may return my money, but that does not cancel our agreement. What you have done is the lowest, most dishonorable . . ."

"Cleopatra's diamond is yours," Molly said. "He wanted you to have it." She spun around and went back to the door where J.J. was standing with such a supercilious grin on his face that she had to bite her lips to keep from laughing out loud. She stole a glance over her shoulder at Louise Hill as she and J.J. headed across the black-and-white marble floor of the vestibule. Had she imagined it, or was Louise Hill about to burst into tears of relief?

Molly could hear the familiar sound of J.J. moving about the drawing room as she started down the stairs. She had reached the landing when the library door opened and J.J. came out into the vestibule. He struck a pose at the bottom of the staircase, one hand gripped over the knob of the balustrade, the other waving a newspaper. "I was coming to find you," he said. "You'll want to read this."

Molly stopped three steps above him. She could feel the blood rushing from her face, and she grabbed the railing to steady herself. Polly Pry— that dreadful woman. If she would only print the stories people gave her, instead of traipsing across the city looking for horrible, embarrassing news that no one needed to know.

"What is it?" she managed, finally taking hold of the newspaper. She sank onto the step and looked at the article that he had folded into place. She had to force herself to focus on the headline, and thank goodness the headline was small—"Actors Plead Guilty to Manslaughter." And thank goodness for something else: There were no sketches.

She felt herself begin to breathe again as she read down the column:

A pair of actors from London, Alex Herron and Kate Dawes, pleaded guilty to manslaughter in the case of fellow actor, Edward Alsop, found shot to death in the alley behind the Oxford Hotel. The couple had come to Denver for a performance at a private gathering, in which the third actor also took part. Evidently, the actors had a falling out over money, and Mr. Alsop attacked Mr. Herron and Miss Dawes, who claim they had no choice but to defend themselves with a small pistol that Miss Dawes carried for protection in strange cities. It was not explained how they happened to be in the alley behind the Oxford, but it would seem that the private performance had taken place nearby. According to Captain McCloskey, the police had acted on an anonymous tip and apprehended the pair at Denver Union Station as they were about to flee aboard the train to San Francisco. Captain McCloskey refused to identify the party that had hired the actors for a private performance. "They have nothing to do with the commission of the crime and must remain anonymous," he said. One can only guess which of Denver's finest had enjoyed a performance staged by murderers!

Molly pushed herself to her feet, hurried down the rest of the steps, and threw herself in J.J.'s arms. "I do believe we are now part of Denver's finest," she said. She was laughing and crying, wiping at her tears and burying her face into the blue serge of J.J.'s waistcoat.

"What are you saying?"

Molly pulled back a little and looked up at him—that same supercilious grin, but mixed now with a genuine look of perplexity. "Isn't that what Louise Hill said?" She was laughing so hard, it took a moment before she could go on. "The mark of the finest is having money. And knowing how to use it."

More from Beyond

Lizzie Come Home

The day the soldiers appeared on the ridge, Lizzie scooped up Little Feather and ran out of the village. In the willows along the creek, she made a leafy bed for the child and snuggled next to him, watching the small brown fingers reach for her red-gold hair and curl into the whiteness of her palms. The willows shaded him from the midday sun that bleached the sky to pale blue. It was cool here; no one could see them.

When she had first heard the rumble of the horses' hooves, her heart had almost stopped. She dropped the moccasin she was stitching and, scarcely breathing, looked toward the ridge in the distance, longing for the sight of Flying Cloud, her husband. But the horses that galloped into view carried three soldiers. The sun glinted off the metal bars of their jackets and caps as they halted to survey the village below, horses whinnying and pawing at the dry earth. Suddenly another rider reined in alongside them, a trader in a buckskin shirt and slouched hat. Like the soldiers, he had a rifle slung across the back of his saddle. In an instant, Lizzie was running to the creek, as her father, Chief Medicine Man, had told her from the time she was a child. "When the white men come to the village," he said, "you must hide yourself. If they see a girl with hair like the sun and skin like the winter snow, they will take her away from us."

Now Lizzie parted the willows and watched the white men ride to the center of the village. Women shooed children into the lodges that stood among the cottonwoods. Except for the clip-clop of horses, the jangle of spurs, and the rush of the breeze, the village was quiet. Medicine Man and the other elders walked toward the riders, hands outstretched in the Arapaho sign of peace.

A soldier as thin as a lodgepole pine swung off his mount and stepped toward her father. The trader followed. Lizzie recognized him. He had come to trade with the *Hi'nono eino* in the time past, before the soldiers had killed the people at Sand Creek, before the worst of the troubles had begun. The harsh sound of voices drifted through the sunshine. Lizzie knew the trader was interpreting the words spoken by her father and the soldiers. Fear as sharp as an arrow shot through her. The traders always lied; they told the soldiers what they wanted to hear.

Little Feather began to whimper. She picked up the child and blew gently on his cheek, lest his cry give away the hiding place. With quick fingers, she loosened the ties on her dress and shrugged the soft buckskin off one shoulder. Then she gave the baby her breast. The small pink mouth tugged at her nipple, making soft, hurried sounds. Stroking the baby's head, she peered again through the willows. Medicine Man and the elders sat in a circle with the white men, heads bent and voices low, like the fading echoes of drums. The cry of a child was of no concern.

She wondered what had brought the strangers to her village. The trader had no goods to trade; he must have come only to interpret the spoken words. But why had the soldiers come? A new fear gripped her. What if they had brought news of Flying Cloud? What if her husband were dead?

Lizzie swallowed back the cry that rose in her throat. Flying Cloud must not be dead! Before he and the other warriors had ridden out of the village, he had come to her lodge. It was the Moon of Ice Breaking on the River, and warmth had begun to seep into the days. She had just given birth to Little Feather and was still gaining her strength. Her husband had lain down beside her on the buffalo robe.

"I go at dawn," he whispered.

"No," she said. "Do not leave me and your new son."

"It must be." His tone was meant to soothe her. "We go to scout for the soldiers on the Sweetwater. When we lead them to the hostiles, it will prove our people only want peace. The soldiers will give us land where we can live without fear that they will kill our people and burn our villages. Little Feather will be able to grow safely into manhood."

She had protested. "They say they will give us lands, but they don't say the truth."

"We have no other choice." His voice was firm.

"But if you . . ." She could not bring herself to speak the words. How could she live with the sadness if Flying Cloud did not return?

She had begun to cry and her husband had gathered her into his arms. He brushed away her tears and kissed her cheeks and the moisture on her eyelids. "You must be brave," he said. "You must believe I will return to you and the child."

Flying Cloud and the other warriors had ridden out of the village in the first light of dawn. Inside her lodge, Lizzie had cuddled Little Feather, listening to the hooves pound through the village and into the silence. Now it was the Moon of the Drying Grass and the prairie lands that stretched away from the village had turned the color of the antelope. Coolness gripped the air, a warning of the cold weather soon to come. Her child's arms and legs had grown fat. He looked at her out of knowing eyes.

She had carried her dread through the passing days. Once, while she was gathering berries near the creek, she had felt the eyes of the other women on her and understood the unspoken words. Who would care for her and the child? Who would bring them flesh and skins from the hunt if Flying Cloud did not return? Which warrior would Chief Medicine Man say must marry her, so that she and Little Feather could survive?

But she was not alone. Other women also awaited the warriors. So many husbands Medicine Man would have to find.

Now she saw the lodgepole-thin soldier jump to his feet and wave toward the lodges, as if he might sweep them away should the notion strike him. The others also got to their feet, and the trader leaned toward Medicine Man, raising one hand in a kind of warning. Abruptly the white men turned and climbed into their saddles. Another moment and they had galloped up the slope and disappeared over the ridge.

A sense of relief flooded through Lizzie. Yet a strange uneasiness nagged at her. She did not want to leave the hiding place. For a long while, she watched the child sleeping in her arms. Her heart swelled with love. Sometimes she wondered whether it was this small human being who inspired such love or the man who had given him to her. He was so like his father: the honey-color of his skin, the bright, dark eyes, and the sureness in the hands clutched into tiny fists. But his hair! His hair was like hers, the bright color of wild berries. Now his hair shone in the sunshine that spattered the willows.

Finally she laid the baby onto the bed of leaves and tied her dress into place. As she got up, lifting the child so as not to wake him, she saw her friend, Kooish, pushing through the tall bushes. There was wildness in her dark eyes; the grandmothers said she was *nohoko*—off in the head— since the terrible day at Sand Creek when the soldiers had killed her husband and shot her baby out of her arms. She had thrown herself in the path of the horses, but a brave had pulled her into the scrub brush and some part of her had survived.

Drawing close, Kooish stretched out one hand and patted the child's head. "So beautiful," she said. Then, a glance at Lizzie. "I heard the men whispering together."

Lizzie said nothing. The only men still in the village, besides the elders, were those of the older generation—not yet wise enough to be elders, not strong enough still to be warriors. Kooish went on, "They are placing bets on who will be your new husband."

"They place their bets too soon," Lizzie said, surprised at a strength in her voice she did not feel.

Kooish shrugged. "Medicine Man calls for you."

Lizzie was trembling as she followed her friend through the willows. What news had the soldiers brought? Already the sadness was coming over her.

As they walked through the village, she saw Yellow Plume, one of the older generation, staring at her from the shadows of his lodge. Round-bellied and thick-armed, he was renowned for the buffalo he had taken. She shuddered at the thought of such a man as her husband. Avoiding his eyes, she hurried past and, after handing the child to Kooish, stepped into her father's lodge.

Medicine Man sat on a buffalo robe across from the opening. On his right was Nee'ma, her mother. Lizzie lowered herself beside the older woman. Thin shafts of sunlight drifted through the opening above and spilled down the center lodgepole, forming a little pool of light on the hard-packed dirt floor. Her heart was like a trapped bird fluttering against her ribs.

Medicine Man cleared his throat. "One day in the long past time," he began, "the people went to trade with the Sioux in a village on the muddy river."

Lizzie reached for her mother's hand, a lifeline to keep from drowning in deepening sadness. If Medicine Man was again telling the story of how she had come to the people, it was because he wanted to soften the blow.

Her father continued. "There in the village was a small girl child with thin shoulders and hair the color of the sunrise and eyes as wide and sad as the sky. I said to the leading man of the Sioux, 'I will give you five ponies and all of my buffalo robes. I will give you the glass beads and tin pans from the white man. You must give me this child.'"

A smile came into her father's eyes. He always smiled at this part. Clearing his throat, he began again. "The leading man said, 'She is not worth the least part of what you offer. But I accept your fool's bargain.' And so I lifted you onto my pony and rode to our village, straight to the lodge of my wife. I said to her, 'Here is a child to replace the one who has gone to the spirit world.' That is how you became our daughter."

Closing her eyes, Lizzie steeled herself against what he would now tell her about her husband. She struggled to make sense of his words. Something about the soldiers coming for a little girl who was now a woman.

Lizzie's eyes snapped opened. A coldness gripped her as Medicine Man explained how a white woman had come to the prairie lands to find a white girl stolen by the Sioux when they had attacked a wagon train on the muddy river.

Lizzie tightened her hold on Nee'ma's hand. A white girl in a wagon train? It meant nothing to her. And yet, a shadow darted at the edge of her mind, the faintest memory of guns firing and men shouting, and she was running, a slow motion across the dusty earth.

"Daughter." Medicine Man's voice called her out of the memory. "The woman says the girl is her own family, that their parents were the same. She has come to take her sister home."

Lizzie stared at her father. "What does this have to do with me?"

"The soldiers believe the little girl has grown into a woman among the *Hi'nono eino*. I said to them, 'The women of our village are Arapaho.' But the white trader told them that once he had seen a little girl with hair like the sun in our village, even though she had run away to hide. I fear he will convince the soldiers he speaks the truth. I fear they will return with the white woman."

"I am not the one they seek," Lizzie said, struggling against the panic rising inside her. "Please don't let them take me."

Medicine Man rose and stepped toward her. "You must listen to me, daughter," he said, touching her shoulder. "Your husband, Flying Cloud, and the others have been away for many days and nights. We have no word of them. We don't know . . ." He stopped speaking a moment, his hand gentle on her. "We don't know if they will return. This white woman comes to take you to another life. A good life."

"No," Lizzie said, shrinking away from his touch. "What do I know of any other kind of life?" She looked from her father to her mother, searching their faces—the narrow, dark eyes, the etchings of the sun on their cheeks, the whitening hair that once was black—for some sign of herself. There was none.

Medicine Man spoke again. "You must decide the best road to follow."

Lizzie got to her feet. She said, "I wait for Flying Cloud."

The early dawn scattered feathers of pink light across the sky as Lizzie carried Little Feather's cradle to the creek. A pair of hawks circled overhead, calling to each other. The child clasped his hands and made happy gurgling sounds. Sheltered in the willows, she removed the shirt she had sewn for him out of the softest deerskin and laid him naked on the bed of leaves. Then she pulled off her moccasins and loosened her dress, letting it fall at her feet. The morning coolness licked at her skin.

She lifted her son and waded into the creek. It was as icy as the streams that tumbled out of the blue-white mountains in the far distance. The baby squealed as she sank down, swishing him gently back and forth. His hands flapped at the water, like small brown leaves caught in an eddy. Balancing him on her lap, she ran both hands over his body to wash him clean. His hair shimmered in the light of the sun creeping over the horizon.

Holding the baby close, she waded out of the creek, her bare feet gripping the slick rocks. The darkness of his skin against hers caught her by surprise, as if she had never noticed it before. She wrapped him in his shirt and laid him on the willow bed. Quickly she pulled on her own dress, wanting to hide the hated whiteness. Yet it remained with her. On her arms. On her hands. What did it matter? she told herself. Medicine Man would never let the soldiers take her. But Medicine Man was growing older, and the warriors were gone. If the soldiers returned, how could her father protect her?

She squatted by the baby and, pushing aside the leaves, began scooping out clumps of dry, brown earth, which she scrubbed on her arms and hands and smeared over the bareness of her neck and face. Scooping up more earth, she rubbed it onto her hair, pulling the strands forward to watch them darken into the color of the hawks. When she was satisfied she no longer looked like the whites, she swung Little Feather's cradle onto her back and started toward the village.

She saw the commotion as she came out of the willows: women pulling down the lodge coverings and packing the travois, children scampering about, men leading ponies from the corral. The village was about to move! She hurried through the cottonwoods toward Medicine Man's lodge, dodging past groups of women, past lodgepoles that stood naked against the sky, skeletons of former homes. The baby's cry was sharp in her ears, an echo of the terror that welled within her.

She found Nee'ma folding the lodge skins into a compact bundle. "We can't leave now," she cried, grabbing her mother's arms.

Nee'ma turned, surprise filling her eyes. She reached out and laid the palm of her hand against the gritty earth on Lizzie's cheek. Then, her voice serious, she said, "Medicine Man says we must go south to the Republican River country."

"But Flying Cloud will come here." Lizzie heard the sobs in her voice. Behind her, the baby's cry lengthened into a wail.

Her mother gathered her close, holding both her and the baby. "Do you really believe the warriors won't find our village? Foolish child. It's the soldiers who won't find our village."

For a moment, Lizzie let herself go limp in her mother's strength. Finally she pulled away and started for her own lodge. It was the only lodge still covered. Inside she worked quickly, filling a parfleche with her extra dress, Little Feather's shirts, and the new moccasins she had beaded for Flying Cloud's return. In another parfleche she packed the cooking pan her husband had gotten from the traders and the spoons and bowls he had carved out of buffalo bones. Setting the parfleches outside, she began rolling the heavy skin coverings across the lodgepoles. Even before she saw the soldiers massed on top of the ridge, she knew by the sudden quiet that fell over the village that they had returned.

Lizzie stopped herself from bolting for her hiding place, afraid the soldiers would notice her darting among the cottonwoods and the bare lodgepoles. Holding herself still, aware of the sighs of the sleeping baby on her back, she asked the earth she had smeared over her skin to hide her as the soldiers rode into the village. In the lead was the lodgepole-thin soldier, the trader, and another rider. They halted close to where Medicine Man stood waiting, arms folded. As they dismounted, Lizzie saw the third rider was a woman. A gust of wind caught at her skirt, billowing it about her legs.

The woman was beautiful, with hair the color of the sun at dusk and hands and face as white as the winter snow. Lizzie's breath stopped in her throat. The woman was like the image she sometimes caught of herself in the creek when it was early morning and the water was more pale than the sky and perfectly clear.

She wasn't aware of Nee'ma at her side until her mother spoke. "Don't be afraid. You have hidden yourself well."

The white woman was glancing about, her gaze taking in the Arapaho women who stood quietly around the lodgepoles, children clutching their legs. And then the woman's eyes fell on Lizzie. Lizzie gasped. The blueness in the eyes, the shape of the nose and chin, strong and defiant. She had seen them before. The faintest image flickered at the edge of her memory. A white girl, older and stronger, who had somehow been part of her.

Suddenly, the white woman seemed to fold into herself. She turned away and was about to mount when Lizzie started toward her, pulled by some force she did not understand. Medicine Man glanced around. "Are you certain, daughter?" he asked as she approached.

The white woman was already moving toward her, fear and joy mingling in her face. Abruptly Lizzie swung around and started for the willows, aware of the snap of footsteps on dry earth behind her. When she reached the hiding place, she turned. The white woman was slashing through the willow branches, as if they were some terrible obstacle to overcome. The breeze plucked at a strand of her red-gold hair.

"Lizzie," she called. Tears filled her eyes and spilled into brown smudges on her white cheeks. Behind her was the trader.

Lizzie stepped back, horrified at what she had done. What had drawn her to this woman from the outside world who was babbling on, sobbing and speaking strange words that called to Lizzie from some past time.

And then the trader began speaking to her in Arapaho, saying her sister had never stopped looking for her, had never stopped believing she would find her. Suddenly, the woman turned to the trader. "Leave us alone," she said. Lizzie felt a prick of surprise that she had understood the strange words.

The trader glanced between them, one hand on the revolver strapped to his belt, as if he feared leaving a white woman in the company of an Arapaho, even one with a baby cradled on her back. Finally he started toward the village. The white woman waited a moment, the breeze sighing in the space between them. "You are my younger sister," she said. "The dirt on your face and hands can't hide the truth. I would know you anywhere."

Lizzie was shaking her head.

"You understand what I'm saying," the woman persisted. "You speak English."

"I learned the white man's language," Lizzie said, surprised again at the ease with which the words tumbled off her tongue. "In the past time," she added.

The woman started to cry. She pressed one fist against her lips to stifle the sobs. Nodding toward the village, she said, "You don't belong here. These horrible savages killed our mother and father. You were so young, you don't remember. But I remember. We had stopped to make camp for the night. It was dusk and very quiet. Suddenly, there was a terrible shrieking and howling, and the warriors came galloping toward us. Father shouted for me to get you and hide under the quilts in the wagon. I pulled you down beside me. I tried to cover your ears so you wouldn't hear Mother and Father screaming as the warriors hacked at them."

The white woman hid her face in her hands. Her shoulders were shaking, and Lizzie fought the temptation to reach out and comfort her. After a moment, the woman looked up. "The Indians poked at the quilts. I was sure they would find us, but they found the bags of sugar and flour Mother had hidden. I always believed they would have gone away if you hadn't . . ." She drew in a long breath. "You were so frightened. You wiggled out of my arms and started screaming, and they grabbed you. They pulled you out of the wagon. You tried to run away, but they caught you, and I—I was so scared, I made myself small and quiet."

The woman was sobbing now. "Oh, Lizzie," she managed, "I let them take you. I'm so sorry."

"They didn't take me," Lizzie said, her voice soft.

Astonishment came into the woman's face. "Of course they took you."

Lizzie said, "My father, Chief Medicine Man, found me with the Sioux. He brought me to the people."

"He's not your father," the woman shouted. Then she stole a glance over one shoulder, as if she feared the trader might return. "Your father was Thomas M. Cook of Chicago, Illinois. Your mother was Mary O'Leary Cook. She came from another country far away from here." She waved toward the plains that stretched into the distances, toward the clouds streaming across the pale blue sky. "We are their children. I am Mary Eileen. You are Mary Elizabeth. We called you Lizzie."

"No!" Lizzie began backing away, nearly stumbling over a low-hanging branch.

"Oh, Lizzie." The woman came toward her. "You will never know. So many sightings of a young white girl in some Indian camp. Traders would see a child that resembled the lost Mary Elizabeth Cook, but by the time the soldiers rode to the village, the village would be gone. Disappeared in the vastness of the plains. And I would receive a telegram about how close they had come to finding you, how they had only missed you by a day or two. And so I decided to come here myself. I knew I would find you."

"You must go," Lizzie said.

"Please." The woman stretched out her arms. "You and the child are my family. You can live in my home. You'll have whatever you want. Your child will go to school and learn to read. You remember, don't you, how Father would set us on his lap and read to us? So many books he read to us."

Lizzie moved backward toward the edge of the creek until the icy water lapped at her moccasins. Her stomach was churning; she felt as if she would be sick. "Go," she said, startled by the harshness in her tone. A part of her did not want the woman to go.

The woman held her gaze a long while before finally turning away. She started through the willows, then swung around. "Before I go," she said, "may I see your baby?"

Slowly, Lizzie took the cradle from her back. She had thought Little Feather was asleep, so quiet was his breathing, but he was awake, his eyes wide and fearful. She set the cradle on the bed of leaves and lowered herself beside the baby. "This is my son," she said.

The woman knelt on the other side. There was the sound of water rushing over boulders, of horses whinnying in the distance. With the tips of her fingers she traced the outline of Little Feather's face—the nose, the square set of his jaw. "So like Father," she said. Then, "My husband and I longed for a child."

"You have a husband?" Lizzie asked. The news filled her with an unexpected gladness. The woman was not alone.

Glancing up, the woman said, "My husband was killed at Gettysburg in the war that just ended. You heard of the war, didn't you?"

Lizzie nodded. She had heard Flying Cloud and the other warriors talking about how the soldiers were killing one another. The war was good, they said. It meant fewer soldiers to attack the villages. But the war had killed the woman's husband. A shiver as cold as an icy stream ran through Lizzie.

"What is it?" the woman asked. Her voice was kind.

Lizzie said, "I think of my husband." She stumbled, groping for words that felt strange and unfamiliar on her tongue. She tried to say that Flying Cloud had gone to lead the soldiers to the hostile tribes in the north country. "I wait for him," she managed.

The woman gasped. "The north country? But that's where the worst battles have been! General Connor has been subduing Indians there all summer. There have been many casualties." A mixture of horror and grief came into the woman's eyes. "Oh, Lizzie," she said, "your husband . . ."

Lizzie held up one hand against the words. The sun seemed to stand still; the breeze stopped in the willows. She got to her feet and walked back to the creek, staring at the dried clumps of grasses on the other bank, at the golden plains that ran into the horizon. What would the world be like without Flying Cloud? There would be another father to show Little Feather the ways of a man. Another husband to provide for her, but the sadness that held her now would be her companion.

The woman was beside her. There was the gentle pressure of the woman's hand on her arm, the soft tone of her voice. "Lizzie, come home."

Lizzie turned to her, trying to imagine—to remember—another world. The warm shelter of the house, the comfort of quilts on the bed, the rungs of a chair against her back, the table where she had taken food and made bright-colored marks on white sheets of paper. It was no longer her world. She was Arapaho. She said, "I am home." And then she added, "Sister."

The woman drew in her lips, as if to bite back a cry, and Lizzie placed her arms around her. They held each other a long moment before the white woman pulled away and started walking back to the village.

Lizzie picked up Little Feather's cradle and swung it on her back. As she started after the woman, she spotted the warriors galloping across the ridge, Flying Cloud in the lead. She knew him at a distance—hair black as the night flying in the wind.

And then Lizzie saw the soldiers whirl their horses about, saw the rifles raised, the heads bent to sight in the line of warriors. She stood frozen to the earth, her mouth open in a scream that locked in her throat.

Running ahead, like an antelope bounding through the grass, was her sister. The white woman reached the lodgepole-thin soldier and yanked at his reins. "No!" she shouted. "Don't shoot." Now she flung herself along the line of soldiers, in front of the guns, waving and shouting, "Friendly Indians. Friendly Indians."

The lodgepole soldier barked words Lizzie struggled to understand, and the others lowered their rifles. She moved closer as the white woman mounted her horse, snapped the reins, and pulled alongside the lodgepole soldier. "Let us leave this village," she shouted. "You've brought me on a wild-goose chase. There are no white women here. Only Arapaho."

Gratitude filled Lizzie's spirit as she watched her sister, surrounded by the soldiers, ride up the slope, pulling to one side to avoid the warriors. She watched until the soldiers reached the top of the ridge, until they disappeared over the horizon. Then she saw other women break away from the village and start to run up the slope. And then she was running with them, catching herself from falling with joy.

Flying Cloud was galloping toward her.

The Man in Her Dreams

Vicky Holden awoke with a start. Her heart thumped at her ribs, like a bird flailing against a cage. The tangle of sheets and blankets was damp with her own perspiration. A wedge of moonlight fell through the window and illuminated a corner of the bedroom. The rest was dark. Red numbers on the nightstand clock glowed into the blackness: 4:23.

From far away came the drone of a truck lumbering along the highway north of Lander. It passed, leaving an empty quiet. Vicky kicked the damp bedclothes aside and forced herself to take deep breaths, willing her heartbeat to slow. It was just a dream.

A dream about a man she didn't know, had never seen before. He had brown hair combed straight back and a long, narrow face. The wide nostrils flared above tightly drawn lips; the dark eyes bored into her with a malevolence that left her stunned and immobilized. It was the man's eyes, she realized, that had tripped her heart into an erratic spin.

The man came walking toward her, kicking up clouds of dust with each step. The dust rose around his boots, licked at his blue jeans and brown corduroy jacket, swirled about his head and shoulders. Still he moved forward, in and out of the dust, eyes fixed on her. She tried to run, but the earth shifted beneath her feet. She couldn't move.

After a while Vicky felt her heartbeat subside to a normal rhythm. She wondered if she had received a vision, then pushed away the idea. In the Arapaho Way, only men received visions. When the warriors went into the wilderness to fast and pray, the forces of nature might reveal themselves and share their power: the strength of the buffalo, the determination of the bear, the cunning of the coyote. Women received dreams. And yet, some evil force had been revealed to her. Its power was mighty. It frightened her.

First chance she got, Vicky decided, she would drive onto the Wind River Reservation north of town and ask Grandmother Ninni to interpret her dream.

Just as no man could interpret his own vision, no woman could discern the meaning of her own dream.

The phone on the nightstand jangled into the early morning quiet, and Vicky realized she had been hearing the noise in the distance for some time. She must have dozed off. It surprised her. She'd given up hope of falling back asleep. Every time she had closed her eyes, she had seen the man walking toward her and felt the evil force in his eyes. She shook herself awake and picked up the receiver.

"That you, Vicky?" A man's voice, someone she must know, but she had no idea who it might be.

She took a deep breath and said, "This is Vicky Holden."

"Darrell Running Bull here. I been tryin' to get ahold of you for thirty minutes or more."

Vicky swung out of bed, muscles tense, senses alert. A call from Darrell Running Bull meant one thing: Richard was in trouble again. Three times in the last four years, Darrell had called about his son. Richard had stolen a car. Richard had beaten up a man in a bar. Richard had been arrested on drug possession. Vicky had managed to keep Richard out of jail on the first two incidents, but he'd done time on the possession charge. "What's going on?" she asked.

"Police got Richard locked up over in county jail." The words came like a burst of gunshot. "You gotta get him out, Vicky. He just got done with prison, and he can't be locked up no more. No tellin' what he might do . . ." Darrell's voice trailed off. She heard a muffled sound, a choked sob.

"Tell me what happened," she said gently.

There was a half second of silence on the line. Then: "Somebody shot Clifford Willow. Police say Richard done it, 'cause it happened over at the construction site where he's been workin'."

Vicky knew the site—a two-block apartment complex on the west side of town. A developer by the name of Stephen Jeffries—she'd heard he was from Los Angeles—had moved to Lander, bought a number of vacant lots, and seemed intent on covering every one of them with buildings. Not everybody liked the idea, but no one could deny that the man had created dozens of much-needed jobs.

"Police jumped to conclusions, all of 'em wrong," Darrell was saying. "Arapaho gets hisself shot. Another Arapaho must've done it. But ever since Richard got outta prison, he seen Willow was leading him down a bad road. He got off them drugs and started a new life. Been goin' to work every day, learning how to be a carpenter. No way he shot that no-good Indian. He don't even own a gun."

A picture had begun to form in Vicky's mind. Clifford Willow sought out Richard at the construction site and they got into an argument over— who knew what? Richard had a violent temper. He whipped out a gun that his father didn't know about and shot the man. But if that were true . . . The picture shifted, like pieces of glass in a kaleidoscope. Why would Richard shoot him at the construction site, where he might come under suspicion? Richard Running Bull might be a hothead, but he wasn't stupid. And he didn't want to go back to prison.

"You gotta get Richard out of jail," Darrell said, his voice tense with fear and hope.

"I'll go see him," Vicky said before hanging up the phone. First she intended to find out what evidence the police had against him.

The skeleton of the apartment complex rose into the steel-gray sky, like an ancient ruin on the plains. Workers in blue jeans, plaid shirts, and hard hats darted among the posts and half walls, shouts mingling with banging hammers and screeching saws. Vicky peered through the Bronco's windshield, trying to spot Detective Bob Eberhart. The desk sergeant at the Lander police headquarters had said she'd find him at the construction site.

She slowed past the pickups along the curb, past the silver trailer that looked dull under a trace of morning dew. Black letters above the door spelled Office. On she drove down the second block. Sounds faded and pickups gave way to three black-and-white police cars at the curb. Yellow tape enclosed a section at the end of the block. She parked behind the last police car and made her way across the hard-churned dirt, loose nails and scrap wood strewn about. Beyond the tape two policemen in dark blue uniforms guided metal detectors over the ground, shoulders stooped to the task.

She spotted Eberhart and another uniformed officer in the shadow of a framed alcove. The detective was a slight man in dark slacks and a tweed sport coat that hung loosely from thin shoulders. As she stepped across the tape, he glanced up and started toward her. "Don't think your legal magic's gonna get Running Bull out of this mess," he said.

"What do you have?" Vicky ignored the comment.

"Your client called Clifford Willow and arranged to meet him here"— a glance at the alcove—"at six thirty last evening. He was looking to buy some cocaine, which Willow was looking to sell. We've been watching Willow. Had a tap on his phone. I had a car over here at six thirty sharp, but Willow had already been shot. A couple workmen flagged down the police car. Said they saw Richard Running Bull leaning over a body. We picked him up just as he was getting in his truck."

Vicky felt her stomach muscles clench. Despite what his father had said, Richard was still using drugs. And the police had a phone tap. Witnesses. "What about the weapon?" She braced herself for the answer.

"Expect we'll find it soon enough." Eberhart nodded toward the policemen with the metal detectors. "Richard shot Willow over by that pile of boards." Another nod. "Soon's he realized somebody saw him, he made a beeline for the truck." The detective raised one hand and traced the direction of Richard's supposed flight. "He stashed the gun right here somewhere. Dropped it in a hole, stuck it under some lumber. Might take a few hours, but we'll find it. Expect we'll find a bag of coke in the same place."

"Wait a minute," Vicky said. "Are you saying you didn't find the gun or any drugs on Richard?"

The detective nodded. "Correct."

"No drugs on Clifford Willow's body?"

"We wouldn't still be lookin' for 'em, now would we?"

"What if Richard didn't make the buy?" Vicky said, marshaling her thoughts. "What if Willow was already dead when Richard got here, and somebody else had taken the cocaine?"

"Nice theory." Eberhart was shaking his head. "I'm willing to bet this badge here"—he patted the pocket of the tweed sport coat—"that soon's we locate the gun, we'll find a baggie of coke. Richard ditched them fast. He would've come back for them later."

Suddenly the officer snapped to attention and stepped out of the alcove. "Mr. Jeffries," he called.

Vicky glanced around. A tall man in blue jeans and a brown corduroy jacket strode toward them, boots kicking up clouds of dust. The long, narrow face, the brown hair flattened along the top of his head, the flashing evil eyes: the man in her dream. Vicky felt her mouth go dry, her breath form a hard rock in her chest. She staggered backward, struggling to find purchase in the chunks of dirt and scraps of wood, stealing herself against the force of evil drawing closer.

"How much longer you gonna keep this area shut down?" The man's voice boomed. "I got fifty men on the payroll sitting on their asses. I'm losin' a lot of money here."

"Sorry, Mr. Jeffries." There was the hint of deference in the officer's tone. "We're still looking for evidence."

Jeffries snorted, then raised a fleshy hand and began patting his nose. He sniffed several times. "What the hell more you need? You got the guy that shot that Indian. I can't afford to pay a bunch of men for not workin'." He was stomping back and forth now, punching both fists into the air.

Eberhart took a couple of steps forward and put out one hand in a gesture of peace. As soon as they found the gun, he began—cajoling, assuring—they would release the area.

Vicky stared at the man. The hair and eyes, the dust billowing around—she had seen it all in her dream. With a certainty that froze her in place, she knew that Stephen Jeffries had killed Clifford Willow.

"You got everything fixed?" Richard Running Bull rose from behind the metal table in the visiting room at the Fremont County jail. He was half a head taller than she was, with a thick chest and muscles that rippled beneath his blue denim shirt. His black hair was parted in the middle and caught in two braids that hung down the front of the shirt. He was about thirty, she knew, but he stared at her out of the solemn eyes of a man twice his age.

"Hello to you, too," Vicky said. She knew he expected her to walk in with a ticket for his release, but it wasn't going to be that easy. The metal door slammed behind her, a low thud that reverberated through the windowless room.

Richard's expression slid from understanding to panic. "I been locked up all night. You gotta get me outta here." He crashed one fist down onto the table. The peaks of his knuckles showed white through his dark skin.

"Sit down, Richard." Vicky nodded toward the chair he had just vacated. She sat across from him and extracted a pen and legal pad from her briefcase. "Let's start at the beginning."

The Indian dropped slowly onto his chair, shoulders hunched, head forward, as if he were about to launch himself out of the room. "They got it all wrong," he said. "I just knocked off work yesterday when these two clowns in uniforms showed up and slapped on the cuffs. Said I shot some Indian named Clifford Willow. Hell"—both hands flew into the air—"I don't know any Clifford Willow."

Vicky locked eyes a long moment with the man. He was lying. An innocent man did not lie. Last night's dream had overcome her ability to think rationally. She shoveled the pad and pen back into the briefcase, rose from the chair, and started for the door. In an instant, Richard Running Bull was around the table, blocking her way. "Where the hell you going?"

Vicky stepped past him, and he grabbed her arm. "I said, where you think you're going?"

"Take your hand off me." Vicky wheeled toward him. They both knew the guard was just outside the door.

Richard let his hand drop. "You got to help me," he pleaded.

"I can't help somebody who lies to me. I want the truth from my client. I want you to tell me about the call you made to Clifford Willow, about the drug buy you set up for yesterday." The Indian flinched, as if she'd slapped him. A look of resignation came into his eyes. He turned and sank onto the chair. "All right," he said.

Vicky resumed her own seat. She retrieved the notepad and pen as he began explaining. He used to hang around with Willow, a long time ago. He gave a little shrug, as if it weren't important. The two of them—well, the truth was, they did drugs together. A little marijuana. Some coke. No dealing. That was Clifford's bag, not his. Just using once in a while, when he got stressed out, when he needed to party a little.

"What happened yesterday?" On the pad, Vicky wrote: *Willow sold drugs.*

The man drew in a long breath. His eyes travelled to a corner of the small room before resting again on hers. "I've been real stressed out lately. The boss, Jeffries, wants more work done every day. Walks around the site shoutin' and yellin'. 'Speed up, speed up. I'm not paying you guys to sit on your asses.' Fact is, he hasn't paid anybody for two weeks. Says his money's all tied up. Says he'll pay us next week. Only reason I been staying around is to get what's owed me."

Vicky wrote down: *Jeffries—money problems*. She said, "So you called Willow."

Richard stared at her a moment, as if weighing his options. "Yeah, I called him. I been clean three months now, and where's it gettin' me? Workin' for a crazy man and not gettin' paid. Willow was supposed to meet me over by the alcove after work, but he didn't show. I waited five, ten minutes. I was heading for my truck when I seen him over by a pile of boards. Geez, there was blood everywhere. I got outta there fast. I was just about to get in my truck when the cops showed up."

He leaned toward her; the black braids drooped along the table. "I swear I didn't shoot him. I don't even own a gun."

Vicky was quiet a moment. Then: "Did Willow know Jeffries?"

Richard blinked and leaned back in his chair. "Yeah, I seen 'em together a couple of times at the site."

Vicky put her things back into her briefcase and got to her feet. She started explaining: He'd had the misfortune to be arrested Friday evening. The initial court appearance wouldn't be until Monday.

Richard had started to get up. He sank back against the chair and put one fist to his mouth. She knew that he knew he would spend the weekend in jail.

She said, "I'll do what I can." A hollow promise, she realized, when he had admitted setting up the drug buy. But he didn't kill Willow. The trouble was, she had no idea how to prove it.

Vicky drove north on the reservation. The foothills of the Wind River Mountains raced by outside her window, a blur of pine trees and scrub brush. Beyond the passenger window, the plains ran brown and humpbacked into the horizon. Every mile or so a small frame house appeared on the landscape, as if it had dropped from the sky. Slowing the Bronco, Vicky swung into a dirt driveway and stopped in front of a white bi-level.

Everything seemed familiar. The dirt yard with a truck parked at the edge, the sheets and towels flapping on the clothesline, the hollow rap on the front door and the footsteps hurrying inside, the feel of Grandmother Ninni's arms gathering her in.

Vicky sat across from the old woman at a small table wedged under the kitchen window. Pale daylight slanted over the walls as she sipped at the mug of tea and told Grandmother Ninni about her dream: A man she had never seen before coming toward her through clouds of dust. The evil in his eyes. She kept coming back to the overwhelming sense of evil. "He's a murderer," she said. "But there's no evidence, and Richard Running Bull is going to be charged with the murder."

The old woman ran one finger around the rim of her mug, as if she were testing the ridge of a tanned hide to which she meant to sew a beaded design. She said, "You must pay attention to what the earth is telling you about this evil man, granddaughter."

Vicky waited as Grandmother Ninni took a sip from her mug. Then she went on, her voice so quiet that Vicky had to lean forward to catch the words. "The earth is angry. It erupts in clouds of dust. You must ask yourself what has made the earth angry."

Vicky gasped. In her mind's eye, as if in a dream, she saw Stephen Jeffries at the site, sniffing and pawing at his nose, striding up and down, shouting, punching the air. A man on cocaine. He'd been getting his supply from Willow—Richard said he'd seen the two men together at the site. He had taken the coke, and then shot the man. And he had hidden the gun in the earth. Stephen Jeffries had defiled the sacred earth.

Vicky clamped down on the gas pedal. The speedometer needle jumped to eighty as she sped south, diving in and out of the black shadows that drifted down the foothills. She slowed at the outskirts of Lander and threaded her way around the trucks and 4x4s on Main Street. A sharp right, then another right, and she was parking in front of the stone building that housed the Lander Police Department.

She found Eberhart in a small office halfway down the corridor, hunched over a desk piled high with papers. "What do you know about Stephen Jeffries?" she said, dropping onto a metal chair.

The detective pushed back in his chair and shot her a puzzled look. "Jeffries," he said. The pencil in his hand beat out an impatient rhythm on the edge of the desk: tap, tap tap. "Newcomer to these parts. Brought a lot of jobs to the area."

"He was high on cocaine this morning."

Eberhart gave a burst of laughter and flipped the pencil across the desk. "The man's always like that."

"Always shouting and stomping around. Always impatient."

"You'd be impatient if we shut down part of your operation."

"He's a man with a drug problem, Bob. And a money problem. He hasn't paid his workers in two weeks. My bet is, the money's gone to cocaine."

"As soon as we find the weapon . . ."

"It's not where you think it is," Vicky interrupted. "Jeffries hid it."

Eberhart raised one hand in protest, but she hurried on. "He saw Willow at the site. He followed him to the alcove, probably figuring he had drugs on him. They had some kind of argument, and Jeffries shot him. He ran off before Richard showed up."

The look of comprehension crept into the detective's eyes, and Vicky wondered how much he already knew. She said, "Jeffries bought drugs from Willow in the past, didn't he? You were tapping Willow's phone."

Eberhart blew out a long breath. "There's nothing to connect him and Jeffries, but . . ." He hesitated. "There was one call from a pay phone a couple nights ago. Some guy begging Willow for cocaine. Willow told him no more until he'd paid what he owed him."

Silence fell over the small office like a dense cloud. After a moment, Vicky said, "I know how to find the gun."

*   *   *

The street was deserted when Vicky parked in front of the silver trailer. A thin light glowed through the front windows. Beyond the trailer, the construction site was quiet, the framed walls and piles of lumber elongating into dark shadows. It was almost six. Jeffries could have left. She could be too late.

As she hurried up the wooden planks that formed the sidewalk, a voice broke through the dead quiet: "I don't want any more excuses." He was still here! She took a deep breath and knocked at the door.

It swung open. Jeffries threw her a glance before turning back to the desk and shouting into the phone clasped at his ear, "You get the framing finished up next week, you hear me? You'll get your money then." He slammed down the phone and, sniffing a couple of times, allowed his gaze to travel over her. "Didn't I see you out on the site this morning?"

"I'm Vicky Holden." She forced herself inside. The trailer was filled with evil, a presence as real as the large, brown-haired man behind the desk. She could hear her own heart beating. "I represent Richard Running Bull," she managed.

The man's eyes bored into her. "What can I do for you, Madame Attorney?"

"Richard needs this job. You'll take him back, won't you?"

"Take him back?" Jeffries let out a long whistle. "That's gonna be kinda hard, with him locked up in prison the rest of his life."

Vicky forced a smile. "I see you haven't heard."

"Heard what?" A wary look came into his eyes.

"The police found the murder weapon today. It wasn't near the alcove where they'd expected to find it, and Richard didn't have time to hide it anywhere else. He'll be released soon and . . ." She allowed the information to float between them. "No doubt the police will arrest the real killer."

The man was quiet. Vicky watched for the slightest twitch of a muscle, the flick of an eyelid. There was nothing. She said, "What about the job?"

"Why not?" Jeffries pinched the tip of his nose between two fingers. "He gets himself out of jail, he's got a job."

Vicky thanked him and backed out the door, pulling it shut behind her. She could feel his eyes on her through the window as she stepped along the planks and slid into the Bronco. She drove a half block and parked behind a Dumpster. There were no police cars about, no sign of anyone, yet Eberhart had said he'd send some officers. For a sickening moment, she wondered if the detective had only pretended to believe her theory.

She let herself out of the Bronco and started across the construction site, picking her way by the light filtering from the streetlamps, past the half walls and the piles of boards, until she had a clear view of the trailer. The front door opened. Jeffries stepped into the doorway, a dark figure backlit by the dim glow inside. He cast his eyes about, making sure the way was clear. Then he stepped out and started toward her. Vicky felt her heart turn over. She pulled back into the shadows and held her breath as he passed. He was so close she could have reached out and touched him.

She watched him head across the site, boots kicking at the wood scraps and bent nails, at the earth, and at the dust rising, rising. And then he was lost in a forest of posts and shadows. She hesitated a moment, half expecting a police car to pull into the curb. Then she started after him, trying not to stumble over the loose boards.

She spotted him leaning over a large wooden box. Metal clanked against metal as he pulled out a shovel. He took several steps to the right—counting the steps, she thought—then veered left a few more steps before he rammed the shovel into the earth and tossed some dirt to the side. Dust rose around him and hung in the faint light.

Suddenly Jeffries jerked about and squinted into the dust. Vicky stood still, praying that the shadows would hide her. Satisfied, he tossed the shovel aside, fell onto his knees, and began pawing at the earth with both hands.

Still no sign of the police. Where were the police? Vicky moved behind a post, her eyes still on the man. In another second he would have the gun. He would dispose of it somewhere, and no one would ever find it.

Jeffries was on his feet. In his hand was a small, dark object. He swung around and started toward her. She had the sickening realization that she'd waited too long, that she was trapped. There was nowhere to run.

The man was coming closer. He saw her now. The brown eyes bored into her with a look of pure malevolence. Slowly he raised his arm and pointed the small object at her. She was frozen in place, her breath stopped in her throat, just as in her dream. The earth shuddered beneath her feet. And then she heard the crunch of footsteps approaching from the side.

"Drop the gun, Jeffries." Eberhart's voice reverberated off the framed walls. Jeffries swung around then let the gun fall to the earth. In a moment, the detective and two officers were surrounding him, clamping on handcuffs, reading him his rights. "You're under arrest for the murder of Clifford Willow," the detective said.

Vicky stepped from behind the post. "I thought you'd never get here," she said to the detective.

"Bitch," Jeffries hissed. In the glare he shot her, Vicky felt the force of the man's evil, but she no longer felt afraid. The dust had settled, the air was clear. She could see beyond the shadows to the light glowing over the street. The earth was strong beneath her feet.

Murder on the Denver Express

"Looks like you got yourself some high-toned traveling companions, Mol," Daniel said.

Molly Brown followed her brother's gaze across the platform of the Leadville depot. The Denver Express stood on the near track, steam belching along the coach and the first-class cars. A plume of gray smoke, dense and ash-scented, cut through the cold morning air. Passengers surged around the conductor at the foot of the steps.

Molly knew it wasn't the miners in bulky coats and slouch hats or the women struggling to hold on to squirming children that her brother was referring to. It was the pair of elderly women starting up the steps, heads aloft under wide-brimmed hats, gloved hands daintily lifting the skirts of their traveling coats, and the handsome middle-aged couple, both swathed in long gray coats, who followed the women into the first-class car.

"You're gonna have yourself a real boring trip," Daniel went on in that teasing voice that had made her pummel him with her tiny fists when they were growing up. "If you wasn't so high-toned yourself, Mol, you'd be ridin' in the coach where you'd have a good visit with some real folks."

"The likes of yourself, I suppose." Molly laid a gloved hand on her favorite brother's arm and tried to ignore the cloud of gloom that always settled over her at the conclusion of each visit home. Leadville still felt like home. The narrow, sloped-roof houses, wagons rattling through the streets, whistles shrieking from mines carved into the mountains above town, miners bellowing outside the saloons day and night—all welcome and familiar, unlike the quiet around her new home on Denver's Pennsylvania Street.

She and J.J. had lived in Denver two years now, since the summer of 1894, after J.J. struck gold in the Little Jonny Mine. The strike had surprised everyone, with the exception of J.J. Leadville was a silver town. Even after the silver market collapsed—plunging Colorado's millionaires into bankruptcy—most mining engineers had clung to the belief that Leadville's mountains would disgorge only silver—not gold. But J.J. had believed otherwise, a happy circumstance that had made the Browns rich beyond imagining.

"Why, there's Charles Langford," Molly said, her attention diverted to the tall, dark-haired gentleman in the chinchilla coat striding alongside the train.

Daniel's expression took on that blank look that always appeared when she had leapt ahead. "President of the Denver Western Bank," she explained. "Must've come to Leadville on business. I saw him yesterday, too, outside the Vendome Hotel." She blinked back the image of Langford darting around the corner of Harrison Avenue. Most likely, he hadn't seen her.

Daniel looked away, but not before she had caught the disappointment shadowing his eyes. "You and J.J. sure got a lot of fancy new friends now," her brother said.

"Oh, I'm sure the Langfords and the Browns will soon be friends." Molly tried for a cheerful tone. "The Langfords live only a block away— on Logan Street. Yes, we're certain to become friends, and you'll surely meet them one day, too." She let her gaze roam over the platform, hoping to see Clarissa Langford. What a stroke of luck it would be to travel with a prominent member of Denver's Sacred 36. Why, she could convince Clarissa that the Browns had more than a gold mine to recommend them to society. After all, J.J. was a brilliant mining engineer. And she had read dozens of books and was learning to speak French.

Molly sighed. Clarissa Langford was nowhere in sight.

As the locomotive emitted a series of shrill whistles, the depot door flew open and two women hurried across the platform. They couldn't have been more than eighteen or nineteen, Molly realized, nearly a decade younger than her. Obviously young women with their own living to get: the black cloaks neatly brushed and patched, the worn, polished boots, the everyday struggle to appear respectable.

For the briefest moment, Molly caught the eye of the smaller woman as she hurried by. She had a pale, delicately shaped face, almost like a child's, and long golden hair that fell around the folds of her hood. She carried a brown canvas grip, holding it ahead of her in both hands. The cloak swung open to reveal a dress as blue as the Leadville sky.

The taller girl had pulled her hood forward around a mass of dark hair. She allowed her companion to board while she stood at the foot of the steps, glancing up and down the platform, eyes wide in fright. Finally she followed the other girl into the coach car.

Molly noticed the round-shouldered man in the red plaid coat standing in the depot doorway, his gaze trailing the two young women. He was hatless, black hair slicked back from a fleshy, mottled face with the gray pallor of a man who had spent too many days underground. He flipped aside a cigarette and started for the train.

"All aboard," the conductor shouted. Molly planted a kiss on Daniel's cheek. No doubt he was right, but she would take a vow of silence before she would give him the satisfaction of hearing her admit that she was in for a boring trip in the first-class car.

The conductor doffed his blue cap as she approached the train. "Welcome aboard, Mrs. Brown."

* * *

Molly tossed aside the small red-leather copy of *Easy Lessons in French Grammar.* She glanced at the silver watch pinned to the bodice of her black traveling dress. Four more hours to Denver. The oil lantern swayed overhead and the sounds of wheels on rails filled the private compartment— clickety-clack, clickety-clack. In the distance, brakes squealed, a whistle bleated. The little station at the top of Kenosha Pass slid by the window, and the train started on the downgrade, winding along a narrow ledge blasted out of the mountainside. Far below a mosaic of sunlight and shadow lay over South Park.

She had been cooped up in the small compartment now for almost six hours, except for the twenty-minute stopover in Como, where she had disembarked and gone to the Pacific Hotel dining room for a slice of apple pie and a cup of coffee. None of the other first-class passengers had left the train. Obviously they were content being cooped up in small compartments.

"What the hell," Molly said out loud, startled by the sound of her own voice. Perhaps there were rules for a lady traveling alone, but sometimes rules had to be broken. She decided to visit the coach car and find some real folks to talk to. She withdrew a silver compact from her pocketbook and dabbed at her cheeks with the powder puff. Tiny laugh lines fanned from the corners of her eyes, which were the blue of morning glories. She patted back the red curls that sprang around her face and fixed them into place with ivory combs. Then she slid the compact back into her pocketbook.

As she started to her feet, the train banked into a curve, swaying on the outside rail toward the mountain drop-off. The lantern swung wildly on its chain. Molly grasped the window bar to keep from being pitched to the floor. She froze, disbelieving her own eyes. Outside, a girl was soaring over the ledge, face turned heavenward, blue dress and long, golden hair flowing in space. In a half instant, she was gone, a bird swooping into the shadows far below.

Molly pressed herself against the cold windowpane. She could hear her heart drumming. "Saints preserve us," she whispered. Either the girl had jumped from the train backward—a notion Molly dismissed as ridiculous—or someone had flung her from the train.

Molly crossed the compartment and threw open the door. "Conductor!" she shouted. From somewhere came the sharp, unmistakable snap of a door closing.

She hurried along the corridor, shouting again for the conductor. As she stepped into the gangway, the rush of cold air whipped at her skirt and plucked her hair loose from the ivory combs. The floor bucked beneath her feet. With a kind of horror, Molly realized she was leaning against the railing over which the poor girl must have been thrown.

"Conductor!" Molly shouted again as she plunged into the coach car. The odors of damp wool, cigar smoke, and sausage filled the air. Heads snapped around, eyes stared at her. The man in the red plaid coat leaned over his armrest and framed her in his gaze. "'Spect you'll find the conductor back with the fine folks," he said.

She swung around and retraced her steps into the first-class car, shouting again and again for the conductor. The door at the far end creaked open, and the elderly women appeared around the frame and stared at her over tiny wire-rimmed glasses perched halfway down their noses. Another door opened. The man in the gray suit stepped out, blocking her way. "What's the meaning of this disturbance?" he demanded.

"A girl's been murdered," Molly said. Her frankness surprised her. She hadn't wanted to admit what she knew must be true: no one could survive being hurled from the train over the steep mountainside. The two elderly women darted back inside their compartment.

"Ridiculous," the man said. "This is a first-class car." Molly felt the pressure of a hand on her arm. "Allow me to be of assistance, Mrs. Brown." It was a man's voice, low and close to her ear.

Molly pivoted about and stared up at Charles Langford, who lifted his chin, as if, with a snap of his fingers, he might banish the cause of her alarm. He was boyishly handsome, with a long, patrician nose, deeply set brown eyes, and sand-colored hair parted in the middle above a high forehead that gave him the look of intelligence. "Whatever is the matter?" he asked.

"A girl was thrown from the train." Molly heard her words tumbling together. Her breath came in quick, sharp jabs that pricked her chest like needles.

"You saw it?" Langford's forehead creased in thought.

"Yes," Molly said. "Well, not exactly. But I saw the girl flying over the ledge. We must stop the train."

"You mustn't concern yourself further, Mrs. Brown," Langford said in a low tone, meant to soothe her. "I'll notify the conductor. You can return to your compartment now."

"Please do so," said the man in gray. "And allow us to complete our trip without further disturbance."

Molly felt a sting of anger and disappointment. "You don't understand." She kept her eyes on Langford. "The girl may still be alive." She doubted that was the case. "We have to go back."

"Now, now, Mrs. Brown." Langford took her arm again and began tugging her toward her own compartment. "The conductor will follow the proper procedures."

"The conductor! He's nowhere around. We have to stop now." Molly jerked herself free and started running along the corridor, eyes fastened on the small box tucked under the ceiling near the gangway door. A red handle protruded from the box, and underneath, black letters swayed with the train: Emergency Brake.

"No!" Langford shouted as Molly reached up and pulled on the handle with all of her strength. The handle snapped downward.

A loud screech ripped through the sounds of the whistle and the blasts of steam coming from the locomotive. The train began to contract and reassemble, swaying sideways, jerking forward and back again. Metal squealed against metal; wood groaned and snapped. Molly huddled against the window as the two men stumbled against her, and then righted themselves. Somewhere a woman was screaming. Gradually the train came to a stop, and the sounds gave way to the shrill blasts of the whistle.

The gangway door crashed open, sending a burst of cold air into the corridor. The conductor stood in the opening, his mouth forming words that appeared to be stuck in his throat. "What . . . What . . . What . . ." he stuttered. "What have you done?" He threw both hands into the air.

"This woman is mad." It was the voice of the man in the gray suit.

"I'm so sorry," Langford said. "I tried to prevent this."

Molly grabbed the lapels of the conductor's blue coat. "A girl was thrown off the train at the big curve. We must back up and find her."

"Back up?" The conductor stared at her with disbelief—she might as well have uttered an obscenity. His massive chest rose and fell as he took in great gulps of air. "That is impossible," he said, withdrawing a white handkerchief from inside his waistcoat and mopping at his face.

"Stout! Where are you?" The man's voice came from outside.

"My engineer," the conductor muttered. He stepped into the gangway, opened the gate, and started down, boots thumping on the steps. Molly followed. She hurried to keep up as they strode alongside the train. Tongues of steam flicked from the underside of the cars, but the wind stabbing at her face and hands was as cold as ice. A few feet away, the ledge dropped off into the chasm below.

The engineer came toward them clapping mittened hands together against the cold. He wore a padded coat buttoned to the neck and a slouch hat pulled low over his ears. "What's the meaning of this?" he yelled. "There's an extra freight coming behind us. If that engineer misses the warning flares I whistled out, we'll be knocked off the mountain."

The conductor tilted his head back toward Molly. "This woman says she saw a girl thrown off the train at the big curve," he said.

Molly stepped forward. "I am Mrs. J. J. Brown," she said, struggling to keep her voice steady in the cold. "I demand you back up and attend to the poor girl."

"J. J. Brown of Leadville?" A look of respect and admiration came into the engineer's eyes.

"Formerly of Leadville. We are wasting time, sir."

The engineer shook his head. "It is impossible to back up, Mrs. Brown. We'll telegraph the police from Pine Grove. Now we must proceed." He gave a little bow and started again for the locomotive.

"All aboard, all aboard," the conductor called as Molly followed him back through the knots of passengers who had also disembarked. Suddenly a chill unrelated to the cold ran down her spine. What had she done? Given the killer a chance to walk away? She stepped toward the ledge, eyes searching the track that stretched out from the train. No sign of anyone walking away. But where could the killer walk to? They were on a narrow ledge, high on a mountainside, miles from the nearest town. No, the killer would wait until they pulled into Pine Grove.

Molly caught up with the conductor. "There's a murderer on board," she said. "You must not allow anyone to leave the train. You must telegraph the Denver police to meet us."

"Madam, you will allow me to do my job." The conductor took her arm and turned her toward the steps where Charles Langford was waiting.

"I'll see Mrs. Brown on board," Langford said, looking back at the conductor. Then he guided Molly up the steps and into the first-class corridor. They stopped at the first door. The sound of three long whistles filled the air as the train started to lurch forward.

Molly said, "I saw the girl boarding in Leadville. She was with a traveling companion, a tall, dark-haired girl."

"A traveling companion." Langford seemed to turn the idea over in his mind a moment. "My dear Mrs. Brown, the authorities will look into the details of this unfortunate incident."

Molly studied the relaxed, confident face—the face of a man who understood a world into which she and J.J. had taken only the first tentative steps. There was so much to learn. Still . . . "It would seem a simple matter to find the companion and learn what she may know," she said.

A gentle smile spread across Langford's handsome face. "If, indeed, the girl was thrown from the train, as you insist, Mrs. Brown"—a slight hesitation—"she could hardly be one of our sort. I am certain Mr. Brown would not approve of your meddling in this matter. Unfortunately you are bereft of his wise guidance at this moment. As a gentleman, I must stand in for your good husband and shield you from your womanly inclinations." Langford opened the compartment door. "Allow me to fetch you a tonic for your nerves," he said, stepping past her. The compartment was almost a duplicate of hers; green plush seat, lantern swaying overhead as the train gathered speed. Stuffed in the overhead rack was the chinchilla coat.

"No need to put yourself to any further trouble." Molly had no intention of drinking something that might dull her senses. She wanted to make certain the conductor did not allow anyone to leave the train at Pine Grove.

"Nonsense. It's no trouble at all. You will find the tonic most soothing." The man had opened a black case on the seat and was pouring a ginger-colored liquid from a small crystal decanter into a glass. A pungent odor that Molly couldn't identify drifted across the compartment.

"Here you are," he said, holding out the glass. "This will help you recover from your shock. You have only to open your mouth."

"Undoubtedly some people on this train would prefer me with my mouth closed, Mr. Langford," Molly said, giving him a polite smile and starting toward her own compartment. Footsteps sounded behind her, and she realized he was following her.

Molly opened her door, then hesitated. A cold understanding flooded over her: the murdered girl's companion was also in danger. Molly had seen the anxious way the dark-haired girl had looked around the platform, as if she had wanted to make certain no one was following. Unfortunately the girl hadn't seen the man in the red plaid coat watching from the depot doorway.

Turning back to Langford, Molly said, "I'm sure someone was after the murdered girl. He must've gotten her in the gangway, where he threw her overboard. He may try to kill her companion to keep her from telling what she knows."

"My dear Mrs. Brown," Langford began, a condescending note in his tone, "you have a most vivid imagination. If you choose to pursue this matter, I must warn you that it will harm your reputation. No one whose name appears in the newspaper in connection with a scandal could expect an invitation to the Christmas dance at the Denver Country Club."

Molly backed into her compartment, closed the door, and leaned against the paneling, marveling at the proposition Charles Langford had made her. She had only to remain in her compartment until the train pulled into Denver Union Station, and an invitation to the Christmas dance would be hers. Hers and J.J.'s, although she knew the real challenge would lie in convincing J.J. to attend.

She closed her eyes and swayed in rhythm with the train, imagining herself in J.J.'s arms, gliding across the polished floor of the Denver Country Club, orchestral music filling the perfumed air, and all of the Sacred 36 admiring the gown she would have made for the occasion. She had waited two years for this invitation.

Her eyes snapped open. She could wait a while longer. The dark-haired girl was in danger now.

Molly flung open the door and hurried to the coach car. At the far end, a small group of miners waited outside the water closet. Other passengers sat upright, eyes ahead, as if on the lookout for the killer in their midst. Molly gripped the backs of the seats and pulled herself along the aisle, looking for the dark-haired girl. She stopped at the vacant seat across from the man in the red plaid coat. Tossed in the seat was a single black cloak, the fabric shiny and thin, a patch neatly stitched to the hood. She felt her heart turn over. The girl was gone.

Molly whirled toward the man across the aisle. "Where is the girl with dark hair?" she demanded.

The man moved his head from side to side as if to bring Molly into clearer focus. "Ain't you the lady that seen her get tossed off the train?" His voice had the scratchy texture of tobacco.

"You're mistaken." Molly held the man's gaze. "The blond girl in the blue dress was thrown from the train."

"Beggin' your pardon"—the man shook his head—"but the pretty one with the long yellow hair got off at Como." Shouts and hard thuds came from the front of the coach. Molly glanced around. Two miners were pounding on the water closet door. Turning away from the commotion, she said, "What makes you believe the blond woman disembarked at Como?"

"I got her grip down from the rack. Took it out to the platform myself." A wistful smile played at the corners of the man's mouth. "She was a pretty thing. I seen her in the depot. Don't mind saying I was looking forward to getting acquainted. Too bad she was only goin' as far as Como."

Molly tried to swallow back the alarm rising inside her. Obviously the man had concocted a story meant to exonerate himself: she had seen the girl flying over the ledge when the train was twenty miles beyond Como. And where was the dark-haired girl? Had he also tossed her from the train?

The shouts and pounding were louder, angrier. Looking around, Molly saw that the conductor had joined the group. She started toward him. "Mr. Stout," she called. "A girl is missing . . ."

"Please, Mrs. Brown." The conductor waved a hand in the air. "One emergency at a time." He turned and rapped on the door. "Open up," he shouted. "There's folks need the facilities."

Molly stared at the closed door. So that was where the dark-haired girl had gone to. She was hiding from a killer. Molly pushed through the crowd of miners and, ignoring the look of astonishment on the conductor's face, knocked hard on the door. "This is Mrs. J. J. Brown," she called. "I know what happened to your friend. No one is going to harm you. You can come out now."

The only sounds were those of the miners drawing in sharp breaths, the wheels rattling beneath the floor. Slowly the door slid open. The girl leaned against the frame, dark curls pressed around a pale face, both hands clasped under her chin. Her knuckles rose in little white peaks.

One of the miners sneered. "About time."

Molly placed an arm around the girl's thin shoulders and drew her forward. As she guided her past the men, Molly called back: "Mr. Stout, please join us in my compartment."

Laura Binkham sat at the far end of the plush seat, huddled against the window. Molly sat beside her, legs tucked sideways to make room for the conductor who leaned back against the compartment door, arms folded across his broad chest. The murdered girl—"A good girl, she was," Laura said—was Effie Rogers. "She never meant to go wrong, but after she was let go . . ." Laura sniffled and dabbed at her eyes with the handkerchief Molly had handed her.

"Let go?" Molly prodded.

"From the grand house where Effie was the second-floor girl. Times got hard after the silver crash. Lots of fancy people couldn't keep help like me and Effie anymore."

Molly pictured the fine mansions in Leadville, the army of former domestics searching for other employment after the silver market had crashed. Even she and J.J. had hit upon hard times, until J.J. had struck gold.

The girl went on: "I was the lucky one. My mistress kept me on at half wages. Leastwise I had a roof over my head. Not like Effie. She caught on at a shop on Harrison Avenue, but the wages wasn't enough to keep her. What choice did she have?" The girl pressed her lips together against the answer; light from the overhead lantern glinted in her dark eyes.

"Effie began entertaining gentlemen friends, is that it?" Molly was beginning to understand: one of the friends was the man in the red plaid coat—a man Effie had most likely rejected.

The conductor shifted from one foot to the other; his uniform made a scratchy sound against the door. "I hardly think any of this matters, Mrs. Brown."

"Please go on," Molly said to the girl.

"I told Effie, you gotta get hold of your gentleman."

"Gentleman?" The man in the red plaid coat was certainly not a gentleman.

"'Cause he's the one that . . ." Laura threw an embarrassed glance toward the conductor, then lowered her eyes. "When Effie was employed in his grand home . . ." Her voice faltered. "I told her, he's gotta help you out, your gentleman. He's gotta take care of you."

The picture was beginning to change, like tiny glass pieces in a kaleidoscope forming and reforming. Molly had misjudged the man in the red plaid coat. She wondered which of Leadville's millionaires had imposed himself on the second-floor girl.

"So Effie sent a telegram to Denver," the girl was saying.

"Denver? You said Effie worked in Leadville."

Laura nodded. "That's right. She come up there after she was let go."

"Did she tell you the gentleman's name?" Molly asked.

"Oh, no. Effie was very protective of his reputation. She always called him 'my gentleman.' And sure enough, he telegraphed her back. Said to meet him at the Vendome Hotel."

"The Vendome?" Molly felt the muscles in her chest contract. The compartment felt warm and close; it was difficult to breathe.

"That's right," Laura said. "Only he never showed up."

"I must return to my duties." The conductor withdrew a gold watch from his vest, snapped open the cover, and peered at the face. "We will pull into Pine Grove in exactly nine minutes."

"One moment, Mr. Stout." Molly patted the girl's hand. "Please continue."

"Well, the gentleman come to the shop and give Effie some money and a one-way ticket on the Denver Express. He says she was not to worry. He was gonna make things right with her in Denver. But she told me he was acting nervous, not like his old self. I think she was scared. So she asked me to come to Denver with her. You know, just 'til she seen everything was gonna be fine. My mistress give me two days off, and Effie used the gentleman's money to get me a round-trip ticket. Soon's the train pulled into Como, she pretended to get off, just like the gentleman told her. When it was all clear, she got back on and . . ."

"And went to Charles Langford's compartment," Molly said.

"I must protest." The conductor's tone was sharp with astonishment. "Surely, Mrs. Brown, you cannot believe this"—he waved toward the girl huddled beside the window—"this domestic's story has anything to do with a fine gentleman like Mr. Langford."

Molly got to her feet. "I suggest we check Mr. Langford's compartment. I believe the murdered girl's cloak and canvas bag are in the overhead, nicely hidden by a chinchilla coat."

The conductor hesitated, then squared his shoulders and threw open the door. Molly brushed past and led the way down the corridor. She knocked sharply on the first door.

After a moment, the door swung open and Charles Langford peered out, annoyance and concern mingling in the handsome face. His gaze shifted from Molly to the conductor. "Yes? What is it?" he asked.

Molly said, "I believe you have something that belongs to Effie Rogers."

Langford looked at her with unconcealed disdain. "I'm afraid your imagination has outrun my patience, Mrs. Brown," he said finally. He stepped back and started to close the door. The conductor rammed his shoulder against it, holding it open, and Molly slipped inside.

Langford faced the conductor. "If you do not remove this meddlesome woman from my compartment, I shall contact the president of this railroad and have you removed from your position."

"Mrs. Brown believes the dead woman's things are in this compartment," Stout said. "If that is untrue, we shall be on our way with my sincerest apologies."

Molly reached up to the rack and pulled down the chinchilla coat. It fell away in great, heavy folds, enveloping her arms and shoulders, the fur tickling at her nose. Her heart thumped against her ribs. The rack was empty. She looked around the small compartment. Nothing, except Langford's black case. He must have already thrown the cloak and canvas bag overboard.

And then she glimpsed the small rectangle of brown beneath the seat. She dropped to her knees and began tugging at the canvas bag.

"Leave that alone," Langford shouted. "It is none of your business."

Out of the corner of her eye, Molly saw the man rear over her, one fist in the air, and the conductor grab his arm. "Now, now, Mr. Langford. We will have no violence."

Molly pulled out the grip, trailing the shabby black cloak across the floor. Then she got to her feet and faced Langford. "Effie threatened to expose your treatment of her, isn't that true? So you came to Leadville with the purpose of murdering her."

Langford turned to the conductor. "I have no idea what this madwoman is raving about."

"Oh, I think you do, Mr. Langford," Stout said, still gripping the other man's arm.

Molly went on: "You couldn't take the chance of meeting Effie at the Vendome after you saw me leaving the lobby, so you decided to entice her to come to Denver and murder her on the train. It was your door that shut just after I saw the poor girl hurled over the ledge. You meant to throw her things overboard, too, but after I started shouting for the conductor, it was too risky for you to attempt to dispose of them. You planned to carry them off the train wrapped in your chinchilla coat. Your plan might have worked, Mr. Langford, if Effie hadn't brought along a companion who knew she did not get off at Como." Langford pulled his arm free and lurched toward the opened door, but Molly threw her weight against it, slamming it shut. The conductor wrapped both arms around the other man's chest and wrestled him onto the seat. Standing over him, he said, "You will remain locked in this compartment, Mr. Langford, for the duration of the trip."

"You'll regret this," Langford shouted, his long legs tangled in the chinchilla coat. "I will see that you never work for another railroad. And this horrible woman will never, never be accepted in society . . ." Suddenly the man doubled over, lowered his head, and began sobbing.

Stout ushered Molly into the corridor. From outside came the mournful sounds of brakes screeching and the locomotive whistling as the train jerked into a slower rhythm. Laura was holding onto the window bar muttering over and over, "He threw Effie off the train."

"He drugged her first, so Effie didn't know what happened." Molly spoke softly. She wondered what would have become of her had she taken the tonic Langford had offered.

Stout inserted a key into the lock and tried the knob. Satisfied, he turned to Molly. "I commend you, Mrs. Brown. The railroad company will honor you."

"Oh, no." Molly held out both hands in protest. "I wouldn't want publicity."

"I quite understand. You are a real lady, Mrs. Brown." The conductor smiled and gave her a little bow. Then he began backing toward the gangway. "We are coming into Pine Grove. I must telegraph the police. Be assured that they will meet the train in Denver."

A Well-Respected Man

The jangling noise grew louder, like a siren closing in from a far distance. Vicky Holden groped for the alarm clock on the nightstand and pressed the button. The noise continued. Struggling upright in the darkness, one elbow cradled in the pillow, she reached for the phone on the far side of the clock.

"Vicky, that you?" A man's voice, the words rushed and breathless. "Oh, man, I thought you wasn't there. They got me locked up in jail."

"Who is this?" Vicky said. She heard the sleepiness in her own voice. The luminous numbers on the clock showed 5:22.

"Leland Iron Wolf." Another rush of words. "You gotta get me outta here."

An image flashed into Vicky's mind: lanky frame, about six feet tall, cowboy hat pulled forward, shading the dark, steady eyes that took in the world on their own terms, thick black braids hanging down the front of a Western shirt. Leland was about twenty-five years old, the only grandson of Elton Iron Wolf, one of the Arapaho elders. The old man had raised the boy after his parents were killed in an accident. Vicky had never heard of Leland in any kind of trouble.

"What happened?" she asked, fully awake now.

Words tumbled over the line: The police on the Wind River Reservation arrested him an hour ago. He was still sleeping, and there they were outside, pounding on the front door. They turned him over to the sheriff, and next thing he knew, he was in the county jail.

Leland hesitated. Vicky heard the sound of incomprehension in the short, quick breaths at the other end of the line. Finally: "They think I shot the boss. Killed him. *Nohoko*."

Crazy indeed, Vicky thought. Killers did crazy things, but Leland Iron Wolf . . . He was not a killer. "Who was shot?" she asked.

"Jess Miller. My boss over at the Miller ranch. I got hired out there a couple months ago."

Vicky knew the place—a spread that ran into the foothills west of Lander. The same spread that Jess Miller's father and grandfather had worked. The family was well respected in the area. Over the years, they had occasionally hired an Arapaho ranch hand.

"What happened?" She was out of bed now, phone tucked under her chin as she switched on the light and began riffling through her clothes in the closet.

"How the hell do I know?" Impatience and desperation mingled in Leland's voice. "I rode in from doctoring calves and picked up my pay at the office in the barn. The boss was alive and kickin', his same old mean self when I left."

"What time was that?" Vicky persisted.

"About seven, almost dark. You gotta get me outta here, Vicky." The words sounded like a long wail.

Vicky understood. For an Arapaho accustomed to herding cattle on open ranges, warrior blood coursing through his veins, there was nothing worse than to be locked behind bars. It was death itself. "I'm on my way." She tossed the jacket and skirt of her navy blue suit onto the bed, then an ivory silk blouse. "Don't say anything until I get there—understand?"

"Hurry," Leland said.

Vicky pushed the disconnect button, then tapped in the numbers of the sheriff's office and asked for Mark Albert, the detective most likely handling the case. He picked up the phone on the first ring.

"This is Vicky Holden," she told him. "I'm representing Leland Iron Wolf."

"Figured you'd be the one calling." Sounds of rustling paper came over the line.

Vicky ignored the implication that only an Arapaho lawyer would take an Arapaho's case. She said, "What do you have?"

"Evidence Leland Iron Wolf murdered one of the county's prominent citizens."

"Have you questioned him?"

"We Mirandized him, counselor, and he said he was gonna call a lawyer." The words were laced with sarcasm.

Vicky drew in a long breath, struggling to keep her temper in check. "Give me the details."

"Donna Miller, that's the wife, found Jess's body in the barn last evening about eight o'clock. Shot in the chest, right in the heart, to be precise. Shotgun that killed him was dropped outside the barn."

Vicky said, "Leland left the ranch at seven."

"Mrs. Miller says otherwise." Vicky flinched at the peremptory tone. Mark Albert was a tough adversary. "The missus was in the kitchen around eight o'clock. Looked out the window and saw Leland going into the barn. Couple minutes later she heard a gunshot and ran outside. That's when she found her husband."

Vicky could feel the knot tightening in her stomach. *His same old mean self*, Leland had called his boss. She said, "What's the motive, Mark?"

"Oldest motive in the world. Cash." A little burst of laughter sounded over the line. "Jess Miller paid Leland in cash every Friday evening. Wife says Indian ranch hands always preferred cash to checks . . ." The unspoken idea hung in the quiet like a heavy weight: local bars prefer cash. "Besides," the detective hurried on, "that's probably the way of Jess's daddy, and his daddy before him. Old families have their own ways of doing things. Point is, the cash box is gone."

"A lot of people must have known about the cash," Vicky said.

Mark Albert didn't say anything for a moment. Then: "There's something else. We got some good prints off the shotgun. They look like Leland's. We'll have confirmation in a few hours."

Vicky stared out the bedroom window at the dawn glowing red and gold in the eastern sky. Prints. Motive. Opportunity. Mark Albert had them all, but that didn't mean Leland Iron Wolf was guilty. "When's the initial hearing?" she heard herself asking.

"One o'clock, county court."

"I want to talk to Leland right away."

"You know where to find him."

The metal security door slammed behind her as Vicky followed the blue-uniformed guard down the concrete hallway. A mixture of television noise, rap music, and ringing phones floated from the cell block at the far end of the hallway. Odors of detergent and stale coffee permeated the air. The guard unclipped a ring of keys from his belt, unlocked a metal door, and shoved it open. Vicky stepped into a small, windowless room. "Wait here," the guard ordered, closing the door.

Vicky dropped her briefcase on the table that took up most of the room. She shivered in the chill penetrating the pale green concrete walls. Leland had been locked up how many hours now—two? Three? He would be going crazy.

The door swung open. Leland stood in the doorway, eyes darting over the windowless walls, arms at his sides, hands clenched hard into fists. He had on a bright orange jumpsuit that looked a couple of sizes too large for his wiry frame. His black hair, shiny under the fluorescent ceiling light, was parted in the middle and caught in two braids that dropped down the front of the orange jumpsuit. He started into the room, shuffling, halting, glancing back.

Vicky held her breath, afraid he would turn around and hurl himself against the closed door. "Tell me what you know about Miller's death." She kept her voice calm, an effort to hold the young man in the present. She sat down and extracted a legal pad and pen from the briefcase.

Leland sank into the chair across from her. He was quiet a long moment, calling on something inside of him. Finally, he said, "Somebody shot him is all I know."

"He was alive when you left the ranch?"

Leland's head reared back. The ceiling light glinted in the dark eyes. "You don't believe me?"

"I had to ask." Silence hung between them a moment. "Where did you go?"

Leland shifted in the chair and shot a glance at the closed door. "Just drove around."

"Drove around?"

"I had some thinkin' to do."

Vicky waited. After a moment, Leland said, "I got the chance to manage a big spread down in Colorado. They need a real good, experienced cowboy, so a buddy of mine working there gave the owner my name. I gotta decide if I'm gonna leave . . ." He exhaled a long, shuddering breath. "Grandfather don't have nobody but me, and he don't have much money, you know. If I go down to Colorado, it's gonna be real hard on him."

Vicky swallowed back the lump rising in her throat. Leland had just confirmed the motive. With several thousand dollars, Elton Iron Wolf could get along for a while and Leland could move away. She pushed on: "Did you stop anywhere?"

The young man was shaking his head. "I think best when I'm just movin', you know." A glance at the walls looming around them. "I drove up to Dubois and back. Got home about ten."

Vicky made a note on the pad. *Dubois. No alibi.* She looked up. "Look, Leland." She was searching for the words to soften the blow. "I'm going to level with you. Mrs. Miller says she saw you going into the barn just before her husband was killed. The detective says your fingerprints are probably on the shotgun."

A mixture of surprise and disbelief came into the young man's face. "My prints are all over that shotgun. I took it out a couple days ago after some coyotes been killin' the calves."

"Who knew you used the gun?" Vicky persisted.

"The boss's kid, Buddy. He rode out with me. Got a real kick outta watching me pick off a coyote. Helps out on the ranch when school's out. Pretty good cowboy for fifteen years old."

"Any other ranch hands?"

Leland gave his head a quick shake. "That's it. Me and the boss and sometimes the kid. We pretty much took care of things. Boss didn't like a lotta people around, poking into his business was the way he put it. Him and his wife and those two kids, they liked their privacy."

"Two kids?"

"Boy's got a sister, Julie. She's fourteen. Real pretty little thing. See 'em comin' down the road together after the school bus let 'em off. Just the two of 'em, like they was each other's best friends. Good kids. Real quiet like their dad."

"You said Jess Miller was mean."

Leland nodded. "Yeah, he could be mean all right, if he didn't like the job you was doin'. About the only time he had much to say was if he wanted to lay you out. Rest of the time, he kept to hisself. Tended his own business."

Vicky could feel the jitters in her stomach: prominent rancher who minded his own business, close family, Indian ranch hand with fingerprints all over the murder weapon and a motive to help himself to the cash box. Selecting the words carefully, she said, "You may have to stay in jail awhile, Leland. Just until I can get to the bottom of this."

Leland blinked hard. "What're you gonna do?"

"You'll have to trust me," she said with as much confidence as she could muster.

*   *   *

The sounds of organ music resounded through the church as Vicky slipped into the back pew. Ranchers in cowboy shirts and blue jeans and businessmen filled the other pews. There were only a few women. Vicky recognized some of the mourners: the mayor was here, the chamber of commerce president, the owner of the steak house on Main Street, all friends of Jess Miller. She wondered if the murderer was among them. What had she expected to find by coming here? She was grasping, grasping for some way to clear Leland.

At the hearing yesterday, the county attorney had trotted out what he called *a preponderance of evidence*, and she had been left to argue that there was some other explanation. "I look forward to hearing it," the judge had said. Then he'd denied bail and remanded Leland to the county jail.

Vicky exhaled a long breath and turned her attention to the Miller family in the front pew: the small woman dressed in black, a black lace veil draping her head, the thin-shouldered boy with sandy hair, the dark-haired girl throwing nervous glances from side to side.

The organ music stopped abruptly, leaving only the hushed sounds of whispering and shifting in the pews. A minister in a white robe mounted the pulpit, eyes trained on the family below. He cleared his throat into the microphone and began a flat, perfunctory talk: fine man in our community, cut down in his prime, loving wife and children, devastated by death. The heavens cried out for justice.

After the service concluded, Vicky kept her place, watching the mourners file past the family, nodding, shaking hands. Suddenly the boy wrenched himself sideways, and Vicky noticed the gray-haired woman approaching him. She bent over the pew, trying to get his attention, but he kept his head averted, as if the woman were not there. She moved tentatively toward the girl, then the mother. Both kept their heads down, and finally the woman moved away. She reached into a large black bag and pulled out a white handkerchief, which she dabbed at her eyes as she exited through a side door.

Vicky hurried out the front entrance and made her way around the side of the church to the parking lot. The woman was about to lower herself into a brown sedan. "Excuse me," Vicky called, walking over.

The woman swung around, surprise and fear mingling in her expression. She pulled the car door toward her, as if to put a shield between her and the outside world.

"I didn't mean to startle you," Vicky said. "You must be a friend of the family."

The woman shot a nervous glance at the businessmen and cowboys filing toward the rows of cars and trucks in the lot. "I would say that family has few real friends," she said. "I came for the children." Slowly she reached a hand around the door. "Elizabeth Shubert. Lander High counselor."

"Vicky Holden." The other woman's hand was as smooth and cool as a sheet of paper. "I represent Leland Iron Wolf."

"I thought that might be the case." Elizabeth Shubert gave her head a slow shake. "I don't believe Leland is capable of murder."

"You know him?" Vicky heard the surprise in her voice.

"I knew him when he was at the high school. A fine boy."

"Mrs. Shubert . . ."

"Miss," the woman interrupted.

"Would you be willing to talk to me?"

The woman sank into the front seat and peered through the windshield. A line of vehicles waited to turn into the street. The hearse that had been parked in front of the church was pulling away. A black limousine followed, three heads bobbing in the backseat. "I shouldn't be talking to you," she said after a moment. "I must get back to school."

Vicky gripped the edge of the door to keep it from shutting. "Miss Shubert, Leland faces a first-degree murder charge. He's innocent." She hesitated. All she had was an instinct that this woman knew something. She plunged on. "Is there anything you can tell me, anything at all, that might help him?"

Elizabeth Shubert was quiet. She reached up and tucked a strand of gray hair into place, her eyes fixed on some point beyond the windshield. "Come to my house at four thirty." She gave the address. "White house on the corner. You can't miss it."

Vicky leaned into the bell next to the blue-painted door. From inside came a muffled sound, like the tingling of a xylophone, followed by hurried footsteps. The door flung open. Elizabeth Shubert stood back in the shadow of the front hallway, allowing her gaze to roam up and down the street. "Come in, come in," she said, in a hushed tone.

When they were seated in the living room, Vicky said, "I couldn't help but notice the way the family reacted as you extended your condolences."

Elizabeth Shubert picked up the flower-printed teapot on the table between them and poured the steaming brown liquid into two china cups. Handing a cup and saucer to Vicky, she said, "I'm sure they must blame me for . . . well, for what happened."

"For Jess Miller's murder?"

"Oh, no." The woman sat up straighter. One hand flew to her throat, and unadorned fingers began crinkling the collar of her white blouse. "For what happened before. You see, I was worried about Buddy and Julie. Whenever there's a precipitous drop in grades and a change in personality, well, naturally, you wish to inquire as to the reason."

Vicky shifted forward. She held the other woman's gaze. "When did this occur?"

"Well, it's not as if they were brilliant students, you understand." Elizabeth Shubert made a little clicking noise with her tongue. "Average, I would say. But they were going along as usual until recently. Several teachers reported they were both flunking classes."

"What about the personality change?"

"Well, not so much the boy." The woman rested her eyes on a corner of the living room for a moment. "Buddy's always been a loner. Tends to his own business. Perhaps he seemed a little more withdrawn and morose lately, but, frankly, I attributed that to the poor report. The change was in Julie. Such a quiet, nice girl until . . ."

Vicky waited, one hand wrapped around the china cup in her lap.

"It's hard to explain," the woman went on. "Julie became very outgoing, I would say. Yes, very aggressive and pushy. You could hear her shouting in the halls. She was distracting in class, giggling and cutting up and generally making a nuisance of herself. She was sent to my office four times in the last two weeks. Well, I thought it was just an adolescent phase." The woman leaned forward and set her cup and saucer on the table. The china made a little rattling noise. "It was more than that."

"How so?"

"The way she flaunted herself. Deliberately provocative, I would say. The tightest, shortest skirts, the lowest-cut tops, that sort of thing." The woman looked away again, and then brought her gaze back. "Believe me, girls can be very brazen these days, but this was not like Julie Miller. It was as if suddenly she had become someone else."

Vicky set her own cup and saucer on the table. "What did you do?"

"I'm not certain I did the right thing." The woman spoke slowly, remembering. "I called Mr. and Mrs. Miller last week and asked for a meeting. I was terribly concerned about the children, you see."

"Yes, of course. What did the parents say?"

"The parents? Well, Mrs. Miller said nothing. She remained silent through the entire meeting. She just sat there, never taking her eyes from her husband. He did all the talking. He was very upset. Accused me of violating their privacy. Said he would tend to his own children. If they were having problems, he would straighten them out, and I should stay out of their business. And that's not all." Elizabeth Shubert looked away again, pulling the memory out of a shadowed corner. "He threatened to bring a lawsuit against me."

"A lawsuit!" Vicky felt a jolt of surprise. "On what possible grounds? That you were concerned about his children?"

"That I had defamed his family." The woman gave a little shudder. "It was ridiculous, of course. But I don't mind telling you, it frightened me. I don't want any trouble with the school district. You see, I'm due to retire next year, and I'm a woman of modest means." She glanced around the living room: the worn sofa and chairs, the faded doilies on the armrests, the gold carpet crisscrossed with gray pathways. "Mr. Miller was a well-respected man, and he was very angry. Unfortunately, he must have thought Buddy had told me something because . . ."

She stopped. Her hands were now clasped into a tight ball in her lap. "Oh, dear." A tremor had come into her voice. "I shouldn't be telling you this. It's exactly what Mr. Miller warned me against. I have no proof of anything." She gripped the armrests and started to lift herself out of the chair, a motion of dismissal.

"Please, Elizabeth." Vicky moved to the edge of her own chair. "What happened to Buddy after the meeting?"

The woman sat back into the cushions. A muscle twitched along the rim of her jawline. Finally, she said: "Mr. Miller punished the boy."

"You mean, he beat him?" A coldness rippled along Vicky's spine. In her mind, she saw the widow and mother, head lowered under a black lace veil. A silent woman. Had she finally had enough? Had she finally decided to protect her children?

"I have no proof," Elizabeth Shubert was saying. "But the boy was absent for two days after the meeting. When he came back, he had a note from his mother saying he'd been home with a cold. But I didn't believe it, not for a minute."

"Did you report this to social services?"

Elizabeth Shubert was rubbing her hands together now. "I took the steps I believed necessary. I called Buddy into my office. I told him of my suspicions. He said his father was a fine man, that I shouldn't say bad things about him, that his father would sue me for defaming the family. He used almost the same words his father had used, and I remember thinking, this poor boy has been brainwashed. But I had no proof. Nothing. Nothing." The woman shook her head; moisture pooled at the corners of her eyes. "Oh, I know I should have reported my suspicions, but what good would it have done? Jess Miller was an upstanding citizen from a very old family. No one would have believed me."

Vicky didn't say anything. She was wondering if Donna Miller had reached the same conclusion: no one could stop her husband.

The woman was crying softly now. "Excuse me," she said, half stumbling to her feet. She disappeared through an alcove. In a moment she was back, blowing her nose into a white handkerchief.

Vicky got to her feet. "You must tell the sheriff what you've told me," she said.

"Oh, I did." An aggrieved note came into the woman's voice. "I called the sheriff the minute I heard about the murder. Not that it did any good." She gave a little shiver.

"What do you mean?"

"I'm sure Mrs. Miller and the children denied everything. They probably said I was a meddling old lady. That's why they rebuffed me today at the church."

"What if . . ." Vicky began, slowly giving voice to the shadowy idea at the back of her mind, "Donna Miller shot her husband to protect her children."

Elizabeth Shubert nodded. "That thought has been tormenting me."

Outside Vicky sat behind the wheel of her Bronco trying to arrange the pieces into a picture that made sense: well-respected man, perfect family with a cancer eating at its heart, mother who knew when Leland Iron Wolf would pick up his pay and who must have known he had recently used the shotgun. She could have waited until Leland drove off, and then gone to the barn, shot her husband—in the heart, Albert had said. She wore gloves, so Leland's prints were the only prints on the gun. After she had hidden the cash box, she had called the police. But who would believe it? Certainly not Mark Albert.

Vicky slammed one fist against the edge of the steering wheel. Leland Iron Wolf was about to spend the rest of his life in prison for a murder he didn't commit. He trusted her, and she had come up with nothing. Nothing but a sense of what could have happened, a vague and unprovable theory. She rammed the key into the ignition. The engine growled into life, and she pulled into the street, turned right, and headed west. She intended to pay a condolence call on the grieving family.

Vicky drove under the wooden gate with the letter M carved overhead. She passed the cars and trucks parked in front of the redbrick ranch house and stopped in the driveway that ran from the house to the barn. As she let herself out, she glanced about, then made her way to the front door.

"What do you want?" Donna Miller stood in the doorway, a small woman with sloped shoulders and sunken chest. She looked at Vicky out of red-rimmed eyes, the most notable feature in a narrow, plain face. Her hair was streaked with gray and brushed to one side, as if it had simply been put out of the way. She was still in the black dress she had worn to the church earlier. A hum of voices came from inside the house.

"I'd like to talk to you," Vicky said. She told the woman that she represented Leland Iron Wolf.

"I have nothing to say to you. I have guests." Donna Miller glanced over one shoulder at the knots of people floating past the entry. Vicky glimpsed Buddy and Julie standing together in the shadows near the staircase.

"I've spoken to Elizabeth Shubert," Vicky persisted.

"Elizabeth Shu . . ." The thin lips tightened on the name. "That woman has no right to . . ." Suddenly she moved backward. "Come in." As Vicky stepped inside, the woman nodded toward the door on the other side of the staircase. "We'll talk in there," she said. The boy and girl had disappeared.

The room was small, with a desk against one wall and two upholstered chairs pushed against the opposite wall. Thick, gauzy curtains at the window gave the air a grayish cast. Donna Miller closed the door and sank back against it. "I know the ugly rumors that woman has spread. The sheriff looked into them and found them completely false."

"Mrs. Miller," Vicky began, struggling against the sense of hopelessness rising inside her. What did she expect? That this woman would incriminate herself? She pushed on: "Leland Iron Wolf has been charged with a murder we both know he did not commit."

"I don't know what you're talking about." There was a rigid calmness to the woman. She stared at Vicky out of gray, blank eyes. "The sheriff has conducted a thorough investigation. He has arrested my husband's murderer."

"What kind of man was your husband?" Vicky asked, trying a different tack.

The woman blinked, as if she were trying to register the meaning of the question. "He was a very fine man. Ask anyone in the area. He was well respected." She tilted her head toward the closed door and the muffled sound of conversations coming from the main part of the house.

"What about your children?"

"My children? They're very well adjusted, ask anyone." Another tilt of the head toward the door. "They were fortunate to grow up on the ranch. They're very close. They never needed other friends. They had each other."

"How did your husband treat them?"

"What right do you have to ask these questions?" Donna Miller said, a shrillness in the tone that seemed to surprise her. She straightened herself against the door. "He was wonderful to the children, of course. He protected them. He protected all of us in our kingdom." One hand fluttered into the room. "He always called the ranch our kingdom where we could do things our own way." A waviness had come into her voice, a hint of tears. "We could live the way we wanted, with no outsiders telling us what we could do."

Vicky waited for the woman to go on, but Donna Miller had sunk into silence. At any moment, Vicky knew, the woman would tell her to leave. She took a chance. "He abused the children, didn't he? He beat your son. And your daughter?" Vicky caught her breath, a sharp lump in her chest. *Such a nice quiet girl. A complete change in personality.* "What did he do to your daughter, Mrs. Miller?"

"That woman has no right to speak such filth."

"You decided it had to end," Vicky said. "You wanted to protect your children."

"No!" The word came like a cry of agony from a lonely, faraway place. "Go away. Go away and leave us alone."

Suddenly the door swung open against the woman. She stumbled, off-balance, and Vicky grabbed her elbow, steadying her. Buddy stood in the doorway, a tall, gangly boy with light hair flopping over his forehead. Behind him was Julie in a tight, black dress with a neckline that dipped into the cleft of round, firm breasts. The boy reached back, grabbed his sister's hand, and pulled her into the room. Then he closed the door.

Turning to his mother, he said, "What's going on? I seen this lady talking to Miss Shubert in the church parking lot. Is she a cop?"

The mother shook her head. "This is Leland's lawyer. She's just getting ready to leave. You and Julie go on out and talk to people."

"Don't you worry, Mother. I'll take care of this. I'll protect you now, just like I told ya." The boy stepped forward, shielding both women. His eyes fixed on Vicky's. "That Indian killed my father and he's gonna get what's coming to him. You best be goin' now."

Vicky stared at the boy, the narrowed shoulders pulled square, the chin jutting forward in shaky confidence. She had it all wrong. It wasn't Donna Miller who had killed her husband, it was the son. Not until afterward, after the terrible deed had been done and Jess Miller lay dying in the barn office, did his wife summon the courage to protect her child. And now, she realized her only hope was that Buddy would insist upon protecting her.

"I know what happened, Buddy," she said, choosing the words carefully, threading a pathway for him to follow to a logical conclusion. "Your mother killed your father, didn't she?" A little cry of anguish came from the woman. Vicky pushed on. "She said she saw Leland going to the barn, but that's a lie. It was dark at eight o'clock, and I doubt there are lights between the house and barn. The sheriff is putting it all together. He's talked to Miss Shubert."

The woman was sobbing now, and Julie had dropped her face into both hands. Moisture seeped through the girl's slim fingers. The boy turned toward them. "Don't worry," he said again, a tremor in his voice. "I'll take care of you."

Slowly he turned back. He pushed back the hank of hair that had fallen forward. A vein pulsated in the center of his forehead. "Me, I could take it, 'cause I'm a man," he said. "But he was always hitting Mom, see, and she's just a little lady. Then he started . . ." He hesitated. His eyes went blank, as if he could no longer take in the reality. "He started hurting Julie, see. And no sheriff or social workers was gonna come out here and tell Jess Miller to stop. Nobody's gonna tell Jess Miller what he can do in his kingdom. That's what he always said. So I took the shotgun that ranch hand had shot off, and I put a stop to it."

Vicky felt a sharp pang of relief and with it, something else—a hot rush of anger that burned at her cheeks and constricted her throat. "All of you were willing to send an innocent man to jail for the rest of his life," she said, the words choked with rage. She backed to the desk and picked up the phone. "I'm going to call the sheriff's office."

She punched in the numbers. From somewhere in the house came the muffled voices of mourners, the clap of a door shutting. She listened to the electronic buzz of the phone ringing on Mark Albert's desk, her eyes on the family huddled together, shoulders touching, hands entwined. Everything suffused with sadness.

"Detective Albert." The voice boomed into her ear, jarring her back to herself.

"One moment," she said, barely controlling the tremble in her voice. She cupped one hand over the mouthpiece and, looking beyond the boy and girl, children yet, she caught the woman's eyes. "Mrs. Miller," she said, "you'll want to call a lawyer for your son."

The Man Who Thought He Was a Deer

She was so pretty.

Her coat was like gold, and sleek. Not the matted, dull coat of the other yearlings. He had been watching over her since the day she was born a year ago June, in the meadow up the mountain. Spindly legs and a little white rump that floated through the wild grasses. She'd moved with such grace and confidence that he'd started crying, despite himself. And he'd made her a promise: "No harm will come to you, pretty one. I'll look after you."

It was his job. Dennis Michael Lockett was his name, but that was in the human world, before he'd become a deer. And not just one of the herd roaming the wilderness of Mount Massive. He was the chief. He took care of the herd. Even the bucks—including the old one-horn that lost half a rack last rutting season—bowed to him. Literally bowed. Bent their front legs and swung their racks up and down. Oh, they understood he'd come into the wilderness to save them from the cruelty of humans. Men tramping up the mountain with guns to harvest the dear. Harvest! Even the word was cruel.

A rifle shot sounded in the distance. Pretty didn't move, but Dennis caught sight of the tremor running along her flank and down her legs. She was waiting for him in the trees up above, head crooked back, brown, patient eyes beckoning him forward. He adjusted his rifle in the sling that he'd buckled over his orange jacket and started climbing. A snowy sky poked through the tops of the spruce trees. He had to duck past the branches covered with last night's snow, his breath floating ahead in gray puffs. He picked his way through the ice-crusted undergrowth so that the scrunching noise wouldn't alarm her.

Maybe she'd let him touch her this time. Pat her back, scratch her ears a little, let her know everything was gonna be fine. He bet she'd like that.

He was close enough to make out the drops of moisture on her coat. Just as he reached for her, she bolted, swinging her head and running for the meadow beyond the trees. She ran like a dancer, high on her toes, gliding around the branches. The pleasure in watching her almost eclipsed the stab of disappointment he'd felt when she'd turned away.

Another rifle shot cracked the air. Dennis held his breath, trying to gauge the distance by the reverberations. Close. His heart felt as heavy as lead. The hunter was coming for his herd. And Pretty—where was she? In the meadow? There were no trees in the meadow, no protection.

Dennis started running up the slope, crashing through the branches that tore at his jacket and scratched his face. He darted out of the trees and into the meadow. The wild grasses rose out of the ground like stalks of ice. Looming overhead were the barren, snow-dusted peaks of Mount Massive. Pretty stood about thirty feet away, her little head lifted toward the dark figure crouched in the outcropping at the far edge of the meadow. The hunter's orange hat bobbed over the boulders.

Dennis sprinted toward Pretty, waving his arms overhead so that the hunter would see him—an orange streak through the meadow.

"Mine! Mine!" he shouted. "Don't shoot."

The rifle shot almost knocked him off his feet. He staggered sideways before regaining his balance. Then he waved his orange cap toward the boulders, shouting and crying, "No! No!"

But it was too late. Pretty was down, her golden body sunk into the grass. He could see the depression, like a grave. He stumbled forward, then dropped onto his hands and knees and crawled to her. She lay on her side, left leg twitching, brown eyes—so sad now—staring at him. He watched her heart thump against the shiny coat a couple times, and then she was still, her eyes frozen and dull. He ran his hand over her flank. Her coat was so soft, it made him weep.

After a moment, he wiped at the moisture on his cheeks with his jacket sleeve and pushed himself to his feet. The killer was crouched in front of the boulders, shoulders and head jutting toward the meadow, as though he couldn't understand why another hunter had claimed his kill. The fluorescent orange jacket and orange cowboy hat shimmered in the flat, gray light.

Dennis reached back, unsnapped the sling, and pulled out his rifle, not taking his eyes off the killer. He brought the orange vest into the crosshairs before his finger squeezed the icy metal trigger.

Holy shit! Mickey Hoffman dove backward and clambered into the boulders. The bullet had whooshed past him like a rocket. His shoulder was burning. He took off his glove and dipped his fingers into the warm stickiness of his own blood. Then he pressed himself against the rough granite surface, unable to stop shaking.

The crack of another shot reverberated around him, bouncing off the trees and boulders. Just his luck to run into some crazy coot. How'd he know another hunter was stalking that little deer? He hadn't seen the guy until he came bounding out of the trees, yelling and hollering. Wonder the deer didn't take off. But she was his kill. So the other hunter was pissed off, so what? He was willing to share the meat.

"Hold on," Mickey shouted. "Let's parley."

The guy fired off another shot. Pieces of granite, sharp as needles, exploded in Mickey's face. What the hell? His heart knocked against his ribs. He had to get out of here before the crazy coot killed him.

There was another shot, then another. He started crawling through the boulders. His truck was in the trees about twenty feet away. He'd have to make a run for it, but the coot would pick him off for sure. Crouching low, he worked his way out of his jacket, then took off his cowboy hat and rolled them together, fiddling with the jacket snaps until he had a floppy basketball, which he threw as hard as he could across the boulders, away from the trees. He sprinted for the truck. The sound of the rifle shot shook the ground under his boots.

He threw his rifle into the cab and, wincing with the pain in his shoulder, jumped in after it. He stomped on the accelerator and headed into a narrow tunnel of trees before turning away from the meadow. The truck bounced over the scraggly brush and up onto the dirt road, tires squealing, rear end slipping on the hard, icy ground. The campsite was five miles away. He hadn't spotted any other vehicles parked in the area. Chances were good the crazy coot was on foot.

Mickey drove with one hand, and clamped the other over his shoulder. The blood oozed through his fingers.

He drew in a long breath. He was safe.

Dennis clambered over the boulders and stared at the pickup bouncing down the mountain, belching black smoke from the tailpipe. The mixture of grief and anger that boiled inside him was so strong he had to hold on to the edge of a boulder to steady himself. Distracting the hunter was the oldest trick in the book, and he'd fallen for it. Even the old bucks knew the trick, but Pretty—she hadn't been on the earth long enough to know how to survive. He should have protected her.

He knew where the killer was going. All them killers stayed at Halfmoon campsite. Five miles down the winding, narrow jeep road. Two miles, the way the crow flies. He could run down the mountain like a deer. He'd be waiting when the killer pulled in.

*   *   *

Deputy sheriff Shelly Maginnis knocked on the front door of the two-story Victorian house on West Seventh Street in Leadville. Strips of brown wood poked through the faded yellow paint on the facade. The once-blue trim around the windows was almost white. She glanced around. Black clouds drifted down the slopes of Mount Massive, west of town. There was a cold bite in the air. It would snow again today. It always snowed in October in deer-hunting season.

She knocked again, wondering what was taking Mrs. Lockett so long to respond. The woman had called the sheriff's department thirty minutes ago. Sheriff Nichols himself had spoken with her, then planted himself in the doorway and surveyed the empty desks in the outer office. The other two deputies were already out on calls. She was the only one free.

"Maginnis," he'd shouted. "Get over to Marybelle Lockett's place. See what the hell's going on with Dennis. Don't know why his mother don't put that boy in an institution. Gonna be the death of her, if he don't kill somebody else first." He'd paused at that, then disappeared back into his office.

Shelly didn't mind taking the call. She'd known Dennis Lockett all her life. Went to school with him, until Dennis dropped out of Leadville High somewhere around tenth grade. Sure, he was an oddball, but who wasn't these days? She'd have a talk with Mrs. Lockett, then talk with Dennis and see what was bothering him. In any case, it felt good to get out of the office. She'd been cooped up indoors with paperwork for two weeks while the other deputies had taken the calls. It wasn't just that she was the only woman: she refused to believe that had anything to do with it. She was the greenhorn, that was all. She still had a lot to learn.

She pounded on the door and pressed her face against the oblong block of beveled glass to one side. The blurred figure of Mrs. Lockett emerged from the kitchen in back and headed into the living room. A second passed before the door creaked open. The woman wasn't much older than fifty, Shelly guessed, but she looked ancient, with deep furrows in her brow and eyes red-rimmed from crying. Her gray hair was pinned back, except for a strand that had worked loose and fallen over her cheek.

She said, "You gotta help my boy."

Shelly followed the woman into the tidy living room with an Oriental rug spread over the wood floor and crocheted doilies on the high-backed Victorian chairs. The air was close and stale, like the air in a museum.

"What's going on?" Shelly waited until the woman dropped into one of the chairs before she sat down across from her.

"Every time hunting season comes around," the woman began, "Dennis gets himself into a tizzy. No telling what he might get up to. You gotta bring him home, Shelly, where I can look after him."

"Where is he?"

"Staying in that old prospector's cabin on Emerald Lake."

Shelly could picture the place. Kids in Leadville grew up hiking in the mountains around town. They knew all the prospectors' cabins and abandoned mine shafts and wagon roads left behind from the time when silver and gold had flowed out of the mountains like molten rivers.

"Haven't seen my boy in two weeks now," Mrs. Lockett went on. "I been taking his food up to the cabin every couple days, but he ain't there. Oh, I know what he's up to." She was wringing her hands in her lap. "He's out with the deer herd."

"Hunting?" Shelly heard the surprise in her voice. Dennis was always a sensitive kid, the perfect target for the other boys to bully. She couldn't imagine Dennis hunting.

The woman leaned so far forward, Shelly thought for an instant that she would tumble out of her chair. "My boy don't go hunting deer. He *is* a deer."

"What!"

"I'm trying to tell you, Shelly, that Dennis thinks he's a deer. He's got himself a human body, but inside, he says, he's a deer. He says it's his job to protect the rest of the herd up on Mount Massive 'cause he's got advantages. He knows all about people. So he wears an orange hunting jacket and cap and goes out with the herd, thinking the hunters'll see him and won't shoot."

"Dennis'll get himself shot by accident."

The woman flinched, and Shelly regretted having blurted out the thought. She would have to learn to keep her thoughts to herself.

Mrs. Lockett drew herself upright, as if she were drawing on some invisible reserve of strength. "I guess he's safe enough with his orange on," she said. "It's them hunters I'm worried about. They come after Dennis's herd, he's likely gonna shoot 'em. You gotta find him before he kills somebody."

Shelly got to her feet. She could see the campers and pickups that had been crawling through town all week, rifles locked in frames across the rear windows. Dozens of hunters heading into the mountains to harvest deer. And waiting for them was a crazy man with a rifle.

"I'll see what I can do," she managed.

She'd started for the door when the older woman propelled herself out of her chair. "Wait a minute," she said, heading toward the kitchen.

After a moment, she returned and handed Shelly a bulky brown bag. "Will you take this here food up to my boy?" she said. "Some bread, vegetables, fruits, nuts. Deer don't eat meat, you know."

"*Deer don't eat meat*?" Shelly repeated the words out loud as she drove south through town on Highway 24. Hard to tell who was crazier, Mrs. Lockett or Dennis. At any rate, Dennis was the one with the rifle, and she was going to have to find him before he killed somebody.

She was halfway to Emerald Lake on the two-lane road that wound around the base of Mount Massive—too far out of town, she hoped, for the sheriff to call her back—before she picked up the radio and called the office. When she had Sheriff Nichols on the line, she told him what Mrs. Lockett had said.

"Soon's they get in, I'll send Ellis or Moore after Dennis," the sheriff said.

"I'm twenty minutes from the cabin." Shelly steeled herself for the reply.

"Damnit, Shelly. The man's dangerous."

"I've known Dennis for years." A man who thought he was a deer? She didn't know him at all. "I'll be okay," she heard herself saying.

"Stay in contact. Oh, and Shelly. You got orange with you?"

Shelly glanced around at the supply kit in the back. "Yeah."

"You put it on, hear?"

Shelly drove the Bronco up what passed for a road, the engine screaming in low gear, tires crawling over the rocks and slipping on the ice. Last night's snow glistened on the branches of the spruce and alpine fir that clawed at the sides of the Bronco. The rock-strewn slopes and shadows of the forest rose on both sides of the road. She had a sense of the mountain itself closing in upon her.

She'd come around a wide bend when she spotted the logs piled across the road ahead. Dennis. He didn't want hunters in the wilderness. She shook her head at the futility: he couldn't block all the roads.

Shelly parked with the front bumper up close to the logs and got out. The snow blowing off the trees felt like ice pelting her face, and the wind pressed her uniform against her skin. Shivering, she pulled on the orange vest over her jacket, glad for the extra layer of clothing. Then she put on the orange cap.

A rifle shot cracked the cold air, followed by another and another. She stared at her own rifle locked in the frame inside the Bronco, debating whether to take it. She had her revolver; she was suddenly conscious of the weight of the gun on her hip. But a revolver in the mountains with the far distances . . .

She unclipped the rifle from the frame, grabbed the bag of food, and headed up the road. The ground was hard with the cold and snow; the pine needles crackled under her boots. After about a half mile, the road veered to the right. She turned left into the forest and started climbing the steep slope. The air was filled with the odors of dense undergrowth and fallen, rotted trees. As she ducked past the branches, snow showered down on her. Icy flakes stuck inside her collar and dripped down her back.

She was breathing hard when she reached the top of the slope. Beyond the tree line, the lake lay quiet and gray under the heavy sky. In the clearing, close to the shore, was the cabin, a lopsided wreck of old logs topped with a rusted tin roof. The place probably hadn't changed much since the day the prospector had walked away a hundred years ago.

"Dennis!" Shelly called. She stayed back in the trees, her eyes searching the cabin and the clearing. No sign of anyone.

Hoisting the rifle, she hurried across the clearing to the cabin and pushed open the door. A column of gray light fell over the bunk against the far wall. In the center were a chair and a table of sorts that consisted of a plank on two upright logs. A dark jacket hung off a hook on the log wall, and next to the jacket was a rack of guns. The top space was empty.

Shelly set the bag of food on the plank table and went back outside. Silence, except for the wind in the trees and the distant crack of a rifle. She looked around, half expecting to spot Dennis lurking about somewhere. She could make out the faint mark of her own boot prints in the snow, and, beyond the cabin, leading back into the trees, another set of boot prints, as clear as if Dennis had left her a map.

She fingered the radio on her belt, debating whether to check in with the office, and then decided to wait. Dennis had probably heard her approaching and was hiding nearby. She wouldn't have any trouble finding him.

She started following the boot prints. For the most part, they moved in a straight line through the trees, but here and there, they doubled back, and then shot ahead again, as if Dennis wasn't sure where he wanted to go. Shelly crouched low, not taking her eyes from the trail. It was easy to get disoriented in the mountains; it happened to hunters all the time, and it was the sheriff's deputies who had to go out and find them.

She could see the boot prints running ahead into a meadow. And there were other prints now: small bisected marks of deer hooves. The meadow was a good hunting place, she thought. Close to the lake, plenty of wild grass. And the hunters had a clear shot from the trees and rock outcroppings around the periphery.

Shelly stopped at the edge of the trees. She could hear her heart thudding in her ears. The meadow was almost a perfect circle, quiet and peaceful, layered with ice that glinted like glass. On the opposite side was an outcropping of granite boulders, and rising over the meadow, the brown, snow-washed shoulders of Mount Massive. The meadow was no place for a human being in hunting season; no place for a man who thought he was a deer.

When she was certain there was no movement around the periphery, Shelly started forward, glad for the orange vest and the too-big orange cap that flopped over her ears.

"Dennis! Where are you?" she shouted. The grass was trampled, as if he'd been running, hitting the earth hard, but he was nowhere in sight.

Then she saw the brown hump. She moved closer. Somebody had harvested a deer: a young doe, probably a yearling, stretched on its side, thin legs frozen in the air, brown eyes staring into nothingness. Odd, she thought. Hunters didn't walk away from the kill. They cleaned the carcass and took the meat.

Dennis had found the animal, probably knelt down, judging by the depressions in the grass. And there was something else: the glint of a gray metal cartridge. She scooped it up and rolled it around her palm. A rifle cartridge. She spotted two more cartridges, which she dropped into her vest pocket with the first. Then she started following the tracks across the meadow, glancing about as she walked. Her skin felt prickly; the rifle a dead weight in her hand.

She reached the outcropping on the far side and made her way around the boulders, losing Dennis' trail, and then picking it up again in the snow. There were other boot prints; hard to tell which belonged to Dennis and which belonged to . . . a hunter? As she came out on the far edge of the outcropping, she spotted the blood-spattered boulder.

"What the hell happened up here?" she said out loud, startled by the sound of her voice in the quiet. She clambered back up onto a boulder and peered around the area. A vehicle had been parked in the trees. She could see the depression made by the tires.

A picture started moving in her mind, like an old film, jumpy and black-spotted, cutting off and starting up again. You had to pay attention to make sense out of it, but it was all there, in front of her. Dennis had found the doe in the meadow and had shot at the hunter. The cartridges were from Dennis's rifle. The hunter had been hit, but he'd gotten to his truck and driven away.

And—the film rolling to the climax now—Dennis had gone after him. Which meant he knew where the hunter was headed. Halfmoon campsite, where most of the hunters in the Mount Massive wilderness stayed.

The hunter was wounded, she reminded herself. If he had any sense, he'd drive straight down to town and find a doctor. But she knew hunters; knew the type. He'd want to collect his camping gear. He'd figure he had plenty of time: he had a vehicle and Dennis was on foot. But Dennis knew every inch of the mountain. He'd head straight downslope, and when the hunter drove into the campground, Dennis would be waiting.

Shelly grabbed her radio and pressed the cold plastic against her face. "Deputy Maginnis here," she shouted into the mouthpiece.

"Where the hell are you?" The sheriff's voice crackled back at her.

She gave her position and told him what she'd learned. "I'm on my way to Halfmoon," she said.

"Negative. Get back . . ."

Shelly cut off. She stared at the inert plastic in her hand, and then clipped it onto her belt. It clanked next to her handcuffs. Mrs. Lockett's voice sounded in her head, as sharp as if the woman were next to her: *You gotta find him before he kills somebody.*

The rifle shot jolted the truck, sending it swerving across the campground. Mickey fought the steering wheel for control and tapped on the brake, finally bringing the truck to a stop next to the fire pit. Another shot crashed through the windshield.

Mickey rammed down the door handle and slid onto the ground, hunkering close to the front tire. He peered around. There was an orange flash in the trees on the north edge of the camp. He spit out the wad of acid that had welled up in his mouth. How the hell did that crazy coot get there so fast?

Mickey gripped his wounded shoulder—it was numb now, and stiff—his eyes following the orange in the trees. Should've gone straight down to Leadville, he told himself. Now he was facing off with a nutcase, nobody else in shouting distance.

Okay. He drew in a long breath; the cold air burned in his chest. He'd faced worse in Nam, gooks in front and gooks in back firing away at him. He'd taken a couple slugs in the gut that made the shoulder graze look like a splinter. He was a survivor.

"Come and get me, you bastard," he shouted at the orange weaving back and forth.

"Why'd you kill Pretty?"

Hello, looney tunes! The guy's voice was as high-pitched as a girl's, and real shaky, like he was scared shitless. Scared killers. In Nam, they were the most dangerous.

"She ain't dead, you fool," Mickey shouted. "Look over there on the right. She done followed you."

A half second was all he needed. The orange jacket hesitated, and then swerved to the right. Mickey reached up, grabbed his rifle out of the front seat, and ran into the trees on the left.

The orange vest had turned around. Mickey saw the rifle come up. Another shot fractured the air between them. A cloud of dust and snow swirled around the front of the truck, and one of the wheels sank into the ground.

"That's right," Mickey said under his breath. "You think you got me pinned by the truck. Come on, bastard. Come on."

The coot stepped out of the trees, hesitated, and then started walking at a diagonal from Mickey, the rifle trained on the truck.

Mickey lifted his own rifle and sighted in the orange vest.

The rifle shots thudded through the trees.

Shelly was running full out down the slope, gripping the rifle in both hands, crashing through the branches and scrub brush. She could see Dennis standing in the middle of the campsite, arms raised into the sky, eyes wide with surprise, like those of a deer suddenly aware he was in the hunter's crosshairs.

A rifle lay at his boots.

She stopped running. Her chest felt like it was going to explode. Someone else—a man—was crouched in the clump of trees directly below, a rifle pointed at Dennis.

"Drop the gun!" Shelly shouted. "Sheriff's officers!" She reached down for a dead branch and threw it as hard as she could to the man's left, desperate to make it seem that there were others, that she wasn't alone.

"We got you covered," she yelled, working her way down the slope.

The man didn't move. His rifle was still on Dennis.

Shelly lifted her own rifle and fired into the air. She scrambled backward with the recoil.

"Set the gun on the ground," she yelled. She was about fifteen feet behind the man. He knew—she could see it in the drop of his shoulders— that she was close enough to blast a hole in his back. He set the gun down.

"Kick the guns to the side, both of you. Do it now!"

The man stuck out his boot and gave the rifle a shove.

"Harder!"

He shoved the rifle again. It was more than an arm's length away.

Dennis was reaching down. "Don't touch the gun!" she shouted. "Kick it away."

"Shelly! That you?"

"Do like I say, Dennis, or we're gonna have to shoot you." Her heart was hammering. There was no *we*.

Dennis prodded the rifle with his boot, then sent it skimming over the ground. "He's a killer, Shelly."

Shelly walked down and picked up the other hunter's gun. She could see the blood-matted spot on the shoulder of the tan jacket. Stepping back, she shoved the gun into the scrub brush.

"I got a right to defend myself," the man said. "Guy's crazy. Shot me up at the meadow."

"Shut up and get down on your stomach," Shelly said, trying to keep her own fear out of her voice. "Face into the dirt." She waited while the man flattened himself around the brush and rocks. Who would believe it? she was thinking. She'd run to the campsite to save some hunter, and now it looked like she'd saved Dennis. She had no idea who the hunter was, but she knew Dennis. She had to take a chance on what she knew.

"Get over here, Dennis," she shouted.

He started walking up the slope, his hands shaking at his sides, as if they'd come unstuck from his arms.

"He killed Pretty." It sounded like a whimper.

"I know."

"I was just gonna punish him."

"You can't take the law into your own hands, Dennis. You know that."

"I got a license to kill that damn deer." There was a hard resolve in the hunter's voice. He was dangerous.

"Scoot yourself over to the truck," Shelly said.

"You alone, ain't you, lady."

"I got this." Shelly fired the rifle again. "Do like I say, or the next shot's for you."

The man started pulling himself forward on one elbow, dragging his wounded shoulder, digging the toes of his boots into the ground. His stomach bumped over the rocks. Finally he lay still next to the truck.

Shelly unhooked the handcuffs from her belt and tossed them to Dennis. "Get a cuff on his left wrist," she said.

Dennis stared at the cuffs as if they were fireworks about to explode in his face.

"Do it, Dennis."

He started shuffling toward the truck, and Shelly moved closer to the man stomach-down on the ground. "One wrong move, cowboy," she said, "and you're a dead man."

Dennis leaned over and clamped on the handcuff.

Shelly said, "Raise your left arm alongside the truck, cowboy."

He started to turn on his wounded shoulder, winced, and dropped his forehead on the ground. Slowly, his left arm started scrabbling up the side of the truck. "You're gonna pay for this." He spit out the words. "I gotta get to the hospital."

"Okay, Dennis," Shelly said. "Cuff him to the door handle."

Dennis looked around, like a deer about to bolt.

"You can do it, Dennis."

Dennis stood frozen in place.

"Come on." Shelly motioned to him with the rifle. "I don't wanna have to shoot both of you."

"For Crissakes," the hunter shouted. He raised himself up on his knees and snapped the other cuff to the door handle. "You happy now? Get this nutcase's rifle before he kills you and me both."

The hunter was right. Dennis' eyes were sliding toward the rifle about fifteen feet away.

"On the ground, Dennis," she said.

"I ain't gonna hurt you, Shelly." Dennis did a half turn toward the gun. She could sense his muscles coiled for the sprint.

"I know that. Your mother sent me up to find you."

"Huh?" He swung toward her.

"Sit over there." She nodded toward a large rock and held her breath. If he went to the rock, she could get between him and his rifle. "Your mother's been real worried about you."

Dennis rolled his head around, as if he expected his mother to walk out of the trees. "She don't understand."

"I understand. You're a deer now."

The man handcuffed to the truck let out a loud guffaw. "What is this, Disneyland?"

Dennis looked as if his legs had started to melt beneath him. He stumbled backward, grabbed for the rock, and dropped down.

"How'd you know?" he said.

"Your mother said something about it." Shelly moved sideways to the rifle. She picked it up, then walked over to the trees and pushed the gun into the shadows, out of sight.

Still keeping her own rifle on Dennis, she fumbled for the radio and called the sheriff.

"Damnit, Maginnis." The sheriff's voice burst through the static. "What's going on?"

"I'm at Halfmoon," she said. "I've got Dennis and another guy covered. They're both disarmed. Could use some backup about now."

"Ellis and Moore are on the way. You gonna be able to hang on?"

"Looks like it." Yes, she could hang on, she was thinking. Everything under control. She heard the sound of her own breathing—slow and regular.

She shut off the radio and smiled at Dennis.

"Tell me about Pretty," she said.

Santorini

Maddie looked gorgeous. Standing in the narrow doorway to my suite, diamond sparkling on the hand that gripped the doorknob, silk dress as blue-green as the Aegean, and silver, high-heeled shoe tapping out my baby sister's impatience. "We mustn't keep the captain waiting, Jules," she said, tossing out the nickname she'd come up with when we were kids, knowing it always made my blood boil.

"Julia," I said, correcting her for the millionth time.

Maddie shrugged and headed down the corridor, leaving the door ajar. I took another look in the mirror, adjusted a piece of copper-colored hair that refused to stay in place, patted a little more powder over the freckles on my nose, and shook my head at the black, go-everywhere dress I'd packed for the elegant evening at the captain's table, which I'd predicted even before we'd booked the expensive cruise through the Greek Isles.

I'd had to do some fast talking to get Maddie to agree. "Think of the sympathy factor," I'd told her. "Wealthy young widow grieving over the untimely, tragic death of her husband, cruising the Greek Isles in search of forgetfulness."

"Just how do you propose we pay for the cruise?" Maddie had flashed her checkbook at me. She hadn't totaled the balance since Norton died, but I did a quick calculation in my head. About fifty-seven thousand dollars, her entire inheritance after the bank canceled the credit cards and she pawned the diamond rings, bracelets, and other jewelry that Norton had given her, and cleaned out the cash that he'd stashed in a bedroom safe. It was enough to play the role of wealthy widow for a while.

"Rich men do not take cheap cruises," I reminded her. "How else do you expect to meet another man like Norton?"

That's when I also reminded her that we had to make certain the next so-called rich man had real money, unlike Norton, who turned out to have a bank account of three hundred thousand, about a tenth of what we'd expected, and about a million dollars' worth of debt. I was at the lawyer's office when he gave Maddie the bad news. She'd almost slid off the leather chair, and I'd had to hold on to my own armrests to keep from sliding with her. We'd had to help each other to the elevator. When we'd gotten to the house in Palos Verdes, which the bank took possession of three days later, I fixed us each a gin and tonic. Then fixed three more. Maddie had gulped hers down in between jags of crying and cursing as it dawned on her that Maddie and Julia were just as broke as when they'd been hustling drinks in the bar at Redondo Beach, gazing up at the big houses tucked into the hills in the distance, sun glinting off the windows that faced the ocean, and swearing that, damnit, there had to be a way to get up there.

Well, we figured we'd found the way. Thad Norton. All two-hundred-and-fifty pounds of fat and bluster, flashing a thick wallet around the bar, buying drinks for the surfers and the tanned, bleached-blond bimbos that crowded into the booths as soon as the sun set, and who partied until we had to sweep them out at closing. Buying drinks for everybody, that was Norton, with his big house and flashy Mercedes, bragging about how he'd made piles of money in the dot-com business, forgetting to mention how he'd lost 99 percent of it, and all the time, not taking his beady, hungry eyes off Maddie.

Maddie was different from the other bimbos in the bar. She had class. She looked like she came from somewhere, not the shithole we actually came from. Norton saw that right away. He was always saying, "What's a beautiful lady like you doing in this dump?"

Maybe Maddie had the class and the looks, but I had the brains. We made a good pair. We'd looked out for each other since we were kids. That is, I looked out for Maddie. I was the one that kept Mom's current boyfriend off her when he was drunk. Pulled her out of the way when Mom went into one of her flying rages. Convinced Maddie when we were fourteen and sixteen that we could make it on our own.

And I was the one that said, *Maddie, all you have to do is get Norton to marry you and we'll be living in his big house up in the hills.* There were a few days when even the prospect of the big house and the credit cards and shopping on Rodeo Drive and all the other stuff we thought Norton could afford didn't stop Maddie from rolling her eyes every time I brought up the subject. It wasn't until I mentioned that she would make a beautiful widow that she got the idea. A beautiful, rich widow.

I gave myself a last go-over in the mirror, wishing that I had half of Maddie's looks, then stepped into the corridor. Maddie was about to swing around the banister and start down the wide staircase, and I hurried to catch up. What an appearance she made, blond hair swept up and clipped into place with a comb that everyone would assume was banded in diamonds, the blue-green dress shimmering against the gentle swells of the Aegean as she strolled along the railing. There wasn't a man in the crowd outside the dining hall whose eyeballs weren't falling out.

Just as Captain Jelenik had run into a little eye trouble when we came aboard this morning. He'd made a beeline through the other passengers, white hat cocked forward, gold buttons about to pop off the white jacket that strained around his enormous stomach. He grabbed Maddie's hand, telling her how pleased—how very pleased—he was to meet her, holding on so long that another officer in a white uniform had finally urged her free of the captain's grasp.

"I give him fifteen minutes," I'd told her when we got to our adjoining suites on the upper deck. I was wrong. Ten minutes later the same officer was pounding on Maddie's door with an invitation for both of us to join the captain for dinner that evening. We were off to a good start. The richest, most important passengers would be at the captain's table on the first night out.

Maddie headed toward the carved double doors to the dining room, passing through the crowd of passengers like the Queen of England, nodding and smiling, with me two steps behind, like one of the royal attendants. The doors swung open, and another officer escorted us across the dining room. The subdued lighting danced over the white tablecloths with their bouquets of pink and white flowers, and shone in the silver and white china and the tall, crystal wineglasses. The knives and forks looked heavy enough to anchor the ship.

Captain Jelenik, in white uniform with gold buttons flashing, was weaving through the tables toward us. "So pleased you could join me this evening," he said, taking Maddie's hand again and throwing a half glance in my direction. The other officer peeled away, and the captain guided us to the knot of people standing around the large round table at the head of the dining room. I did a quick count: two balding men with their dumpy, thick-waisted wives, and a single man, at least six feet tall and handsome, with a broad forehead, hair as thick and black as the night, and dark, intense eyes, which were fastened on Maddie.

Captain Jelenik introduced us to Mr. and Mrs. Robertson, Mr. and Mrs. Shea, and, finally, to Peter Hainsworth from Philadelphia, who held Maddie's hand between his own for a long moment, saying how the captain had told him many fine things about Mrs. Thad Norton and how sorry he was to hear of her husband's death. At that, the double doors swept open and the other passengers plunged toward the tables, filling the dining hall with the buzz of voices and the scrape of footsteps on the carpet.

Maddie was seated to the captain's right, next to Peter Hainsworth, with both men vying for her attention through the hors d'oeuvres and salad, the filet mignon and pyramid of mashed potatoes, the crème brûlée and coffee that smelled as if the beans had been picked yesterday, and glass after glass of heavenly wine. I, on the other hand, was stuck between boring Mr. Robertson who went on and on about the flour mill he'd inherited from his grandfather and built into a multinational processed-food empire, while his wife nodded and grinned, and the even more boring Mr. Shea of the Shea Timber Company of northern Minnesota. Surely I had heard of the company. Who hasn't? I asked, giving the fool and his equally foolish wife my best smile, and all the time, keeping one eye on Maddie. Oh, yes. Maddie had Peter Hainsworth in the palm of her dainty, manicured hand.

"I've met Mr. Perfect." Maddie rushed past me and dropped onto the edge of the bed in my suite, crossed her shapely legs, and smoothed the front of the blue-green dress, which had most likely gotten mussed in saying her good-nights to Peter Hainsworth.

I closed the door and settled back into the chair at the desk. After dinner had ended and Maddie and Peter had excused themselves—Peter saying that the ship's orchestra was too good to miss on such a beautiful night—I managed to escape from the Robertsons and Sheas and even from Captain Jelenik, who'd obviously decided that he was striking out with Maddie and maybe her sister wasn't so bad. I'd headed for my laptop.

"Well, tell me all about him," I said, hoping Maddie had learned more than I'd managed to pull up on the Internet. My search for Peter Hainsworth had produced fifteen links, which meant that the man could be any one of fifteen different people, including Realtor, guitar player, expert on eating disorders, or athlete.

"He's rich. What else do we need to know?"

"How did he get his money?"

"The old-fashioned way, Jules. He inherited it, and now all he has to do is manage it." Maddie gave a little laugh and smoothed the blue-green silk over her lap. "Imagine having so much money that you have your own company to manage it."

"Company name?" I turned back to the laptop and curled my fingers over the keys.

"Schiff Investments."

"Schiff," I said, about to ask Maddie to spell it, then laughing at the idea of my sister spelling anything. I typed in what I thought might work. The laptop went through its gyrations, text appearing and disappearing, and finally the notice: no matches found. I tried another spelling. Still nothing, so I typed in, Private Investment Company. Now I had a screen full of names, but nothing that resembled Schiff.

"So he manages his investments." I turned to Maddie, who was leaning back on both elbows, swinging a silver high-heeled foot into the space between us. "That doesn't prove he's rich."

"Peter comes to the Greek Isles three or four times a year," Maddie offered. "I'd say that takes money."

Okay, she had me there. It took money, but the question was still how much money? I could see by the stars dancing in my sister's blue eyes that if Peter Hainsworth had a bank account big enough to pay the grocery bill, it would be enough for her.

I jumped up and went to her. "Listen," I said, slipping my arm around Maddie's shoulder. "Don't go falling for this bozo . . ."

"Bozo!" Maddie shrugged away and glared at me. "Peter's wonderful, Jules. He's handsome and smart. If he says he's rich, then he's rich. He wouldn't lie to me."

"You've known the man for like ten minutes."

"Long enough." Maddie pushed herself to her feet. "Trust me, Jules. I know what I'm talking about. When we dock tomorrow morning at Mykonos, Peter insists we spend the day together." Maddie pivoted around and started for the door.

"Wait a minute." I went after her. "Let's say you're right and Peter Hainsworth has money to burn. If you fall for him, all our plans go out the window. Even if you get him to marry you, he'll be the one in control of his fortune."

"Jules. Jules." Maddie was shaking her head. "All that worrying's gonna give you a lot of wrinkles. So what if I fall for him?" Maddie flung open the door. "I figure I'll have about three great months as Mrs. Peter Hainsworth . . ." She headed into the corridor and tossed the rest of it over one shoulder: "Before I'm a widow again."

Maddie and Peter spent all of their time together, strolling the narrow, steep alleyways of Mykonos, past the whitewashed houses gleaming in the sun, with the Aegean lapping at the beaches far below. I followed at a discreet distance, trying to fend off the Robertsons and Sheas and two or three men traveling alone, who, I suspect, had decided that the sister of Thad Norton's wealthy widow might also be floating on a sea of gold.

The next day we put in at Patmos, and the day after that, we were in Rhodes. It was always the same, following Maddie and Peter up and down the narrow streets that wound past arcades and courtyards to ancient churches and temples. Peter, handsome even in his walking shorts and open-neck shirts, and Maddie, turning everybody's head with her blond hair trailing down her back, the short shorts that showed off her long legs and slim hips, and the tight, sleeveless tee shirts. They would hold hands, then slip their arms around each other as they paused on the top of a steep hill to gaze across the sea at the dark smudge of another island rising between the water and the sky. Before returning to the ship, they would duck into a taverna where I would join them for a plate of meze and a glass of Greek wine. We'd sit on a balcony and watch the sun light up the sea like fire as it dropped below the horizon. Oh, Greece. What happy memories for a while.

In the evenings, while Maddie and Peter danced or walked along the decks, I hit the laptop and tried to confirm whatever new information Maddie had gathered. At one point, Peter let slip that he'd graduated from Princeton, the definitive proof to Maddie that he was rich. "They don't let poor people into fancy colleges," she said, giving me one of her looks that meant, I told you so!

I searched for Peter Hainsworth and Princeton. Bingo! Class of 1990, president of half a dozen clubs as well as the drama society. The senior photograph showed a younger version of the man, smiling good looks and laughing eyes, the kind of guy everybody loved. What was not to love? I shut down the computer with the sense that maybe Maddie had hit the jackpot.

It was over wine one late afternoon, above the bay on Crete, that Peter turned to Maddie and said, "Tell me about your husband, sweetheart."

I don't know who was more startled, Maddie or me. I figured she'd already told him how Norton had made a gazillion dollars in his dot-com business, leaving out the part about how he'd lost it, but obviously that wasn't what they'd been discussing when I heard them in the corridor at night. Always the swish of Maddie's door opening and closing, followed by the kind of absorbed stillness that meant she wasn't alone.

"Oh, Norton was quite successful," Maddie said, using her best adoring wife tone.

"Did he hang on to his money?"

Something in Peter's voice made me wonder if he hadn't also been searching the Internet, and I jumped in. "A lot of dot-com guys lost money," I said. "But not Norton. He was fortunate enough to sell out before the company crashed." Also fortunate, I was thinking, that Norton never took the company public, so chances were good that Peter Hainsworth hadn't found any more about the company than I'd been able to find on Schiff Investments.

Peter laid a tan hand over Maddie's. "How did Norton die?"

Maddie blinked a couple of times, then took her eyes away and stared out at the Aegean. Very effective, I thought, but then I'd seen her play the part dozens of times in the months since Norton's accident. She had it down pat, even to the slight moisture pooling at the corners of her eyes. "Norton loved to sail," she said finally. "He always wanted to take me sailing."

Well, that was a lie. The man couldn't swim, hated the water, and had never been in a sailboat. Maddie and I, on the other hand, had become pretty good at sailing, after she hooked up with the guy that rented out boats near the bar. For a while he took us out sailing every week and taught us how to crew, and in return Maddie spent the night with him, which she didn't mind since he wasn't half-bad looking and we were both under the impression that he was Mr. Rich. The arrangement ended, along with our sailing lessons, when my laptop coughed up the fact that Mr. Rich didn't own the boat rental business. He was paid by the hour, same as Maddie and me. But by then, Thad Norton had wandered into the bar.

"One day, Norton begged me and Jules to go sailing."

We were the ones begging Norton. "It'll be such fun," Maddie had said, leaning over his chair so that he got a good look down her shirt and planting a kiss on the freckled bald spot on his head.

"It was such a pretty day that we agreed to go. Isn't that right, Jules?" Maddie glanced at me.

"I wish we'd talked him out of it," I said, playing my part pretty well, too.

Maddie was going on: How we were a good three or four miles out and running full with the wind and what fun it turned out to be after all, Norton looking like a real sailor, except that he was standing up straight, which he shouldn't have been doing, when the jibing boom bonked him in the head and pitched him into the water.

Bonked him in the head, all right, after I yelled, "Jibe ho," and pulled the tiller windward, which brought the boom swinging hard across the cockpit straight at Norton. Of course Maddie had neglected to center the boom.

"God, we tried to circle into the wind and luff up alongside him to pull him out," Maddie said, her voice quivering. "But he'd already disappeared beneath the waves."

Disappeared, all right, as Maddie and I were racing away. And who could prove that it wasn't an accident?

"What a dreadful experience," Peter said, lacing his fingers into Maddie's. "Poor man."

Yes, Maddie and I both agreed. Poor Norton.

Maddie turned her still-moist eyes back to the man beside her. "How did your wife die, Peter?"

This was the first I'd heard of a wife, but it made sense that a man like Peter Hainsworth had a few women in his past. Why not a wife?

"Also terrible," Peter said. "Annette was out shopping one day. A little boutique she liked to frequent a few miles from home. She was walking back to her car when she was struck by a hit-and-run driver. She never regained consciousness."

Now Maddie's tears actually seemed real. "Oh, Peter," she said. "We're both wounded spirits."

From the distance came the bleat of the ship's horn. We finished our wine and started for the dock.

Later that evening, while Maddie and Peter were dancing on the upper deck, I checked the Internet for Annette Hainsworth and drew about ten links, none of which seemed likely. Annette Hainsworth, veterinary assistant? I didn't think so. Then I found the website of the *Philadelphia Inquirer* and hit pay dirt. The front-page headline screamed in black type, Socialite Victim of Hit and Run. The socialite part was good. It was looking more and more like Peter Hainsworth really was rich.

I read through the two-column article, which confirmed what Peter had said, and added some details he'd left out. His wife, who went by the name of Annette Schiffler, had been run down by a rental car, later found abandoned two miles from the accident. Witnesses said that the driver was a woman with long black hair, the same woman, a police spokesman said, who had rented the car that morning using a stolen credit card and driver's license. The victim was the daughter of the late Owen Schiffler, who built Schiff Telecommunications Company, which he sold for thirty million dollars. Annette Schiffler was survived by her husband, Peter Hainsworth.

I shut down my laptop. Well, well. We'd found the perfect husband for Maddie. Only one thing kept me from going to bed smiling: Maddie had fallen for the guy.

Three hours later, a loud pounding interrupted my dreams. I managed to swim up into consciousness, stumble through the bedroom and sitting area to the door, while, at the same time, trying to clear my throat and mumble, "Who's there?"

"It's me, Jules." My sister's voice, as cheery as the sunshine that wouldn't appear for another two hours.

The *me* turned out to be Maddie with Peter hovering at her shoulder, a wide grin plastered across his handsome, half-drunken face.

"You have any idea what time it is?" I asked as they loped inside.

That's when Maddie, posing next to the sofa like a model on a runway with adoring fans at her side, announced that she and Peter were getting married. Then she shoved out her left hand, flashing a diamond ring that shone like a headlight and, unlike the diamond on her other hand, was most assuredly real. For once, I didn't know what to say, which is what I said.

"How about, you're happy for us," Peter suggested.

"Yes, of course." The announcement had come sooner than I'd expected. "When's the big day?"

"Day after tomorrow." Peter again.

"Wow. That soon?"

"We'll be docked at Santorini for two days," Maddie said. "Captain Jelenik will marry us in the morning. Peter insists that we spend the first night of our honeymoon"—she paused and gave her future husband a look promising especially great sex—"on Santorini. Peter loves Santorini," she hurried on. "It's so romantic. He always spends time there when he's in the Greek Isles."

Well, what could I do but order champagne, and join in the small talk about the upcoming nuptials and the dress that Maddie would wear—the pink chiffon that looked great with her blue eyes, and the pink high heels.

We chatted about the other arrangements. How, after the ship docked at Piraeus in Athens, Maddie and Peter would fly to Philadelphia to begin their life together in a house that Peter called "the estate," which I took to mean the kind of mansion Maddie and I had dreamed about. I assured her that I would pack her things and have them shipped to Philadelphia, thinking that should take about five minutes, with what the creditors had left her.

Finally, a sleep-addled steward delivered a bottle of chilled Dom Perignon on a tray with three crystal glasses, and I toasted the happy couple.

The wedding went off as planned, with Maddie and Peter pledging their vows on the upper deck, the turquoise Aegean swelling and murmuring around us, and the little houses like white cubes piled on the cliffs of Santorini coming closer and closer. Maddie looked gorgeous, as usual, holding a bouquet of white and pink flowers, and Peter—well, Peter was a knockout in his white morning coat. Captain Jelenik looked both pained and proud, and the Robertsons and Sheas and other passengers stood around with looks of rapture on their sunburned faces, witnessing the true love of the most beautiful woman and the most handsome man on the cruise. I had to blink back the tears. We were so close to our goal, Maddie and me. She'd be Mrs. Peter Hainsworth of "the estate," and I'd be lucky if she remembered her older sister with a check now and then.

Afterward, the little wedding party adjourned to the dining room for brunch, courtesy of Captain Jelenik. I plied myself with five or six glasses of champagne, picked at the omelet and croissants, and listened to the inane toasts. Finally, Maddie and Peter began to make their getaway. Santorini was waiting. But as my sister moved around the back of my chair, she leaned down.

"Trust me," she whispered in my ear.

The next day, while I was walking up the narrow, winding path to the town of Fira, I understood. Above me, on a lookout that dropped a thousand feet into the sea, were Maddie and Peter. Maddie stood back, her head bent into a camera. Peter was at the lip of the edge, so that behind him was nothing but the endless blue sky dropping into the sea, and below, the black, jagged rocks. One slip—a sudden push—and Peter Hainsworth would disappear into the abyss.

But not yet. Peter Hainsworth visited Santorini two or three times a year. "Three months as Mrs. Peter Hainsworth," Maddie had said. "Then we'll all go to Santorini, and I'll become a wealthy widow."

It was two and a half months later when Maddie called. She caught up with me after my shift at the restaurant on Wilshire, which had patrons several notches in class above the bar in Redondo.

"We're in Santorini," Maddie said, her voice faint against the bleat of music in the background, as if a band were marching down one of the narrow streets. "Peter's waiting for me in the lobby. We're going to hike around the caldera. Can you come over afterward?"

"Afterward?"

"When it's over, Jules."

"I was supposed to meet you there, Maddie. You can't do it alone."

"I can handle it," she said. I could barely hear her. It was hard to make out the rest of it—something about an overlook that makes the perfect photo opportunity.

"I thought you loved him."

"And we were going to live happily ever after?" My sister made a noise that sounded like she was choking. Her voice was so faint I had to press the phone hard against my ear to catch what she was saying. "I admit I had second thoughts for a while, until I caught him with his girlfriend. The bastard brought her into our bedroom. Some tramp with black, stringy hair, and the way she acted, like she owned the place, I got the feeling that she's been around for a long time. Of course Peter insisted he still loved me, but I started thinking that the girlfriend was going to make it a lot easier."

Girlfriend. I felt my chest tighten, as if something had gotten caught in my windpipe. My heart was pounding against my ribs. It was a moment before I caught my breath. "Listen to me, Maddie," I shouted. "You've got to get out of Santorini."

"I told Peter I was going back to the room for my sunscreen." Her voice had started going in and out. Peter. Room. Sunscreen. I had to fill in the rest. Maddie's new husband did not like being kept waiting.

"Peter killed his wife, Maddie. He had his girlfriend drive the car."

"What? Jules, what . . .?"

"Don't hike up over the caldera, Maddie!" I was screaming, the pieces of the puzzle falling together in my head. It was so clear. Why hadn't we seen it before? "Can you hear me? Peter's wife probably inherited a fortune, and he killed her for it. But he didn't get it, Maddie. You hear me?" I felt like I was screaming into the wind. "He didn't get the money. That's why he went on the cruise. He was looking for another rich woman."

"Jules? Jules? You're breaking up. Everything's . . . fine. Okay? Okay? Don't worry." She sounded like she was in the middle of the sea, and I had the terrible feeling that my sister was fading away from me. "I've got to go."

"No, Maddie! Peter thinks you've got Norton's money. He's gonna push you off the cliff. You won't have a chance . . ."

I was shouting into a dead phone. I pushed the redial key and closed my eyes, listening to the buzz of a phone ringing in an empty hotel room somewhere in Santorini. God, they could be staying in any one of dozens of little hotels. It could be a short hike to the caldera overlook.

I hit the end button and spent the next fifteen minutes trying to connect with the Santorini police, not taking my eyes off the clock. Maddie and Peter were on their way to the overlook.

Finally, a man's voice on the line, and me shouting about how an American named Peter Hainsworth was going to an overlook on the caldera to kill his wife, how he planned to push her over the edge, and the voice saying, "Eh? Eh?"

"English!" I shouted. "Get me someone that speaks English."

And the voice saying, "No Inglish," and me continuing to shout even after I knew the line had gone dead. Twenty-five minutes had passed. They would be at the overlook by now. Maddie waving toward the edge of the cliff that dropped into the Aegean and saying, *Stand over there, Peter*, and Peter saying, *Let me get your picture first, sweetheart. I insist.* And no one would be able to prove that it wasn't an accident.

I threw the phone hard against the wall and watched the black metal break into pieces, as if it had been dropped off a cliff.

Essays

The Birth of Stories

She was beautiful, just as I imagined Sacajawea must have been. The sculptured bronze face and dress and moccasins shimmered in the August sun. She stood in the cemetery named for her—the Sacajawea Cemetery—looking out over the rolling brown plains. The wind was blowing hard, I remember, the way it often blows on the Wind River Reservation. In a cradle strapped to her back was the figure of her child, Jean Baptiste, born a few weeks before the Lewis and Clark expedition left the Mandan village in North Dakota. She had gone with the expedition, the only woman among thirty-two men, an infant on her back. By the time she returned to her village, Jean Baptiste was eighteen months old, a dancing child, Clark called him. Something about the sculpture gripped me, tugged at my heart. A woman—a girl, really; she was sixteen years old—departing on a 5,000-mile journey with a baby. These were the facts, and I knew the facts would never let me go until I had worked them into a story.

Stories arrive out of nowhere, out of a cemetery in the middle of an Indian reservation in the middle of Wyoming. It is always exciting for authors, the moment when a story arrives and we know we must write it. Stories come with their own urgency: they must be written *now*. We have to trust that it will all work out somehow, even if, in the grip of that initial idea, we're never quite certain how the story will unfold.

This was a phenomenon I had often experienced and never understood until I began writing about the Arapahos. They believe that the universe is filled with stories. From time to time, stories allow themselves to be told, and when they decide to be told, they choose the storytellers. When I first heard the explanation, I thought, of course. What else could explain authors working away sometimes for years writing stories that have nothing to do with them and that may not even be published? Look at the works of almost any author: Shakespeare writing about a Danish prince, or a Moorish general, or star-crossed lovers and doomed kings. Larry McMurtry writing about a nineteenth-century cattle drive. Evan S. Connell re-creating the life and death of General George Armstrong Custer. What explanation other than that a story had allowed itself to be told and had laid hold of an author's heart and said: you are the one.

What else could explain why, on that hot August day, I stood in front of a bronze sculpture of a girl who lived two hundred years ago and knew that it was incumbent upon me to write a story about her? It had to be done. I remember speaking to her out loud: *What is your story? Tell me your story.*

For me, a story starts in the actual world, a piece of information or random fact—a small kernel that might grow and bear fruit. I had happened upon a kernel, the fact of a girl and a baby and a journey, and something so poignant about it, so terribly human. But where was the entrance into the story itself? What exactly was the story and how did it want to be told? I needed more facts, so I began reading about Sacajawea and the Lewis and Clark expedition, getting a sense of the young girl with the baby, drawing closer with each book and article. I spent a week in Montana floating the Missouri River, stopping along the way where the expedition had stopped, camping under a field of stars that blazed in a clear black sky, listening to the river lap at the banks and knowing—

knowing—Sacajawea had been to this place. She had seen these stars; she had listened to this river.

Then I found another fact, another kernel: a notebook had once existed. An old Shoshone woman had come onto the Wind River Reservation with her people in 1868. She had told wondrous stories, this old woman, about going with the soldiers on a long journey. And remember that the Lewis and Clark expedition was a military affair. She spoke French, and we also have to remember that Sacajawea's husband, who was on the expedition, was Frenchman Toussaint Charbonneau. She told about walking over mountains and floating down rivers in pirogues the soldiers had carved out of trees. She told about eating horsemeat in blizzards, hunting for wild vegetables in the warm weather, locating familiar mountain peaks and streams when the expedition reached the territory of her people, the Shoshones.

And when they reached the mouth of a great river and set up camp, she had gone to Captain Clark himself and demanded that she be allowed to go with the men to see the waters that wrapped around the world. To have come all that way and endured all the hardships, yet not see the great waters, she said, would be very hard. So she went to the Pacific Ocean. She saw the bones of a whale, which she called a fish as large as a house.

All of the old woman's stories are discounted by historians, who offer evidence that the Shoshone wife of Charbonneau died at Fort Manuel in present-day South Dakota in 1812, six years following the expedition. They cite a notation written by Clark in 1828 that Sacajawea was deceased. The problem with these pieces of historical evidence is that Charbonneau was a much-marrying man. Even the historians admit that he had more than one Shoshone wife, and the wife who died in 1812 is unnamed. In any case, whatever the historians might believe makes no difference to the Shoshones and Arapahos on the Wind River Reservation. They have their own stories, they say, passed down by Sacajawea herself.

The wife of the government agent at the time recognized that the stories the old woman told were important. They were history, eyewitness accounts of marvelous events. The agent's wife started recording the stories in a notebook, eventually filling twenty-five pages, the notebook becoming more precious with each story, more laden with history. She had to keep it safe, she must have told herself, because she placed the notebook in the agency building. One night, the building burned down.

This was the salient fact—a notebook that once existed—that revealed the entrance into the story. I write mystery novels and short stories, all set in the West because I'm a westerner to the bone, a fourth-generation Coloradan. Stories about the West are part of my DNA. They forever capture my imagination, all those bigger-than-life western people and the western landscapes that go on forever and stun you with their beauty. I had been following Hemingway's advice to "write what you know" before I had ever heard of it. Now another story of the West had found me. I would write a mystery novel based on a beautiful bronze girl with a baby and a notebook filled with her experiences on the Lewis and Clark expedition.

I began by asking the what-if questions. What if the notebook hadn't been destroyed in the fire after all? What if someone had rushed into the burning agency building and carried it to safety? What if the notebook had been passed down from generation to generation, a family's precious treasure? What if someone outside the family discovered the notebook's existence and recognized its value? What if someone was willing to kill for it?

The answers eventually worked their way into the plot for *The Spirit Woman*, a mystery novel set in the present, yet intertwined with the story of a girl two hundred years ago, embarking on a journey with an infant on her back. But the story was also about the journey that my fictional characters embarked upon as they set out to locate a priceless notebook believed to have been destroyed, with a killer tracking their footsteps.

The stories that find me—novels, short stories, nonfiction pieces alike—begin with that tiny bit of information that springs in front of me, blocking my way and drawing me into a conspiracy to bring forth a story. One morning a professor loomed out of a black-and-white photo in a newspaper. All white hair and beard flowing about his shoulders and chest, a little stooped over with wrists handcuffed over his belly, being led to a waiting car by three or four men in dark, serious suits. The headline blared something like: "Drug Lab Busted in Kansas Field."

A small article on an inside page, but it had taken hold of me. A professor of chemistry whose brilliance had gone unrecognized and who had been unfairly compensated at numerous universities and scientific laboratories. But a drug cartel had recognized that brilliance and built a state-of-the-art lab for the professor in the middle of a Kansas cornfield. Compensation was in line with talent: jets to Mexican beaches and Monte Carlo casinos. All he had to do was manufacture fentanyl, and he was very good at the task until the gloomy day the FBI knocked on the laboratory's door.

The idea of such a man—a small kernel—grew into a novel called *The Ghost Walker*. The character based on the professor turned out to be a minor character, yet the whole idea for the novel—a fentanyl lab on the Wind River Reservation run by an unappreciated genius—came about because, one morning, I happened to pour another cup of coffee and linger a little longer over the newspaper.

I've learned over the years that when this happens—a kernel springs in front of me—there is nothing to be done except to surrender because there will be no peace until the story is written. The girl in bronze with a baby on her back and the genius professor with the flowing white beard will walk through my dreams, dance about on my dashboard as I drive down the road, and meet me at every corner. And always the urgency to write the story *now*. But now isn't always the best time. Now is when I'm in the grips of writing another story, and for me there's no breaking stride once a story is under way. So I make notes about this new kernel, jotting at a furious rate with the urgency of it all. I clip the newspaper articles, look up the books I will have to read, jot down the names of experts I must contact. All of which goes into a file folder that is now fat and overflowing, taking up half of a drawer by itself, a constant reminder of the stories demanding to be told.

I've also learned that kernels can appear anywhere—in a newspaper, magazine, book, on a billboard. I suppose I am always expecting them, always on the lookout. They might jump out from the present or from the past; they aren't particular about the century from which they emerge. But the kernels that come to me have one thing in common—they are connected to the West. The professor's lab stood in a Kansas cornfield, but the idea translated easily westward, where the remote spaces of Indian reservations had long been hospitable to clandestine drug labs.

But stories come to different authors in different ways. I've heard authors talk about the characters that walked into their heads. Sitting at an intersection, waiting for a green light, listening to the motor idling, and here comes a character. Not anyone the author knows or has ever met in the actual world, the character is someone new, a new man or woman born fully grown. The author Mark Spragg has said that, out of the blue, the image of an old man came to him. But the kernel that caught Spragg's attention, grabbed onto him, and tugged at his heart was this: the old man seemed so sad. Why was he so sad? The answer that came out of that question led to the novel *An Unfinished Life*.

Any kernel or notion or idea, any image that appears out of nowhere, is only the beginning, the entrance into a story. And at this point the author's imagination must take over. To paraphrase Wordsworth, imagination is the art of seeing what is there. Not everything that matters is apparent at first, but that doesn't mean it isn't there. Imagination looks beyond the obvious and sees the connections and relationships that might go unnoticed. Imagination sees below the surface into the heart of things. Imagination is like a muscle. The more you use it, the stronger it becomes. When people say to me, *I don't have any imagination*, my response is always, *Maybe you're not using it.*

For a story with a mystery at its heart, I turn my imagination loose on the what-if questions, never censoring or blocking any ideas that come to me. At this point, everything is on the table; everything is possible. This is the time for ruminating, taking long walks and letting the story begin to play out in my head the way in which it wants to play out. This is the time to watch the story people going about their lives, like watching actors

on a stage. Such surprising people step out of the wings and do such surprising things! Now, why would she do that? Why did he go there? What
is she doing here? You keep watching. You can't turn away because you
are in the grip of the story. What is driving these interesting people?
What will become of them? Gradually you begin to see beneath the surface into the hearts and minds of these story people. You build a relationship with them.

Stories depend upon relationships and connections, all the invisible
strings that bind human beings to one another. Pull on one string at the
beginning of a story, and somewhere in a following chapter, a character
will cry. E. M. Forster put it best when he differentiated between facts
and stories. The king died and the queen died are facts, Forster said. But
a story is this: The king died and the queen died *of grief.* An essential
connection exists, an invisible thread that binds the events and characters,
and it is the author's imagination that sees beyond the obvious to that
connection.

As an author who has carried on a love affair with history my entire
career—I've written books on history; I've woven the past into every
novel—I sometimes think that I might die of grief over the way so many
academic history books are limited by facts. Lists and lists of dead, dry
facts. No wonder kids think history is boring. Facts can be boring. The
way in which the facts are connected is what brings history to life and
allows Custer to ride again over the rolling hills to his death and the warriors to rise up and defeat the 7th Cavalry, knowing even as they do so
that in the very victory they will lose the war, and with the war, an entire
way of life. How could any of this be boring, pulsing with life as it is?
What is boring is the list of facts bereft of the author's imagination, bereft
of connections and, consequently, bereft of meaning.

I am not suggesting that any author writing a story about actual events
jettison the facts. The facts must stand; they are what they are and what
happened, happened. But I am suggesting that before writing any story
based on actual events, authors must read widely and deeply and do the
necessary research for the imagination to make the connections—to *see*—

what the facts alone may obscure. Because Evan S. Connell allowed his imagination to see into the connections and relationships among the facts, a sense of the truth of what happened at the Battle of the Little Bighorn shines through the novel *Son of the Morning Star.* This is the author's responsibility to the story itself—the responsibility to bear witness to what occurred in such a way that the reader understands what happened and why it matters.

By the time I sat down to write the biography of an Arapaho leader, Chief Left Hand, I had spent four years on the research. I had surrounded myself with facts—boxes of filled notebooks and stacks of photocopies, hundreds of names and dates and events. But not until I began writing the story—which is when the imagination goes to work—did the connections and networks and relationships among all the seemingly disparate facts begin to show themselves. Take two events in particular: the Camp Weld Council, September 28, 1864, and the Sand Creek Massacre, November 29, 1864. The authorities in Colorado had met with Arapaho and Cheyenne leaders at Camp Weld and instructed them to take their people to an area in southeastern Colorado, near Sand Creek. The white authorities would then begin negotiations to make peace on the plains. But after the tribes had complied with the instructions, the Third Colorado Regiment had attacked the villages and massacred 160 people, mostly women, children, and old people.

What I had was a set of facts about two events with an obvious relationship. The Camp Weld Council precipitated the Sand Creek Massacre in that the tribes would not have been camped at Sand Creek if they had not been instructed to go there. But there were other facts, small and obscure—casual remarks in letters, reports of overheard conversations, veiled phrases in memoirs and journals—which depended upon imagination to make the connections that revealed the true depth of the relationship between these events, to *see* that all the time the white authorities were assuring the tribal leaders of their good will at Camp Weld, they were condemning them and their families to death at Sand Creek.

Strange and inexplicable, the way imagination connects the facts that allow the truth to shine through. But it happens because authors live inside the story, with all of their antennae finely tuned, as alert to nuances and stolen glances—maybe even more alert—as in their own lives. Authors move through the worlds inhabited by story people, live in their houses and apartments, walk down their streets, experience their hopes and dreams, see through their eyes. While I wrote *Chief Left Hand*, I lived in my imagination on the plains with the Arapahos. I experienced the hope and the dejection, the fear and the anger, of a people watching their way of life begin to slip away. Story worlds are real and true, sometimes even more real and truer than the author's own because there is no place for story people to hide, no room for denials and circumlocutions. Even when story people attempt to hide from the truth, the author's imagination allows the reader to see through all the attempts at obfuscation to the truth of the matter. Nothing is hidden in the shadows.

In the months that author Jane Barker spent researching the life of Mari Sandoz for the novel *Mari*, she kept running into a brick wall. None of the facts explained a period of time when Sandoz seemed to have stepped off the earth. Where had she gone? What had she done? Why had she wanted to disappear? But in writing the novel, Barker's imagination saw the connections among the facts, and the connections exposed the truth. She knew how Mari Sandoz had spent the time when no one had any idea of where she was with as much certainty as she knew the details of her own life. And she wrote the story that she was certain was true.

Just as the novel was published, a packet of letters written by Mari Sandoz came to a Nebraska library. Moldering in someone's attic for decades, unknown and unread, the letters told about the period when Sandoz had needed to disappear. And they confirmed the truth that Jane Barker's imagination had discovered.

As fragile as air, stories, and yet necessary. Growing out of nothing but snippets of information or impressions that flitter through an author's mind—a beautiful bronze girl with a baby on her back, a crazed-looking professor with flowing white hair, an old man who seems sad—accumulating details that fix them in the world and depending upon imagination to make the connections, stories tell the truth. And it is in this feat of truth telling, at looking at the world as it is, at exploring hopes and dreams and laying bare the human heart, that stories speak to us and help us to understand the stories of our own lives.

The West of Ghosts

On the wall of my study is a framed, bronze-toned illustration by Frank McCarthy, titled "Beneath the Cliff of the Spirits." Six Shoshone warriors are riding across the lower half beneath stark cliffs emblazoned with petroglyphs. Both the warriors and the ponies are painted, and the warriors brandish spears partly wrapped in leather thongs tied to eagle feathers that wave overhead. Eagle feathers sprout from their headdresses, but the lead warrior wears the head of a gray wolf, signifying that he is the leader of the scouts, like the alpha wolf, scouting the prey or the enemy.

The petroglyphs represent the spirits of the ancestors, and native people will tell you that petroglyphs are chiseled by the spirits that dwell in the rock. The spirits manifest their presence by making the petroglyphs visible when they choose and to whom they choose. If you have ever gone looking for petroglyphs among the remote cliffs and rock formations in the West, you know that sometimes they can be seen and other times, even when you are certain they are present, they remain invisible. What makes McCarthy's illustration so powerful is that the spirits have obviously chosen to show themselves to the warriors. They ride alongside and float above, always staying nearby.

The illustration captures my own sense of the West where I was born and have spent my entire life—the Rocky Mountains and the vast, still mostly empty plains of Colorado. My West is a place of ghosts, a place where the ancestors hover nearby. It is a multilayered place with the present rooted in the past and the past always working its way into the present. Past and present—two sides of the same old coin. It's possible to look at only one side, say the present, which might seem a rational approach, but the past is still there, shaping the heft and size, the depth and overall configuration. This is the West that I try to bring to life in my novels and short stories, in nonfiction books and articles and essays, the West that McCarthy so eloquently brought to life in the illustration.

That ghosts from the past inhabit the West seems obvious. The past is everywhere. It is part of the landscape from the high mountain valleys to the bluffs and arroyos that break up the plains. It is even part of the highways and roads. The multi-lane, congested I-25, on which a never-ending stream of cars, SUVs, and semis moves up and down the front range of the Rockies from the southern reaches of New Mexico to the northern part of Wyoming, follows an Indian trail. For two hundred years, Arapahos and Cheyennes rode the trail up and down the front range. They had made the trail, those people of long ago.

There are other old Indian trails that have metamorphosed into highways and hundreds of two-lane roads that wind through the mountains and shoot across the plains, following the rivers, or what passes for a river in my part of the West but is often nothing more than a dry streambed. Out on the plains, the roads run past clusters of cottonwoods where Arapaho and Cheyenne villages once stood, and probably the camps of Sioux, Kiowa, Apache, and Pawnee hunting parties. It's possible to imagine—at least I think so, each time I drive past a stand of cottonwoods close to a stream—the white tipis sheltering in the shade of the trees, the sound of babies crying, dogs yapping, and horses neighing in the corrals.

Or to imagine the warriors riding across the horizon on their way back to the village after the hunt.

There are stretches of ranchland across the plains, open, windblown places with a scattering of sagebrush and a few dried, gnarled trees— virgin land much of it, unplowed and untouched—that probably look the same as when the warriors rode out to fight the enemy or hunt the buffalo, or when the soldiers attacked a village. Such a place is the site of the Sand Creek Massacre in southeastern Colorado, where the Third Colorado Regiment attacked the Cheyenne and Arapaho village in the freezing dawn of November 29, 1864. When the attack ended, at least 160 Indians lay dead, mostly women and children. The elders say that you can still see the spirits of the women and children running through the thin stand of trees at the site, frantic to escape the soldiers bearing down on horseback.

In November 2000, Congress passed a law designating the more than 12,000 acres on which the Sand Creek Massacre occurred—the massacre that ignited twenty years of war on the plains—as a national historic site. A place of the past will be preserved for the future. Eventually the National Park Service will build an interpretive center where people can learn about what happened there and why it mattered, where people can touch the past as they do at the site of the Battle of the Little Bighorn.

In my West, such places are everywhere. They number in the hundreds, and I have visited many of them. They are the places that inspire me in my writing, the places where I can *feel* the past. Take the confluence of the South Platte River and Beaver Creek, near the town of Brush in northeastern Colorado. Every summer, the Arapahos held a trading fair on the site. Tribes came from the north and south to barter and exchange goods—ponies and buffalo robes, tin pots, glass beads, Mexican silver or serapes, bolts of trade cloth, tobacco. And the visiting that went on back and forth among the tipis, the exchange of news and gossip, the kids romping together. A county fair, we would call such an event. There is something about the site today—the gurgling creek, the wind brushing the leaves of the cottonwoods, and the lone black bull that sometimes grazes the wild grass—that retains the exuberance of those gatherings, as if the crowd had just packed up the tipis and trading goods and ridden away. It's the feel of a stadium after the crowd has departed.

A couple of years ago, I set out with my husband, George, to locate the place where the Arapaho Chief Left Hand had died and was buried. My first book, *Chief Left Hand*, published in 1981, was both a biography of this English-speaking diplomat and a history of his turbulent times. Left Hand became prominent in the mid-1800s during the time of the Colorado Gold Rush, when nearly two hundred thousand Americans— mostly men, armed to the teeth—scrambled onto the empty plains and into the mountains expecting to scoop up gold nuggets scattered at their feet, wash chunks of glittering gold out of the streams, and head back East wealthy men. The reality turned out to be different. They soon discovered that the gold, silver, lead, tungsten, molybdenum, and other minerals that would eventually be mined in Colorado were embedded in hard rock deep inside the mountains and that more than pickaxes would be needed to dislodge the riches.

The influx of gold seekers changed the lives of the Arapahos and Cheyennes on the plains and the Utes in the mountains in ways that the Indians could not have imagined. After the gold rush came homesteaders fencing off farms and ranches, wagons and animals of the "overlanders" clogging the trails, tent settlements and tar-paper and plank-board towns springing up literally overnight, Army troops riding out from newly built forts to protect the newcomers from the depredations of Indians whose lands they had taken, and iron rails flinging themselves across the plains and through the mountains, black smoke from the locomotives belching into the air. All of which squeezed the Cheyennes, Arapahos, and Utes into smaller and smaller areas until, finally, after all of the skirmishes, battles, and massacres, the survivors found themselves on reservations, the "reserved" portions of their once-vast lands. As one Arapaho put it at the time, the Indians thought that all the white people in the world had come to their lands.

In the four years I spent researching *Chief Left Hand*, I was able to locate evidence never before published that Left Hand had been mortally wounded during the Sand Creek Massacre, but had made his way north, along with a handful of survivors, to a large Sioux camp on the Smoky Hill River where he had died. He was buried in the ground there, according to the Arapaho Way.

By the time the book was published, I had visited most of the places where Left Hand had lived his life, but it was not until ten years later, on a ninety-degree day in August, that I found the place where he had died, which today is part of a ranch near the small town of Cheyenne Wells. After obtaining permission from the rancher to scout the site where the Sioux camp had stood, George and I bumped over dirt roads in our Blazer, raising clouds of dust, and when we ran out of road, we got out and started walking. It was about noon, the sun white-hot overhead. All around us, the glass-blue sky dipped over the empty, endless plains, with nothing to interrupt the horizon.

As we trekked along, we realized that we were not alone. Flying with us, perching on the little sand hills and clumps of brush, watching from no more than twenty or thirty feet away, was a large, wide-eyed owl. Apart from an occasional prairie dog or the buzzing of a bee, there was no other sign of life. We veered in one direction, then in another, hoping to stumble onto the Smoky Hill, which we knew would be nothing more than a dry bed. No matter how many zigzags we took, the owl stayed with us. The afternoon wore on with no sign of the riverbed, but instead of feeling anxious, I felt only peace. The Arapahos say that the ancestors may choose to accompany you on your way, and if they do, they usually choose to come in the form of an owl. I had no doubt that somewhere in the glare of the sun and the sameness of the brown plains, we would stumble onto an indentation, like a scar running over the land, that would lead us to the site of the Sioux camp.

We found the riverbed and followed it to the wide bend where the camp had been located. We knew from the old records that the river had bent around the camp, but we hadn't known that the river bent around a bluff, and the camp had been on top. From a distance on the plains, the cuts and rises in the land meld into the vastness. We hadn't seen the bluff until we'd bumped up against it. We started hiking up the sliding dirt slope, the owl already perched on the edge above. When we reached the top, we stood perfectly still, unable to speak, hardly able to breathe. Rising above the brown plains that ran as far as we could see in every direction was a field of wildflowers—yellows, purples, reds, oranges, blues, vermilions, and whites—that swayed against the blue sky. It was there that Left Hand had died, and there, somewhere among the wildflowers, his body lay buried.

When we looked around, the owl was gone.

Not all of the ghosts in my West are Arapahos, however, or other Indians who had lived on the plains and in the mountains of Colorado. There are the ghostly trails of the trappers, people like Jedediah Smith and Jim Beckwourth, who made a living of sorts trapping beaver in the streams, and the traders, like the entrepreneurial Bent Brothers—William and Charles—who, in 1830, built Bent's Fort, an adobe structure on the Arkansas River and the first permanent structure in United States territory west of the Mississippi. Santa Fe, still part of Mexico then, was already two hundred years old, already filled with its own ghosts of the Spanish, Mexicans, and Indians who had settled the place and whose descendants moved up and down the Santa Fe Trail with wagon trains of trade goods, always stopping at Bent's Fort.

A few years ago, I spent an evening at the reconstructed Bent's Fort, after the enormous gates had swung shut on the last tourist, leaving the fort to the imaginations of a group of western history buffs. We ate dinner in the courtyard, with campfires burning along the side and buffalo meat sizzling on a grill, Mexicans in sombreros strumming guitars, and the last of the summer sun flaring red on the adobe walls. It was easy to imagine—as I suspect everyone of us did—that the present and past had traded places, and that we were caught in the past, that in the rooms around us were the traders who'd come from Santa Fe or St. Louis or an Indian village, speaking a medley of languages—Spanish, French,

English, Arapaho, Cheyenne—their horses grazing on hay in the corral, and William Bent himself upstairs in the corner room entertaining Kit Carson with a game of billiards at the only billiard table west of St. Louis.

There are also the ghostly trails of the gold seekers who clambered through the mountains, cutting burro roads high above the timberline, up and over jaw-dropping-steep peaks. You can hike to the top of those peaks and look down over miles and miles of old roads still visible in the fragile tundra and imagine the burros straining at the head of wagons loaded with ore that might contain a little gold, or might not. You can see the century-old tailings still spilling from mines cut into the sides of rock-strewn mountains so formidable that you wonder how anyone had reached them. Yet the gold seekers had made the roads and sunk the mines in a feat of daring and endurance that can only be a tribute to the power of greed, or to the depth of the desperation that drove the gold seekers on.

Traces of the old narrow-gauge railroads also cling to the mountains—roadbeds no wider than a wagon hung on the mountainsides, switching back and forth on themselves as they climb higher and higher before plunging down the other side. We've hiked and Jeeped many of those old railroad beds. We've even dropped down a rocky shaft with miner's lamps on our heads to illuminate the blackness and walked the length of the Alpine Tunnel—as long as six football fields, burrowed beneath the continental divide—and as we walked and explored, we could imagine the Denver, South Park, and Pacific trains churning through the tunnel at five miles an hour, ferrying cars of gold, silver, and coal through the mountains.

Even the cities that I know best are shaped by the past. I'm a city girl, raised in Denver, a sprawling city of freeways and suburbs and skyscrapers that some might argue would be the same if it were transported to the deep south or set down somewhere in the Midwest or anywhere else, for that matter. I would argue that Denver would not be Denver without its ghosts. Take the spit of land at the confluence of Cherry Creek and the Platte River on the edge of downtown, crowded with trendy shops and blocks of warehouses turned into upscale lofts and condominiums where people like bankers, lawyers, and software engineers live. On that same spit of land stood an Arapaho village, within shouting distance of the tent and log cabin towns of Denver and Auraria, which eventually melded into Denver. They were traders, the Arapahos, the "businessmen of the plains," the newcomers called them, and they wanted to live near their trading business, just as, I suspect, many of the people in today's condominiums want to live near downtown.

Or take the variety of people—characters, many of them—who had come West, settled in the new town of Denver, and left their personalities forever stamped on the city. The cowboys who drove their cattle down Denver's dirt streets to graze in pastures in the middle of town, the gunslingers like Doc Holliday and Wyatt Earp who happened through town, the gamblers and flimflam artists like Soapy Smith who ran the games of chance on Larimer Street, which is now a restored historical district of boutiques and restaurants. People like Molly Brown, whose husband, J.J., had struck gold in Leadville, confounding all the experts who said that Leadville was a silver city, which it was, and would remain a silver city, which it didn't. The stone lions still grace the mansion that J.J. purchased for Molly on Pennsylvania Street.

Or Henry C. Brown, no relation to Molly. Henry and his wife had traveled by wagon on the overland trail from the Midwest and stopped off in Denver, intending to rest awhile before crossing the mountains and continuing on to the California goldfields, their real destination. But when Mrs. Brown awoke on her first morning in Denver under a sky as big as the outdoors and the clearest blue she could imagine, she said to Henry: "You may proceed to California, Mr. Brown, if such be your wish. I shall remain here." Henry decided that he would also remain. He would go on to build the Brown Palace Hotel, a still-elegant visitor from the past that has stayed on.

Such visitors can be found everywhere in Denver. The white-bricked Tivoli building, for example, with its blue-tiled roofs, built by German immigrants more than a century ago, still looming like a Bavarian castle over today's Auraria campus near downtown; or the spire of the Daniels and Fisher Tower, nineteen stories high, soaring high above the city in 1911, the highest building then on the Great Plains, and a re-creation of the Campanile in Venice, proving to the world that Denver was a city of culture, not just a cow town. The golden dome of the State Capitol shines at the other end of Sixteenth Street, the dome paved with real gold, the exterior built of granite, the interior decorated with red and white marble, all spewed out of Colorado's mountains. Such a grand capitol building would symbolize the best of Colorado—state officials overseeing construction in the 1890s actually expressed such sentiments—a gift from the nineteenth century to future generations. It took almost two decades to finish the capitol, with every penny accounted for and no hint of corruption or scandal—an astonishing accomplishment for government officials in the Gilded Age. Indeed, in any age.

Out of the parade of such westerners—builders, gold seekers, traders, cowboys and Indians, characters with personalities larger than life, the Molly Browns and Henry Browns, the English-speaking diplomats who happened to be Indian chiefs—the myth of the West grew up, helped to maturity by the writers of pulp novels and the movies of John Ford. It has always seemed to me the myth of the West was about freedom. Where else could people be free enough to test their own mettle, to prove the stuff they were made of without the social constraints of propriety, the accepted wisdom that life should be lived in prescribed ways? In the wide-open spaces of the West, waiting to be conquered, developed, and stamped with your personality, you could figure out your own way to live. Where else could Custer have been free enough to plunge headlong into his last battle? Or railroad magnates push the tracks of a transcontinental railroad through the wilderness one mile each day, no matter the weather and damn any other obstacle? Or J. J. Brown and H. A. W. Tabor, the silver king, and hundreds of other poor men get rich quick?

Where else could women vote in the nineteenth century, except Wyoming and Colorado? Where else could women acquire their own land, except by homesteading what was usually the hardest-scrabble land available after men had fenced off the best sections? But it was land women could own outright, their piece of independence. Where else could women herd cattle, rope calves, and become dead-eye shots, outshooting all the men, as Annie Oakley did? For that matter, where else could women mount a horse and ride alone into the plains and mountains, as the St. Louis–bred Susan Magoffin had spent her days at Bent's Fort in 1848, leaving behind a journal that bursts with the exhilaration of being free for the first time in her young lady's life. Free. Free. Free.

But the myth of the Old West—aren't we endlessly reminded by revisionist historians?—failed to take into account some uncomfortable facts, such as the decimation and near extinction of the Native Americans, the rape and destruction of the landscape, the pollution of the streams and rivers, the near destruction of entire species of animals, including the buffalo and wolf. All true no doubt, and yet that myth of freedom, born out of the larger-than-life characters who settled the Old West and proved that people could be free, refuses to die. Perhaps the reason is that those larger-than-life characters were real.

We knew them. That is, my family carts around an enormous bag of stories that we pass from generation to generation about a lot of western characters. Most of my ancestors had trickled into Colorado in the 1860s and 1870s, when bands of Indians could still be seen riding across places like the South Park, which, not long before, had resembled a brown ocean of buffalo. My father's family had moved from Pennsylvania as far west as a rock-strewn farm in Missouri—the kind of Missouri farm that had led Ulysses S. Grant to rethink a career in the Army—so that, in 1883, my paternal grandfather became the last of my ancestors to reach Colorado. So the miners and railroaders and cowboys, the independent women—these were the people among whom my family had lived, worked, and prospered. In fact, these were the people that they were. Larger-than-life, real westerners.

Back in Missouri, my great-grandfather had hoisted a rifle on the front porch of the farmhouse and ordered Cole Younger and his gang off the land. That was prior to 1876 when Younger's attempt to rob a bank in Northfield, Minnesota, landed him in prison for the next twenty-five years. One great-aunt was a longtime friend of Molly Brown's. I have a photograph of my mother's father as a young man, posing with three other young men, all dapper and well-scrubbed and cocky-looking, staring into a bright future. Three of them would hit it rich in the gold mines and establish families whose names are still found in Denver's social register, but my grandfather wasn't one of them. I remember the tobacco-spitting, leather-faced cowboys at the stock shows and the rodeos we went to—all friends of the family—and the old-timer who had worked with my father's father on the narrow-gauge railroads, then spent years tearing up the rails after the mines closed and the railroads went bust. I remember the tales of the mountain lions and bears he'd fought off to bring the iron rails out of the mountains.

In one way or another, the ghosts of these western characters trail through the different kinds of stories that I've written over the last twenty-five years. I started my career as a journalist, chronicling the accomplishments and peccadilloes of modern characters for a weekly newspaper in a Denver suburb, then began contributing articles on the West to national newspapers and magazines, such as the *New York Times*, *Christian Science Monitor*, and *American Heritage of Invention and Technology*. In everything that I wrote, I was drawn to the past. I wanted to evoke the past that had formed my own imagination, not a country of dead people that the rest of us can hurry by, but a country that seemed alive and still mattered. I wanted to write about how our past has shaped who we are in the West, why the past matters.

I have always followed the old maxim preached to every aspiring writer: write what you know. I write about a West that I know in my bones, that I've been breathing in since I drew my first breath, a West of stories intertwined with the stories of my own family. Yet I was drawn to writing about the Plains Indians, whom I knew very little about. But they seemed so attuned to the past. After all, it is the Cheyenne and Arapaho elders who see the women and children still fleeing the soldiers at Sand Creek. So I decided to follow a contradictory maxim: write what you don't know, because then you will have the pleasure of finding out.

I wanted to find out about the Plains Indians. The more I learned about the tribes that had moved through Colorado—Cheyenne, Sioux, Kiowa, Apache, Pawnee, Arapaho—the more interested I became in the Arapaho. I liked the way they raised their children: "the easiest way," they called their method, which meant talking to them, explaining how the world worked, why it was good to do one thing and not another. I liked the mixture of practicality—the business part of their makeup—and the deep spirituality that saw all creatures, including the two-leggeds, the four-leggeds, and the wingeds, as relatives, connected to one another. I liked the ideal of living in beauty. Even the simplest tools or items of clothing should be beautiful, the women said, since they were seen every day. I liked the way they taught their children to live in harmony with one another and the earth. Did Arapahos always live those ideals? Of course not. They're people, not saints. They stumbled and fell like everybody else, but what was important, it seemed to me, was that they never gave up their ideals.

Everything I read about the Arapahos in the mid–1800s, at the time of the gold rush, mentioned one of their leaders, a man named Left Hand, a man fluent in English. Fluent in English? I'd learned enough by then to know that only a handful of Plains Indians ever became fluent in English. They didn't have to learn English or any language other than their own. They used the sign language to communicate with other tribes and with the traders and the other Americans coming onto the plains. Yet Left Hand not only spoke English, I learned later; he also spoke Cheyenne and Sioux. I set out to find out about a man who was interested enough in other people to learn their languages. What kind of man was he? Where were his villages? Which battles did he fight? How did he learn English? What became of him?

It was the finding out, the learning what I hadn't known, that resulted in *Chief Left Hand* and launched me into an adventure that continues today. I wrote other nonfiction books on the history of Colorado, with the ghosts of the gold seekers, railroaders, and builders all making their presences felt, but I kept returning to the Arapahos, where the lines between past and present seemed blurred, one melting into the other. When Arapahos from the Wind River Reservation in Wyoming head south to visit relatives in Oklahoma, they go by way of Sand Creek to pray for the people who died there. The Sand Creek Massacre took place one hundred and fifty years ago—eons ago, in the view of most people speeding along I-25—but to the Arapahos, it still matters.

Some years ago, I happened to hear Tony Hillerman speak about writing mystery novels set among the Navajos. I remember sitting in the middle of a large conference room surrounded by other writers, all of us wondering what we might write next, and thinking that I might write a mystery novel set among the Arapahos. It would be a contemporary novel, I remember thinking—laying my plans there in the conference room—but it would also be about the past. It would be both sides of the same coin.

This seemed like a good idea. I had no idea of how to go about writing fiction, but I liked reading mystery novels. They were fun to take to the beach or to curl up with in the evenings. How tough could one be to write? I was going to find out, but not before I figured out what I would write about. For inspiration, I began digging into my research for *Chief Left Hand* and came upon something that had taken place when the Arapahos and Cheyennes were moved to reservations. I had only mentioned it in *Chief Left Hand*, but I remembered being stunned by the information, and angry. I knew that someday I would write more about it, thinking that I would write an article or include it in another book, neither of which happened. Instead, it became the basis of the plot for *The Eagle Catcher*.

What I'd uncovered was this: Soon after the treaties that sent the tribes to reservations were signed—the Arapaho and Cheyenne chiefs making their X's on the word of government translators who assured the chiefs that they were signing what they thought they were signing—the government sent out agents to "make the reservations ready for the Indians." The agents carried out the assignment by carving off the lands with water and timber for their own ranches and leaving the less desirable lands for the tribes. This at a time when the Plains Indians had just been defeated in a war, huge numbers of their warriors dead, the buffalo dispersed and slaughtered, the children crying with hunger. This was the remnant that struggled onto the reservations: the wounded and demoralized, the old and sick and hungry. "We were a pitiful lot," is the way that Virginia Sutter, an Arapaho friend, described the nine hundred Arapahos who came to the Wind River Reservation in 1878.

The story I set out to tell in *The Eagle Catcher* was not just the history of how sections of reservation lands were stolen, but the way in which crimes of fraud and deceit that occurred more than a hundred years ago echo through the present. My novels since have reflected the same theme: the ghosts of the past that hover around us. When I'm looking for a plot of a new novel, I look into the bitter period between the time when the Arapahos roamed the plains—when, as they put it, they were free—and the early years on the reservation.

One of my novels, *The Story Teller*, is about the ledger books that the Arapaho, Cheyenne, Kiowa, Crow, and Sioux *wrote*. They wrote in pictographs, intricate and detailed, that filled the pages of ledger books they had obtained in trade with traders, homesteaders, and Army officers. They used crayons and pencils to tell the stories of battles and heroic exploits and the intimate accounts of village life. Two thousand Plains Indian ledger books, scholars say, once existed on the plains. Today there are fewer than three dozen, mostly in museums, some in private collections. A complete ledger book can be worth a million dollars. Pages razored out of ledger books are also in museums, but they turn up from time to time in galleries in places like Santa Fe and Aspen. At least three pages are known to exist from a ledger book account of the Sand Creek Massacre.

For all of my stories and novels, I start with questions of What If? For *The Story Teller*, the questions were, What if a complete Arapaho ledger book on the Sand Creek Massacre were found? What if the Arapaho tribe wanted to reclaim the book as part of their cultural and historical heritage? What if someone else wanted possession of a book worth a million dollars? Out of the answers to those questions came the plot for a novel that wove the importance of the ledger books to our knowledge and understanding of past events like the Sand Creek Massacre.

I remember standing at the granite stone marking the grave of Sacajawea on the Wind River Reservation and asking myself, What if Sacajawea had found her way back to her people after the Lewis and Clark expedition and lived to be a very old woman, as the Shoshones and Arapahos believe? What if she had dictated her story to the wife of the government agent, who wrote the story in a notebook, as historical records say had happened? What if the notebook had been rescued from a fire at the agency, instead of destroyed? What would Sacajawea's account of the expedition be worth today? The answers became *The Spirit Woman*.

All of my other novels, *Wife of Moon*, *Killing Raven*, *The Shadow Dancer*, *The Lost Bird*, *The Thunder Keeper*, *The Dream Stalker*, *The Ghost Walker*, and the novel that I'm currently writing are rooted in the past. With fiction, I'm no longer limited to narratives of what might have happened. I can plumb the meaning and imagine how a past event might continue to affect individuals and families. In all that imagining, I believe every fiction writer would agree, it is astonishing how often we hit upon a kernel of truth and how often readers say: "How did you know that's how it was? How did you know we felt that way?" After publication of *The Lost Bird*, which dealt with the crime in the recent past of infants being stolen from reservations and sold on the black market, I received a call from an Arapaho woman. "You wrote my story," she said. "How did you know my story?" I didn't know her story. I had imagined how such a crime would affect everyone involved.

The stories that I imagine keep me moving between the past and the present: the past of the Arapahos on the plains and their life today on the reservation. I spend part of every summer visiting the reservation, catching up with friends, talking with people, and, most of all, listening to what they have to say and the way in which they say it. George and I have driven the roads that my characters drive; we've visited the sites that I write about—the towns and community centers, the rivers and bluffs and petroglyphs. We've gone to the powwows and the rendezvous; we've taken part in the sweat lodge; we've sat and listened to the elders. We've attended the Sun Dance, and in all of this, we've touched a past threaded through the present.

I remember the July day we came over a rise on Ethete Road on our way to the Sun Dance. Spread through a scattering of cottonwoods on the Sun Dance grounds below were several hundred tipis, white and gleaming in the sun. We stopped the Blazer and got out, struck by what we saw. We could hear voices carried on the breeze, the sound of infants crying. People were moving about among the tipis, ducking in and out of the brush shades where food would be constantly available. In the center was the Sun Dance lodge, the sides fashioned of willow branches that the men had cut in the riverbeds and the sacred pole rising overhead, rainbows of cloth offerings tied to the roof poles and billowing against the blue sky. We might have been looking down at an Arapaho village in the Old Time about to begin the holiest of ceremonies, the Sun Dance.

As the Arapahos would say, the ancestors are always with us.

CREDITS

"Bad Heart," signed special limited edition with introduction by T. Jefferson Parker, Arapaho Commandments Series, ASAP Publishing, 2004.

"The Birth of Stories" first published as "Anatomy of a Story" in *An Elevated View: Colorado Writers on Writing*, edited by W.C. Jameson, Seven Oaks Publishing, 2011.

"Day of Rest," signed special limited edition with introduction by C. J. Box, Arapaho Commandments Series, ASAP Publishing, 2005.

"Dead End," signed special limited edition with introduction by James D. Doss, Arapaho Commandments Series, ASAP Publishing, 1997.

"Hole in the Wall," signed special limited edition with introduction by Edward D. Hoch, Arapaho Commandments Series, ASAP Publishing, 1998.

"Honor," signed special limited edition with introduction by Jan Burke, Arapaho Commandments Series, ASAP Publishing, 1999.

"An Incident in Aspen" in *Murder Here, Murder There*, edited by R. Barri Flowers and Jan Grape, 2012.

"Lizzie Come Home" in *How the West Was Read, Vol. II*, audio book edited by Robert J. Randisi, 1997.

"The Man in Her Dreams" in *More Murder, They Wrote*, edited by Elizabeth Foxwell and Martin H. Greenberg.

"The Man Who Thought He Was a Deer" in *Wild Crimes*, edited by Dana Stabenow, 2004.

"Molly Brown and Cleopatra's Diamond" first published in *Watching Eagles Soar: Stories from the Wind River and Beyond*, ASAP Publishing, 2011.

"Murder on the Denver Express" in *Crime Through Time, Vol. III*, edited by Sharan Newman, 2000.

"My Last Good-bye," signed special limited edition with introduction by Nancy Pickard, Arapaho Commandments Series, ASAP Publishing, 2002.

"Nobody's Going to Cry," signed special limited edition with introduction by Craig Johnson, Arapaho Commandments Series, ASAP Publishing, 2006.

"Otto's Sons" first published in *Watching Eagles Soar: Stories from the Wind River and Beyond*, ASAP Publishing, 2011.

"Santorini" in *Dry Spell: Tales of Thirst and Longing*, a selection of short stories by members of Rocky Mountain Fiction Writers, 2004.

"St. Elmo in Winter" in *Ghost Towns*, edited by Martin H. Greenberg and Russell Davis, Kensington Publishing, 2010.

"Stolen Smoke," signed special limited edition with introduction by Marcia Muller, Arapaho Commandments Series, ASAP Publishing, 2000.

"A Well-Respected Man" in *Women Before the Bench*, edited by Carolyn Wheat, 2001. Reprinted in *The World's Finest Mystery and Crime Stories*, edited by Ed Gorman and Martin H. Greenberg, 2002.

"The West of Ghosts" first published in *Hot Coffee and Cold Truth: Living and Writing the West*, edited by W.C. Jameson, University of New Mexico Press, 2006.

"Whirlwind Woman," signed special limited edition, Arapaho Commandments Series, ASAP Publishing, 2007.

"The Woman Who Climbed to the Sky," signed special limited edition with introduction by Tony Hillerman, Arapaho Commandments Series, ASAP Publishing, 2001.

"Yellow Roses" in *A Dozen on Denver: Stories to Celebrate the City at 150*, edited by Sandra Dallas, 2008. Published in *The Rocky Mountain News*.